OFF SEASON
AN EXTRA INNINGS NOVEL

AK Landow
AK LANDOW AUTHOR

OFF SEASON: An Extra Innings Novel

Published by Author AK Landow, LLC

ISBN: 978-1-962575-23-2

Edited By: Chrisandra's Corrections

Proofed By: Sarah Watt

Cover Design & Illustration By: K.B. Designs

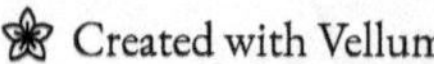 Created with Vellum

DEDICATION

To all the women out there who have a different version of happily ever after. It doesn't have to be anything other than what makes you happy.

"We must recognise that there are no hard and fast rules for how women should live their lives." ~Eleanor Roosevelt

BASEBALL/ SOFTBALL GLOSSARY

WORD/PHRASE	DEFINITION
Gassed	Nothing left in the tank. When a pitcher is spent.
Bomb	A hard hit home run
Contact Hitter	A batter who often makes contact & puts the ball in play
Sacrifice Bunt	Deliberately bunting the ball, before 2 outs, to advance baserunner
Bases Loaded	Runner at first, second, & third base.
Hit Away	When the batter is told to freely swing in the at-bat
Grand Slam	When a batter hits a home run with runners on first, second, & third bases
Showboat	When a player excessively celebrates their accomplishments
Five-Six Hole	The area on the field between the shortstop & third baseman
Softball IQ	Situational intelligence to make smart & fast decisions in a game

PROLOGUE

CHRISTMAS EVE

KAMRYN

I stare at my peacefully sleeping sister, willing her to wake up. I'm all jittery. I need her.

I'm twenty-eight years old and today will be the first airplane flight in my life that I will take without Bailey. What's worse? I'm a nervous flyer. A *very* nervous flyer. She's the only person who can soothe me. How am I going to get through this without her? My crutch. My teammate. My best friend. My twin. My soulmate.

Cheetah asked me to come home with him for Christmas. His family lives in Galveston, Texas and we're supposed to fly there from Philadelphia in a few hours. He has five hundred siblings. Okay, it's six, but they're all married with kids, so it feels like five hundred. He's the black sheep of the family because he's still single. Apparently, his mother's mission in life is to see him married. She even has the woman picked out for him. He begged me to come home with him and pretend to be his girlfriend for a few days to get everyone off his back. He even promised me an all-expenses-paid trip to Jamaica afterward as *payment* for agreeing to accompany him and being his fake girlfriend for five days. I would have done it for him without the promise of Jamaica, but there's no need for me to tell him that.

Cheetah, everyone's nickname for superstar, speedy professional baseball player Cruz Gonzales, is a tall, dark, and handsome blue-eyed Latino man. I call him kitten just to fuck with him, but the man is no kitten. I was instantly attracted to him when we met. Both his looks and his larger-than-life personality drew me in. Admittedly, no man has ever made me laugh like he does. After toying with him for a few months, we eventually became casual fuck buddies. That's all I'm capable of, and he seems good with it.

I'm attracted to both men and women, depending on my mood. What I really like is having the autonomy to do what and who I want, whenever I want. In the handful of weeks since we started our casual encounters, Cheetah hasn't once tried to rein me in. That's the kiss of death for my bedmates. I'm wild. Untamable. Anyone who challenges that will be left like yesterday's news.

I carefully crawl into Bailey's bed, creepily taking in her familiar, comforting scent. My body immediately relaxes. Her eyes mercifully blink open, and she reaches for my hand. She croaks out, "Stop worrying. You'll be fine. It's safe."

"Safe? There's nothing safe about being tens of thousands of feet up in the air at the mercy of some random person you've never even met. Maybe they were out all night on a bender. What if they were last in their class in pilot school? What if they were absent the day they taught landing? What if they broke up with their significant other the night before? I wouldn't know because you never get to see the pilot, a stranger, before the flight takes off."

She gives me a sleepy smile. "I researched the statistics." She knows I'm a big stats person. "Your odds of crashing in a plane are, like, one in eleven million compared to your odds of getting into a car crash, which is one in five thousand."

I exhale a long breath. "I know. I get it in theory. I just hate having no control. It's not like you get into cars with strangers though."

She gives me an unimpressed look. "You Uber."

I twist my lips. "Hmm. Valid point." I squeeze her hand and whisper, "I've never done this without you. I...I don't know if I can do it."

She pulls me close into her comforting arms. "You can. I briefed Cheetah on how to manage you. He knows what to do."

"What did you say to him?" I ask accusatorily.

"Nothing for you to worry about, but he's aware of what he's getting himself into."

"What about you? Will you be okay flying without me tomorrow?" She's flying to Colorado with Tanner Montgomery, a sports agent to all the top athletes. Bailey nannies for his seven-year-old daughter and is now secretly sleeping with Tanner. She won't give me any real details but has finally admitted it's happening. They're heading out west with his daughter and her friend to ski for the holiday week.

"I'll be fine. I'm only a call away, so don't freak out." We've never spent an entire week apart in our entire lives. In fact, we've never spent more than a night or two apart.

I nod. "I know. We'll talk every day, right?"

"Of course."

"Even with the time difference?"

"It's one hour."

I sink my head into the pillow. "Ugh. It might as well be a million."

I hear our front door open and a deep voice yelling out, "It's time, Kam bam. Get your hot ass up and ready to board the Cheetah kidney-buster."

I perk up at the simple sound of his voice and purr, "In here, kitten."

He walks into Bailey's bedroom with his trademark enormous grin. "Morning, ladies. Merry almost Christmas. May Santa come long and hard down your chimneys tonight."

Oh right, it's Christmas Eve.

I scrunch my face. "That was kind of a boring entrance. Do you have anything better to say? Maybe a holiday poem?"

He toggles his head back and forth in contemplation for a minute. "Hmm. Santa's suit is red, but the mistletoe is greener. When I think of you, I play with my wiener."

Bailey giggles and I can't help but smile. "You're a modern-day Robert Frost. Thank you."

He nods in satisfaction. "You're welcome. By the way, I bumped into the weird ginger across the hallway. He scowled at me. I feel like he might murder me in my sleep one day."

Bailey shakes her head. "Stop it. Justin is a sweetie, but he's in love with Kam. She constantly walks around half-naked. He runs out into the hallway every time our door opens. I think he's hoping to get a look at her."

I scoff. "Yeah, kitten, be nice to him. The poor guy will probably die a virgin. What's the difference between a brick and a male ginger?"

Cheetah thinks for a moment. "I don't know. What?"

I answer, "The brick gets laid."

He chuckles. "Good one." He peeks out the bedroom door. "By the way, there's something boiling on your stove. It looks like it might overflow."

I pop out of Bailey's bed. "Oops, I almost forgot about my stew."

Bailey moans in malcontent. "Ugh. Make sure that's cleaned up before you go."

As I approach the door, I notice that Cheetah is clean-shaven. I've never seen him this way before. I rub his face. "What's with this? It's not very sittable."

"Sorry. My mother likes it when I shave. I indulge her for the holidays. Look at the bright side. It will be more like sitting on a woman's face for you."

"If I wanted to sit on a woman's face, I would. Half your appeal is the scruff rubbing me in all the right places."

"What's the other half?"

"Hmm. Your stamina." *The guy can fuck me for hours.*

He winks before I make my way to the kitchen with him hot on my heels. I quickly turn down the dial on the stove.

He approaches me from behind and looks over my shoulder. "Holy shit. Is that a boiling pot full of dildos? And I thought you didn't cook."

I turn my head and smile. "Dildo stew is my specialty."

Bailey walks out of her room with messy hair and in an oversized T-shirt I know isn't hers. I raise an eyebrow. "Is that Daddy Tanner's shirt?"

She rolls her eyes and points toward the stove. "Seriously, don't leave me with a pot full of your nasty dildos. I'm never cleaning that again. I have PTSD from that one time."

I shake my head. "I just boiled them. They're not nasty, they're clean. Sanitized."

Cheetah continues to stare in bewilderment at the big pot full of seven giant dildos in multiple colors. "Care to explain, Kam bam?"

"I wanted them clean for when you let me peg you as a thank-you for pretending to be your girlfriend this week."

His eyes widen, and I burst out laughing. "Just kidding, kitten. I only use them on the ladies. At least once a month, I like to sanitize my dildo collection. In case our plane crashes, I wanted to make sure all the dildos were clean. I'm getting my affairs in order."

Bailey deadpans, "Getting your affairs in order means cleaning your dildos? What about something useful like making amends with Mom?"

My face falls at the mere mention of that woman. "Beverly

Hart is no mother to me and never has been. I care more about the silicone in this pot than I do about her."

Cheetah rubs my arms. Clearly noticing I need a distraction, he asks, "Are you all packed? We should get going soon."

"Ugh. Are you one of those people who likes to get to airports overly early?"

He nods. "Yes, I am. Let's tear off the Band-Aid of the undoubtedly long goodbye to your sister and get going."

Lots of crying and two hours later, we're sitting at our gate. Cheetah looks over at me. "Let's run through the members of my family again."

I shrug. "I've got it all down. No need."

"You know the names of my six siblings, their spouses, and their seventeen combined kids?"

"Plus, your aunts and uncles. I told you; once it's in my brain, it never leaves."

He crosses his arms in challenge. "Let's hear it. I'll settle for just my siblings and their spouses."

I smile, knowing I've got it down perfectly. "You've got three older siblings. Luna, Alejandro, and Santiago. Their respective spouses are Armando, Ana, and Gabriela. Your three younger siblings are Ruben, Adriana, and Camila. Their spouses are Lola, Santos, and Fernando. You're closest with Ruben and dote on Camila 'cause she's the baby of the family."

He narrows his eyes. "I never told you that." He then mumbles, "But it's true."

"Told ya so." I thump my head. "Steel trap. I don't miss a thing. I even remember you mentioning once that everyone gets along well except for Adriana and Camila."

He gives me a very impressed look. I'm not sure why people,

particularly men, always underestimate my powers of retention. I have a bit of a photographic memory.

I haven't told him yet that I taught myself Spanish too. I'll wait until the family doesn't think I understand what they're saying before I reveal that tidbit. I'm hoping they talk shit about me and then I can shock them.

He nods. "Well done. You've earned playtime."

"Ooh. What does playtime entail?"

"We're going to have some fun airdropping weird dick pics to random people nearby and watching for their reactions. The game is identifying who it went to."

My mouth widens in shock. "What? Is that a thing?"

He nods. "Yes. I do it all the time."

"Do they know who it comes from? Isn't your name on your phone?"

"I changed the name on my phone to *Bad Ass Motherfucker*."

"Genius."

We then proceed to spend the next thirty minutes downloading photos of nasty-looking penises and airdropping them to random people around us. We laugh as we both scramble to be the first to find the poor unsuspecting souls. I'm already having a blast. I always do with him.

They eventually call for first class to board the plane, and Cheetah stands. "That's us."

"Ooh, fancy. I've never sat in first class before."

"Yep. That's how I roll. Does it turn you on? I'm more than ready to taxi down your runway."

I smile. "Only if your tray table is in its upright position."

"Is it ever not?"

I stand, grab my backpack, and nod in agreement. "Fair point."

We board the plane and settle into first class. This is usually when the anxiety starts to kick into high gear for me. It's the takeoff that freaks me out the most. It's like we're defying gravity by getting something this heavy to fly into the air like a simple kite.

My heart begins beating faster and faster. I can feel my face redden. A sheen of sweat forms over my skin. I get up to do my regular pacing, but he grabs my arm before I can fully stand. "Relax. Look at the flight attendant. He's bringing us drinks."

As if on cue, the flight attendant walks over and delivers two beers and a blanket.

Cheetah spreads the blanket across our laps and nods for me to drink my beer.

I happily take a huge gulp. Several huge gulps. "I can't believe you get booze in first class. Before the flight even takes off. In a fancy beer mug."

He winks. "That's not all you get."

His hand under the blanket slips into my leggings and then under my panties. I suck in a breath at the surprise intrusion. "Oh shit." I look around to see if anyone has noticed. They haven't. "What are you doing?"

He leans over and whispers into my ear. "Just relax. Spread your legs a little bit more." As soon as I do, his finger slides into me. Deep into me. "An orgasm at takeoff should cure you. I can give you something Bailey can't."

I tilt my head back as he begins to establish a rhythm with two fingers now inside me and his palm rubbing against my clit.

I'm gripping the armrest for dear life. My stomach is clenching, and my toes are curling.

Taking deep breaths, I look over at him, into his blue eyes. They normally sparkle with mischief, but right now his heated gaze is so damn erotic. And obvious. I'm definitely the better actor of the two of us. But I can't deny that I love how into this he is.

He's slow and methodical in his movements. He's practically massaging my insides with his expert precision. I can feel my pussy contracting around his fingers.

"You won't come until I say it's time. But when I do, come right away."

Damn it, I love when he gets bossy in bed. I laughed the first time he ordered me to come, thinking he was insane, but my greedy whore body obeys like a well-trained service dog. In fairness, his body obeys my command as well.

I think I feel us moving, but I'm not sure because I'm being finger-fucked in a plane of over three hundred people, and I can't really focus on anything else around me.

I can both feel and hear how wet I am. This is crazy hot.

His lips brush over my ear. His hot breath gives me shivers as he asks, "Are you ready to let go?"

I can only manage a nod, fearful that anything I say will come out in a loud moan.

"Imagine it's my sausage in there. Fucking your pink velvet sausage wallet the way you like it."

I manage to grit out, "But I kind of prefer just the tip of your sausage. You know how strongly I feel that just the tip is such an underrated sex move."

"Fine, then imagine it's my sausage link."

I let out a laugh, but he bites my earlobe, quickly bringing me back into the moment. And then he goes and curls his fingers in the exact spot he's learned so well. I'm officially a goner.

He commands, "Come. Now."

I squeeze my eyes shut to try to keep myself from shaking or yelling out as an electric current blissfully runs through my entire body, and I come all over his hand.

I take a few long breaths and blink my eyes open. Immediately looking out the window, I see that we're in the air. Above the clouds. "Holy shit. You're a fucking genius. Orgasm therapy. You should patent that shit, Dr. Gonzales."

He smiles and winks. "Happy to be of service, ma'am. Be sure to tell your sister that I'm now the king of Kam control."

"Ha! Kam control. As if."

ABOUT FOUR HOURS and one hand job later, we land in Texas. I text my sister that orgasm therapy will now be my go-to method of overcoming my fear of flying. She texts back that I'll have to find someone besides her to do it.

We Uber to his parents' house. It's more modest than I would have thought, considering the fact that Cheetah makes millions of dollars each year. As if reading my mind, he says, "They won't let me buy them a nicer home. I've offered thousands of times, but they're proud, and they've lived here for over forty years. We settled on me paying off their mortgage so at least they're debt-free."

They're humble. I immediately know I'll like them.

He carries our bags to the front door. He looks a little uncharacteristically nervous. Maybe it's because I'm not Latina and we're faking being in a real relationship. All his siblings married within their ethnicity.

He sets the bags down and has a sheepish look on his face. After pulling something out of his pocket, he grabs my left hand, brings it to his lips, and kisses it. "Thanks for doing this. I really appreciate it."

I smile. "My pleasure. You're a good guy, kitten. I'd do anything for you."

"I'm glad you feel that way because—"

Before he can finish his sentence, the door begins to open. He hurriedly shoves something onto my ring finger. I look down and notice a giant diamond ring encircling it.

My eyes widen in shock, but he simply throws his arm around me as a woman comes into view.

"Hola, Mamá. Te presento a mi prometida, Kamryn Hart." *Hi Mom. Meet my fiancée, Kamryn Hart.*

What. The. Fuck.

CHAPTER ONE

KAMRYN

"Blow jobs are my love language with men. With women..." I twist my lips, "hmm, maybe making them squirt."

Ripley, Arizona, and Bailey all burst out laughing. My waterbed is shaking because they're all sitting on it laughing so damn hard.

Ripley wheezes, "Blow jobs and squirting aren't love languages, you lunatic."

I pinch my eyebrows together. I wasn't trying to be funny. "What are love languages?"

She answers, "I texted you all the test last night and told you to take it. There are five love languages. Physical touch, quality time, words of affirmation, acts of service, and receiving gifts. The test shows you how you prefer to be loved. Everyone is different and it's all on a sliding scale. We like a little of each, but usually, there's one strong leader in the pack."

I pull up our group chat, see the link to the test, and click on it. I'm answering all the inane questions while I hear them chatting about their results. Ripley's number one love language is words of affirmation. That makes sense for her. Ripley is the curviest of the four of us and has always suffered from body image issues over her larger six-foot pitcher's frame. I imagine she'll need someone who makes her feel comfortable in her own skin. She's a gorgeous, curly-haired redhead, and I don't know why she doesn't see it, but she doesn't. I hope she finds a man who makes her feel as beautiful as she is, both on the inside and outside.

Bailey and I met Ripley and Arizona ten years ago during our freshman year of college at UCLA. We all played on the UCLA softball team. Ripley and Arizona grew up together in Northern California while Bailey and I grew up in Southern Florida. Bailey and I played professional ball in Chicago for the past six years after we graduated from college. Arizona played in Southern California while Ripley played in Houston, Texas. A few weeks ago, we all signed with a new team, the Philadelphia Anacondas, and moved to Philly last week. Bailey and I live in the apartment next door to Ripley and Arizona. It's so fun to be reunited with our close friends as we begin training for the Olympics in four years. It's something we've been talking about doing together since the day we all met. Well, maybe not all of us. My sister is a bit indifferent, but the rest of us won't accept anything besides Olympic gold.

Arizona, a tall, blonde-haired, blue-eyed beauty, answers, "My primary love language is physical touch." She sighs. "I do miss the touch of a man."

She had a bad breakup with her fiancé last year, and it's taken a toll on her. I don't think she's dated much since, though I know Ripley is hopeful that this move will break Arizona out of her fog. And she had a big date last night that she's been tight-lipped about this morning.

Bailey holds up her phone and, to no one's surprise, proclaims that quality time is her primary love language. My sister, the much kinder, sweeter, more subdued twin, loves spending time with the men she dates. I'm the exact opposite. One, I don't date. Sexual encounters are all I'm interested in. Men or women, I don't care, but I'm a hit-and-run kind of girl. Two, the last thing I want is to spend quality time with someone. Sex? Yes. Anything more? Absolutely not. It's a waste of my time and energy.

After answering the series of questions, the online calculator spits out my answer. Lifting my head, I say, "According to this, I'm forty-three percent interested in a partner providing me with acts of service. What does that mean?"

Ripley answers, "You're most interested in someone taking care of you."

"Well, duh. They need to make me come. That's *all* I want from anyone. It should be a hundred percent."

My sister rolls her eyes. "It's not only physical needs. It's more. This is kind of sweet, Kam. You get off on someone who considers *all* your needs." She wiggles her eyebrows. "All hope isn't lost for you."

I throw my phone on my bed and cross my arms. "Whatever. This is dumb. I don't need a partner to take care of anything for me beyond the bedroom. I'm an independent woman. I can take care of myself."

I don't want to talk about this anymore, so I turn to Arizona. "How was your date with the one and only Layton Lancaster last night? *Please* give us a few juicy details."

Arizona went on her first date in forever last night. Not just any date. She went to a huge public event with one of the biggest, hottest professional baseball players on the planet. Their pictures are all over every gossip site this morning, with lots of speculation about a budding relationship.

She nervously tucks her hair behind her ear. "It was...umm... fine. He was sweet. Respectful."

Weird answer. "Did you bang him?"

She rolls her eyes. "No. Absolutely not."

"Why not? He's so hot. I'd sit right on that square chin of his if I were you."

She and Ripley exchange an indecipherable look before she

turns back to me. "We had a nice time. We're going to see each other again, but you know I'm just getting back into the dating pool. I need to take things slowly. While we're on this topic, he invited us to hang out with him and his friends tonight. They're going to the same bar, Screwballs, that we went to the other night."

Bailey and I instinctively look at each other and communicate without words or actions, as always. I nod. "Sure, we'd love to. I hope his friends are hot too."

She smiles as she stands. "Great. I'm having brunch with my brother. I'll see you guys later."

I wink at her. "Tell sexy Quincy that we say hello."

She narrows her eyes at me. "Off limits. My brother is off limits to you. He can't handle you." She mumbles, "I'm not sure anyone can."

I simply smile at her. Quincy Abbott is a pitcher for the Philly Cougars. He's hot as hell, extremely tall, with blond curly hair and Arizona's same bright blue eyes. But I would never go there. I simply enjoy fucking with her. Besides, I've gotten the feeling that Ripley has a crush on him. She's never admitted as much, but I have my suspicions.

Arizona leaves and Ripley, Bailey, and I all lay back on my brand-new king-sized waterbed. I've wanted a waterbed my entire life. So much so that I asked for a waterbed and a puppy for Christmas every single year of my life. My parents never considered indulging me on the waterbed. When Bailey and I signed our contracts with the Anacondas, the biggest of my life, I decided to finally treat myself to one. It arrived yesterday and I'm obsessed with it.

I turn on the vibration setting, and Bailey starts giggling. "I can't believe your bed vibrates. I think this will be my last time on it. I'm afraid of what will happen on this bed."

I blow out a breath. "I can't wait to have my first non-self-induced orgasm on it. It's going to be epic. I'm glad we're going out tonight. I'll bring someone home for a little surfing fun. I'm feeling like I want a woman tonight." I wiggle my hips. "I need it a little gentler as I learn the motion of this ocean."

Ripley asks, "How do you know when a woman is interested? I guess I assume most women are into men unless there's some obvious signal."

I shrug. "I don't know. I guess I assume everyone is open-minded. If they're not interested, they can let me know and I'll back off. I frankly think everyone is on a sliding scale of sexuality. Your exposures and experiences dictate what you do and don't indulge in."

She twists her lips. "Hmm. That's an interesting perspective. What do you look for in a woman?"

I smirk. "Women should be like swim goggles."

Bailey sighs. "Oh god, don't get her started."

I giggle. "Yep. Goggles. Tight, wet, and on my face."

Ripley smiles. "Seriously. I want to know."

I sigh. "It's no different from what you look for in a man. A spark. Some attraction and chemistry. I don't need much more. I'm not marrying them, I'm fucking them. I won't ever see them again after we're done."

She asks, "What's the deciding factor each night whether you go home with a man or woman?"

"I don't know." They always have questions about this. "I suppose at times it depends on my mood. One night, I might want to do squat thrusts in the cucumber patch, and other nights, I want to stir the bean curd."

Ripley lets out a laugh. "Ha. I've missed your euphemisms for sex. I'm so happy to be reunited with you two. I've missed you so much. And I think this change of scenery is needed for Arizona."

Bailey's face turns serious. "How's she doing?"

Ripley shakes her head. "She's been a mess. I want my best friend back, and this move is just what the doctor ordered. We need to make sure she's pushing herself on the social front. She's been a clam all year."

"At least she went on a date last night. That's a big deal for her," I add.

Ripley slowly nods. "I guess."

Something is off about this situation. Why isn't she elated that Arizona went on a date last night, especially with a stud like Layton Lancaster?

Bailey and I exchange glances. I know she's thinking the same thing I am.

CHEETAH

I'm at the stadium with Layton in our training facility, getting electric stimulation on our sore muscles. It's the all-star break in professional baseball. It takes place every year at the halfway point in the season. It's a time for baseball to celebrate the best players in the league with a friendly game. There are always parties and other fun activities associated with the event for those who are selected for the teams.

For those who aren't, it's four days off from the grind of a long one-hundred-and-sixty-two-game season. I've been having a good year, but not all-star worthy. Our young, popular shortstop, Avery McNeil, as well as one of our relief pitchers, both made the team. Our new pitcher, Quincy Abbott, should have made the team but didn't. He was traded to us from Houston before this season. He said he'd rather save his arm for the second half of our season, but he still should have been offered the roster spot. He's having a career year and has become our ace on the mound.

Layton made the all-star team for ten straight years but hasn't in the last few. He used to be the biggest star in baseball, but at thirty-four, I imagine retirement is around the corner for him. He's one of my best friends in the world. I can't imagine ever playing without him, but that day is coming sooner rather than later.

He's got ice on his knees and the e-stim hooked up to his quads, which is pretty standard for catchers. It's the most physically demanding position. I've got the e-stim on my hamstrings, which feel a little tight. I'm a speedy center fielder, a position you can play for much longer than a catcher. I've had years where I led the league in stolen bases, but turning thirty has made it so my muscles don't recover as quickly as they used to. The e-stim helps them loosen up a bit.

I woke up this morning to a flood of online photos of Layton with Quincy's little sister, Arizona. Apparently, they attended an event in New York City last night, and the paparazzi went absolutely wild for them. I guess it makes sense; he's a good-looking fucker who was the face of baseball for a long time. She's a professional softball player and, judging by her photos, is incredibly beautiful. I haven't met her since she just moved to Philly. The internet practically exploded this morning. I can't imagine Quincy is thrilled about it. When it comes to women, Layton is the biggest player on the planet; he's with a different girl every single night.

I ask, "How did you end up with Quincy's sister last night? Was she cool?"

He smiles. "Very cool. I briefly met her…once before, but then management introduced us yesterday and asked us to attend the event together. We hit it off and are going to hang out a bit."

"She's fucking hot."

He wiggles his eyebrows. "No shit."

"Speaking of shit, is Quincy losing his?"

He winces. "She's telling him this morning. I'm going to head home soon, anticipating an angry Quincy stopping by.

We can talk, man to man. I'm not planning to dick her around. I wouldn't do that to Q."

I nod in understanding. "Honestly, I'd fucking throttle you if you went out with any of my sisters."

He winks. "It's a good thing they're all married. You'll meet Arizona tonight. She and her friends are meeting us out."

"Sweet. Hot girls usually hang with other hot girls."

"I thought you were hanging out with that girl, Brianna."

I raise an eyebrow. "Have you ever known me to be truly serious with anyone? The front doors are always open for business on the Cheetah bus to Manchester."

There's a reason it's been a long time since I've had a serious girlfriend. I'm a lot to handle. I know that about myself. I like to have fun. I want to be the life of the party. I say and do crazy things. Putting all that aside, I hate hurting people. I hate confrontation. When a relationship goes to shit, which it always does, I allow it to go on longer than it should because I don't want to hurt the woman. In the end, we both end up mad or hurt. I've stopped trying.

Layton smirks. "You'd be serious if it was a clone of Gemma DePaul."

I give him the finger. They all like to rub my nose in the fact that I have an innocent crush on teammate Trey DePaul's wife. She might also be the reason I don't date. No one measures up to her. She's perfection.

"She's just a friend."

He chuckles. "I know, but how much porn do you watch that has brunettes with great tits?"

I scrunch my face. "A lot. You know I like to watch the ultimate act of intimacy."

"You like to watch porn. Nothing intimate about that."

Yes, I'm a normal, red-blooded man who likes a healthy dose of porn. Admittedly, I put it on in hotel rooms when we travel, but I mostly do that just to fuck with the guys. They think it's crazy, and I've got a rep to protect as the funny, nutty teammate.

He continues, "You're a kinky motherfucker, Cheetah. Just admit it."

I shake my head. "Kinky sounds dirty. I prefer...erotic. It's a sexier term." I gyrate my hips back and forth suggestively, and he laughs.

He shrugs. "Whatever, dude. Is there even a difference between erotic and kinky?"

I roll my eyes. "Of course there is. Erotic is teasing your woman with a feather, driving her crazy with desire. Pushing her to the edge before you give her what she needs. Kinky is using the whole fucking chicken for some messed up shit. Big difference."

He starts laughing hysterically. I notice our trainer, Jeffrey, biting back his smile.

Like I said, I have a rep to protect.

IT'S NIGHTTIME, and we're sitting in our regular booth at Screwballs. The owner always ropes it off for us, loving the attention we bring to his bar. It's a huge booth. Not only can we all fit in it, but there's plenty of room for any guests we invite to join us. It's often a few random girls, but not tonight. Tonight, it's Arizona Abbott and her friends. I'm kind of excited to meet professional softball players. I don't know any.

Quincy is running late, but our teammate, Ezra Decker, is with us. He's our second baseman and good friend. He's a shy, understated man from the Midwest who happens to be one of the nicest guys I know.

I ask Layton, "Can you tell us their names again?"

He scoffs in annoyance. "Arizona is my girl. Ripley is the tall redhead. The brunette identical twins are Bailey and Kamryn. I only met them briefly, but I think Kamryn is the outgoing one. I can't tell them apart though."

"Are they hot?"

He nods. "All four of them are hot. I think the twins might be up your alley. They're sexy brunettes."

I wiggle my eyebrows. "I had sex with twins once. It was amazing."

His lips curl up in amusement. "You did? Could you tell them apart?"

I smirk. "Yep. Maria had a nose piercing and Marco had two balls."

He and Ezra start laughing but I hold up my hand. "Just kidding. There are always subtle differences in twins. You need to find them. It's like a treasure hunt." I look around and innocently ask, "Are Trey and Gemma coming?"

Trey is our third baseman, and his wife of a few years is Gemma. They used to come out all the time, but they had a baby a few months ago and don't go out as much. I obviously see Trey in the locker room and on the field, but I miss Gemma. She's the coolest chick I've ever met. She's a super smart lawyer, but also a down-and-dirty secret romance author. I love her sense of humor. She may be the most beautiful woman I've ever seen. I admittedly have always had a crush on her, but Trey staked his claim the second he laid eyes on her. Layton wasn't wrong earlier today. Gemma is the reason I've had a several-year brunette fetish.

She and I have a lot in common, and she's become one of my best friends. I decide to text her.

> Me: You guys coming out?

Gemma: Sorry, no sitter. Fletcher is asleep,
and Trey wants me to himself. He's not home
many evenings during the season. I need to
get my fill of my sexy man when I can.

Me: Okay. Book club meeting this week?

Gemma and I have lunch once a month to chat about the romance books we're reading. I love reading romance books. It's like porn with a storyline. I also think it gives insight into the minds of women. I try to tell the guys that all the time, but they don't listen. They never read anything except fantasy football magazines.

Gemma: Yep. Come by my office and we'll
grab lunch one day.

Me: Yes, Mommy.

Gemma: Such a good boy.

I smile as I place my phone back in my pocket. She always has a comeback for my comments. Yep, Gemma DePaul is a unicorn. What I wouldn't give for a woman with a dirty yet smart mind like Gemma's.

Layton announces, "Here they are."

I look up and see four women walking toward our table. Four gorgeous women. What's cool is that they're dressed casually, not like the usual women in the bar who dress more provocatively. The four women are all in sweatpants, but it's the one brunette in a cropped T-shirt catching my attention. She's fucking beautiful, with long hair, huge golden-brown eyes, a button nose, and a body built for sin. There's something about the twinkle in her eyes and the confident way she's walking that tells me she's a little crazy. Just how I like them.

Layton introduces all of us and I take Kamryn's hand in mine. A lot of women get shy or awkward when meeting famous baseball players, but she doesn't cower at all. In fact, she licks her lips like I'm her next meal.

I squeeze her hand a little harder and ask, "Do you know the difference between a cheeseburger and a boner?"

She smiles. It's mischievous, and I love it. "Do tell."

"You're not giving me a cheeseburger right now."

She giggles. "I like you, Cruz."

"I like you too, Kamryn. How old are you?" She could be twenty-two, too young for me, or thirty, I have no idea. Though I'm thinking older, given her confidence.

"Old enough to remember when saying *shove it up your ass* was an insult, not a pickup line."

I can't help but chuckle. She's a hellcat. I think I'm in love.

Rubbing my scruff, I ask, "But are you old enough that you still type a double space after a period?"

She lets out a laugh. "*Definitely* not."

"Hmm. I'd say that makes you roughly twenty-nine."

She nods. "Close. Twenty-eight going on twenty. How old are you? Forty? Fifty?"

She's fucking with me. Love it. "Thirty, going on eighteen. A perfect match."

"Thirty, and you're using cheesy pickup lines about cheeseburgers?" She tsks.

"You liked it."

She bites back her smile. "Pickup lines aren't really my thing. I'd rather be pinned down than picked up."

I chuckle as I finally release her hand. I think I may have just found my soulmate.

Quincy arrives and everyone is chatting, but I can't take my eyes off Kamryn. There's something extra about her.

At some point, the conversation steers toward walkup songs. At the beginning of each season, a ballplayer selects a walkup song. At every home game, just as he's walking from the dugout to the batter's box, that specific song of his choosing is played. It sounds like the girls have them too.

Arizona mentions that she plans to use "Smooth Criminal" by Michael Jackson this season. I ask, "Are you a speed player?"

She nods. "Yep. I usually lead the league in stolen bases."

"Ahh. That song is perfect. Damn, I wish I had thought of it."

She smiles. "Use it next year. Luke Combs's version of 'Fast Car' that you're using this year is a good one. Plus, you do your whole dance bit during the seventh-inning stretch of every game. They don't ever show it on TV though. I only see them on TikTok. I'm excited to catch a few games in person so I can watch you in action."

"You'll have to come dance with me sometime," I offer.

Her face lights up. "I'd love to."

I turn to Kamryn. "What about you? What's your walkup song?"

She smirks. This woman oozes trouble, and I'm so damn attracted to it. "I like to ruffle feathers with my song selections. Last year I did 'Barbie Girl' by Aqua. It made me laugh every time I stepped to the plate. The year before I used 'Pony' from *Magic Mike*."

I chuckle. "What about this year?"

"You'll have to come out to the ballpark to find out. I've got a special one this year. I think you might like it."

"Maybe I *will* come watch you play."

She tilts her head to the side. "Why do they call you Cheetah?"

I give her a cocky smirk. "Because I'm fast. *Very* fast." Cheetahs are known to be the fastest animals. I've been called that since middle school.

Without an ounce of hesitation, she brings her face

within an inch of mine. "No one likes a man who's fast, *Cheetah*."

"On the field, sweetheart. In bed, I'm more of a tiger than a cheetah. A different feline, but an animal nonetheless."

She then starts calling me kitten. Fuck, I love it. It makes my dick swell in my pants.

She motions her head toward the dance floor. I see some chick I hadn't noticed staring at our table. It's not exactly unusual for women at this bar to stare at a table of professional baseball players. I think I'm desensitized to it at this point. I hate when women make it too obvious and easy for me. The chase is half the fun.

Kamryn asks, "Do you think that attractive woman over there is looking at me or you, kitten?"

My head toggles between the two of them as realization hits. Shit, Kamryn likes women. "Is that what you're into? Explains why you're busting my balls instead of gargling with them."

She calmly sits back in her seat and slowly sips her beer, though I notice a slight curl of her lips in amusement. She places her beer on the table, never breaking eye contact with me. "Sometimes I like a banana in my fruit salad, and sometimes I like to dip my toes in the kitty pool. It depends on my mood." She stares at me with a mixture of both fire and mischief in her eyes. "I'm a mood fucker."

Where has this woman been hiding all my life?

She continues, "How about a little wager, kitten?"

"What do you have in mind, Kam bam?" Not the best nickname, but if she's calling me kitten, I need to call her something besides Kamryn. Her friends have been calling her Kam. I'm just adding the bam.

She smiles. "If our lady friend wants *you*, I'll let you come home with me tonight to break in my new waterbed. If she wants *me*, you need to come to our first game with my name written across your chest in thick Sharpie. It has to read, *Kam's Kitten.*"

This sounds like a win-win for me. I hold out my hand. "Deal. You and I will be riding that wave within the hour."

She shakes my hand in return as something electric passes between us. We both feel it but then break apart, stand, and race toward the brunette, who I have zero interest in. It's Kam I want, but if leading this random girl on is what I need to do to get Kam under me, then so be it. I'll make sure to at least buy the woman a drink or two after I win the bet. I'm not a total asshole.

I get to her a hair ahead of Kam and give her my big, trademark smile. One that admittedly gets most ladies swooning over my dimples. I gently place my hand on her waist and pull her close to me. "Hi, beautiful. What's your name?"

She bats her long eyelashes at me. "I'm...I'm Stephanie. Ohmigod, you're Cruz Gonzales, the star centerfielder."

I nod. "Yes, I am. You can call me Cheetah." I whisper in her ear, loud enough for Kam to hear, "You'll be screaming it later."

Her eyes light up as she runs her hand across my chest. I place my hand over hers. "What does my shirt feel like?"

She pinches her eyebrows together. "Umm...cotton?"

"No, sweetheart. It's boyfriend material."

Kam lets out a laugh as she uncaringly enters our space and tucks Stephanie's hair behind her ear, brushing her fingertips across her cheek as she does so. "I'm Kamryn." She leans toward her ear and whispers in the same louder tone I did, "I'll be the one making you scream later, but the S will be silent."

Stephanie's face flushes as she stares at Kam and licks her lips. Her breathing picks up.

What the fuck is happening here?

I stand there in awe as Kam works her magic with

Stephanie. She's putty in Kam's hands. Kam is funny, sweet, charming, dirty, and all-around awesome. I'm not sure I care about losing anymore. I'm simply enjoying watching her in action.

Stephanie is laughing. I can't get in a word. Who is this enigma that is Kamryn Hart?

At some point, Kam brushes her lips over Stephanie's. Stephanie runs her hand over Kam's bare waist and moans into her mouth.

I'm not sure whether I'm incredibly insulted or incredibly turned on. Judging by the sudden tightness of my pants, it's quite possibly both.

Within minutes, Stephanie has agreed to go home with her. I nod at Kam. "You win. Let's go back to the table."

She winks. "Sorry, kitten, I have a much better offer." She grabs Stephanie's hand and makes her way toward the front door.

I barely got in a word with Stephanie. More importantly, I didn't get to talk to Kam as much as I would have liked. That woman has more game than anyone I've ever seen.

I drop my head and walk back to our booth. Layton looks at me in shock. "Did you lose?"

I motion toward Kam and Stephanie at the entrance, and admit, "I did."

Kam gives us the Cougars' famous claw sign and then starts laughing as they leave. I can only shake my head as I ask no one in particular, "What does she have that I don't?"

Arizona answers. "A vagina."

I purse my lips. "Hmm. Fair point.

Bailey rubs my back. "She's bizarrely charming, isn't she? It's infectious. She's been this way since we were kids. Don't take it personally. She always gets the person she wants and *never* strikes out."

I sigh. "She likes men too, right?"

Bailey nods. "Yes, but you might not want to waste your time. She rarely sleeps with someone more than once. She had her heart broken to shreds in high school and hasn't been in a single relationship since. Don't fall for her. Her heart is gold when it comes to her friends and stone when it comes to physical relationships."

Layton smirks. "Cheetah doesn't do relationships either. Unless Gemma DePaul also has a twin, he's not the commitment type."

I narrow my eyes at him. He didn't need to out my crush to our new friends. I mumble, "Dick."

He chuckles as he wraps his arm around Arizona and pulls her close to him. I look at Quincy, who's staring at them with daggers in his eyes.

We end up having a fun night. It's nice hanging out with female athletes. The girls are all cool and fun, but it's the one who already left that I can't get out of my mind.

CHAPTER TWO

I run as fast as my ten-year-old legs allow as I find my way back to the dressing room where she told Bailey and me to wait. I'm trying to make sense of the bits and pieces of a conversation I just overheard.

Bailey's worried eyes lift from her book and widen when I breathlessly return and close the door behind me. "Where have you been, Kam? Mommy said to stay put."

"Bails, something is wr—"

Before I can finish my sentence, the door reopens and Mommy walks in. She grabs my hand. "Kamryn, come with me. We have a wardrobe fitting." She gives her fake smile which I've come to learn is not a good thing. "It looks like you two have secured a spot in a television show. It's premiering after the Super Bowl. It will catapult both of you to superstardom."

Bailey and I look at each other, exchanging a million words without having to utter a single one. We overheard our father bargain with our mother that if we didn't get this television show, she'd give in and let us go to regular school. We've been homeschooled by our mother to allow us the flexibility to go to auditions and *attend modeling shoots. Despite our protests, we've been in dozens of commercials and print ads over the years.*

Mommy now wants us on a television show too. She doesn't care that we don't want it. We want to be normal kids.

We're sick of being on sets. We're sick of Mommy trying to teach us math in between takes. She doesn't even do it right. When we get home every day, I teach Bailey the right way. The same goes for grammar.

We've been purposefully messing up at this all-day audition, hoping they would select other child actors for the role. We were terrible. Why would they hire us?

She sneers, "You should look a little more appreciative. You two are about to become the biggest child stars on the planet. You'll be set for life. You won't struggle like I've had to."

I ball my fists and grit out, "We don't want to do it. I want to play softball. Bails wants to play basketball. We both want to go to real school and do fun activities. We want more time to be with our friends." Tears threaten my eyes, but I don't like to cry in front of her. "We want to be...normal."

She scrunches her face in complete and total disgust. "You're too pretty to waste your time on sports and other nonsense. Trust me, beauty fades. You should take advantage of it while you can. Why be ordinary when you two have the faces to be extraordinary?" She holds her hand out to me. "Now come on, Kamryn. Let's go to the wardrobe room."

I cross my arms in defiance. "What about Bailey? She needs to be fitted too."

Mommy shakes her head. "You're the same size, and the room is too small for so many bodies." She grabs my wrist and pulls me. Hard. "Let's go. We can't keep them waiting. Your sister will read her book while we wait, won't you, sweetie?" Her eyes move to my sister.

Bailey forces a frightened smile. "O...okay, Mommy."

I shake my head emphatically. "I don't want to leave my sister. This place gives me the creeps."

Mommy grits her teeth. "Kamryn! I'm not up for your shit. Now!"

Bailey worriedly whispers, "Just go. I'll be fine." Bailey hates it when I get into trouble, which happens nearly every day.

I swallow hard and let my mother pull me down the hallway. I have a bad feeling about this. There's something inside me telling me I need to get back to my sister. I need to protect her.

I look up at Cruella, my nickname for our wretched mother. "Mommy, I need to go to the bathroom. I'll meet you in the dressing room in five minutes. Go pick out the outfits you like."

She narrows her eyes at me. "You never let me help pick your wardrobe."

I give her a fake smile and bat my eyelashes at her while I lie, "I trust you, Mommy."

She slowly nods before making her way toward the dressing room area. As soon as she rounds the corner, I quickly make my way into the kitchen and start opening drawers until I find something useful.

I then sprint back toward my sister, immediately seeing Shrek about to turn the knob on her dressing room door. Shrek is what Bailey and I call the casting director. He's a big-eared, old, ugly guy with more nose and ear hair than hair on his head. He's always smelly and always sitting too close to us. I love making Bails laugh by making gagging faces behind his back.

Marching right up to him, I shove the fork into his upper thigh. Not hard enough to break the skin, but hard enough to cause a little pain.

He freezes in shock.

With all the bravado I can muster, I say, "If you go near my sister, it will be the last thing you ever do."

He looks down and scowls at me. I can see his nose hairs too close from this angle. Gross.

His mouth twitches a few times before snarling, "Go find your mother, little girl."

"I'm here for my sister, and there's not a chance in the world

I'm leaving without her. If you don't walk away right now, I'll start screaming at the top of my lungs."

He stares at me with pure venom. I don't care at all. I'm standing my ground. This man will not go into that room with my sister.

Eventually, he turns and walks back toward his office. I let out a huge breath of relief.

Opening the door, I see Bails sitting on the couch, innocently reading her book. Holding out my hand, I say, "Come with me. I won't go anywhere without you again. Ever."

My eyes pop open, and I sit up, breathing heavily. My clothes are sticking to my sweaty body like a second skin. I look around. It was just a nightmare. It's been eighteen years since that day, but the nightmares never leave me. What was he doing there? What if I didn't come back for her? I vowed that day to never leave her side, and I never will.

It's also the last day I ever called Beverly Hart mother.

Looking back at that day through the years has given me perspective. Some days, I hope I misinterpreted the situation, but most days I'm confident I didn't.

At least this nightmare was true to the events of that day as I remember them. Sometimes I have them where I don't come back for Bailey. After those, I don't let myself sleep for a week.

I look at the clock. It's three in the morning. I got three hours of sleep. That's not bad for me. I've been an insomniac since that day. Half because of the nightmares, and half because I have this constant need to check on my sister to make sure she's okay.

I get up and tiptoe over to her bedroom. Quietly opening her door, I see her peacefully asleep. Relief washes over me. She's so pure and good-hearted. I know I've manipulated things in our lives to keep her close to me, but it's because I love her and want to keep her safe.

She was a great basketball player in high school. An all-state basketball player. I knew we weren't going to end up at the same college if I didn't do something drastic. I all but forced her to start playing softball so we could be together. Even though she's the better overall athlete, I was a superstar softball player with offers from every top college softball program in the country. I chose the best school that agreed to give my sister a scholarship too. I knew she'd end up a star. She can do anything she sets her mind to.

When we graduated from college and she considered getting her masters in childhood education, I again manipulated things to make sure we were drafted by the same professional softball team out of Chicago and begged her to come with me. The thought of living far away from her was adding to my always-present anxiety.

And when Reagan Daulton, the owner of the Philly Anacondas, called me about signing me to her team, I let her know we were a package deal. In fairness to Bails, she's become an elite softball player too. Mrs. Daulton was more than happy to acquiesce to my demand.

Here we are, ten years removed from high school, and Bails and I never do anything without each other. She doesn't know exactly what happened that day, but at the time, she suspected something had gone down. That's when I stopped considering Beverly Hart my mother, and I wasn't afraid to make it clear. It's also when I started truly acting out so we could eventually stop being pushed into something we hated. It took two more years, but we finally enrolled in regular school and were able to participate in activities of our choosing. That's when our mother started hitting the bottle. Hard.

Grabbing my laptop, I plop down on the couch and do what I do almost every night.

WE'RE in the locker room about to head out to our first game of the season. The first game ever for the Philly Anacondas franchise. It's kind of cool to be a part of history. And our team is good. *Very* good. Even though Bailey and I haven't played with Arizona and Ripley in six years, it's as though no time has passed. There's a chemistry between the four of us that you can't manufacture. It's just there.

Coach Billie walks out of her office. She's about fifteen years older than us. She is a former Olympic outfielder. She's tiny, with light hair and blue eyes. She's got more energy and enthusiasm than a brand-new puppy.

She smiles at me. In her cheery demeanor, she asks, "How are you feeling, Kam? Ready to kick ass?"

"Always, Coach Billie."

She does her trademark pump of her fist. "Excellent. You're the shortstop. That means you're the team leader. Our general. King Cobra, if you will. The younger players on the team look up to you, Bailey, Ripley, and Arizona. You're all legends and seem likely to be on the Olympic team in four years. I need you to teach them. To guide them. To lead them."

I salute her. "Yes, commander."

Her steadfast smile falls a bit as she rubs my back. "Is everything okay? You look tired."

I've been tired for eighteen years. I force out a smile. "I'm fine. I didn't sleep well last night."

"Must be the new city. I think it's an adjustment for everyone."

I nod and lie, "Probably."

She must pick up on something because she says, "Kamryn, my door is always open to you. I love being your biggest cheerleader, but I can also be a friend when you need one." She looks over at Bailey, Arizona, and Ripley. "Maybe when you need one who isn't quite as entrenched in your life."

"Thanks, Coach. I'm good. I'm excited about the game."

"Fantastic."

As she returns to her office, I walk over to my friends who are talking to our young third baseman. Her name is Amber, and they seem to be consoling her. I pinch my eyebrows together. "What's wrong?"

Arizona winces. "Her boyfriend just broke up with her."

I shake my head. "Asshole. Just before opening day? What a prick. We can key his car after the game. Ooh, maybe we'll pour some sugar in his gas tank." Unbeknownst to Bailey, I did that to her ex-boyfriend in Chicago. He dicked over the wrong woman. "Is this the guy you said moved in with you a few months ago?" I ask.

Amber visibly swallows. "Yes. He said he's moving in with someone else. And before me, he was living with another woman."

I give her a knowing smile. "Ahh, I know guys like him. They're called hobosexuals."

She has a look of confusion on her face. "He's not gay."

"Not *homo*sexual. *Hobo*sexual. It's a person who jumps from relationship to relationship so they have somewhere to live. He didn't even pay rent, did he?"

She shakes her head.

"Yep, a hobosexual. Such an asshole move. Don't take it personally. He's basically a con artist."

Bailey stares at me. "You do have a gift for making up words, but this one is dead-on accurate. What a great term."

I take a bow. "Thank you, but I can't take credit. That's an Urban Dictionary term. I'm fluent in Urban Dictionary, arguably the greatest work of literature in the twenty-first century." I look back to poor Amber, knowing I need to turn her frown upside down. "I bet I can put a smile on your face in under ten seconds."

She whimpers, "Doubt it."

"What does the receptionist at a sperm bank say when a man is walking out the door?"

"W...what?"

"Thank you. Come again soon."

Amber lets out a giggle, as do Arizona and Ripley. Bailey rolls her eyes at me but knows I was doing what was necessary to snap Amber out of it.

It works.

WE'RE ALL in the dugout now just before our game is about to start. I keep an eye on Amber. She seems to be okay, smiling with the other young players on the team.

The franchise owner, Reagan Daulton, walks into the dugout. She's in an Anacondas blue pantsuit with matching heels. She's an imposingly attractive woman with perfectly blown-out blonde hair, blue eyes, and makeup that looks like it was professionally applied. What's even more shocking is that she's only a few years older than us.

She gives us a genuine smile and says to no one in particular, "Are you ready for the first-ever game of the Philly Anacondas?"

We all nod. Arizona answers, "Yes, ma'am."

Mrs. Daulton scrunches her face. "Don't call me ma'am. It makes me feel old. Reagan will be just fine. Anyway, I wanted to wish you luck. I know the stands are only half full today, but I'm confident I've assembled a team and a marketing plan that will fill them in no time. Don't be discouraged."

I wonder if she realizes that half-full stands are considered good in professional softball. Even during our playoffs, we don't get many more fans than this. Softball doesn't get the same attention that baseball does.

She motions to me. "Kamryn, can I speak with you for a moment?"

I nod. "Of course."

We step aside, out of earshot of any of my teammates. She places her hand on my shoulder. "Coach Billie tells me that you're the team leader."

I can't help but smile with pride. "It's nice to hear that. I do what I can."

"I have really high goals for this team, for you as individuals, and for women's sports in general."

I have no idea what that means, but I respond, "That all sounds good to me."

She nods. "I know you have a background in modeling."

"It's been a hot minute, but yes. I dabble now and then. Nothing too serious. I take a few jobs here and there to make ends meet."

I didn't do any modeling for about a decade after we finally got to go to real school and do real activities, but I've done a little in the past few years to help pay the bills in the off-season. Always on my terms though. Bailey refuses to do any modeling. She usually finds nannying jobs both during and after our seasons. She loves little kids. As good as she is with them, that's how bad I am with them. I honestly don't know why she enjoys the little monsters as much as she does.

Reagan studies me carefully. I can almost see the wheels turning. "I've watched a few of your postgame interviews from over the past few years. There's something extra about the way you conduct yourself. You're quite witty. You have an outgoing personality and enjoy the limelight. What are your plans for life after softball?"

I haven't told another living soul what I'm planning, and I'm certainly not going to start with Reagan Daulton. I shrug. "I'm not sure yet. For now, I'm focused on making this team a success and, hopefully, making the Olympic team in four years."

She tilts her head to the side. She's trying to read me, but I'm not giving anything away. No one has a better poker face than me. I don't care how smart this woman is, she won't get what she wants from me right now, and that's information.

Eventually, she gives me a small smile and says, "I've been keeping a close eye on you. I know what you're capable of. Go out there and put on a show they won't forget."

I think she means more than the softball, but she doesn't elaborate further, and I'm not about to ruffle feathers with someone as powerful as her.

I reply with a simple, "Yes, ma'am...err, Reagan."

She lets out a laugh as she exits the dugout, and we make our final preparations for the game.

As we take the field for the top half of the first inning, I see commotion in the stands behind our dugout. It's Layton, Cheetah, Quincy, and Ezra. People must be excited to see four famous baseball players. That's not the norm at professional softball games. It's great that they're here supporting us.

I learned the other night that they're truly nice guys. In fact, we're supposed to go out with them again after this game.

As soon as Cheetah's eyes find mine, he smiles. He has the biggest, most genuine smile I've ever seen in my life. It's equal parts playful and sexy. And his dimples? Holy shit, they're hot.

I was immediately attracted to him when we met. So much so that I didn't want to go home with him. I knew if I did, I'd be done with him when it was over, and I'm just a little too interested to see how much tension we can build before we inevitably get to the main event. Besides, he strikes me as the type of guy who likes a little chase. I plan to give him the chase of his life.

Once he notices me looking at him, he immediately pulls his shirt over his head. Wow, he's ripped. He's tall and not as broad as some of his teammates. I know he's a speed player, so I assumed he'd be scrawny, but he's not. He's got muscles and washboard abs. Yummy.

Sure enough, in thick, black Sharpie, he has *Kam's Kitten* written across his chest. What the hell? I think he also has a huge snake drawn on there like it's going into his pants. It looks like it was professionally done.

Standing on his chair, he lifts his arms and yells out, "Kam bam is the bomb! Go Anacondas! I love softball!"

He then takes it a step further and does a little dance number that would make *Magic Mike* jealous. All the fans are watching him with amusement. He obviously loves being the center of attention. This guy definitely makes me laugh.

The game begins. Ripley shuts down our opponent with

three strikeouts to begin the game. She's throwing heat right now. Unhittable. She's only getting better with age. She's truly a generational pitcher. If any of us will be in the Olympics, it will be her.

We head to the bottom of the first inning. Arizona leads off with a perfect bunt and then steals second base. Our two-batter grounds out to shortstop, but Arizona doesn't advance to third on the play.

Bailey then steps into the batter's box. Four pitches later, she hits a bomb that falls just over the left-field wall for a home run. I throw my hands in the air. "My fucking sister!"

In her always-classy, demure way, she quietly and quickly rounds the bases until we all greet her at home plate to congratulate her. I love watching her excel. I wish she took a little more joy in it.

Now it's my turn to bat. I selected "Save a Horse [Ride a Cowboy]" by Big & Rich as my walkup song. Cheetah and the boys all start laughing when they hear it. Naturally, Cheetah stands again and dances like a cowboy, complete with his pretend lasso that he mock-throws my way before reeling me in.

I inwardly laugh before stepping into the batter's box. I dig in and get set. The first pitch comes in, and I crush it. It's a no-doubter over the centerfield wall. Back-to-back home runs for my sister and me. I love it when that happens.

I make a spectacle of flipping my bat and holding my arms in the air as the crowd stands and cheers for me. They play "Save a Horse" on the speakers again as I slowly trot around the bases, enjoying my moment. The stadium may only be half full, but everyone there is dancing and having a great time. It's been a while since softball was this much fun.

I'м with Arizona, Ripley, and Bailey. We're walking down the city block, about to meet the guys at Screwballs to celebrate our big victory tonight.

Some random man in a bunny costume runs down the street screaming about the Cougars. I've learned quickly that this city has a lot of personality and a lot of crazy characters. It's got a completely different vibe from Chicago. It's grittier, and I like it.

Bailey shakes her head in disbelief. "I guess the Easter Bunny is out in July in Philly."

I twist my lips. "Does anyone find it weird that the Easter Bunny hides eggs?"

Ripley shrugs. "Why is it weird?"

I answer, "Rabbits don't lay eggs. Where did they come from?"

Her jaw drops. "Holy shit. I've never thought of that."

Bailey sighs. "This is the crap my sister contemplates when she's up all night. One night last week, I woke up and she immediately asked me if I've ever considered what *strap-on* backward spells."

I see Ripley and Arizona trying to figure it out. They both start laughing hysterically when they do.

I nod. "Crazy, right?"

Arizona lifts an eyebrow. "You? Yes."

"Judge all you want, but I gain an extra eight hours of knowledge every night that you guys don't."

Bailey shakes her head. "Because the human body requires sleep to function. You're supernatural."

I wiggle my eyebrows. "I've had a lot of men and women tell me that."

We approach Screwballs, and as soon as we step inside, the entire bar stands and claps. We all swivel our heads and look at each other. What is happening? Why are they clapping? Did someone famous walk in behind us?

The owner, an older man, approaches us with a giant smile on his face. "We had your game playing on all the televisions tonight.

It was my first softball game. I can't get over how great you ladies play. Everyone was mesmerized by the way you dominated the other team." He holds up a camera. "Can we get a picture of you for you to sign that I'll hang on the wall?"

We look at each other in a bit of bewilderment before we all happily agree and then pose for several photos with some of the patrons. I see the guys in our big booth, smiling throughout the interaction. They cheered like madmen tonight, and it's cool that they're being so supportive.

After the impromptu photo session, we make our way to the booth in a straight line, with me in the far back. Layton smiles. "Kam, you're technically the last to arrive."

When Arizona and Quincy were kids, their mom created a game in which the last person to arrive at the dinner table had to tell the group some random fact. This game not only enforces good habits about being on time for things but also forces you to constantly have random facts on hand.

I've seen it in action at the Abbott house. Frankly, it's interesting. I love learning new, random things.

Apparently, Quincy has carried the tradition to every team he's ever played on. The guys get a kick out of it. By virtue of friendship, it's carried through to us as well. I don't mind. I always have random shit churning through my head.

"Hmm. Let me think." I briefly tap my lip before a good one occurs to me. "Do you know why bananas are crooked?"

Cheetah smiles. "For the same reason Ezra's penis is crooked. Nature hates him."

Ezra smacks Cheetah's arm. "My dick isn't crooked, asshole." Then he mumbles, "Maybe a little, but at least I don't have elephantiasis of the nuts."

The guys all laugh while Cheetah gives them the finger. Men are such idiots.

I place my hands on my hips. "Does anyone want to know the answer?"

They all nod.

"Because of two interconnected reasons. One, they grow upward in opposition to gravity, which is always pushing against them. And two, they move toward the sunlight. Those two facts together cause them to be crooked."

Cheetah shrugs. "That's not why Ezra's penis is crooked. He has no game and therefore never has a reason for it to grow upward."

The guys all chuckle again. Even Ezra laughs this time. Men are so different from women. I would never insult my friends like that.

I force Cheetah to lift his shirt so I can see the writing and the artwork closeup. The snake is really good. He denies having it professionally done, but I'm confident he did.

After I take several pictures with Cheetah and his bare chest, which has my name on it, we have a few rounds of drinks, good conversation, and even a little dancing mixed in.

We're on the dance floor, and Cheetah has his eyes on me the whole time. He happens to be a really good dancer. I ask, "Were you one of those weird kids who took ballroom dancing lessons as a kid? Did you wear tight pants and have slicked-back hair?"

"No." He shakes his hips. "I'm Latino. Dancing and hip action in general are in my DNA. I've got a secret for you though. Trey was one of those weirdos. He can legit ballroom dance. You should have seen the two of them at their wedding. It looked like an episode of *Dancing with the Stars*."

I look over at Trey and Gemma, who joined us tonight. He's twirling her all over the place while they both smile and laugh.

"Wow, they're amazing."

He nods. "They are. You're a good dancer too."

He grabs my hips and moves them to the beat of the music.

I place my hands on his shoulders as we continue dancing. "I'll give you a confession, kitten. I wanted to take dance lessons as a kid, but our mother wouldn't allow it."

His face falls. "Why not? My sisters all took dance lessons when they were really little, though only one was any good."

"Our mother was a controlling asshole. We weren't allowed to participate in normal activities until we were twelve. That's kind of late to start dancing, and I really wanted to play ball. I had to choose."

"That sucks. All kids should do whatever activities they want. They should try everything."

I shake my head. "We couldn't do anything. *Anything*. Hell, I had to stash Reese's Peanut Butter Cups beneath my floorboard in my room because she wouldn't let us have candy."

"Best candy ever."

"Agreed. But only the dark chocolate kind."

His lips form an O. "Oooooh. Hard to find, but very good."

I nod. "I'm all for anything dark chocolate, but my mother monitored our diets like a hawk. She feared us gaining weight and losing modeling jobs."

"Your mom sounds like a peach."

"You have no idea. Speaking of peaches. What do you think of that blonde over there?" I nod toward an attractive woman who's shaking her ass.

His face scrunches. "I'm not into blondes. I feel like they're all fake. What do you call a blonde doing a handstand?"

"What?"

"A brunette."

I giggle. "Nice. Hmm, I don't know. I'm into blondes. Maybe it was my time in

California. How about another bet?"

His lips curl up in amusement. "Same terms?"

"Same terms, kitten."

CHAPTER THREE

CHEETAH

I'm standing in my bathroom, shaving the word *Kam* into my hair. The result of yet *another* lost bet with her from after their game the other night. She got the girl... again. Kamryn Hart has my number. I can't beat her.

Admittedly, I'm enjoying watching their softball games. I don't think I've ever appreciated how talented the girls are. I can't wait to go to more of their games. It's hard with our schedule, but we plan to go anytime we can.

Kam's on-field presence is amazing. She's the clear team leader, always talking to the younger players. Always giving them instructions and making them laugh. It's a good trick with newer players to keep them loose. There's a smart maturity to her game that you'd only notice if you play yourself.

She wears her hair in these Princess Leia side buns. It's so fucking hot with the tight pants showing off her ass. She blows bubbles with purple bubblegum. I swear, my dick twitches every time that bubble forms from her lips. I can't take my eyes off her.

After hearing Kam's walkup song at their first game, I did buy myself a nice cowboy hat to wear. It brought a smile to her gorgeous face when she saw me arrive with one on my head.

My Kam daydreaming is broken when my phone rings, and I glance at the screen to see that it's my mother. I hit the accept button. "Hola, mi madre bonita." *Hello, my beautiful mother.*

"Hola, mi hijo guapo." *Hello, my handsome son.* In her Spanish-accented English, she asks, "What are you doing?"

"I'm shaving."

"Oh good. I hope that filthy malandro look is gone." She hates my scruff.

"I'm not shaving my face."

"Dios mio, I don't need to hear about that."

I let out a laugh. "My hair. On the top of my head. Just giving myself a little...trim." I leave out the part about it being the name of the hot chick who won't give it up to me and went home with yet *another* woman, causing me to lose *another* bet, and that's why I'm shaving her name in my hair.

"Ahh. That could use a trim too, but I love seeing your handsome face. I don't know why you hide it."

Because women love sitting on it when it's a little rough. Possibly something I shouldn't share with my mother.

"How's Papá?"

She sighs. "Stubborn as a mule. His truck is acting up again. He's in the garage trying to fix it, making all kinds of unruly noises."

"The truck is almost as old as me. It's not fixable. Let me buy you a new one."

"Ay, no! Your money is for your future familia. For when you buy a house near ours and raise your family. We have plenty. He'll fix it. I have no doubt. If you need money for the house, let us know. We have some saved for you just in case."

I shake my head. Sometimes I truly wonder if they realize how much money I make. More than I could spend in ten lifetimes.

Hmm, I think I know what Santa will bring them this year. I make a mental note to call Uncle Roddy. He's a car salesman. Getting my father a new car and my uncle a little business. Sounds like a win-win.

Ignoring the comment about me buying a house near them, I say, "I'm sure he'll fix it. He loves a good challenge. He married you, after all."

She giggles. "I'm not that tough. I'm a softie."

I let out a laugh. "I love you, Mamá, but there's nothing soft about you."

"My stomach is soft. And too round."

"That's because you're such a great cook. I learned from the best."

"You flatter me. Speaking of cooking, are you cooking for anyone special right now? I can't wait for the day you move back here with your wife and children, but you need that wife first."

I roll my eyes. That's now twice she's mentioned me moving home in less than three minutes. That might be a record, even for her.

I'm not sure if that annoys me more than her constant questions about the status of my love life. She asks about it every time we speak, which is a few times a week.

Never one to ruffle any feathers, I answer, "No, Mamá. I can't find anyone as perfect as you."

"You're full of mierda." She gasps as if what she's about to tell me is important. "I almost forgot to tell you. Mariana and her mother stopped by last week. We were making empanadas. She's a wonderful cook, and she's gotten even more stunning. She asked for you."

Mariana is the younger sister of a childhood friend of mine. She's best friends with my baby sister. Mariana has always had a crush on me. She's attractive, but I just don't see her *that* way. She's kind of...boring. I like a woman with a big personality. One who can match mine. My mother knows all this, yet she still tries to shove Mariana down my throat.

I do my best to remain polite. "Please give her my best."

"You should do that in person. It's time to settle down, mi hijo. Make me grandbabies."

"You have seventeen grandbabies. You're being greedy."

"It's my greatest joy in life. And who wouldn't want a few more Gonzales niños blessing this world?"

"Better get Adriana or Camila on it."

"You're very funny."

I chuckle. "I think so."

"Well, when you come home for Christmas, we'll see where things go with Mariana. I may invite them to join our family dinner."

Oh no. She's made it so obvious and uncomfortable that I rarely go home anymore. "I gotta run, Mamá. I have lunch plans."

"With a woman? A date?"

"Yes, I have a lunch date with an amazing, perfect woman, so don't invite Mariana just yet."

She gasps. "How wonderful. Tell me about her."

"She's a stunning brunette and has an *outgoing* personality." I try to stress the last part because Mariana does not have an outgoing bone in her body.

"I assume she's not Latina. Does she at least speak Spanish?"

"I'm not sure. I've never asked."

"Send me photos."

I sigh. "Not a chance. I'll talk to you soon. Love you."

"Love you too."

THIRTY MINUTES LATER, I walk into Gemma's office building. Andrew, the longtime receptionist, greets me with a big smile. "Hey, Cruzy."

He started calling me that a few years ago. Even though he has a boyfriend, he seems to have a bit of a crush on me and isn't shy about it. I happily indulge him.

I look his body up and down in a way that makes him blush. "Have you been working out, Andrew? You're looking buff. I don't know if I can keep up with you anymore." I flex in my tight T-shirt just to make him happy. Yep, I'm a true humanitarian.

His face lights up. "I have. Thank you for noticing. You look good too, Cruzy."

"Thanks, buddy. Is my favorite girl around?"

"She's expecting you. She said that you can head straight back to her office but that you *shouldn't* hit on the cute brunette assistant in the cubicle outside her office. She very specifically told me to convey that to you."

I chuckle. "Thanks, handsome." I wink at him. "No brunette woman could ever be as cute as you, Andrew."

Andrew practically giggles in glee as I walk past him and back toward Gemma's office. Sadly, the cubicle outside her office is empty. In fact, it doesn't look like anyone is working there. It's just Gemma fucking with me. She loves to do that.

Her door is opened a crack, so I push it all the way open. Stunning Gemma DePaul is sitting at her executive desk like the badass attorney she is. As always, she's in a high-fashion business suit looking like she's a runway model. Though she's built more like a swimsuit model, with curves and huge tits. Her hair is in an elegant chignon, as it often is during the workday. Her full lips are painted in her signature red color. She has this old-school, classy Audrey Hepburn look, though Audrey has nothing on Gemma.

She smiles when she sees me and holds up her finger. "Trey, Cheetah just walked in, no more dirty talk." She wiggles her eyebrows at me.

He yells out, "Why are you in my wife's office, asshole?"

I yell back, "I'm trying to steal her. She needs a real man."

Gemma simply shakes her head. "Baby, Cheetah and I have our monthly book club meeting. You know that. I need to run. Love you." She loudly whispers to him, "You can pick our trope tonight. Make it extra dirty."

I yell out, "You should try why choose. I volunteer as tribute."

Gemma points at me. "Don't poke the bear."

I chuckle. "I love you too, Trey."

He grumbles. "I hate you. Make sure you go somewhere public."

Gemma giggles as she ends the call. She shakes her head at me. "Why do you start with him? You know how jealous he gets of our friendship."

I smile and answer, "Because he's an easy target...and I'm waiting for you to leave him for me."

Without an ounce of shame, she asks, "Have you pierced your dick yet?"

I reluctantly shake my head. "Hmm. Nope."

She shrugs. "Well, then...no. I won't leave him for you. He'll always have that on you. And I also happen to love him more than you could ever possibly imagine. He's my forever. Sorry."

My shoulders fall. "Ugh. Fine." I mumble, "Such bullshit. I saw you first." And I was there when he got his dick pierced for her. I passed out cold the second the needle touched his dick. I can't believe he did that for her...before they went on their first date. He overheard her on the phone saying how much she liked it and went that night to get it done. What a psychopath. A lucky-in-love psychopath, but a psychopath nonetheless.

She gives me a small smile. "We'll always have our book club lunches." Throwing the strap of her purse over her shoulder, she offers me her arm. "Shall we? There's a new oyster bar around the corner. Let's go there."

I thread my arm through hers. "Ooh. An aphrodisiac. Good idea. You'll be gagging for me within the hour."

She giggles while we leave her office. As we're making our way toward the elevator, we see her boss walking out of her office. Her face is flushed, and her hair is messy. She's a sexy-as-hell middle-aged woman. Like Gemma, she's a brunette with green eyes and killer curves.

Her face lights up when she sees me. "Cruz! Good to see you. You guys are having an amazing season."

"Thanks, Darian. The team is great this year. Hoping we make a run."

She nods. "Me too. Did you know that my daughter is one of the new owners?"

My chin drops. "Really? Which owner?"

"Reagan Daulton."

"I guess both brains and beauty run in the family. Speaking of which, are you ready to leave your husband for me yet?"

A deep voice grumbles, "Not a chance, hotshot."

I turn and see her husband, Jackson Knight, walking out of her office fixing his tie. His face is also flushed, and his dark hair is messy.

I look at Gemma and widen my eyes. She smirks and gives me a subtle nod that they were, in fact, just getting it on in Darian's office. We both have to bite back our smiles.

Gemma waves. "We're headed to lunch."

Jackson winks at Darian. "I just had lunch. It was delicious."

After ten minutes of gossiping about how her boss often has lunchtime sex in the office, we're seated at the restaurant, and each of us orders a glass of wine. I ask, "How's Fletch?" Their son, Fletcher, is about six months old.

She has a dreamy look on her face. "Amazing. You can't imagine how much you're capable of loving a child until you have one. I want to eat him up. He's got Trey's chin dimple. So freakin' cute. And seeing Trey with him is probably my favorite thing in the world. The two of them are on their way to the park right now. I hope they send pics."

"Oh, he'll definitely send pics, trying to interrupt our lunch."

She nods in agreement. "Yep, he will. How are things with you?"

"Good. The team is on fire. Layton is starting to play better than he has in years. Adding Quincy to the pitching rotation has been a huge boost. I think we'll make a run."

"I didn't mean baseball. I know how *that's* going." She leans forward a little. "I meant life. I'm not a fool. I've noticed the way you've interacted with Kamryn Hart. You're crushing on her. Big time."

I shrug. "I am, but I don't think she's into me. She keeps going home with other people. Other *women*."

She contemplates my words for a moment. "She's a different bird. I haven't quite figured her out yet. I've spent more time talking to her sister, but I think Kam goes home with women to mess with you. And, just like in kindergarten, when a girl messes with a boy...you know what that means..."

I pinch my eyebrows together. "That she likes me?"

Gemma nods. "Absolutely. Call it a woman's intuition."

"I hope you're right. She could be the woman to help me get over my crush on you."

Gemma winks at me. "Fingers crossed. Tread carefully. Kamryn is likely a little damaged."

"Really? How so?"

Gemma shrugs. "I don't know specifics, but she is. I can tell. When a woman has that much masculine bravado, there's usually other things going on. They're hiding something. I like her for you though. She's got a great personality and will keep you on your toes. We both know you like a bit of a challenge. Don't give up."

I exhale a breath. "I won't. Now onto the topic at hand. Did you finish our book of the month?"

She smiles. "I sure did. You can't ever go wrong with a Jade Dollston book. And I know exactly which scene was your favorite."

"Which one?"

"When her mother walks into her apartment and her man walks out naked stroking himself, not realizing the mom is standing there. He epically fails at trying to cover his giant body and erection, and then her cat jumps into his arms."

I start laughing. "You know me well. Classic Dollston humor. And you know I love a good scene where a couple is walked in on while they're in a compromising position."

She nods. "Yep. That's why I have at least one in all my books. They're *always* funny, right?"

"Every. Damn. Time."

We're approaching the seventh-inning stretch of our game. It's a tradition at all professional baseball games that there's a pause in the game between the top and bottom halves of the seventh inning. As a song plays, the crowd stands and sings along. It's considered a time to stretch their legs and have a little fun. It's also a time for the grounds crew to clean up the field a bit. Each individual stadium has a song they play for every seventh-inning stretch in a given season. It usually doesn't vary from game to game, only season to season, and each team has a different selection.

It's become a bit commonplace in Philly for me to dance with a fan during the break. It started a few years ago when Chris Brown dropped the song, *Cheetah*. I mentioned it to then-owner Harold Greene, and he loved the idea of playing the song during the stretch and me picking a fan at each game to dance with. We've been doing it ever since. It's usually a random stranger, with all the ladies clamoring for the spot, though it's been my mother a few times and Gemma twice just to piss off Trey. I even danced with Gemma's grandmother, Grammy Jane, one time. She's a hoot. She lives in Florida, but she and Gemma are extremely close, and she visits once or twice a year. In fact, I think she'll be here in a few weeks. Assuming she comes to a game, I'll have to remind the field crew to bring her down to dance with me again.

I told the crew where Kamryn will be sitting for this game. Now that Arizona and Layton are dating, the four girls have season passes to the best four seats in the stadium, right behind our dugout. The cameras have started to find them since the Anacondas are steadily growing in popularity. I want to have her brought onto the field to dance with me tonight.

As the top half of the inning ends, I see them escorting her onto the field. She has a huge smile on her beautiful face. She knows what it means to be brought out here at this point in the game. She even shimmies her way to me on the field. Most of the women who do this are a little embarrassed and shy, but not Kamryn Hart. She's going to own this.

She's in cutoff jean shorts that show off her long legs and a tight, tiny Lancaster jersey. I think it's even bedazzled. She's so hot, though she'd be hotter in my jersey. I make a mental note to have one sent to her.

As she approaches, I wink at her. "Just so you know, my safe word is *harder*."

She lets out a laugh. "You like to be a bottom, kitten? I would have taken you for an on-top kind of man."

I take her hand and kiss it. "Kam bam, a great pancake isn't done until it's flipped on both sides."

She runs her full, sexy bottom lip through her teeth. "Is that an offer?"

"It's a promise."

Her eyes flash with amusement. She's got the most expressive eyes I've ever seen. They tell a thousand stories, all of which promise fun. It's the biggest difference between her and Bailey. Even though they're identical, I can easily tell the difference from their eyes. Bailey's are soft and sweet. Kam's make all the blood in my body rush below my belt.

She reaches for my baseball hat and turns it backward. "Ooh, I like that much better, though not as much as the cowboy hat."

"I know you like to ride cowboys. You can ride me anytime you want, Kam bam."

Her lips curl in amusement. "Did you know that the most dangerous way to have sex, as measured by hospitalizations, is reverse cowgirl?"

I shake my head. "I didn't."

"If you can't ride a cowboy properly, you shouldn't. It's a good thing my riding skills are top-notch."

Fuck, I'm getting hard in a stadium in front of tens of thousands of people.

Our bodies are close, and we're staring at each other. She

must feel the same chemistry I'm feeling. It's oozing from both of us.

Our intense stare-down is broken by the music beginning. I twirl her around while all the fans sing along and clap as Kam and I put on a full show. Definitely the best one in all the years I've done this for our hometown fans. There's even a touch of dirty dancing involved. She can really move her hips and does so without an ounce of embarrassment.

We're both smiling and laughing throughout the whole song, having a great time. I can't remember the last time I had so much fun with a woman...while vertical.

When it's over, our lips are only an inch or two apart. I want to kiss her, but something tells me that Kamryn wouldn't like being put on the spot like this in front of forty thousand fans. She likes to maintain control. This has to be on her timeline. I won't force it.

I kiss her cheek, by her ear, taking in her peach scent while whispering, "Thanks for the dance, Kam bam."

I feel her warm breath on me as she whispers back, "Anytime, kitten."

CHAPTER FOUR

CHEETAH

I'm at Tanner Montgomery's house tonight for our monthly poker game. He's my agent and has been since I started playing ball. He's only thirteen years older than me, but he's always been a surrogate father to me since mine lives so far away.

He likes to host a few of his local clients every month for a poker game full of good food, good drinks, bad smack talk, and the best of friends. He has a high-end man cave, complete with a poker table, pool table, and a full bar. It's me, Layton, and Trey from the Cougars, as well as Vance McCaffrey and Daylen Humblecut from the Philadelphia Camels, the local professional football team. Vance is their quarterback, and Daylen is their tight end. Both are among the biggest stars in the league.

Vance is a little grumpy, and Daylen is a lot goofy, but they're great guys, and I consider them friends. The two of them are the best of friends, even if a bit of an odd couple with their vastly different personalities. For some reason it works, and they're inseparable.

Vance is from Montana and can often be seen at public events in a cowboy hat and cowboy boots, paying homage to his roots. He's got dark hair, a little long but in style. Daylen, on the other hand, has wild blond hair that I don't think I've ever seen cut or styled in the same manner two times in a row. He messes with it as much as he messes with his facial hair.

We're headed out on a road trip tomorrow so I'm happy to be having a fun night with my friends, full of laughs and shit talk. It's always plentiful during our poker nights. The Anacondas are on a road trip right now, which is why we're meeting tonight. Layton hasn't otherwise torn himself away from Arizona since they started dating. I've never seen him like this with a woman. They return late tonight. Layton has been counting the seconds.

Daylen is talking about their teammate, Presley, whose wife is newly pregnant. Presley apparently just made his first-ever trip to the OBGYN with her and was dumbfounded by it. Daylen chuckles. "He couldn't get over the fact that the doctor literally stuck his hands into his wife. I guess it's one of those things you sort of know about but don't truly appreciate unless you witness it."

Hmm. I've never thought about it. "Was the doctor younger or older?" I ask.

Daylen shrugs. "I don't know."

I nod. "I've heard that women prefer old OBGYNs."

Daylen looks at me skeptically. "Why is that? More experience?"

I smirk as I wiggle my fingers. "Shaky hands."

Everyone except Trey and Tanner laugh. Tanner simply rolls his eyes at us. He's a single father with a seven-year-old daughter.

He sighs. "I went to Fallon's appointments when she was pregnant with Harper. It's very clinical."

Trey nods his head. "Agreed. You morons are a sad group."

Daylen responds, "Sad? We're not sad. Sad is when a nymphomaniac says *let's just be friends*."

I chuckle as I toss my cards on the table and fold my hand. "I'm out. You fuckers are taking all my money tonight."

Trey throws his cards on the table. "I'm out too. I think I'm going to head home."

Tanner scoffs. "It's been less than an hour. Why are you leaving so early?"

"Gemma made me come here. Said I needed a chill night with boys, but I want to get home before she goes to sleep."

The guys all give him shit for being whipped, but if I had Gemma DePaul at home waiting for me, I'd feel the same.

I nod at him, and with a straight face say, "Tell my future wife that I said hello."

He gives me the finger, and I smile. I do enjoy ruffling his feathers.

A FEW HOURS LATER, I'm tossing and turning in bed. It's one of those nights where you wonder what you're doing with your life. I'm a successful baseball player. That was my childhood dream, and I achieved it. I've made more money than I'll ever need in my life. I live in a gorgeous condo with amazing city views. I have a great group of friends and a wonderful family that I love. Yet for the first time in my life, I feel like something is missing.

If I'm being honest, that feeling started a few years ago when Trey met Gemma, and I had a front-row seat to watch their love story unfold. While most of the guys on the team are married, my inner circle isn't. Layton is a thirty-four-year-old career bachelor. So are Vance and Daylen, for that matter. Ezra never dates. Our newest close friend, Quincy, goes home with a different woman every night. I saw the emotional toll Tanner's divorce took on him. It's made him swear away all relationships.

Trey was just like the rest of us, moving from woman to woman, until the second he laid eyes on Gemma. He was a goner from that point on. I joke about my crush on Gemma, but it's their relationship I envy.

And then one gorgeous face pops into my mind.

KAMRYN

It's the middle of the night and I'm awake, as always. I have a million things running through my head.

The first few weeks of our season have gone well, and we all seem to be acclimating to our new city. When neither of our teams are on the road, we tend to go out with the guys on the Cougars. They're a fun group.

I'm sitting on my sofa typing away on my computer when I notice the screen on my phone light up. I pick it up to see that a text came through.

> Unknown: It's Cheetah. You awake?

I decide to fuck with him and type back.

> Me: I know a lot of cheetahs. None of whom I've given my telephone number to. You'll have to be more specific. Maybe something only one individual cheetah would know.

Unknown: This Cheetah knows that you're a vagitarian.

I can't help but laugh.

Me: Hmm. Not true. I like a meaty burger too.

Unknown: Meaty burgers are good for you. You know what I don't like about Philly?

Me: What?

Unknown: There's no In and Out Burger. I guess that means I'll have to go in and out of you.

Me: Ohhhh, I only know one cheetah with cheesy pickup lines. A cheetah who recently sent me a very tight, youth-sized jersey with his name on the back. This must be Cruz Gonzales. I have you in my contacts as kitten.

I don't, but I will in a second.

Kitten: I bet I can make you purr like a kitten.

Me: No easy task, especially for men. Where are you?

Kitten: On the toilet. Just letting you know you're my number one while I make a number two.

Me: So romantic. Every woman dreams of a man saying things like that to her.

Kitten: I know. I do my best work on this toilet. Why are you awake?

Me: I rarely sleep.

Kitten: Why?

Me: Because I'm busy washing my hair.

Kitten: Are you in the shower now? FaceTime me if you are.

Me: Whoops. Just got out. Sorry.

Kitten: Damn! Are you liking Philly?

Me: I think I like it better than Chicago.

Kitten: Why?

Me: I don't have to see the Chicago Bulls logo anymore. It's all over the place in Chi-town. Have you ever looked at that sucker upside down? It looks like a robot defiling a crab.

It's silent for a few minutes. He's definitely googling the logo and turning it upside down.

Kitten: Holy. Fucking. Shit. You're right.

Me: I know. I usually am.

Kitten: You just blew my mind.

Me: My blowing skills are often praised.

Kitten: I'm willing to give a firsthand evaluation whenever you're up for it.

Me: Good night, kitten.

Kitten: Sweet dreams, Kam bam.

I'M on the couch working on my laptop when my sister wakes up and sleepily walks out of her room. She stretches and yawns, "Morning."

I lift my head and turn it to her. "Did you know that semen is low in calories?"

She twists her lips. "Hmm. Is that your way of telling me that we're having semen for breakfast today?"

I let out a laugh. "Not today. There are a bunch of sliced pineapples on the kitchen table." We've been eating pineapples in mass quantity since I discovered that it's supposed to make the taste of your vajayjay better when someone goes down on you.

"Thanks. What are you up to today?"

"Not much. What about you?"

"I'm heading over to the Montgomerys's house."

Bailey just started nannying for the famous sports agent Tanner Montgomery. He's a single father to a seven-year-old daughter. I think she already has a crush on him.

"How's your zaddy doing?"

She rolls her eyes. "He's just my boss. Nothing else."

"Bull-fucking-shit. I know you have a crush on him. You've always been into older men. Hell, you saw an older guy on the television the other day and were salivating. I had to tell you it was for a Depends ad."

She lets out a laugh as she makes her way to the kitchen and yells back, "That guy was, like, forty-five. He didn't need Depends."

I shout back, "Try seventy-five." Okay, maybe he was only sixty, but it was still funny that she was so into a guy in a Depends ad.

She walks back in with a few pineapple slices in hand. "I'll admit Mr. Montgomery is handsome for an older man."

I nod. "Fuck yes. I internet stalked him. He's McZaddy."

She giggles and mumbles, "Truth." She nods toward my laptop. "Did you sleep at all?"

I bite my lip. She hates it that I don't sleep. "Maybe an hour or so. I just don't need as much sleep as regular people."

"What do you do on your laptop all night?"

Besides what happened that night in the studio when we were ten, this is probably the only secret I've ever kept from my sister. I'm not ready to tell her about it just yet.

I twist my lips and come up with something believable. "I watch a lot of porn and get myself off."

"Do you watch girl porn or guy porn?" she asks.

"Depends on my mood." I wiggle my eyebrows. "Sometimes both at the same time. That *really* gets me going."

Our conversation is cut short by a knock at our door. I get up to answer it, assuming it's going to be Ripley or Arizona, but it's Justin, our redheaded, nerdy neighbor from across the hallway.

His eyes widen and then move up and down my body. I'm in panties, no bra, and a T-shirt that just barely reaches my waist. Whatever. I'm wearing more than a bathing suit.

He starts physically shaking with nerves. "G...g...good morning, Kamryn."

I give him a sexy smile because it will probably be the only time a woman ever smiles at him in his life. "Hey, handsome. What can I do for you?"

He hands me a plate of something covered in aluminum foil that smells good. "I made pineapple muffins. I know how much you love pineapples. I see you buying them all the time."

Oookay. Sort of creepy that he knows about my purchasing habits.

"Aww, thanks, Justin. That was really sweet of you. They smell amazing."

He smiles like I just told him I'd have sex with him.

I hear a door in the hallway opening and then closing just before I see Arizona and Ripley approach. Arizona looks at my state of undress and raises an eyebrow before turning to Justin. "Good morning, Justin."

"Umm...good morning, Arizona. Do you guys have a game today?"

She shakes her head. "Not today. Rip and I are heading over to the stadium for a little training. I just wanted to see if Kam and Bailey wanted to come with us."

I nod. "I'll go with you. Bails is headed to Daddy Montgomery's house." I look back at Justin and hold up the plate. "Thanks for these. Have a good day."

He hesitates briefly before turning and walking back into his apartment with his head down. Ripley and Arizona walk into ours before I close the door. Ripley shakes her head. "The poor guy is in there jerking off to images of you dressed like this."

I scrunch my face in disgust. "Ugh. A ginger penis is unappealing. It's probably like a raw carrot. Crooked and discolored."

Ripley scoffs. "Stop being mean to gingers. Once again, I'm one of your best friends and I'm a ginger."

"You know it's just the men who give me the willies." I shiver. "Ugh. Do you know why ginger men all smell so bad?"

She lets out a long breath. "God help me. Why?"

"So blind people know who to avoid as well."

She pinches her lips together, clearly fighting a smile.

"How does a male ginger high-five his best friend?" I ask.

She raises her eyebrows in question.

I answer, "He claps his hands."

She spits in laughter. "There is something really wrong with you, Kam."

"Agreed." I sigh. "Just messing with you. He really is such a sweetie...in a Ted Bundy, serial killer kind of way. I almost feel like we should give him an SOS."

Arizona does her trademark snort-laugh. "Holy shit. I totally forgot we used to do that." She covers her eyes with her hand. "It's embarrassing how many times we've done that."

In college, we performed a bit of a *community service* for nice, nerdy guys who had no chance of getting any action. We would each kiss him. All four of us, one right after the other. Full kisses; tongue and everything. We called it an SOS, as in us saving the person. Arizona and I were amused by it while Bailey and Ripley did it because they felt like we were genuinely helping the poor guys.

Ripley winces. "It's kind of disgusting when you think about it, but if there was ever anyone in need of it, it's poor Justin."

I nod. "Truth."

My close friends are all busy tonight, so I agreed to go out with my teammate, Amber, and her friend, Trisha. Trisha is very introverted and could use a little help in the confidence department, but she's not my mission this evening. My mission is to find Amber a man. I don't spend too much time in clubs anymore, mostly because my sister and friends don't like it, but I wanted to take Amber out and help her move on from her hobosexual ex. She deserves a little fun.

I'm in a short black skirt and backless, midriff-baring sparkly silver halter top. The club has a great vibe and is completely packed. The music is blaring, and people are drinking, dancing, and talking, as is normal at a club like this.

We're on the dance floor, having a blast. We've had a few drinks. Amber has let loose, but this Trisha chick is super uptight, constantly wanting to move off the dance floor and sit down. She's kind of a drag.

At least seven guys have approached me and asked me to go home with them. They didn't even ask for my name. It's not like

I'm into that get-to-know-you chit-chat much, but a fucking exchange of names and a few sentences would be nice.

Why am I so off-put by guys tonight? I'm definitely taking a girl home with me.

I'm swaying my hips to the beat of the music when a familiar, extremely attractive, very muscular, tall man with shaggy blond hair approaches me and places his hands on my hips without invitation. He gives me a bit of a goofy smile. "Wow. You're stunning. I'm real life swiping right on you."

I let out a laugh. "That's funny, but I'm not a Tinder girl. I don't need an app to get laid."

He smirks. "No doubt. I've watched you swat away man after man all night."

"Well, some guys are real assholes. Like...every single one of them in this club." I look down at his hands on my hips and raise my eyebrow.

He takes the cue and immediately removes them. "I promise you; my friends and I aren't assholes. We're just here to have a little fun. We have a booth. Come have a drink with us." He holds out his hand in a more respectful manner. "I'm Daylen."

I narrow my eyes at him. "You look familiar, Daylen. Have we met before?"

He shakes his head. "Nope. Trust me, I'd remember meeting you. No bullshit, you're the most beautiful woman in this club. What's your name?"

At least this guy asked for it.

"Kamryn. My friends call me Kam. You can call me Kamryn."

He smiles before lifting my hand and kissing it. "Come. Have a drink with us, Kamryn. I'm hoping you'll let me call you Kam by the end of the night. Worst case scenario, you'll have a few drinks and a few laughs."

I place my hands on my hips. "I have two girlfriends with me."

"Bring them. The more the merrier." He points toward a back corner area. "We're right up there."

I look up and see a booth that is clearly being guarded by

security. I know enough to realize they must be famous or they wouldn't have a roped-off booth at a club with security surrounding it. Given the size of this guy, he must be a professional athlete.

I shrug. "Maybe in a little bit. Let me check with them."

The cocky bastard smirks again before he walks away. Amber and Trisha run up to me, practically bouncing on their feet. It's the only smile I've seen Trisha crack all night. Amber excitedly screeches, "Holy shit, Daylen Humblecut just hit on you. What did he say?"

"He invited us to sit with him and his friends. Who's Daylen Humblecut?"

Amber gives me an incredulous look. "Only one of the most famous football players on the planet. He's the tight end for the Camels." She fans herself. "Why is that such a hot position? Between him, Travis Kelce, and Axel Broxton, I don't know who's the hottest, but they are *big* boys, and I like me a good old-fashioned big boy."

I look up toward the booth again. It's crowded. It must be filled with famous football players. Could be fun. I'm not feeling it, but this will be good for Amber. She's a pretty girl with long, straight, auburn hair a few shades darker than Ripley's. Guys dig ginger women. Trisha has no shot, but who knows what will happen?

I wave. "Follow me."

Trisha fiddles nervously with the bottom of her *looks-like-she's-about-to go-to-church* floral sundress, complete with a white cardigan sweater. "I think I might leave."

I shake my head. "Nope. You're staying. Push yourself out of your comfort zone. Will you let me help you a bit?"

She pinches her eyebrows together. "How so?"

I take Trisha's hand and pull her toward the bathroom. I spend about ten minutes doing the best I can with her hair and makeup, pulling her frizzy brown hair into a more stylish ponytail and adding a little color to her pale skin. It's a vast improvement.

Amber fixes her already perfectly applied makeup, accentuating her big, green eyes. She's adorable. I make it a policy to never sleep with teammates, but I'd be totally into her if I met her at a club.

After finishing up in the bathroom, I lead us toward the booth. Daylen's face lights up as we approach. Like Cheetah, he has one of those larger-than-life smiles.

Now my mind drifts to Cheetah. I can't shake him, and it's annoying me. Maybe I should go home with one of these guys tonight. I need Cruz Gonzales fucked out of my system.

Daylen stands. "Kamryn, please meet Vance, Beau, and Presley." He points to each of them. "The beautiful lady next to Presley is his wife, Layla."

Presley wraps his arm around her proudly. "My *pregnant* wife, Layla."

She's got a very small baby bump. I wouldn't have known she was pregnant if he didn't mention it. She looks familiar to me, though I can't place her. They're an attractive Latino couple.

Vance rolls his eyes. "He manages to sneak in the fact that he knocked her up into every conversation."

Okay, I definitely recognize Vance McCaffrey. He's a super famous quarterback. A fucking hot-as-hell famous quarterback with longer, dark hair. Good lord, he's sexy in a cowboy way. While the rest of the guys are dressed more stylishly, Vance is in old jeans, a flannel top, and cowboy boots, giving off that *I don't give a fuck* allure.

While Daylen smiles, Vance scowls. He's broody. I can tell. Not my usual type, but I might make an exception to get that rugged, sharp jawline between my legs.

I nod toward Amber and Trisha while I introduce them to the gang.

Daylen motions for me to sit next to him, but I push Amber to do so. Daylen reminds me too much of Cheetah. I need the opposite of Cheetah tonight.

I sit near Vance and stare right at him. His face is still sour.

"What crawled up your ass, cowboy?"

Daylen starts laughing hysterically. "Oh, shit. She's got your number. You better be nice to her, McCaffrey. The last hot chick who gave you the time of day has been ghosting you ever since."

Vance narrows his eyes at Daylen. "I'm not getting ghosted. My texts are just so interesting that she's taking time to think about her reply."

He says it deadpan. I'm trying to hide my smile, not knowing if he seriously believes that.

Daylen lets out a deep, booming laugh and Vance cracks a small, crooked smile. Okay, grumpy bear has a sense of humor. I like that.

Vance throws his arm around me. "You're just sour that your crush sat next to me, Humblecut. Must be your teeny weenie."

Daylen asks, "What do you call a woman who likes small dicks?"

Vance cautiously responds, "What?"

"Your last girlfriend."

I spit out laughing and Vance glares at me. I sheepishly admit, "Sorry. That's funny."

He raises an unimpressed eyebrow. "Do I look like the type of man who has a...teeny weenie?"

I slowly and obviously rake my eyes up and down his big, thick body. He most certainly doesn't.

Daylen breaks me out of my ogling by asking, "Are you a model, Kamryn?"

I turn my head to him. "At times, yes, but my real job is being a professional athlete, just like you."

His eyes widen in shock. I get that reaction all the time.

"What sport?"

"Softball. I'm on the new team in Philly. The Anacondas." I nod toward Amber. "So is she."

Amber isn't listening, too engrossed in a conversation with Beau. He's cute in a more militant way. He's got a buzz cut and a giant body. He must play defense. Amber said she likes a big boy.

While all the guys sitting here fit the bill, he's certainly the biggest of them all.

Daylen widens his eyes as if something just occurred to him. "Ahh, you're friends with Cheetah and Layton, right?"

I nod. "I am. My friend is dating Layton."

Vance and Daylen look at each other as something passes between them.

Vance slowly removes his arm from around me and says, "They're good friends of ours too. We all share the same agent."

"Tanner Montgomery?"

He nods. "Yes. Layton and Cheetah are like brothers to us."

I study his face. He's not going to make a move on me because of Cheetah. Fucking guy is cockblocking me even when he's not here.

I swear, I've had it with men.

A cute girl walks by. She's walked by this table at least three times. I assumed she wanted the guys' attention, but this time, she winks at me. Fuck these guys. If they're not going to touch me because of Cheetah, I'm bailing. I'm going to talk to the hot girl. I said I wanted a woman tonight anyway.

I stand. Amber and Trisha immediately begin to follow me. I point at them. "You two stay."

Amber leans over and whispers, "I used to date a guy named Beau. I can't do anything with this one. It would be weird."

I shake my head. "If you sleep with two people with the same name, they cancel each other out and lower your body count."

She pinches her eyebrows together. "Is that true?"

I nod. "Yep." I just made it up, but the girl needs some action to help her move on from her ex, and Beau is just what the doctor ordered.

She agrees to stay. Trisha says she's grabbing an Uber, and I don't bother to stop her. She's nice, but without a little help from me, this will be nothing but awkward for her. I feel bad leaving her, but I came here tonight to get Amber laid, and she looks well on her way. Now it's my turn.

CHAPTER FIVE

KAMRYN

The guys have been on a long road trip. Arizona has been missing Layton. I think she's falling for him. I hope she doesn't get hurt. Layton Lancaster is a well-known playboy. Admittedly, he outwardly appears devoted to her. I hope his feelings are genuine. I'd hate to see her suffer any more heartbreak than she already has.

Fortunately for her, we're leaving for a road trip, and we happen to be staying at the same hotel as the Cougars. Arizona has been bouncing around all day, excited to see Layton.

Due to an airport delay, we don't end up arriving at the hotel until the middle of the night.

Arizona is my roommate for this trip. I'm getting into bed when she looks at me from hers and bites her lip. "Will you cover for me?"

"Ooh. Sneaking into your boyfriend's room for some action? How very high school of you."

She giggles. "It's been eleven days and seven hours since he's been inside me. I need him."

I lift an eyebrow. "That was freakishly accurate. You do realize you went over a year without sex, and now after eleven days and seven hours you're gagging for it?"

She gives me a dreamy smile. "Well, I've never gotten it as good as he gives it to me." She sighs. "It's more than the incredible sex. I...just...need him. I can't explain the inner peace I have when I'm in his arms. The noises in my head go away."

I roll my eyes at the ridiculousness. "Fucking hell. You're dick-whipped. Are you in love with him?" Even when she was engaged to her shitbag ex, she wasn't like this.

She shrugs. "I'm not sure I know the difference between like and love anymore. What do you think the difference is?"

"You're asking me? You know I'm not the right person to ask. The only difference I see between liking and loving is spitting and swallowing."

She lets out a laugh before smiling. "Spitters are quitters."

I nod enthusiastically. "Damn straight they are. What's the point in doing all that work just to spit it out?" I wave my hand at her. "Go have fun. I'll cover for you. Have a few orgasms for me."

She stands and salutes me. "Will do, sergeant. Thanks."

After propping a few pillows under her blankets to make sure it looks like she's sleeping in her bed just in case the coaches check, I attempt to fall asleep in mine.

At some point during the night, I feel a warm body slip into my bed and a hand rubbing my hip. Assuming it's Arizona messing with me, I wiggle back but feel a large erection on my ass. Huh?

I quickly lift the upper half of my body and snap my head around. "Cheetah? What are you doing here?"

"I just watched Layton and Arizona have sex. I'm so fucking turned on."

I turn all the way around and shove his chest. His shockingly solid, broad chest. "Go choke the chicken like a normal person."

"I did. While watching them. I'm still turned on. Those two fuck like rock stars. My dick won't go down. Want to give him a little attention?"

"I'm not having sex with you."

He gives me a playful smile. "I know. Honestly, I was just jealous watching them peacefully sleeping together, so I stole her room key. Can I sleep here? I'll play with your fun sponge if you want."

"Cheetah—"

"I'm just kidding. I know you're not into me. Can't we cuddle like friends?"

It's not that I'm not into him. I'm too into him.

I point to the exceedingly large tent in his shorts. "You have a boner. Friends don't let friends get boners around each other."

"I will always have a boner around you. You're legit the hottest woman I've ever met. I can't control it. It's physics."

"It's not physics, dipshit, it's biology."

He chuckles. "I love how smart you are. I never get to spend time with smart women."

"That's because you bang skanks from bars and clubs who are only interested in your bank account."

"That's a valid point." He tucks my hair behind my ear. "I do enjoy your brain though. I like how it works."

That may be the first time in my life a man has complimented me on something other than my looks. I know for a fact that my brain has never been complimented, despite the fact that I'm at least twice as smart as every man I've ever met.

The big softie is getting to me. I can't believe I'm considering letting him stay. I need to fuck with him first though.

"I like how funny you are. If you make me laugh, I'll let you stay. If I belly laugh, I'll even let you grab a boob."

His face lights up. "Hmm. Let me think. If sex with three people is called a threesome, and sex with four people is called a foursome, what's sex with me?"

"What?"

He holds up his hand. "Handsome."

I swallow down the laugh bubbling in my throat. "Nope. Didn't do it." I point toward the door. "See ya around, kitten."

His adorable face falls and he sticks out his pouty lower lip. "One more chance? Please. I want to stay with you."

He then busts out the dimples. Fucking dimples.

"Fine, but then you leave. Last chance. Don't bring out the dimples if you fail. That's not playing fair."

He silently laughs. "Deal. This one is a guaranteed stomach clencher. A young guy goes to a library and shamelessly walks right up to the librarian and asks, 'Do you have a book for men with small dicks?' She begins typing away on her computer before saying, 'I don't think it's in yet.' He perks up and replies, 'Yep, that's the one.'"

I burst out laughing. Damn it. He got me. He smiles in victory before holding out his arms for me.

Plopping down onto the pillow with my back to him, I reach behind me and give his dick a quick tap. "You earned your stay but keep the bishop in the castle."

He sucks in a breath. "If you touch the bishop again, no castle will keep him contained. But if you're into medieval play, I'm down with that. I'll wear one of those armored outfits if it's your thing."

"Stop talking. It ruins your appeal."

I wiggle my ass on his dick. He warns, "Kam—"

I giggle as I snuggle into him. I even grab his hand and place it on my T-shirt-covered boob. "Payment for services rendered. I never go back on my word."

"Umm. You have great tits." He squeezes it a few times. "I wasn't sure they were real, but I feel they are. They defy gravity."

"I'm twenty-eight, not eighty-eight."

He thrusts his hard dick onto me again. "You like numbers? I'm eight inches if you want to check. Nine when covered in Kam bam fluids."

I gulp. Nine inches. That's tempting, but I know it's a mistake. Our groups hang out too much. I don't want issues. At least that's what I'm telling myself.

"Good night, kitten."

He kisses my head and squeezes my boob again. "Good night, Kam bam."

His arms are around me, his hand is on my boob, and his hard dick is pressed to my ass. I don't think I've ever done this with a man where it didn't lead to sex.

Naturally, I can't sleep. I eventually whisper, "Kitten? You awake?"

"Yes."

"Tell me something real about you. Something I can't find on Google."

"Have you been googling me?"

"Maybe."

I feel him smile into my hair. "I'm an endangered species."

"Nine-inch dicks are rare but not endangered."

He chuckles. "I didn't mean that. I'm a blue-eyed Latino."

"I didn't realize that was on the endangered list."

"It is. I'm the only one in my immediate family. Besides one cousin and an aunt, I don't know any others, and I know *a lot* of Latinos and have a *very* big family."

"I hope the mailman didn't have blue eyes."

He snorts in annoyance. "There's no joke you can tell that I haven't already heard. My brothers are relentless about it."

"I would be too if I were them. It's cool. I love your eyes. Tell me something real though. Something deep."

He rubs his thumb over my nipple. Suddenly his alleged nine inches are sounding mighty appealing.

In a low, quiet voice, he admits, "I've never been in love."

"A lot of people haven't."

"I'm thirty. It's weird. I feel like something is wrong with me."

"Have you ever told a woman you loved her?"

"I just said I've never been in love."

"Doesn't mean you haven't said it. Men say it to me five minutes after meeting me. Women say it right after I go down on them."

He lets out a laugh. "You must give good head."

"The best." I flick my tongue a few times on his forearm.

He sighs. "How did you know you liked both men and women?"

"I don't know. I was always attracted to both. It's not like I woke up one day and decided to be something mainstream society doesn't understand. I just am. Honestly, I think all people are bisexual."

"I'm not. I don't like men."

"Your hand is bisexual. It likes pussy and dick."

"Huh?"

"Where was the last place your hand was before you walked into my room?" I wiggle onto his dick again.

He breathes, "Holy shit. You're right. My hand is bisexual. It likes dick and pussy."

My body shakes in silent laughter.

He squeezes my boob. Again. "Tell me something about woman-on-woman sex that most people don't know."

"Don't you watch porn?"

"You know I do. But I also know that's sensationalized. Tell me something I can't learn from the highly educational porn websites."

I smile to myself. "Scissoring isn't real. No one does that. It's something men think women do but they don't. It's fake news."

He gasps. "What? For real?"

I nod. "Yep."

"You guys don't ever rub against each other?"

"Of course we do. It's not different from hetero-sex in that regard. You're grinding your dick on my ass right now."

He thrusts his dick onto me for added effect.

I continue, "The proper term is tribbing. I might rub my clit against some part of her and she might do the same to me, but it's never clit to clit. Think about the body part involved in that. It doesn't give you the needed friction to feel good. It's like trying to put two electric sockets together to make a spark. It doesn't do anything. A thigh is so much better for that."

"Hmm. I guess that makes sense. You've officially blown my mind." He continues rubbing my nipple through my shirt. "Have you ever been in love, Kam?"

I stiffen a bit, though I bizarrely feel comfortable confiding in him. "Once. Dak, my high school sweetheart. My heart was shattered beyond repair." I'm quiet for a second. "I've sworn away any and all commitment since. It's not worth the pain. I'll never give up control again."

I take a few deep breaths. I haven't thought about Dak in a while. My heart starts racing. Fuck, why does it still get to me?

As if sensing my need to get back to silliness, he says, "Kam?"

"Yes?"

"I'm a poet."

"You are? Tell me one of your poems."

"Roses are red, violets are blue, even when I use my hand, I'm thinking of you."

I let out a laugh. "Cruz Gonzales, now *you've* truly blown *my* mind."

"Anything else you'd care to blow?"

I smile as I shake my head. "Not happening. Nighty night, kitten."

He pulls me as close to him as possible. "Nighty night, Kam bam."

WHEN I EVENTUALLY BLINK MY eyes open, I notice it's light out. It means I got at least four hours of sleep. I can't remember the last time I slept for four straight hours.

It occurs to me why I slept so well. Cheetah was in my bed holding me—and my boob—all night.

I don't feel him on my back anymore. I reach behind me only to realize he's gone, but it's still warm. He didn't leave that long ago.

I turn around and see Arizona's still not in her bed. She better get back soon before the coaches wake up.

Something orange on the night table catches my eye. I focus on it and realize that it's a bag of dark chocolate Reese's Peanut Butter Cups. There's a note folded under it which I open and read:

Hope your dreams
were as sweet as
mine. Thanks for the
squeeze.
XOXO

How the hell did he find a bag of dark chocolate Reese's in the middle of the night? I'm teetering between confused and touched when the door opens. Fortunately, it's Arizona.

I smile at her and joke, "Ooh, look who broke curfew. You're a black-bottom-ho this morning." She knows that's my phrase for women who go out at night in heels, go home with someone, and then have to walk home with no shoes on. The bottom of their feet gets dirty. That's why they're black-bottom-hoes.

She wiggles the bottom of her feet at me. "Nope. All clear."

"I guess you got *#LaidByLayton*?" That hashtag is always trending with the skanks of Instagram.

She gives me a mischievous smile. One I haven't seen from her in a long time. "Nope. He got *#AttackedByArizona*."

It's good to see her like this. "Look who's back. Arizona *fucking* Abbott, ladies and gentlemen."

She's glowing in a way I haven't seen since before her failed engagement. *Well* before her failed engagement. I'm so happy for her.

I play ignorant. "Who was Layton rooming with?"

"Cheetah. The fucker watched us have sex. I think he was jerking off to it." She bites her lip. "Honestly, it was kind of hot. I've never been watched before. I'm not saying I want to make a habit of it, and Layton tried his best to keep me covered, but I definitely got off on it. Do you think that's weird?"

"Fuck no. It's hot as hell. In fact, if there's a job opening, I'd love to watch you guys have sex sometime too. You're both so damn sexy. I bet the sex is smokin'."

She giggles. "Not happening. Nice try."

AFTER A FEW DAYS on the road, we're finally on the way to the airport to fly home. Though my flight anxiety really kicks in when we board the plane, it sometimes revs up once we arrive at the airport. I need a distraction and often get it by pranking my sister. Embarrassing her at airports has become a bit of a team joke at this point. I'm always researching new ways to humiliate her, and I've been sitting on this one all week. With our outbound flight being delayed, I decided to save it for the return trip to optimize the number of people at the airport.

Given how much I like to slip things into her carry-on bags that she takes through security, Bailey now checks her bags thoroughly before we leave the hotel. I have to discreetly slip things into her bag on the bus ride.

I motion to Arizona to distract Bailey, and she nods before turning to Bails. "How is it going with Tanner Montgomery?"

Bailey's whole face lights up. "Great. I adore Harper. She's so much fun. And so damn smart. She's the smartest kid I've ever been around."

I give a mock gasp. "Smarter than I was? Can she do calculus at seven years old? I could." That's a slight exaggeration, but not too far off.

Bailey raises her eyebrow. "No calculus, but her vocabulary is amazing. She has word-of-the-day toilet paper and learns a new crazy word every day. She always remembers them and then uses them appropriately in sentences. It blows my mind."

"Give me an example of one."

She twists her lips as she thinks. "Hmm. She had a good one last week. Noctivagant."

I narrow my eyes at her. "You're trying to stump me. Even if I don't know a word, I can figure it out. It's the one perk of having taken Latin for so many years. Nox means night, and vagus means wandering. I'm guessing it has to do with night wandering. Someone like me who doesn't sleep and gets shit done at night."

She scrunches her face. "Fuck, I hate how smart you are. It's annoying. Mr. Montgomery is the same way. He knows *every* single word. He hasn't missed one yet. He's incredible."

"Does he know you have a daddy fetish too? That you want him to stick his bald-headed giggle stick into your Mary-Ellen?"

She rolls her eyes at me. "Where do you come up with this shitake?"

She now substitutes all curse words to force herself to not use any in front of Harper.

"Urban Dictionary is my bible."

She sighs. "No doubt." She then turns back to Arizona and talks more about how much she's enjoying Harper and Harper's two best friends, Andie and Dylan. How they remind her of our group of friends.

While she's distracted, I slip a little something into her bag. She's going to freak out at me. I love it.

Once we're at the airport, I make sure to get through security a few people ahead of her. I then quickly pull out my phone and press the necessary buttons to effectuate my plan.

Just as Bailey's bag enters the security scanner, where she can no longer access it, I hit the final button, and the sounds of a woman orgasming ring loudly in her bag. She dives for it but it's too late. It's already in the x-ray machine. While all eyes move to her, hers snap toward me as I simply stand there smiling while videotaping the whole scene.

She yells out, "Kamryn Sarah Hart, what did you do?"

The whole team starts laughing as the sounds of sex continue playing loudly. The TSA agents are scrambling to get her bag through as quickly as possible. There are a hundred people staring at Bailey, who's beet red in mortification.

The bag eventually emerges on the other side, and the TSA agent quickly grabs it before unzipping the bag. She pulls out the Bluetooth speaker I snuck into it. The sounds of ecstasy increase in volume as she scrambles to turn it off to a sea of laughter.

Damn, I love fucking with my sister.

CHAPTER SIX

CHEETAH

We're out on the field, late in the game. We're up by one run. Quincy is pitching one of the best games of his life. In fact, he's been doing it all season. He might single-handedly carry our team to a World Series title this year.

He's starting to get a little tired though. I'm not sure why the coaches are keeping him in the game. It's the seventh inning, and he's gassed. If I were the coach, I'd pull him now.

Sure enough, he walks the next two batters. There are two outs with two runners on base. Quincy throws a pitch and the batter crushes it. It's a line drive to the left-center gap. If it drops, two runs will be scored.

Our left fielder was shading toward the foul line. He has no chance of catching this ball. I tuck my glove under my armpit and run as fast as I can. As the ball sinks toward the grass, I lay out, completely parallel to the ground. Just as the ball is about to land, I get my glove under it for a spectacular catch that I know will be on ESPN later. More importantly, it saved us two runs and ended the inning.

All the fans are standing and cheering for me. As I run in, Quincy practically tackles me with excitement. "You're the fucking bomb, Cheetah. Thank you."

I smile at him. "Anything for you, big guy."

Just before I enter the dugout, my eyes find Kamryn's while she's jumping up and down with excitement. With a huge smile on her face, she blows me a kiss. I catch it and then slap it over my heart before she turns around and shows me my name on the back of her jersey.

She looks so sexy in the ridiculously small jersey I sent her. There's something incredibly hot about seeing a beautiful woman wearing your number. I want to fuck her while she's wearing it.

I don't think I've ever wanted a woman as much as I want her. Want isn't the right word. It's a deep attraction. It's not just about sex. I need to spend more time with her. She's an enigma. A puzzle I want to solve. A present I can't wait to unwrap.

Inexplicably, the coaches leave Quincy in the game at the top of the eighth inning, where he promptly gives up a two-run home run. He yells and curses at himself as he's removed from the game. It's not his fault. Coach Steel should have pulled him. Quincy has about ninety to ninety-five pitches in him before he tires. He must be well over a hundred now.

We head toward the bottom of the inning with our team now down a run. I need to get on base. I represent the tying run.

I hit a single to lead off the bottom of the eighth. The next batter pops up but the batter after him walks. Layton then steps into the box and smacks a three-run bomb, securing our victory. He's in the middle of his best hitting streak in years. I'm so happy for him. I guess there's a little gas left in his tank after all.

We all head to Screwballs after the game to celebrate the big victory. Not only did Layton have the huge hit, but we're about to clinch a spot in the postseason.

We're all engaging in our usual banter and chit-chat. When Trey disappears, Gemma starts talking about his birthday. I crack a few jokes, but he's lucky to have someone who cares enough about his birthday to want to celebrate it. My birthday is the day before Thanksgiving this year. I'm never home for it because I go home for Christmas and that's about all I can take of my mother's pressure, but my friends are often out of town because it's our off-season. It tends to be a lonely time of year for me, though Layton is usually around and we do something fun together. Unfortunately, he won't be around this year. He and Arizona are doing some sort of bathing suit campaign, and the photo shoot is overseas during that time. I'll probably be alone for my birthday. It's kind of depressing.

Though Gemma doesn't usually talk about her writing in mixed company, she ends up discussing her books with Kamryn. Somehow, that morphs into Kamryn learning that I read Gemma's books. She busts my balls about it for a bit. Nothing new.

I'm feeling a little down tonight. Perhaps it was the birthday talk. I think I should head home. It's unusual for me to leave early, but I need to get away from Kamryn. Some guy sitting at the bar has been staring at her all night, and I saw her looking at him. She's just going to fuck with me and then go home with someone else. I can't bear to watch it again.

I start to stand but Gemma grabs my arm and quietly asks, "Where are you going?"

"I'm sick of her rejecting me. I'm going home."

She rolls her eyes in obvious annoyance. "Don't you read my books?"

"I've read every word you've ever written. Multiple times. Sometimes clothed and sometimes naked."

Gemma bites back her smile. "Then you should understand signals. She's been staring at you all night. She wants you."

I shake my head. "She doesn't. I think I've been friend-zoned."

"What do you want to bet that you end up having sex with her tonight?"

I wiggle my eyebrows. "What are you thinking?"

She twists her lips. "Hmm. If I'm right and you have sex with her tonight, you have to babysit Fletcher on a night of my choosing."

"I'd do that anyway."

She smacks my arm. "Shush. We're making this interesting."

"Fine. If I win, and she doesn't sleep with me, you have to leave Trey for me."

She lets out a laugh. "Umm, no. Never. But I'll let you name my next male main character."

My eyes widen. "Anything I want?"

She nods. "Anything."

"C. Mike Rack?"

"No problem."

"Ben Derhover?"

"Sure."

"Buster Cherry?"

"If that's really what you want."

I smile as I hold out my hand. "This is a no-lose scenario for me. You're on, DePaul."

She shakes my hand in return with a sparkle in her green eyes. "Don't ever doubt a romance author," she whispers. "We're like sex hound dogs." She sniffs a few times. "We can smell it coming from a mile away. Pun intended."

I chuckle before clearing my throat to get Kam's attention. With nothing to lose, I ask, "Hey, Kam, what's your story? Are you riding the pole or picking flowers in the lady garden tonight? I need to know where to spend my time."

Her face lights up. I love how much she enjoys the ridiculous way I talk to her. It's always like a heavyweight fight between us as to who can come up with more crazy shit. It's a battle of euphemisms, and I've never met a woman with more in her arsenal than Kamryn Hart.

She slowly downs the rest of her beer before looking at me. "I'm not sure what I'm in the mood for. Maybe both. What do you have in mind? You can't possibly want to lose another bet."

I look around until I locate the cute blonde, Olivia, who I spent time with years ago. In fact, she came up to me when we walked in and asked me to hang out tonight. She's definitely straight. I'll win this wager. I motion toward her. "She's cute."

Kam couldn't possibly look any less interested. "Are you seriously looking to make another wager? Your hair just grew back. What's left? Tattoos?"

For her, I'd get a tattoo. Wait, did I just think that? Shit, and I berated Trey for piercing his dick for Gemma before they even had their first date.

I exhale a long breath. "One of these days I'll win, and then I'm going to jam your clam so hard that you'll never be able to look at a fishing pole without thinking of me. It's worth the small sacrifices along the way." I turn my head in the direction of Olivia. "Same rules?"

Kam taps her chin a few times before leaning back in the booth. "Meh. She doesn't do it for me."

Ugh. I can't even get her to bet me again. The one time I know winning is a sure thing.

She continues, "I think my lady garden isn't feeling like a vegetarian tonight. She needs a little meat. Maybe some big Mexican salami. Know where I can find one?"

My eyes widen and I glance at a smirking Gemma. She's a sex witch. She's all-knowing. I'll never doubt the sex master again.

I look back at Kam. "Are you fucking with me right now? Is this for real?"

She stands and leans over so I can see down her shirt. Licking her lips, she says, "Alright, guapo. Let's see if you can handle me. You better be the tiger I've been hearing about for months." She fucking winks at me. "Game on, motherfucker."

Like a starving man who's being given a chance at a juicy, Grade-A piece of steak, I stand on the cushion of the booth and leap all the way across the table. Everyone is laughing at my enthusiasm, but I don't give a shit. Kamryn just said yes. To me.

I grab her arm. "I hope you've got vet insurance, Kam bam, 'cause I'm about to tear that pussy up. Let's go, momma."

At that, I physically throw her over my shoulder and sprint out the door of the bar.

She's laughing the whole time.

I growl, "God, I love your laugh, but I think I'll love your moan even more."

"You're that confident you can make me moan?"

"It's a guarantee."

Once we're outside, she smacks my ass. "Put me down, you gorilla."

I slowly slide her down the front of my body. I'm already rock hard, and she undoubtedly feels it, not that I care. Fuck, I want her so badly. I don't know where to start.

I quickly scan the area. I know her apartment is close by, but if there's a hotel closer, I'll book it. Anything to be with this goddess as quickly as possible before she changes her mind.

She leans her body into mine and runs her fingers through my hair before grabbing two fistfuls in the back and tugging them hard. "We haven't even kissed." She playfully nibbles on my lower lip. "I can't fuck you if you're not a good kisser. House rules. You better kiss me so I can sample the goods. Now."

I feel like I need to do something grand to impress her. I've played this out in my mind a thousand times, ultimately determining that Kam needs a man who likes to take over so she can simply enjoy herself. She's always got the upper hand in relationships. She decides when and where, but once the decision is made, she needs someone who keeps her on her toes. Someone who gives her unimaginable pleasure. I'm guessing that she likes to give up a little bit of control when it comes to sex. And she toys with people. Maybe she needs to be toyed with a little to get off.

I wrap my arms around her body, lift her, and move us to the brick wall of the building where I place her down and cage her in. Grabbing her wrists, I pin them to the wall on either side of her hips.

Her eyes flutter as she licks her lips in anticipation. I bring my mouth less than an inch from hers. Our collective breath is comingled. Hers is a mixture of mint and the orange from the beer she was drinking.

She leans her mouth toward mine, but I pull back a drop and don't connect them. Not yet. I slowly pepper soft kisses along her jawline and eventually down her neck and chest. Reaching the top of one of her breasts, I suck hard enough to leave a mark.

She lets out a moan and thrusts her hips forward to meet mine. Moving back to her lips, she moves her head forward, again assuming I'm going to kiss her, but I simply allow our now-ragged breaths to comingle again.

I repeat the same slow, tortuous path down her jawline, neck, and chest, this time leaving a mark on the top of her other breast. All I really want to do is rip her shirt open. It's taking every ounce of restraint I have not to. I feel like I'm getting one chance to do this right and I need it to be everything.

She moans, "Cruz. Kiss me. Please."

She never calls me Cruz. She's feeling needy. I can't help but smile as my lips move back up her body until they're a hairsbreadth from hers.

Releasing her wrists, I grab the side of her face and run my thumb along her lower lip. "I've never been around a more incredible woman than you. It's not just your obvious beauty." I kiss the corner of her mouth. "It's your talent." Kiss. "Your charm." Kiss. "Your wit." Kiss. "Your big heart." Kiss.

A look of disbelief flashes over her face. I'm surprised. Kamryn is confident. It's one of her most attractive qualities. She must know how perfect she is.

She whispers, "You don't need lines anymore. I told you I'm in."

I shake my head. "They're not lines." I softly kiss the center of her lips this time. "Que," I kiss them again, "perfecto."

My tongue traces a line on her lower lip, teasing her just a little longer before my lips finally meet hers. I keep it soft for the first few seconds before deepening it, dying to taste every inch of her.

My tongue prods her lips until it finally meets hers after all this time. I can feel us both physically give in to the sense of relief that feels so damn right. Her taste is intoxicating. Her body fits on mine.

Que. Perfecto.

KAMRYN

Fuck, he can kiss. He has no idea what teasing does for me, and yet he just managed to tease me enough to have me soaking my panties for a damn kiss. A kiss that is likely the best I've ever had.

He tastes so good as his soft-yet-demanding lips dominate me in every way possible. His lips and tongue move over mine like he's truly savoring it. Like if we only kissed right now, he'd be okay with it.

It's too intimate. I need to change course. Grabbing his ass hard, I pull him to me. I want a dirty kiss not an epic kiss, but the smooth fucker manages to keep it controlled and...and...perfect.

His tongue moves through my mouth with something more than lust. It's need. It's desire. It's too fucking much. I'm not sure my heart has ever pounded so strongly from a simple kiss.

Fuck, I can't do this.

I shove his chest and the kiss is broken. He tilts his head to the side and gives me a look of concern.

After taking a few labored breaths, I breathe, "You're good. Now take me home and fuck me hard and dirty." I stare at him, needing to make my intentions clear. "*Only* hard and dirty."

Ten minutes later, we're crashing through my apartment door, tearing each other's clothes off. We're kissing, but it's more frantic and animalistic now.

Yes. This is what I want.

I'm in my bra and panties by the time we reach my room. He's in his boxer briefs and thank fucking god he's packing heat. It would have spoiled the illusion and the weeks-long buildup for tonight if I didn't see a giant bulge in his underwear. I felt it on my ass in the hotel but seeing it with my eyes is a whole other thing.

I grab for his cock and mumble into his mouth, "I need to suck your dick."

He growls before pushing me down onto my bed. My body flows up and down with the ripples of the water.

He laughs. "Holy shit. You really do have a waterbed."

"Fuck yes I do. Time to get your fishing rod all wet in these waters." I smile. "Be careful; there are sharks in here." I chomp down hard with my teeth a few times, making a clacking noise.

He glances down at his cock, looking like it's going to poke a hole in his boxers. "I've got a lot of meat for the sharks. Hope they can handle it."

I motion toward the severely tented boxer briefs. "I can see that. I might gag on your megalodon."

He smirks. "Sweetheart, gagging on my dick during a blow job is the official signal of love."

"How so?"

"You're choosing me over oxygen."

I giggle. God, I love how much he makes me laugh.

He flicks his tongue suggestively. "Time to go deep sea fishing."

He reaches down and violently pulls my panties down my legs before tossing them aside. I did want to suck him off first, but I can go with this change in course.

He falls onto my bed with his head between my legs. The whole bed ripples again. I love this freakin' bed.

Pinning my legs wide apart, he takes a long, slow lick through me, leaving no inch untouched before lifting his head and wiggling his eyebrows up and down. "Que deliciosa."

I don't speak Spanish, but I can figure that one out.

I'm feeling very happy about my recent pineapple intake. "Do I taste sweet like candy? Which brand? Maybe something fruity? Maybe chocolaty? Which is it?"

His blue eyes lift and meet mine. "You taste like pussy, and that happens to be my favorite flavor, being a cheetah and all." He clacks his teeth like I did mine earlier.

He then drops his head and plunges his tongue into me. Fuck yes. I lift my hips a bit to allow him deeper access.

He knows what he's doing in there, hitting every spot I need. His fingers gently brush over my clit every few seconds, teasing me, making me crave his touch all the more.

His whole demeanor is making my pussy leak. I'm so turned on by him.

Women are usually much better at this than men, but not this man. Cheetah knows the right buildup. I hate when men go right to the main event thinking you'll come faster. It has the opposite effect. They should have classes for men on the importance of the slower buildup.

After minutes of teasing, he slowly works his tongue up to my clit. I look down at him. He's got ecstasy written all over his face. I love that he enjoys it.

His tongue lightly grazes my clit several times. I'm writhing, desperate for more. I can't take it slow anymore. Eventually, I grab his hair and push his face into me.

He chuckles before finally giving me what I need. God damn, it's good. His tongue works at a perfect pace while his fingers now tease my entrance. It's like this fucker is inside my brain, knowing how much I need the slower escalation.

His fingers gradually move deeper and deeper until I can't take it anymore and I explode all over his face. I yell out and thrash throughout my entire orgasm.

He looks up with a face covered in me. "I like the way you come."

"I like it when you make me come. Let's do it again."

He smiles as he stands. I immediately sit up and pull his boxer briefs down his legs. His cock springs free. It's big, really big, but that's not what's catching my eye. It's his balls that stand out. They're enormous. I've never seen balls this big.

"What the fuck am I looking at? Do your balls have their own passport?"

He lets out a loud laugh. "Yep, having big balls isn't just a figure of speech for me. I literally have big balls. Always have."

I'm fascinated by this. "And you're sure there's nothing wrong or you're not growing a small family inside there?"

He shakes his head. "Nope. I've had it checked many times, all with the same diagnosis. I just have big balls."

I contemplate the logistics of what it must be like for him, and ask, "If you pass gas when you're lying on your back, is it a scrotal eclipse of the fart?"

He starts laughing hysterically while grabbing his stomach. "Oh my god. That's a good one. I've heard almost everything, but not that one. Want to know a secret about them?"

"Obviously."

"They're sensitive."

"All balls are sensitive. They call a man a pussy if he's soft, yet pussies can take a pounding. It's a man's dick and balls that can't. When someone is soft or a wimp, they should call him a dick or balls, not a pussy."

He twists his lips. "Hmm. That's a bizarrely valid point."

I nod. "I know, right?"

I love that we're both naked, I came seconds ago, and we're minutes from doing the dirty deed, yet our banter doesn't stop. I don't remember ever being this comfortable with someone.

He continues, "I don't mean normal-balls sensitive. I mean turn me on like crazy sensitive."

"You have a g-spot on your balls?"

He nods. "Something like that."

I crook my finger, indicating he come to me. "Step into my office. I'll need to do a full examination to determine the veracity of your statement."

He bites his lip. "Hmm. I love it when you talk smart to me."

"If that's the case, then know that I'm about to titillate your gonads."

He smiles as I drop down to my knees and immediately run

my fingernails and then tongue across his balls. He shivers a bit before precum leaks from his tip. I breathe out, "Holy shit."

I take his extremely thick shaft in my hand and give it a few long pumps as I continue to worship his balls with my lips, tongue, and free hand. He gathers my hair in his fist and starts letting loose a string of what I assume are Spanish expletives. It's hot as hell. I took Latin in high school, not Spanish, though I suddenly want to know what he's saying.

He constantly jerks when I give attention to his balls. They're crazy sensitive. This is like a whole new world. I feel like Aladdin, eager to explore it with my magic carpet.

Before I can get into any kind of groove, he lifts me and throws me on the bed. I widen my eyes. "What are you doing? I want to suck your dick."

"Too bad. I want to pound your pussy. Next time you can suck my dick."

I lift an eyebrow. "You assume there will be a next time?"

He smirks. "There will be. Once you get a taste, you won't be able to deny yourself."

"I promise there won't be any issue walking away from you. I don't need you getting all clingy on me. I don't do relationships, Cruz. Before you glaze my donut, I want to be super clear about that."

"It's a good thing that I don't do relationships either. We're a match made in heaven." He runs his hand up my leg. "I've waited for this. It's happening. There is zero chance I won't be sending an email to your spam folder tonight. Voy a abrirte ese coño y golpearte hasta someterte." *I'm going to spread that pussy open and pound you into submission.*

What the fuck did he just say? Even though I have no idea, it's so damn hot that my eyelids involuntarily flutter. I think my pussy does too.

His dimples make an appearance as he moves to lie on top of me. I push his chest hard so he falls back on the bed, and his body ripples with the motion of the water. Climbing on top of him, I say, "I only come when I'm on top, kitten."

He smiles as he rubs his hands together. "Sounds like a challenge, Kam bam."

I roll my eyes. "Every guy says that, and none have ever come through for me. I'm on top first. It's my home field tonight. My rules."

He bites back a smile and nods as he settles in on his back, looking like a kid about to enter a candy store. I quickly reach over to the drawer in my night table and open it. Reaching inside, I feel around for the big box on the far right, the magnums, for tonight.

He lifts his head and looks in the drawer. "I love that you have three boxes organized by size."

I nod as I tear the condom open and roll it onto him. "Little known fact. There are actually four sizes of condoms, but if we get to this point and the smalls are needed, I bail."

"Has that actually ever happened?"

I nod. "Twice."

"Poor guys."

I shrug. "Not having sex with me is the least of their problems."

He reaches around and smacks my ass. "Glad I can make a dent in the big boy box. Now get on me and give yourself the first of what I promise will be many orgasms." He winks. "Though I suppose technically it will be your second orgasm of the night."

"You're very sure of yourself for a man who is proudly nicknamed after the fastest animal on the planet."

He simply smiles. I do love his smile. It's big and expressive, with his sexy dimples and blue eyes that promise craziness.

I settle my knees on either side of him before grabbing the base. He places his hand over mine. "I like to do it together."

Damn. Why is that so hot?

Together, we move his tip to my entrance, and I begin to sink down onto him. Fuck, it's been a while since I've had a non-silicone big boy inside me.

He moves his hand, grabs my hips, and helps me rock side to side until I manage to wiggle all the way down onto him. "Te sientes tan apretada y cálida. Como en el cielo."

I bite my lip. "What did you just say?"

"That you feel so tight and warm. It's like heaven." He reaches up for my breasts and rubs my nipples between his thumbs and pointer fingers.

I let out a moan and can feel my pussy constrict around him.

He sucks in a breath at the sensation. "Your nipples are sensitive. I love that. Qué jodidamente caliente." *So fucking hot.*

My pussy constricts again at his words. "And...new kink unlocked."

He pinches his eyebrows together in question.

"I won't lie. The Spanish is hot. It's doing things to me."

The corners of his mouth raise in amusement. "Good to know. Mueve tu coño hacia arriba y hacia abajo sobre mi verga gorda." *Move your pussy up and down on my fat cock.*

I don't know what he said but his hands encourage my body to begin my movements. In no time, I'm alternating between bouncing up and down and rocking back and forth on him, taking what I need to get off. The waves of my bed only add to the movements and gratification. Have I mentioned that I love this fucking bed?

He lifts the top half of his body and says, "Voy a chupar tus lindas tetas rosadas." *I'm going to suck on your pretty pink tits.*

He then buries his face in my chest and begins flicking his tongue over my nipples.

He's got one hand cupping the breast of the nipple he's lavishing with attention, and the other moves down to my clit to begin rubbing it.

It takes no time before I'm shattering into a million pieces, screaming out his name. Interestingly, I yell Cruz, not Cheetah or kitten. I wasn't sure which way it would go, but in the moment, his real name was the only one finding my lips.

Before I fully regain my vision, I feel him flip us over. I assume he'll position himself between my legs like every other man in America, but he doesn't. He pulls my right leg over so that my legs are closed together on the left side of my body. My top half remains flat with my back on the bed, and my bottom half is twisted to the side. I've never had sex like this before, but it feels good.

"What is this move?"

He wiggles his eyebrows up and down. "It makes you that much tighter, and now I can see your ass, tits, and face all at once."

He spanks me with one hand and wraps the other around my neck. "I can spank you and choke you at the same time."

I croak out, "Holy. Shit. You're a genius. A pioneer. An innovator."

He nods. "I really am. Now hold on tight. You're about to come again."

I shrug in an unaffected manner. "Best of luck venturing into unchartered waters."

He narrows his eyes at me. "Christopher Columbus said the same thing before he discovered America."

I shake my head. "Fun fact, he didn't actually discover America first. It was the explorer—"

Before I can finish, he slams into me and steals my breath. I manage to mumble, "Oh shit, that's good."

Over the next I don't know how long, it could be ten minutes, it could be an hour, Cheetah fucks the living daylights out of me. His nickname isn't Cheetah because he comes quickly. It's Cheetah because he's able to piston into me at an inhuman pace for an inhuman length of time.

My waterbed is bouncing and sloshing in a way that I'm confident is against the manufacturer's warranty. We're both being thrown around a bit by the motion of the water. It's amazing. I feel my body opening up. I can't believe it. I'm about to come while being on the bottom. This will be a first for me.

My body is metaphorically lifted and then physically lifted as the motion of the bed raises me a bit, like a wave cresting. At the exact same time the crest is about to fall over, Cheetah slams into me and...POP!

Holy. Shit.

My waterbed explodes. Water spurts up in the air like a geyser before beginning to flow out on the ground like the ocean coming into shore.

So. Much. Water.

Cheetah lets out a huge scream. He jumps off me and starts running around naked and waving his arms like a madman. All while still screaming like a little girl.

I can't stop laughing. This is epic. His response is even more epic.

A few seconds later, he returns from my bathroom and starts throwing towels at the oozing water as if they'll make a dent in the over-two-hundred gallons of water currently spilling from my bedroom.

He runs back and forth between my bathroom and bedroom, throwing towels. I simply sit there and watch with amusement. There's nothing we can do to stop this, but he remains steadfast that the towels will get the job done.

Eventually, I nonchalantly walk out of my bedroom naked simply to continue to enjoy watching Cheetah act like a lunatic. My sister comes running out of her room. She gasps as she takes in the whole scene.

I straighten my shoulders and proudly announce, "He fucked me so hard that my waterbed burst. Damn, I was seconds away from another orgasm. Such a bummer."

She grits out, "*That's* the bummer? That you didn't have *another* orgasm? Not the flood happening in our apartment or the one below?"

I can't help but giggle. We both stand there and watch

Cheetah running around the apartment finding every towel in sight and throwing it at the Atlantic Ocean washing through our apartment. I half expect marine life to start tumbling through my bedroom door.

She looks at Cheetah closely and narrows her eyes. "Why are his balls absurdly large?"

Hmm. Maybe we can use them to plug the hole in my bed.

CHAPTER SEVEN

"Katie, you promised me that my waterbed could withstand rough sex."

I hear the saleswoman on the other end of the phone let out a long breath. "Kamryn, I've been doing this for over twenty years. Barring the use of something sharp penetrating the bed, I've never once heard of one popping from the simple act of sex. Are you certain there were no knives or other sharp objects involved?"

"I'm a freak in the sack but knife play isn't my thing. I'm telling you; he was fucking me hard and the damn thing popped."

I hear her talking to someone, but I can't make out exactly what she's saying. She's clearly covering the phone.

When she returns, she asks, "Were you wearing heels?"

"No. I was naked as the day I was born, as was he. Did you get the pictures I sent?"

"Umm, yes. They're inconclusive."

"I filled out the damn thirty pages of information online. I gave you everything you asked for. Now get me my new bed."

She sighs. "Kamryn, I'm not sure the warranty will cover a new bed."

"Listen, bitch, I know my rights. I can fucking read my warranty policy. Chapter eighteen, subsection D, roman numeral four specifically states that if the waterbed pops during appropriate bedtime *activities*, it's covered. Activities are defined in the appendix as sleeping, lying, sitting, reading, sexual intercourse, and a few other irrelevant items. I specifically asked you when I bought the waterbed about rough sex. You laughed while you said, and I quote, *no one has ever had sex rough enough for a waterbed to pop*. Well, welcome to the motherfucking exception. I expect my new waterbed to arrive within a week."

Again, it sounds like she's talking to someone else, but the phone is muffled. Eventually, she says into the phone, "Does next Tuesday early in the morning work for delivery?"

I smile in satisfaction. "It sure does. Let me know if you need a photo of my face for your waterbed-popping wall of fame. I get paid to promote products, but for you, I'll do it for free."

I end the call with a big, satisfied grin on my face. Bailey looks at me. "You're mighty happy with yourself right now, aren't you?"

"Fuck yes I am."

She zips up her bag. "I'm heading to the Montgomerys's. I'll see you at practice tomorrow morning, Joan of Arc."

Our apartment needs major repairs. While that happens, Arizona offered us her bed. She's staying at Layton's place. After sleeping with me for one night, Bailey asked Tanner if she could stay in his guest room ahead of our road trip this week. He was fine with it, so she's staying there.

"Are you staying in McZaddy Tanner's bed?"

"Of course not. The house is enormous. It has a million bedrooms. I won't even be on the same floor as him and Harper."

"Whatever you say. Are you coming to the Cougars' game tonight?"

She shakes her head. "I can't. Mr. Montgomery is working late. I have Harper. It's supposed to storm. Be careful."

"Yes, Mom."

"Speaking of parents, have you spoken to Daddy lately?"

"Not since our last FaceTime together. We texted though. Why?"

She shrugs. "Not sure. Something is off with him."

"Something has been off with him for as long as I can remember. If you were married to that psychotic drunk witch, you'd be fucked up too."

Her shoulders fall. "We haven't seen her in ten years, Kam. Do you think maybe it's time to mend fences? They won't be around forever."

I pinch my eyebrows together. "Are you fucking nuts? Bails, Mom is a pill-popping, raging alcoholic. She's fucked up more times than I can count. And she won't get help. It's not like I cared for her when she was sober, but I would *never* remotely consider any type of reconciliation unless she got clean and came apologizing to us on her hands and knees. Do you realize she's never once seen either of us play ball? How fucked up is that?"

After our father finally intervened, we quit acting for good at twelve. We went to a regular public school and were able to play sports and participate in other activities of our choosing. We got to be the "normal" kids we always wanted to be, but our mother hated it.

Bailey answers, "That's not true. She came a few times."

"Plastered. She came plastered. She once drove her car straight onto the field and almost killed three kids, you included. I don't know how Daddy kept her out of jail on that one."

She twists her lips. "That's true. I think he told them she mixed up her meds."

"Her cocktail of meds would kill most cattle. It's amazing she's upright, assuming she still is."

Once we quit acting, I think our mother lost her sense of purpose. She started hitting the bottles, both alcohol and painkillers. I don't remember a day from the time we were twelve through us leaving for college that she wasn't drinking at least one bottle of vodka a day, along with popping pills like they were Tic Tacs. Our father tried to get her help, but she wouldn't do it. And he wouldn't report anything to child protective services for fear of losing us. He had to be both our mother and our father for years, all while working long hours at a shitty job that he was way too smart for. He would never have had to get a job like that if she hadn't trapped him with her pregnancy. She's a soul-sucking piece of shit.

The list of embarrassing, horrific, and crazy things she did is a long one. The highlights include her accidentally setting the house on fire when Bailey and I were asleep upstairs, crashing her car into our kitchen, killing my dog, and the final straw for Bailey, showing up to our high school graduation completely fucked up and making a hugely embarrassing scene that I don't think Bailey and I will ever get over.

Smaller things such as weaving into school parking lots, forgetting to pick us up, leaving bags of groceries in a hot car for hours, and not getting us to doctor's appointments were the regular course of business for us growing up.

She wouldn't give us rides when we needed them. It was a constant struggle just to get to practices and the like. Fortunately, we were both such strong athletes that coaches ended up driving us most of the time, not wanting either of us to miss our respective sports.

And then there was the odd handful of times that I would just take her car and drive us, years before I had a license to do so. She was too blitzed to even notice. I got busted by the cops once, but they let me off with a warning. I wouldn't let Bails do it because I didn't want her to get into trouble.

Bailey nods. "I know. You're right. She has to help herself before we can consider any communication with her, but I'm worried about Daddy. Something is off. More than usual. Before I leave, can we call him? He's probably in the car on his way to work. You won't have to see her. I just want you to gauge if something is wrong like I suspect it is."

"Of course. Maybe we can talk him into coming up for a

game or two." I hold up my finger. "But not her. She's not welcome."

She nods. "Okay."

She opens her laptop and clicks on the FaceTime app before selecting his name from her contacts. After just one ring, he answers right away. It looks like he's in their kitchen. Fuck. She might be there.

His face lights up. "Hi, girls. How are you?"

We both return his warm smile. Bailey answers, "We're great. How are you, Daddy?"

He sighs before whispering, "Plugging along." He holds up his finger like we should give him a minute before he steps out onto their back patio and sits on a chair. "Sorry, I didn't want to wake your mother."

Wake her? He was in the kitchen. "Was she passed out on the kitchen floor?" I ask.

Bailey sighs. "We're happy we caught you. We just wanted to catch up. I thought you'd be on your way to work."

"I have to take your mother to an appointment this morning. I'm only working a half day."

I look at Bailey and then back to him. "Any chance it's AA? Assholes Anonymous or Alcoholics Anonymous. Both are fitting. Maybe NA, Narcissists Anonymous or Narcotics Anonymous, both work."

He simply shakes his head at me. "Don't worry about it. I saw you two went back-to-back again the other night. You both have so much power. You're the best two hitters in the league. I'm so proud of you. I'm more confident than ever that you'll be on the Olympic team in four years." Tears fill his eyes. "Won't that be amazing?"

I nod. "You should ditch the bitch and come up for a live game."

Bailey hits my leg. "What she means, Daddy, is that we'd love for you to come see us in person."

His face falls. "It's hard for me to leave, and I can't afford it.

I'll try my best." We hear a clanking noise, and then he looks up, beyond the camera. His shoulders fall as he says, "Listen, girls, I need to run. I love you both so much. I hope you know that."

Bailey fights back the emotions I know are bubbling at the surface for her. "We do. Love you too."

She ends the call, and tears immediately fill her eyes. "He's so unhappy, Kam. Can't you see it?"

My face falls as my heart breaks for our father. "I do. Part of me feels bad for him, but part of me doesn't. He can leave her, Bails. I semi-understand why he didn't when we were kids, but it's been ten years since we left. He's choosing this life. I know he feels a sense of obligation, but at some point, you need to choose yourself. You need to create your own happiness."

She nods as she appears to consider my words. She knows I'm not wrong. You can't help someone who won't help themselves.

I wrap my arms around her. "Thank god I have you. I love you, big sis."

She cracks a smile. She always does when I refer to her as my big sis. It's only by nine minutes, but I'm sure at times it feels like nine years for her. She's always taken care of me. I can only hope she knows on some level that I've done the same for her.

She whispers our often-repeated line from our favorite movie, *Titanic*. "You jump, I jump."

Shortly after she leaves for the Montgomery house, Arizona comes home to trade out her clothes. She wiggles her eyebrows at me. "How's my friend who took squirting to a whole new level?"

I smile at the burst-waterbed reference. "How's my friend who finally found a man who makes her squirt?"

She giggles. "I'm more than good. What about you and Cheetah?"

"What about me and Cheetah?"

"Are you interested?"

"Interested in what?"

She sighs. "In spending time with him."

"Have you ever known me to dip into the same well more than once?"

"Your well is still seeping into the hallway. He's good for you and—"

I hold up my hand at her to stop her from continuing the thought. "Pass. Moving on."

Her shoulders fall. "Was the sex bad?"

Not even a little bit. It was on its way to being the best of my life when the damn bed exploded. It was the universe's way of reminding me not to entertain notions of considering more with him.

He's been blowing up my phone since, but I haven't responded. I can't. Now it's going to be weird when our groups hang out together. This is why I was avoiding sleeping with him in the first place.

"It was...explosive."

CHEETAH

All of us older guys are in the training room ahead of our game tonight, getting treatments for our various ailments, each on our own training table. Getting old sucks. My body used to recover much more quickly. I'm also potentially depressed because Kamryn won't return my calls or texts. The sex was amazing until the bed exploded. I thought for sure she'd want to give it another go.

I feel my phone ping. Like a teenage girl, I grab it, hoping Kam is responding to my texts. Much to my disappointment, it's simply *another* real-estate listing from my mother. I click on it and notice that it's four doors down from them.

Feeling defeated, I place my phone down and look over

at my best friend. Layton is sitting on the training table, smiling like a lunatic. I shake my head. "What's wrong with you? You look like Jack Nicholson in *The Shining*. It's giving me the creeps."

Trey lets out a loud laugh. "He's in looooove. It finally happened."

Layton doesn't bother to deny it; he simply sits there grinning like a fool, now purposefully trying to look like Jack.

One of the rookies, Jimmy, walks in with messy hair and Sharpie smeared all over his face. He's wiping it with a wet towel. Trey looks at him. "What the hell happened to you?"

He scrunches his face. "I fell asleep in the locker room, and someone drew a penis on my face. I need something stronger than soap to clean it." He looks at our trainer. "Do you have anything I can use?"

Jeffrey nods while I shake in laughter. Layton and I share bemused looks. Quincy loves to do that to young players who stay out too late and fall asleep in the clubhouse.

I ask Jimmy, "What's worse than waking up with a guy's hammer drawn on your face?"

Jimmy scratches his head. "What?"

I smile. "Finding out that it was traced."

We all laugh but Trey shakes his head. "That's definitely not long quail Quincy's hammer. That fucker would wrap around his entire face and then down his neck. He's got the longest babymaker I've ever seen."

I nod in agreement. "That's the truth. It must be Ezra's, though it's too straight to be his."

Ezra flips me the bird.

Jimmy scrunches his face. "Oh my god. I hadn't considered that it could be traced." He scrubs his face even harder. "Gross. I need to find someone who saw him draw it on me. I won't sleep tonight if that giant python was on my face."

We all laugh hysterically as he runs out of the room in a complete panic.

Layton shakes his head. "Rookies. They're so much fun to fuck with."

I nod in agreement. Rookie hazing is commonplace. We're always trying to come up with new and creative ways to torture them.

Layton asks, "Are you all good to begin the festivities at my place for the party this week?"

Layton and Arizona did a photo shoot for the *Sports Illustrated* couples' body image issue. Apparently, they were half-naked the whole time. I can't imagine how hot it's going to be. Actually, after seeing them in action in the hotel, I can imagine it, and it's hot as hell.

This week, a huge reveal party is taking place in New York City. We're all going up on a big party bus. Layton asked that we meet at his place as a starting point before we pick up the girls, who are getting their hair and makeup professionally done.

We all nod, and I answer, "Yes. Can't wait to see you two naked." I wink at him since I've already seen them naked.

He scowls at me before narrowing his eyes. "What happened with you and Kam the other night?"

Quincy walks in just as the words are trickling out of Layton's mouth. "Oooh, did Cheetah dip his toes in the crazy pool? Knowing Kam, *she* probably did *him* doggie style."

I'm not having this conversation with them. I need to redirect their attention. "Do you know why they call it doggie style?"

He twists his lips. "Because the receiver is on all fours?"

I shake my head. "Nope. It's because *I don't want to look at your ugly face* didn't have a nice ring to it."

He chuckles. "I stand corrected." Fixing his backward baseball hat over his trademark longer, curly blonde hair, he says, "Look, man, I've known Kam for ten years. There's a screw loose with that chick. You might want to steer clear. I used to think every single thing in a woman's life could be fixed by one of two things. Dick or food. But with Kamryn Hart, it's more than that. You're a nice guy. You should be with a nice girl."

Trey nods. "Agreed. The momma's boy needs someone to dote on him like his mother. Kam isn't that person."

Layton slaps my back. "Nah. Cheetah needs a deaf woman to drown out the things that come out of his mouth."

Ezra chuckles. "Or one who doesn't mind being spanked with big balls while he's fucking her."

They all laugh at my expense. They don't know shit about what I need.

CHAPTER EIGHT

Tonight is the big *Sports Illustrated* reveal party. I'm so excited to see Kamryn that I can hardly contain myself. I'm doing my best to play it cool on the party bus though. Layton and Trey are practically salivating to get to their women. I'm sure they're not noticing me equally as worked up.

We arrive at Kamryn's apartment building, and the five girls walk out. Arizona, Ripley, Gemma, and Bailey all look stunning, but it's Kamryn Hart who steals my breath. She's in a tight, gold strapless dress that leaves little to the imagination. She looks like a golden goddess. I can't take my eyes off her. She's so fucking beautiful.

Trey and Layton jump off the bus before it even stops moving to ogle and fondle their women. Knowing Kamryn wouldn't appreciate the same treatment, I stay seated and watch her step onto the bus with all the confidence in the world. It's like she's moving in slow motion with her hips swaying and her hair flowing in the gentle breeze. Her full lips are painted red. Her eyes, which always tell a million stories, are particularly vibrant tonight. My mouth is wide open as I take her in.

She doesn't make eye contact with me as she walks through the bus. I can't help but reach out and attempt to pull her onto my lap. I whisper in her ear, "You're stunning. I've missed you."

She coldly shoves me away, crossing her arms in defiance. "Nope. You had your shot, kitten. You blew it. Literally."

Trey lets out a laugh. "Did things end, *prematurely*? Shame on you, Cheetah."

Fuck this. I turn to him. "It ended because her bed exploded. *Literally*. Her waterbed burst. I had to surf out of her bedroom. Naked."

They all start laughing. It's not funny. Why is she pushing me away? What am I missing? Was she not feeling what I was the other night? There's something real and special between us. She must realize that.

She pays me no attention as the crew temporarily moves on to other topics. *Temporarily*.

As I suspected it would, the topic eventually returns to the bursting waterbed and Kam gives them a detailed account of what happened. Everyone is in a fit of laughter.

Layton slaps my back with a huge grin on his face. "You finally got a girl wet. It only took you thirty years." He laughs hysterically at his own joke.

Quincy shakes his head. "Cheetah, you give a whole new meaning to the term *diving in*."

Gemma gives me more of a compassionate smile. "Look at the bright side. At least you made a woman squirt. Very few men accomplish that."

I can't help but let a small smile creep out at that one. I suppose the whole situation is funny.

Fortunately, they move on to other topics. The ninety-minute ride to New York City is full of drinks and laughs.

Everyone is having a great time. I really do like our growing circle of friends.

At some point, Kamryn turns to me and playfully narrows her eyes. "Stop staring at my tits."

I feign shock. "I'm staring at your heart. It's my favorite thing about you. I can't help that it's covered by your glorious snuggle pups."

She smiles. Hopefully the tension will be broken between us.

As we exit the bus when we arrive at the event, she even straightens my tie. "Your tuxedo suits you."

I smile. "You should see what it looks like rolled up in a ball on the floor."

She rolls her eyes but lets me take her hand as we walk as a group through the paparazzi line. Everyone except Arizona and Layton. They hold back a few minutes so they can make their grand entrance.

We're reboarding the bus at the end of the night. Arizona and Layton were revealed to be the cover couple for the *Sports Illustrated* issue. It's not just any cover though. It's the most erotic cover in the magazine's long history. They're half-naked, looking seconds away from having sex. I think there were three hundred chins on the floor when they unveiled the cover. I'm happy for my best friend. He's gotten a career resurgence, and I think he found his soulmate. I've never seen him happier.

I end up being the last to board the bus. Everyone immediately heckles me for a fun fact.

I plop down on the seat next to Kamryn, and say, "Statistically speaking, male homosexual marriages have the lowest rate of divorce of any pairings. Lower than female homosexual marriages and much lower than heterosexual marriages. Do you know what this tells us?"

Layton responds, "What?"

"That blow jobs are the key to happiness."

Everyone laughs but Trey has a huge shit-eating grin on his face. Way more than is normal.

I turn to him. "Why are you so fucking happy?"

He smirks at Gemma, and she simply shakes her head. "I woke him up this morning by swallowing his baloney pony, and he's been grinning like a fool ever since."

I chuckle. Is there any woman better than Gemma DePaul?

I shrug my shoulders and joke, "I don't know, Gem, was he conscious enough to give consent? I think we have a legal issue here. You're the attorney. You tell us."

Trey lifts an eyebrow. "It's part of the *any clause* in our marriage contract."

"Any clause?" I question.

"She can swallow my baloney pony *any*time, *any*place, *any*where."

Layton nods in agreement. "Morning blowies? Hell yes. We're like 7-11. Always open for business."

"Hmm." I turn to the girls. "How do you ladies feel about it? Receiving some lickin' lovin' while unconscious."

Kam blinks her eyes a few times. "Being awakened by someone we're already in bed with by him or her calling for Connie Lingus?"

I nod. "Yep."

"In the wise words of Dr. Suess, *I like it here, I like it there, I like it even if I'm unaware.*"

I stifle my smile. "My mom didn't read me that one as a kid. Which Dr. Suess book is it from?"

She deadpans, "*The Grinch's Nine Inches.* It's a classic."

I chuckle. She's got a line for everything.

Everyone falls into their own conversations. Though

some are more physical. Trey and Gemma are practically having sex in a dark corner while Layton and Arizona are grinding at the other end of the bus. Ezra and Bailey are being touchy-feely. I didn't think she was into him. Even more surprising, she gets off the bus with him at his house. Kamryn doesn't look happy about it, but it still happens.

It's now just me, Kam, Ripley, and Quincy left on the bus. I turn to Kam. "I'm not tired. Want to hit a club with me?"

Her eyes light up. "Hell yes. I can never get those girls to go with me. I have to go with younger players if I want to have some extra fun."

She asks Ripley and Quincy to join us but they both decline. I'm sensing some tension between the two of them. I wonder if they're secretly bumping uglies.

We instruct the bus driver to drop us at Club Liberty. It's a Philly staple and always has a line around the block.

Kam grabs my hand and pulls me toward the front door, not the end of the line. I'm a famous baseball player; it's easy for me to butt in line, but I don't love doing it.

I ask, "Are you using my fame to skip the line?"

She lifts an eyebrow and points up and down her own body. "I've never in my life waited in a line. In case you haven't noticed, I've got a lot going on." She winks at me.

I can only nod as I take in her flawless figure. "Believe me, I've noticed. All fucking night."

As soon as we approach the front door, the bouncer rakes his eyes up and down her body, immediately opens the rope, and lets us in, much to the audibly groaning malcontent of those in the long line.

As we enter the club, the music is pumping and there are bodies everywhere. I immediately spot Daylen on the dance floor. He's kind of hard to miss, always towering over everyone. The man is a flat-out giant.

Daylen and Vance had a late practice tonight, or they would have joined us at the event.

He grins widely as he sees us approach. "If it isn't the big *pussy* cat." He nods toward the VIP area. "Vance has a booth and is holding court up there. Warning, he's in a pissy mood."

I let out a laugh. "He's always in a pissy mood."

"It's a little extra today. I had to force him to come out." He kisses Kam's cheek and says to her, "Looks like you're slumming it tonight."

She smiles at him. "I'm open for business. You looking for some fun, hot stuff?"

I tighten my hold on her, but Daylen simply lets out one of his booming laughs. I know he would never go there. To his core, he's a great guy.

He simply shakes his head. "No, but it looks like you are."

"I'm always looking for trouble, you know that."

I tug on her hand. "Let's go find Vance."

She shakes her head. "I'll meet you up there. I want to dance for a bit."

"I'll dance with you."

She pulls her hand away. "Don't suffocate me. Go up to the booth. I'll be there in a bit when I feel like it."

THIRTY MINUTES later I'm sitting in the booth with Daylen and Vance. Daylen is swallowing some poor girl's mouth whole, but Vance is looking at what I've been staring at since I sat down.

Kamryn is grinding between a man and a woman on the dance floor. The man is rubbing himself all over her ass, and she's kissing the woman. Open-mouth, full tongue kissing. Kamryn's hands are squeezing the woman's ass.

Vance lets out a moan. "Is it wrong that I'm completely turned on by this?"

I shake my head. "I might jerk off to this image every night for the rest of my life. Though I could do without the guy."

He nods. "Yep, though I'm jealous of him."

Kamryn breaks the kiss and looks up at me. After briefly making eye contact, she moves her body around so she's now kissing the guy while the woman fondles her body. I turn my head. I can't watch her kiss another guy. For whatever reason, watching her with a woman doesn't bother me but a man does.

After fifteen more minutes of torture, she makes her way up to the booth with a big smile on her face. "Hey, boys. What are we drinking?"

I nod toward the beer bottle. "I ordered you your favorite beer."

"Thanks, kitten. Find any hotties to your liking?"

I shake my head.

She shrugs. "You need to get laid. You're bizarrely uptight tonight. You should find someone to take home. I might go home with that guy I was dancing with. He has a new puppy. I'm obsessed with puppies. I'm getting dozens of them the day I retire."

Daylen breaks his game of tonsil hockey in time to say, "Vance and I were walking down the street the other day and saw the cutest puppy licking his own balls. Vance said that he wished he could do that. I told him he should probably just pet the puppy."

Kamryn starts laughing along with Daylen while Vance flips him the bird. Daylen's laugh can probably be heard from ten miles over. It's a good thing because it's masking the sound of my heart breaking.

CHAPTER NINE

KAMRYN

I'm sitting in the stands at Bailey's basketball game, cheering for my sister. She's a true superstar. One of the best basketball players in the country. I'm so proud of her. I love watching her shine doing what she loves.

There are two rows of college coaches watching her play and she's only a freshman in high school. I find myself calculating which of those colleges also have great softball programs. I need to end up at the same college as my sister. She's too naïve and innocent to be in the real world without me protecting her. I think we're both good enough at our respective sports to earn scholarships.

Running through the list, I'm realizing that there's no overlap. I'm being recruited by schools on the West Coast and in the Deep South. She's being recruited by schools in the Northeast and Midwest.

I start feeling anxious. Sweat pours from my body at the thought of four years away from the other half of my soul. I can't imagine it. There will be people lined up to take advantage of her innate kindness.

My mind drifts to that night five years ago. The one that

haunts me every single night of my life. What would have happened to her if I wasn't there?

Nope. Not happening. I need to find a way to keep her by my side.

I smile as an idea starts to take form in my head.

I jerk awake in the middle of the night. Looking around, I realize that I must have fallen asleep on our couch. The words on the laptop lying across my stomach are staring at me in the face.

A suffocating feeling of guilt washes over me for manipulating my sister into playing softball. It wasn't her passion, basketball was. It still isn't her passion, working with children is. Yet I continue to push her to play. I'm such a horrible person. Sometimes I truly hate myself.

Suddenly there's a soft knock on my front door. I look at the clock on my laptop. It's three in the morning. Who the fuck is knocking at this hour?

I look down at myself in sleep shorts and a tank top with no bra. I notice that my nipples are visible. Standing and wrapping a blanket around myself, I open the door a small crack and see bright carrot-orange hair.

Opening the door a bit more, I scrunch my eyebrows together. "Justin? What are you doing here in the middle of the night?"

He twists his lips. "I saw your light on." He offers me a mug with steam billowing out of it. "I made you some warm milk. It sometimes helps me."

"Oh...umm...thanks." I reach for it. A normal woman would assume she's about to be roofied, but I'm a good judge of character and I think Justin is harmless. He's just fucking weird. That, and he's so scrawny I know I can beat the shit out of him, even if I'm drugged. "Do you want to come in?"

He gives the sweetest smile. "I would love to."

He steps inside, and I notice he's wearing an Anacondas T-shirt and gym shorts. Yep, fucking weird.

Looking around, he says, "Wow, you guys did a great job with this place. I have the same layout, but this looks so much better."

I'm just now realizing that I've never invited him inside despite the fact that he's brought me dozens of goodies throughout our first few months here. I'm sort of an asshole.

I shrug. "My sister has a good eye. We need to keep it down. She's asleep." And I want to make sure he knows we're not alone in this apartment in case he's related to Jeffrey Dahmer.

He lowers his voice to a near whisper. "No problem."

"Can I get you anything?"

He shakes his head. "No, I'm good."

I sit in a big chair so he can't sit next to me. Curling my legs in, I tightly wrap myself in the blanket and sip the milk. It's actually pretty good. No signs of poison, but I'll wait another minute or two before I take another sip just in case.

He happily plops himself down on our sofa before looking at me. "You don't sleep either?"

I shake my head. "No. Not for years."

"How come?"

He doesn't need my deepest, darkest secrets.

"I'm just one of those people who require very little sleep to function. I should have been a doctor. What about you? Why don't you sleep?"

He looks down, breaking our eye contact. "Let's just say that I've endured a good amount of bullying in my life, including a time in high school when the entire football team snuck in through my bedroom window and beat the shit out of me in the middle of the night." He points to the large scar on his forehead and another through his lip. "I left that town behind, but some scars never heal."

My heart breaks for him. I give a hopeful smile. "For what it's worth, women love scars. Men too. Whichever you prefer."

He offers a nervous laugh. "It's women, not that any notice me."

"Do you go out? I've never seen you leave your apartment." Not once.

He shakes his head. "I've had some...anxiety since that night. I work from home. I've lived here for a year, but I don't have any friends. It's a little daunting to go out alone in a big city."

This poor guy. He's got to be in his mid-twenties and all he does is sit home alone. I'm so sad for him. I have a sudden urge to help him as an idea occurs to me. "Do you ever come to our games?"

"No, but I watch them all on TV." He smiles. "You're amazing. All four of you. I feel like I live across from huge stars. I was never into sports, but I've researched softball since you moved in, and I think I mostly understand what's going on."

"The fourth game of our championship series is tomorrow night. I'm going to leave you a ticket at the box office. I have a friend who's coming alone. Will you sit with her to keep her company?"

We cruised through the first few rounds of the playoffs but are down two games to one in the best-of-five championship series. We need to get our acts together and take the next two games in a row. The next game is at home, and then, if we win, a winner-take-all game five in Miami.

The Cougars are in the World Series. Philly is electric for both teams. Our popularity has continued to surge throughout the season. We're now sold out for every single game. I have a handful of endorsements and am making decent money. At Bailey's request, Tanner Montgomery has been helping to negotiate my contracts, as he does for Ripley and Arizona. My sister continues to refuse to do any modeling.

Justin's eyes widen with concern. "Her?"

I nod. "Yes. She's kind of shy too. Can you help me out? I'd really appreciate it."

He gives me a nervous smile. "O...okay. If it helps you, I'll do it."

"It does. What's your last name? I'll need it for the ticket."

He winces. "It's...umm...Bieber."

I swear I try hard not to laugh, but a small one bubbles in my throat. "Your name is Justin Bieber?"

His shoulders fall as he nods. "Yep. It's been a big problem for me for a long time."

Poor guy. He's a nerdy ginger and has the same name as a person famous for basically being attractive. I suppose there's some talent there, but he wouldn't have become a star if he wasn't cute. Not so much in my opinion, but most people consider him to be.

"I think it's cool. I'm a Belieber. You should grow your hair like his and lean into the whole red-headed Justin Bieber thing."

He laughs. "I don't think I could pull it off."

"You never know until you try." I stretch and yawn like I'm tired, even though I'm not. "I'm going to head to bed. I'll leave you the ticket and look for you in the stands."

He gets up from the sofa and smiles. It's the biggest smile I've seen from him yet. "Great. Thank you. I'm really excited to watch you play."

"Thank *you*. You're the one helping me. Just remember, she's super shy. I need you to be the one to break the ice and talk to her."

He visibly swallows. "I'll try."

As soon as he leaves, I pull up my text string with Amber.

> Me: I need your friend Trisha to do me a favor.

THE COUGARS HAD a home game this afternoon which they won. They're now up two to one in the World Series' best-of-seven.

The good news about them having an afternoon home game is that they can come to our game tonight. If we win, we'll head down to Miami, so this is the last time they'll watch us play this season.

I see all the guys sitting together with Tanner and Harper. Cheetah and Harper are laughing and dancing together. He's cute with her. He's kind of the perfect man. Too perfect for me.

I know my ghosting him the way I have is upsetting him, but it's better this way. It's funny how much shit the guys give him when he's far and away the classiest of the bunch. First-class men deserve to be around first-class women, and I'm no such thing.

It's been weeks since that night in the club. I put on the performance he needed to see to hopefully move on. I felt bad doing it to him, but I'm doing this *for* him.

I do get a kick out of the fact that he's wearing a cowboy hat, as he has for every game he's attended since he heard my walkup song. I love watching him laugh. His smile lights up everyone around him.

Maybe in a different life, if I were a different kind of woman, I would be worthy of someone like Cruz Gonzales. In this life, I'm not.

As I throw my grape bubblegum into my mouth, I look over to the front-row seats I left for Justin and Trisha. She's seated, looking uptight and nervous. He's walking down the steps, looking at me. I wave to him. He smiles and waves back, but he loses concentration and trips down three steps.

Fucking hell. This poor guy is hopeless.

He lands right at his seat on the aisle, so Trisha immediately moves to help him up. He seems okay. Maybe this will be a conversation starter for them.

I look around the stadium. It's filled to capacity. I feel so fortunate.

Arizona throws her arm around me. "Isn't it amazing how many fans we have? We're so lucky that we get to do this for a living. Sometimes I need to pinch myself."

I nod. "I was just thinking the same thing." I nod toward Ripley warming up in the bullpen. "What's going on with her?"

Ripley is the best pitcher in softball. There's no denying that. But she's been distracted this week and isn't throwing her best stuff. I would never blame any loss on one teammate, but her being distracted has undoubtedly played a significant role in us being down in this series. We're the better team.

Arizona shakes her head. "I don't know. Something is up but she won't talk to me about it. She was on the phone with June all morning chatting about her mechanics, so maybe she'll get it together for the next two games."

I gasp. "Mama June!" I *love* Ripley's mom. June St. James is the mother I wish I had. She's a great mom and one of the funniest, least-filtered people I've ever met. She was an Olympic pitcher who coached Arizona and Ripley from their early childhood until they left for college. She still lives in their hometown in Northern California. She embarrasses Ripley, but I love her sense of humor, playfulness, and adventurous side. She and I ended up dancing topless on a bar one night when she visited us in college.

Arizona nods. "Yep. Let's hope June fixed her."

I see Reagan Daulton approaching us with a tall, attractive, muscular, older blond man. She smiles at us. "Kamryn, Arizona, are we ready to kick a little ass and get back into this series?"

We both nod, and I answer, "Hell yes. It's in the bag, your highness."

She smiles while the man chuckles. Reagan points to him. "This is my uncle, Declan McGinley."

"The photographer?" I ask. Declan McGinley is a well-known professional photographer. He's unique in that he photographs both landscapes and models. Most photographers do one or the other.

Reagan nods. "The one and only. At my gentle urging, he was just commissioned by Hubba Bubba. As in five minutes ago." She points to her private club box in the stands. "The CEO is my guest tonight. He's flipping over the excitement for this game. Kamryn, keep blowing big bubbles and hitting bombs. I'm this close," she pinches her thumb and index finger so they're close together, "to selling you as their next spokesmodel. It would be real money for you. Do your thing."

I smile. "Thanks for the added pressure. Lucky for you I'm a diamond and thrive under pressure."

Declan, who I assume is in his fifties, gives me a big smile. "I like you, Kamryn. I hope this works out. I'd love to photograph you."

"Are you flirting with me, Declan?"

He lets out a laugh before he winks at me. "I don't think my beautiful wife, the love of my life, would like that."

Reagan lets out a laugh. "Yep, his wife definitely wouldn't like it. She's my mom's husband's ex-wife. She's also one of my mom's best friends."

We give her a dumbfounded look and her smile widens. "Welcome to my crazy, fucked-up family tree. My mother's other best friend married my stepbrother." She wiggles her fingers. "Anyhoo, have a great game. Kick some ass."

She and Declan laugh in amusement as they walk away.

Arizona and I stare at each other. She fans her face. "I have no idea what she just said, but fuck, he's hot. He should be in front of the camera, not behind it."

I nod. "Totally. Too bad I don't have a daddy fetish like my sister."

As if on cue, Bailey walks over to us. "Who was that guy with Reagan? He's so sexy."

Arizona and I both start giggling uncontrollably. Of course my sister is attracted to the old fucker.

Coach Billie calls us into our pregame huddle. With determination written on her face, she commands, "Ladies, it's time to show the monkey the snake."

What the fuck does that mean? I look around in bewilderment and notice all my teammates with equally baffled expressions on their faces. Coach Billie has a knack for making weird snake puns. I'm usually able to figure them out, but not this one.

She continues, "I'm proud of every single one of you. You've worked your asses off, and I don't mean only this season. All I ask of you is that you leave nothing on the table. Don't walk off the field with regrets. Nothing is worse in life than missed opportunities. You've sacrificed too much. Take advantage of it. As a new franchise, people assume you're undeserving of winning a championship. You haven't bled enough for it. I call bullshit. They don't know shit about you. You deserve to be here. Every single one of you. Keep the negative voices out and just hear my voice. You. Deserve. Everything."

She makes eye contact with each of us, ending with me. Frankly, I'm not sure if she's talking about the game or life.

She places her hand in the middle. "Spear them with our snakes on three."

CHEETAH

This is the most edge-of-your-seat, exciting game of softball I've ever watched. I take in my surroundings. The stands were half full at their first game three months ago, and now they're packed to the gills. There are both Cougars and Anacondas signs everywhere in town. It's so awesome.

I still can't take my eyes off Kamryn. The tight pants and those Princess Leia hair muffs never fail to send my dick into overdrive. And then there are the constant purple bubbles. She's effortlessly sexual. Every single thing she says and does. I wish she'd give me a second chance. I can't even look at other women. No one does it for me like she does, even when she's being cold to me.

I'm wearing my *K. Hart*, number nine jersey, along with my cowboy hat. I'm holding out hope that one day she'll want to ride this cowboy again.

Before the game started, Layton, Ezra, Quincy, and I all removed our shirts to reveal a huge continuous anaconda painted across all our chests. The tongue is on me. Harper was laughing hysterically when I rolled my belly, making the tongue move with it. She's so freakin' cute.

We're down one run in the bottom of the last inning. My heart is pounding so hard. I want them to win this game to send it to a decisive game five down in Miami. Unfortunately, we'll play at the same time as them, so we won't be able to watch it, but I want this for them. They deserve it.

Arizona and Bailey are on base with one out when Kamryn makes her way to the batter's box. They start playing her walkup song "Save a Horse [Ride a Cowboy]". Harper and I are dancing to the music, though we're holding hands because we're both so nervous. I hear Tanner tell Harper that Kamryn is the best hitter in the league. This is who they want up to bat in a big situation.

My chest swells with pride. Kamryn *is* the best hitter in the league. She's so fucking awesome.

I take Harper's hand and cover my eyes. I can't watch. She giggles as we all stand and clap for what we hope will be a big moment.

After the first pitch is called for ball one, the second pitch comes in and Kam smacks it for what will likely be a double to the left-center gap. Arizona easily scores to tie the game. It should move Bailey, the winning run, to third base.

Suddenly, the third base coach inexplicably sends Bailey home. What is she doing? Bailey will be out. We all look at each other in bewilderment.

If it's possible for twenty thousand people to collectively hold their breath, that's what's happening. The ball beats

Bailey to home plate by a mile, but she does some sort of Olympic-worthy gymnastics somersault up and over the catcher and then slides in safely across home plate. Game over. Anacondas win on a walk-off double by Kamryn and a Cirque du Soleil move by Bailey.

Kam lifts her hands in the air in victory as the dugout empties and piles on top of her. She's the big hero.

Kam is now being interviewed by every news channel. She tries to pull Bailey into the interviews, calling her the real hero, but Bailey is content to let Kamryn shine. Bailey hates the limelight. Kam was born for it.

I can't tear my eyes away from her as she makes every newsperson interviewing her laugh with her larger-than-life personality. Fuck, I've got it so bad for her.

We're waiting on the field for them to finish interviews and other postgame business. Harper and I do a little dance number while we wait.

Bailey makes her way to Harper. Their mutual affection is more than apparent. I notice Tanner running his eyes up and down Bailey's body. Hmm. Interesting. Layton mentioned that he thinks Tanner has a thing for Bailey. Perhaps we should talk to Tanner about it. Bailey is an awesome chick. Maybe she could bring Tanner out of his self-imposed post-divorce funk. It's been over four years. It's time.

Kam is giving what appears to be her last interview. I make my way over to her and tip my cowboy hat. "Howdy, ma'am. I'm a cowboy offering riding services."

Without hesitation, she jumps on my back and shouts, "Yeehaw."

The reporter laughs and asks, "Are you two an item?"

I wink at her. "Not yet."

Kam answers, "Not ever."

THE GIRLS PLAY in Miami tonight for the decisive fifth game. We have a game, but management said if the Anacondas are winning, they'll momentarily stop our game and play the last out on the big screen.

That's exactly what happens. Our game is stopped as we all, and I mean all players and all forty thousand fans, have our eyes glued to the big screen.

On a great defensive play by Arizona, their game ends in an Anacondas league championship. We watch on while the girls all pile on top of Ripley as they celebrate.

Our dugout is full of smiles, none bigger than Layton's. He's playing the best ball he has in years, he's happily in love, and his girl just won a league championship. My heart swells for my best friend and his happiness. He deserves this.

The universe must have had other plans in mind because less than an hour later, Layton breaks his leg in the worst sports moment I've ever witnessed. His leg is twisted at an angle that is hard to watch. Tears stream down my cheeks as I watch an ambulance leave the field with him inside, knowing that it's likely the end of his career.

The team couldn't get it together after the loss of our leader, and we lost the game. I've been at the hospital all night with Quincy, Ezra, Trey, and Tanner.

Arizona arrives, and once Layton awakens, she kicks us all out. It's the middle of the night as I exit the hospital. The guys offer me rides, but I tell them I'd rather walk. It's a good two miles, but I need the fresh air to try to wrap my mind around what happened to my friend and the uphill battle he's about to endure.

A few hours ago, he was playing in the World Series, watching the love of his life win her league, and in about two weeks, he was supposed to leave for a two-month worldwide swimsuit photo shoot with Arizona. He'd have his hands on her mostly naked body all day long while posing on some of the most beautiful beaches in the world. They'd undoubtedly stay in five-star hotels and eat amazing food. Now he'll spend the next two months in bed, unable to move. Life can be cruel sometimes.

I'm only five steps out of the hospital front door, just getting lost in my thoughts, when I hear a familiar voice shout, "Why doesn't a snake have balls?"

I snap my head up and see Kamryn sitting on a bench outside the hospital. "What are you doing here? You should be partying in Miami."

She shrugs. "Once news of Layton's injury broke, the party atmosphere kind of fizzled. Arizona left right away with Reagan Daulton. A bunch of the girls flew home early commercially. I decided to join them."

"Why?"

She runs her lip through her teeth as she looks down at the ground for a moment before looking me in the eyes. "I know how much he means to you, Cruz. I thought you could use a friend."

I try to swallow down the obscene happiness running through my body that she cared enough about me to do that. I look at her and deadpan, "No, not why are you here, why doesn't a snake have balls?"

She smiles, knowing that I'm lightening the mood. "Because then it would look like a penis."

I let out a laugh. I'm realizing it's the first time I've smiled in hours.

She stands as I approach her. Wrapping her arms around me, she says, "I'm sorry. It must have been even worse to watch it in person. I know he's your best friend. What can I do to help?"

I squeeze her in return and take in her unique Kam

scent as tears pool in my eyes. "You're doing it. Thanks for being here, Kam bam. I know you should be celebrating."

She's always in a rush to pull away from me, but not right now. She's letting me hold her and it's everything.

She rubs my back. "Why don't we find something where we can be both sad and happy at the same time?"

"At three in the morning?" I ask.

She pulls back and nods. "There's an all-night diner with shockingly good ice cream sundaes near my apartment."

"I'd like that."

She reaches for her suitcase, which I'm just now noticing. She must have come here straight from the airport. My heart swells at the notion as I immediately take it for her.

We sit in the diner until sunrise, talking, laughing, and eating way too much ice cream. Even though I'm slightly disappointed that she sends me on my way when we leave, the whole experience was just what I needed, and I'm grateful to her for being here. I know she cares about me.

And I may fall just a little harder for Kamryn Hart.

CHAPTER TEN

KAMRYN

From the confines of our couch, I look up from my laptop at Bailey walking out of her bedroom. "Are you going to Daddy Tanner's for a little harpooning of the salty longshoreman?"

She recently started fucking her boss and sleeps there when Harper isn't around. She's being extremely tight-lipped on the details but finally admitted she's sleeping with him.

Bailey gives me an incredulous look. "I have absolutely no idea what the hell that means."

I smile. "I think you do, you dirty little girl. Does Daddy Tanner make you dress up in a school uniform while he defiles you? Do you wear pigtails and a plaid skirt?"

She bites back her smile. "There is something seriously wrong with you."

I let out a laugh. "More than one thing, big sis."

She tilts her head to the side. "Who was that guy that approached you at lunch today? Do you know him? He was creepy and kept calling you Carmen?"

Bailey and I worked out today and then grabbed a bite nearby at the same diner Cheetah and I went to a few weeks ago after Layton's injury. Some random guy kept walking by me and touching some part of my body. My back, my shoulders, and even my ass seemed to be fair play until I turned around and told him off.

I shake my head. "I don't know him. I think I met him at a bar one night and rejected him. He didn't like that."

"He kept touching you even though you clearly weren't into it."

"If you haven't noticed, a lot of guys do that without invitation."

She shakes her head. "Not to me. Maybe they're not into me like they are you."

"We're identical. I suppose I invite it with my demeanor. And I tend to wear more revealing clothes than you.

She looks down at herself in small spandex shorts and a tight tank top. "I don't think so, little sis. Frankly, you could walk around naked with your legs spread wide open if you wanted, it doesn't give anyone the right to touch you without your permission."

I nod in agreement. "You're right. It's one of my biggest pet peeves. I like to be touched but on my own terms. I think I'm giving up on men. I'm going full lesbo moving forward, though I suppose women aren't much better." I blow out a breath. "Maybe I'll be celibate." I wiggle my eyebrows. "Or maybe I should develop a daddy fetish like you and find myself a *mature* man."

"I don't have a daddy fetish."

"Are you or are you not currently fucking a man fifteen years older than you who is, in fact, a daddy? Who's only, like, seven years younger than *our* daddy."

Her face and neck flush. She must be getting it good. I don't know why I can't get any dirty details from her. I hope she's not in too deep.

My face turns serious. "Don't fall for him, Bails." I couldn't handle her heart being broken again. It's not like she'll end up with a man like Tanner Montgomery.

She shakes her head. "It's casual. He doesn't want the same future I do. We've discussed it."

"The problem is that you don't do casual."

She narrows her eyes at me. "Maybe I'm turning into you."

"Don't you dare ever turn into me. You're a thousand times better than me. Don't you forget it."

She plops down next to me and pulls me into a hug. "I hate when you say things like that. There's a lot of love living inside you, Kamryn Hart. You don't have to seal it away like you do. Maybe if you opened your heart just a little, you'd see that not everyone is bad. Most people are good."

"A lifetime of evidence to the contrary, big sis."

"What about Cheetah? I see the way he looks at you. You've been blowing him off since the waterbed night. You're obviously attracted to him. Why not give things a go?"

I shake my head. "Cheetah is a great guy. He's way too good for me. He deserves someone who will give him everything he wants and deserves."

Her face looks pained. "You have more to offer than you think, Kamryn. Whether it's Cheetah, some other man, or a woman, I hope one day you give it to someone."

I swallow down my emotions, hating for anyone to see me as emotional as I'm feeling right now. "I save all my love for you. When I'm an old cat-lady spinster you'll let me live above your garage, right?"

She lets out a laugh. "You'll be a dog-lady spinster, not a cat lady."

"But the garage is still on the table, right?"

"I'll always be there for you, little sis. You jump, I jump."

I smile at her. "Want to watch a movie?"

She looks at her watch. "I've got about two hours until I need to be at Mr. Montgomery's."

Without any more words needing to be exchanged, I turn on

Titanic and we cuddle together like we've done thousands of times before.

THREE HOURS LATER, Ripley and I are walking to Screwballs to meet the guys. They're hoping to cheer up Layton, who's miserable without Arizona. She was contractually obligated to go to that worldwide photo shoot while Layton is stuck home recovering from his injury. To add salt to his wounds, they replaced him with the insanely hot Butch McVey, the biggest star in professional baseball right now. The guys said that Layton has been a jealous mess.

I wrap my jacket tightly around me on the cold fall night. "Fuck, it's getting cold. I thought Philly was supposed to be warmer than Chicago."

Without any expression, she mutters, "It's a big city."

What? "Are you listening to me, Rip?"

She blinks a few times. "Sorry. What were you saying? Something about Chicago and coldness. Yes, it's cold as hell."

"The expression is cold as hail, not hell."

She pinches her eyebrows together. "For real?"

"Yep. Hell is hot. Hail is cold."

She mumbles, "Holy shit. I never knew that."

"Hot as hell. Cold as hail. Now you'll never forget." I hold out my arm and stop her from entering the bar. "What's wrong with you? Something is off. Something has been off with you for weeks."

Tears immediately fill her eyes, but they leave as quickly as they come. "I'm fine."

I place my hand on my friend's shoulder. "You can talk to me, Rip. I'm here for you. Always."

She visibly swallows before nodding. "I know. Thanks. I'm good. I promise."

"You're not good. We've been friends for ten years. I would know. Whenever you're ready to talk about whatever has been going on with you the past few weeks, let me know. No judgment. Only love."

I suddenly feel a hard spank on my ass and turn around to see a blond man, likely in his early twenties, smirking at me. He laughs with a group of guys around his age.

As he slowly walks backward while facing me, he says, "Sorry, but you have a great ass. It was begging for a little attention. It's good to see that the front side matches the back side. We should hang out, sexy."

I grit my teeth and point my finger at him. "Listen, you motherfuck—"

I'm a millisecond from beating his ass when I feel Ripley wrap her arms around me and interrupt, "He's not worth your breath. Let's get out of here. The *real* men are waiting." She yells louder. "The kind who know it's not ever okay to grope women without invitation. The kind who know that women could have you arrested for sexual assault if you don't get out of our faces in the next three seconds."

The group of guys all turn and run away. I think I've officially lost all faith in men. I'm genuinely at my wit's end.

Ripley takes my hand. "Are you okay? That was fucked up."

"What is it about me that makes men think it's okay to do that to me?"

"It's not you. It's them. Come on. Let's get inside and get you a drink."

A few seconds later, we walk into the bar. I see Cheetah, Quincy, Ezra, and some random girl sitting in our regular booth. I have a tinge of jealousy at the possibility that she's with Cheetah. I'm already on edge tonight. I don't think I could sit there and watch another woman touch him.

He and I had the best time at the diner the night of the accident. I don't know why I got on that plane with Ripley and

Bailey, but I did. Something inside me told me that he needed a friend, and I was right.

We talked about anything and everything all night. And then, at our team's victory parade a few days later, he celebrated with us like he was the one who won the championship. His genuine joy in our triumph was touching.

My resolve is weakening when it comes to him. I find myself wanting to spend more time with him. It both excites and terrifies me. I haven't felt this way about someone since high school, more than ten years ago.

As we step further inside, Ripley turns to me. "I'm running to the bathroom. I'll meet you in the booth. Try not to screw with Cheetah too much in my absence."

Well, fucking with Cheetah happens to be my favorite pastime. Trading barbs with him warms my soul like nothing else.

He warms my soul.

I walk toward the booth and Quincy looks up at me. "Where did Ripley go?"

"To perform brain surgery. Where do you think? The bathroom."

I am absolutely convinced that the two of them are secretly fucking. It's like a cheesy Hallmark movie. Each of them stares at the other when they aren't looking. I bet there's a good story there. They've known each other since they were little kids. She probably secretly lost her virginity to him.

My Hallmark reel is broken by Cheetah flicking his tongue suggestively at me. "Damn, Kam bam, you look good enough to drink up tonight."

But he doesn't touch me. He *never* touches me without invitation. As much as the two of us trade suggestive comments, he somehow manages to do it respectfully. It's *always* done in good fun. There's something so different about Cruz Gonzales from every other man I've ever known.

I gently pat his hand like I'm expressing sympathy for him.

"Are you jealous because my heart is pumping inside me and you're not?"

His adorable dimples come out just as he lets out his sweet, distinguishable laugh. One that soothes me for some odd reason.

We trade a few more sexually laced comments, per always. He's the only man who has ever been able to go toe-to-toe with me in that department. I think his witty yet dirty mind is almost as attractive to me as his sexy exterior and genuine interior.

God, he makes me laugh. No one in my life has ever made me laugh harder than Cruz Gonzales.

It turns out the girl in the booth is with Ezra. She's a childhood friend of his and is allegedly in a relationship with another guy, but she and Ezra are all over each other. I'm just happy to see him with a woman. I think Bailey broke his heart. He's wanted her since we moved here, but she's friend zoned him. Now that she's doing the deed with Daddy Tanner, Ezra doesn't stand a chance. I doubt he ever did.

Ripley returns to the table and Layton wobbles in on his crutches looking like someone shot his puppy. He whines about missing Arizona terribly. He's such a goner for her.

Some skank tries to hit on Layton, but Ripley stands up to her on Arizona's behalf. After which, the skank makes some nasty comment about Ripley's weight. I'm about to beat this bitch up when Quincy then takes it to a whole other level by physically threatening the woman and then having her booted from the bar by the owner before grabbing Ripley's hand and disappearing toward the bathroom area.

Yep. They're fucking. Not a doubt in my mind now.

Cheetah brings me back to the present by once again asking for another chance with me. Should I give it to him? In fairness, the sex was amazing before my waterbed popped. I don't usually like to have sex with someone more than once because it leads to expectations, but I suppose we didn't technically finish.

Wait. What happened to me being off men? What if he turns

out to be just like the rest? I feel like I'll truly lose all faith in mankind if he ends up being a typical asshole.

I know he's not. That's the problem.

I exhale a long breath and cross my arms in challenge. Narrowing my eyes at him, I say, "I've got one for you, big mouth. Tell me two authentic things about me that have nothing to do with sex, my body, or my current softball team. If you *actually* know *anything* substantive about me, I'm yours for the night to do with as you please."

His entire face lights up like it's Christmas morning. Like he's been waiting his whole life for this question.

He makes a big fucking show of stretching like he's about to run a marathon. He then picks up his beer and makes another show of handing it to Ezra with nothing but pure Cheetah mischief in his eyes. "Hold my beer."

He places his hands on the table and leans toward me, so his handsome face is right in mine. His dimples briefly come out before he begins his little speech. "Kamryn Sarah Hart, age twenty-eight, is the younger of identical twins by nine minutes. Incidentally, that's also your number, but we're not talking about the Anacondas. Your parents are Beverly and Chris. They still live in the same Southern Florida house that you grew up in. You have no other siblings. You were the Gatorade Player of the Year in the state of Florida during your senior year of high school. You had your choice of full athletic scholarships to any college in the country. You chose UCLA because they were willing to take Bailey, who, at the time, wasn't considered as strong of a player as you. You like dark chocolate, not milk chocolate. It's your comfort food. Milk chocolate makes you gassy. You love dogs but realize you can't have one right now because of your life on the road. When you retire, which you plan to do after the twenty-eight Olympics, your first order of business will be to adopt a dog. You smell like peaches, and I know firsthand that you taste like them too, but I'm not allowed to talk about your body. You don't like Doublemint Gum. You and Bailey were in a commercial for it when you were little kids, and they made you chew it for days until it started to physically make you sick. You refused to ever chew it again. You chew grape bubblegum on the field and blow giant bubbles that make my dick hard because I've never been more jealous of a piece of gum in my life. You hate it when—"

I sit there flabbergasted through his speech. I've never felt more seen by a man in my entire life. A woman either, for that matter.

Yes, we've had a bunch of conversations, but he actually listened to the small things and remembered them. Even the tiniest details. And the Gatorade Player of the Year thing? I never told him that. Or the Doublemint commercial thing. He thinks about me when we're not together. Enough to google me.

The gum comment is my final tipping point. Before he can get out the next sentence, I practically crawl across the table and smash my lips to his.

As if we're not in a crowded bar, he grabs my waist and pulls me to straddle his lap. I slide right down onto his hard dick and let out a moan into his mouth.

I forgot how good he tastes and how perfectly he kisses. Our tongues invade each other's mouths as my hands move up and under his sweater, running my nails down his broad, bare chest. His hands squeeze my hips hard while we shamelessly grind onto each other.

Fuck, we're in the middle of a normal bar. This might be acceptable behavior for a dark club but not a regular sports bar. I'm not sure I give a fuck, but I don't want any blowback on him. I mumble into his mouth, "Get me out of here and fuck me senseless."

He lets out a growl before standing with me still wrapped around him. We don't break our kiss or bother to say goodbye to anyone as we leave the bar. I think I hear them all laughing, but I don't give a shit. Laugh away, suckers. I'm about to get it good.

As soon as we're outside, he pushes my body against the brick wall of the building and kisses down my neck. "You have no idea how badly I want you. I can't stop thinking about you."

I can't deny that I've wanted him too. "Let's go back to my place."

He breathlessly lifts his head, so our eyes meet. "There is zero chance of me attempting this again on your waterbed."

I can't help but giggle.

He gives me a serious look. "Come back to my place. My couch doesn't pull out, but I do."

"Hmm, tempting," I sarcastically respond. "You sure you don't want to be an interior decorator and paint my insides white?"

He smiles. "No, but I do believe in love at first choke."

I bite back my smile as I contemplate going home with him. I really do prefer having the home-field advantage. It's usually a stranger and I don't ever go to a stranger's home. I suppose if there's anyone I can trust in this situation, it's him.

He rubs his thumb over my lip. "Get out of your head. I'm not going to hurt you. Just the opposite. I want nothing other than to make you feel good." He softly kisses me. "Let me in."

I think for a moment before eventually nodding. "How far away do you live?"

"Hmm...a few blocks."

"Let me down. I'll walk."

"Nope. I'm not giving you the chance to change your mind and run away. Hold tight, princess. We're going for a ride."

I left my jacket inside. It's freezing cold out here. I should go grab it, but being wrapped in his warm arms sounds like a better idea to me. I'm sure Ripley will grab it for me.

He basically runs, while holding me, for what must be at least ten blocks. It's way more than *a few*. He manages to do it while barely breaking a sweat.

I look down at him while playing with the back of his hair. "This bodes well for your stamina, kitten."

"Baby, I'm going to fuck you all night. Prepare for your first bottom orgasm."

I shrug. "Hmm. We'll see. You couldn't close the deal last time."

He scrunches his face. "You were close. If the bed didn't explode, you would have."

"Maybe yes. Maybe no."

He eventually stops at a large skyscraper and smiles warmly at the doorman as if I'm not wrapped around him. "Good evening, Evan. It's a nice night, isn't it?"

The doorman, a big-bellied middle-aged man in a green uniform complete with a doorman's cap, nods. "It's a little cold for my old bones, Mr. Gonzales. You seem to have grown a pretty lady since you left."

"I sure did. This is Kamryn Hart."

I smile. "Nice to meet you, Evan. He won't put me down. He's basically kidnapped me. Can you please call the police?"

Cheetah shakes his head. "Don't listen to her, Evan. She likes to play pretend. Tonight we're going to pretend that she's a cell phone and I'm going to be the charger."

I can't help but giggle at his ridiculousness. "I didn't know you wanted to play pretend, kitten. Why don't we pretend that I'm the egg and you're the chicken? Then we'll know once and for all who comes first."

Evan lets out a deep laugh. "Ooh. You've found your match in this one, Mr. Gonzales."

Cheetah sighs. "Evan, I've told you a thousand times. Don't call me Mr. Gonzales. Call me Sir Cruz Gonzales, Knight of South Philly."

Evan laughs again as he opens the door for us. "You two kids have fun. Try not to bring the building down tonight."

I shrug. "It sounds like he's challenging us, kitten."

Cheetah nods. "Sure does. Challenge accepted, Evan. Prepare for this building to crumble."

We can hear Evan still chuckling as we make our way across the giant marble lobby and into the elevator.

I take in the opulence and let out a whistle. "Damn, this place is fancy."

"I ooze class and sophistication, don't you think?"

"Totally."

He runs some sort of key card over a scanner on the button pad and the letters *PH* appear on the screen. Penthouse. Of course he's in the penthouse.

As if reading my mind, he says, "It doesn't stand for the penthouse."

"No? What does it stand for?"

"Penis hard."

I giggle as I tighten my legs around him and can feel that his penis is, in fact, very hard. "This is the smartest elevator ever."

He nods. "I know, right? Sometimes it reads B when I have a boner. It's like it always knows when I'm aroused." He gently rubs the side of the elevator. "I think she has a thing for me, don't you, baby girl?"

I laugh harder. "Wow. You must pay a lot for a building that has an elevator like this."

"You bet your soon-to-be-orgasming pussy I do."

I shrug. "Maybe PH stands for pussy handler."

He gasps. "You're right. Aren't you happy you came to my place? I never would have known."

I smile as the elevator pings our arrival and the doors open straight into his apartment. I can't even call it an apartment. It's like a floating mansion.

I breathe out, "Holy shit. This place is insane."

There are floor-to-ceiling windows everywhere with amazing views of the city. The entire floor plan is open. It's modern and massive.

Again, as if reading my mind, he asks, "Can we tour later? I want you naked ASAP."

"You're lucky I like being naked more than I like real estate tours."

He speed-walks us down the hallway and into what I quickly learn is his bedroom. It's nice but not over the top and not bachelor pad looking. Everything is in perfect order, and it appears like a decorator had a hand in it.

He walks us over to the bed but still doesn't put me down. He simply stares at me. "I'm so happy you're here."

"It was the promise of orgasms that won me over."

He wiggles his eyebrows. "This kitten is going to make *you* purr."

We both smile as our lips meet and we fall onto the bed with him between my legs. I expected it to be frantic like it was the first time, but it's not. He's taking his time as if he's savoring every second of it.

We kiss for minutes on end. Our lips and tongues ever so slowly explore each other's mouths. Our hands move all over each other's bodies, both over and under our clothing. I can't remember the last time I did this with a partner. Everyone is always in a rush to get to the main event, but not Cheetah.

He eventually kisses down my neck. "God, you smell so good. I think about your peach scent all the time."

He moves down my body, lifts my sweater, and peppers the softest kisses over my stomach. Suddenly my head starts spinning. I can't do soft and sweet. I *don't* do soft and sweet.

I shove his shoulders. "Stop."

He lifts his head and furrows his brow. "What's wrong?"

I slide away from him toward the middle of the bed and sit up. "Don't treat me like this."

"What did I do wrong?"

"You're...you're...you're being too nice."

He lets out a laugh. "Too nice? What kind of monsters have you been with?"

"The kind I need. The kind I deserve. I like to be fucked, Cruz."

He stands as he holds up his hands in surrender. "My bad. I apologize for wanting to take my time with you. For not wanting it to be over too quickly and for you to leave a trail of smoke in your wake as you hurry out of here."

Tears fill my eyes. "I'm sorry. It's just the way I am. The way I've always been. I told you that I'm fucked up."

He takes a few long breaths. "Do you want this, Kamryn? As much as I want you, I'm certainly not the kind of guy to force anything."

I nod as I hug my knees to my chest. "I do want you, but I need it to be like it was last time."

He gives me a small smile. "Can we compromise?"

I lift an eyebrow. "Are we in a sex negotiation?"

His smile widens. "I suppose we are." He lifts some sort of remote control off his nightstand and presses a button. Slow, sultry Latin music begins playing. He holds out his hand for me. "Dance with me. Let me seduce you for a bit, and then I'll give you what you want. I'll do you hard and dirty."

"You don't need to seduce me. I'm already in your bed."

"I *want* to seduce you, Kamryn."

He motions his hand again for me to take it. This time I do, and he pulls me to stand and then into his arms.

He immediately begins swaying us to the provocative beat of the music. His hands roam up and down my body, both over my clothes and up the back of my sweater. His lips drag along my neck and jawline.

Okay, this is nice. This I can handle. I would do this in a club with someone I'm attracted to, so why not here with him?

He effortlessly moves us around, helping our hips move in unison. He really is a good dancer.

He practically purrs, "He soñado con tenerte en mis brazos así." *I've dreamed of holding you in my arms like this.* "Eres la mujer más hermosa que he visto en mi vida." *You're the most beautiful woman I've ever seen.*

I whisper. "What did you say?"

He smiles into my neck. "That I'm going to pound your pussy until you can't walk straight."

I'm more than confident that he didn't say that, but I appreciate the fact that he knows what I need to hear. Maybe I should learn a little Spanish. In fact, I'm going to do that right away.

As the first song ends and another begins, he turns us so that my back is to his front. He lifts my sweater over my head and tosses it to the side. I feel his bare chest on my back. I guess he removed his sweater too.

After making quick work of my bra, he cups my breasts, though he never stops swaying our hips to the beat of the music.

He rubs his thumbs over my rapidly hardening nipples. "Me dejas sin aliento." *You take my breath away.*

"What did you say?"

"Umm...that I'm going to fuck these tits later."

I giggle. "You definitely didn't say that."

I can feel him silently laugh on my back as he kisses his way down it. I feel his fingers move to unbutton my jeans. Now we're getting somewhere.

He slides my jeans and panties down and off my legs until I'm standing there completely naked.

His fingers run up and down my thighs. Each time they almost reach their final destination but never quite get there. The anticipation is killing me. I'm practically panting. I'm dripping for it.

His warm breath skirts past my ear. "Tell me you want this. Tell me you *need* my cock inside you."

I manage to nod.

"Words, Kamryn. I need your words."

I breathe, "I want it."

His fingers lightly brush by my center. "Do you *need* it?"

Asshole. I grit out, "Yes. Give it to me."

Before I know it, my front is shoved hard against his wall and his naked body is pressed to mine. He grabs my chin and turns my head. "One last kiss."

His lips first brush over mine before they latch on and his tongue sweeps through my mouth. He really is a good kisser.

So good that I'm a little lost in it and don't realize that he's lifted one of my legs and his somehow sheathed tip begins to breach my entrance. In and out, just the tip, over and over.

I can't help but smile into his mouth. "Just the tip is my favorite game."

He smiles back into my mouth. "Just the tip. Just for a second. Just to see how it feels."

I let out a laugh. "The mantra of every teenage boy on the planet."

He nods. "Yep."

For minutes on end, he teases me until I'm confident that I've never been this drenched with desire. Panting for him to push all the way in. "Cruz, please. I want you."

He breathes, "Paciencia," as his fingers graze over my clit and begin to circle it.

My fingers are now clawing at the wall. I can't get enough of this. Of him.

He grumbles, "When I tell you to come, you're going to come for me."

I shake my head. "That's not how it works."

"It is when you're with me."

His strokes over my clit intensify, yet he never pushes more than his tip into me. Fuck, this is good. I'm so close.

"Give me your words, Kamryn. Tell me how it feels."

I breathe out, "It feels good."

"Give me more. You're a smart girl. Hit me with some big words."

"Your joystick and digits are profoundly satisfying to me."

He chuckles. "We'll work on that. Córrete para mí. Come for me, Kamryn."

Like an out-of-body experience, my vision becomes spotted

and my body opens up. I yell out his name while I come long and hard. I can feel my juices dripping down my leg. My whole body shakes through it all.

As soon as I start to regain my senses, he shoves his fingers into my mouth. "Lame tu corras. Lick your come."

I run my tongue over his fingers, enjoying the salty taste of my pleasure. As I begin to suck harder on his fingers, I feel his cock push further into me. He lets out a long groan of pleasure. "Ahhh."

With his other hand, he lifts my leg even higher as he begins his long, hard, deep, purposeful strokes inside me, eventually building to a near-inhuman pace. I tilt my ass back to give him the best angle possible, trying to bounce on him as best as I can at this angle.

My body bangs against the wall with each lunge. My hands search for leverage, but they find none. I can only dig my palms in and push against each punishing thrust, savoring every second of this onslaught.

Our bodies begin to slicken with sweat. The sounds of him pounding into my body overtake the music, the force of it lifting me inches off the ground each time.

This is hard fucking. This is animalistic. This is what I need.

He barks out, "Es esto lo que quieres?"

"Hmm?" No clue what he asked.

"Is this what you want?"

"Fuck yes. As hard as you can. Don't stop."

He hammers into me over and over. His stamina is insane. He's so damn strong.

The only time I've ever come during penetrative sex has been when I'm on top. I was close to coming when the waterbed broke. I think I'm about to come now.

I'm definitely going to be bruised all over, but I don't care. I'm completely absorbed in the pleasure of what he's doing to my body. I think I broke a nail or two, but I can't feel anything but what he's doing to me.

"Tell me how it fucking feels."

He likes words. I grit out, "You're pulverizing my pussy," before yelling out, "Pull my hair."

He immediately obliges. If possible, he thrusts in deeper until I have no choice but to let go and come. I'm on one leg because he's still holding up the other. I feel like I might collapse but his grip on my hair tightens and his body weight on me intensifies.

I can feel my insides spasming around him.

He shouts out, "Fuck yes!" as he continues pounding into me all the way through my orgasm.

His thrusts begin to slow down, and I lean my head back on his shoulder, breathing heavily. "That was amazing."

"We're not done."

I turn my head and look at him. "You didn't come?"

He shakes his head. "Nope. Not yet."

How is that physically possible?

He pulls out and picks me up by the waist. I screech as he throws me onto the bed and instructs, "Get on all fours, wench."

I take in his sexy body. He's fucking hot, all sexed up and covered in sweat. I want to lick it off him.

We were like animals the first time. I remember thinking his body was better than expected, but I didn't truly appreciate it. His hips are slender, but his thighs are thick like a ballplayer. The giant dick in the middle only adds to the allure. His broad, muscular chest has a smattering of hair. He's the perfect male specimen.

"Don't make me spank you. Get your sexy ass on all fours."

I smile as I place my index finger on the corner of my mouth, and innocently respond, "What if I want to get spanked, Daddy?"

He grabs me by the hips and spins me until I'm on all fours, manhandling me like I weigh nothing. I giggle until I feel the delicious pressure of his cock breaching my opening before he pushes back inside me.

I spread my legs wide and tilt my ass in the air.

I feel a hard spank and let out a moan. Ooh, I love that.

"Put your legs together."

"What?"

"Put your fucking legs together."

Okay. This is new.

We both maneuver ourselves until his knees are on the outside of mine. My legs are pushed completely closed.

"Cross your ankles."

I do. Holy shit. It feels like his already enormous cock just grew threefold inside me. I'm both sore and sensitive from the pounding I just received, but my legs closed with him inside me makes the ache intensify that much more.

I turn my head back. "You're very innovative. This is the second time you've put me into a position I didn't know existed."

He slides out and then slowly inches his way back in. His eyes flutter. "Te sientes tan jodidamente apretada como esta." *You feel so fucking tight like this.*

My body is stretching in ways it never has before. I don't know if it's the new position or the fact that he's undoubtedly the biggest man to ever be inside me, but the result is euphoric.

His thrusts into me begin to increase in pace. It goes from slow to fast in mere seconds. I'm bounced forward with every thrust. I can feel his enormous balls smack into me each time. They're close to my clit. It actually feels good. I grip the buttery soft sheets so damn hard that I feel like I might tear them.

His hands begin on my hips, but as we continue, one grabs a fistful of my hair. It didn't take him long to realize how much I love that, and he does it properly. So many guys grab small handfuls. They're fucking clueless.

"Tu coño está tan jodidamente apretado. Estás ordeñando mi polla ahora mismo."

I breathlessly plead, "Tell me what you said. Please. It's so hot. I need to know."

"Your pussy is so fucking tight. You're milking my cock right now."

It sounds hot in English, but in Spanish, it's on a whole other level. Fucking hell. He's blowing my mind.

I do my best to squeeze him inside me. I want this to be as good for him as it is for me.

"Oh, fuuuuuck. I need you to come. I'm close."

I pant, "I've already come twice. I'm not sure I have another in me."

He spanks me again and pulls my hair hard...and I stand corrected. The whole scene pushes me over the edge again, but this time he comes with me on a very loud growl that I'm confident Evan must have heard sixty floors down.

We both breathlessly collapse onto the bed in a heap of sweat and my fluids. He immediately pulls the condom off his dick and tosses it toward the bathroom area. "Fuck, that was good."

I pat his leg. "Aren't you glad I made you fuck me?"

His eyes close but his dimples come out. "I took it easy on you." Huh? "Round two will be much harder."

What the fuck?

His smile widens. He's fucking with me. He chuckles. "We didn't bring the building down so my work here isn't done."

He rolls over onto me and slips down my body until his face is between my legs, and his tongue licks through me.

My mouth widens. "You must be kidding me."

His tongue sweeps through me again. "Oh, Kam bam, we're just getting started."

CHAPTER ELEVEN

CHEETAH

I wake up in the middle of the night and reach over to the other side of the bed for Kam, but it's cold and empty. Did she leave? Why does the thought of that hurt so much?

Would she really just leave without a word? The sex was off the charts. She can't possibly consider walking away again.

I quickly scan my bedroom floor and see the pile of our clothes as we left them. She's still here.

Even though I'm naked, I get up and quietly walk out of my bedroom and into my living room. I immediately see her standing at my most central floor-to-ceiling window, which overlooks the Philly skyline and the river. The view is spectacular and I'm not talking about what's outside the windows.

Her back is to me and she's naked, but her hourglass figure is illuminated by the city lights. What I'm looking at right now is far too beautiful to be real. It's like a painting. I would pay big money for a piece of art that looks just like this.

"That view is what sold me on the place."

She turns her head enough so that I can see her softly smiling profile. "It's stunning. I like that the city is still bustling with excitement yet it's peacefully quiet up here. I almost feel like a voyeur." Her smile widens. "Now I know why you like it here so much."

"You know I like to watch." I walk up to her and rub her arms from behind. "Can't sleep?"

She turns her face back toward the window and mutters, "I never sleep. Not since I was a little kid."

"Why?"

She's quiet for a brief moment before saying, "I guess my mind is always churning. It's hard to turn off."

I wrap my arms around her and kiss her shoulder. "It must be exhausting. Anything I can do to help?"

She leans her head back on my shoulder and looks up at me. "I wish. Sometimes it feels like I've been tired for eighteen years."

I wonder what happened eighteen years ago.

"What do you think about when you're awake?"

She lifts her head and stares out the window again. "It's not what I think about when I'm awake. It's what I dream of when I'm not."

"And what's that?"

She turns around and wraps her arms around my neck while pulling me close so her soft body is flush to mine. She shakes her head. "Nothing I care to talk about." She softly kisses my lips before her uncharacteristically softened eyes meet mine. "Thanks for reminding me that there are a few good guys still out there." She pats my chest with her hand. "But I should leave and let you sleep."

I catch sight of the time on the clock in my kitchen. "It's after three in the morning, babe. I'm not letting you leave alone in the middle of the night."

She raises her eyebrows. "Letting me?"

I rub her back. "It's not safe. Don't go. Please. I'll make us a fire." I smile. "I'll even build a fort. I happen to be a great fort builder. Professional-level fort engineering is my specialty. You know I have six siblings and seventeen nieces and nephews, so creating mansion-quality forts comes easily to me."

Her eyes light up. "Well, I suppose I need to see what professional-level fort engineering looks like. I'll grab us some clothes."

"Ooh. That's a no-no. My adult forts are nudist forts. No clothing is allowed, and cuddling is mandatory. Oh, and there's a confidentiality clause. Whatever is said in a fort stays in a fort. No exceptions. It's like a mafia fort."

She lets out a laugh. "There are a lot of rules in your nudist mafia fort. I'm not much of a rule follower."

"What if I were to tell you that naked fort dwellers are permitted to make s'mores, but at the Gonzales nudist colony fort, we make s'mores with dark chocolate instead of milk chocolate?"

She runs her bottom lip through her teeth, and I have to will my cock not to ruin our moment by poking his head out. She's just so damn sexy.

Her eyebrow then lifts slightly. "I suppose most nudist colonies prefer any food over *weenie* roasts."

I chuckle as I nod in agreement. "True. And most nudist colonies screen *Free Willy*."

She silently shakes in laughter. "Alright, kitten. Let's see your fort and fire-building skills. They better be top-notch. I'll be leaving a review online."

Fifteen minutes later, a gigantic fort and a roaring fire are built. I used the all-white bedding from one of my guestrooms. The floor is covered in blankets and pillows. I have the white sheets hanging from chairs so that everything is covered except the opening facing the fireplace. I even found some LED fairy lights that I had bought when my nieces visited last year and strung them along the top of the fort. I'm happy with my finished product.

I grab the s'mores' necessities as I join Kam inside the fort. She's happily facing the fire, lying with her hands behind her head on the bed of pillows I created. I love how she's completely exposed but confidently lays there as though she isn't. I can see the reflection of the fire in her big, light brown eyes. It makes the gold flakes come out in full force.

I crawl into the fort with my hands full of food. "Impressed?"

She shrugs. "Only a little. Being naked while carrying two hot chocolates and twelve donuts at once," she looks at my semi-hard dick, "*that* would impress me."

I let out a laugh. "Fair enough. I'll be sure to keep more donuts on hand if you promise to come back again."

I place everything on the blanket and lie down next to her. Our heads and shoulders are touching but the rest of our bodies aren't. We both quietly stare into the fire for a minute or two before she sighs. "Why do you want me to come back?"

I turn to look at her, my face only a few inches from hers. "Is it so hard to believe that I enjoy spending time with you? That I've never met anyone like you? That I'm fascinated by you?"

She turns her head toward me and steels her face. "You just want to fuck me again."

"That too because I'm wildly attracted to you," I admit, "but I'm equally happy to talk to you, Kamryn."

"What do you want to talk about?"

"Tell me why you don't sleep."

She turns her head away from me. "I have a lot of demons, *Cruz*. You don't end up as fucked up as I am with a normal, healthy upbringing."

"Does this have to do with your mother?"

She turns toward me again and pinches her eyebrows together. "What makes you think that?"

"I don't know. I've listened to every word you've ever said. You and Bailey are unusually tight, and I know you both are close with your father, but you never go home. You haven't since you left for college. You never talk about your mother; except the one time you mentioned her not allowing you certain kid-like liberties when you were young. But I know she exists. I guess I simply put the pieces together." And I may have googled Kam. Anytime she's been asked about her family in interviews, she mentions her sister and father, never her mother.

She exhales a long breath. "I guess you're not just a pretty face with a great ass and giant beach balls. Yes, we adore our father. Yes, Bailey and I are unusually close, even for twins. We've had to rely on each other for as long as I can remember. Our mother is a piece of shit, but that's all you're getting from me. Now it's your turn. How's your relationship with your family?"

I shrug. I've got nothing to hide. "Pretty good. My family life was always chaotic. You know I have a lot of siblings. I'm the middle one."

"I can't imagine. That must be crazy."

"Good crazy. Two of my sisters butt heads a bit, but everyone mostly gets along well. My father is a mechanic who still works his ass off. My mother helps babysit all the grandkids. I talk to her a few times a week. I'm the only one of my siblings who lives out of town. I'm most definitely expected to move back when I retire. My status as an unmarried man who hasn't given her more grandkids is a constant topic. Like you, she doesn't sleep well. She obsessively cooks during the night, though I think she mostly stays up and dreams of ways to marry me off. I know she means well, but she drives me nuts about it."

"At least she cares about you. Be thankful."

"I know, but it's excessive. It's the reason I only go home once a year for Christmas. In part, I can't handle the pressure, but I also feel like I'm a disappointment."

She rolls her eyes. "You're a superstar baseball player who has a fuck ton of money. And you happen to be a good guy. A great guy. Why in the world would she be disappointed?"

"Money means nothing to them. Familia. Niños. Those things are success to them. In that sense, I'm a failure."

"That's nuts."

"That's my family. My mother even has the woman picked out."

She scrunches her face. "Ouch. Is she a troll?"

I let out a laugh. "Not even close. She's beautiful, sweet, and comes from a good, honest family."

"What's the problem?"

I look Kam in the eyes. "I don't know that it's the life I want. What they want for me doesn't excite me. As for the woman, she doesn't challenge me. She doesn't make me laugh. She's...kind of boring."

"Vanilla sex?"

"I wouldn't know. I've never even kissed her. I've known her for all of her twenty-five years, and I've never once come close to touching her. I won't lead her on. You can't force it. I refuse to marry someone for anything other than true love."

"Is that what you want? Marriage? A family? True love?"

"Doesn't everyone want that?"

She shakes her head. "I don't. Fucked up people shouldn't bring kids into this world. My mother is exhibit one. I refuse to be exhibit two in the Hart family."

"Everyone is a little fucked up."

"Well, I'm a lot of it."

"Then what is it that you do want?"

She thinks for a moment. "To make a difference."

Not the answer I expected. "How so?"

She's quiet for a moment. "If I tell you something, can I trust that it stays between us? No one knows this, not even my sister."

"Of course. I promise. I told you, what happens in a fort stays in a fort. Standard fort rules." I make a show of crossing my heart.

She briefly covers her eyes with her hands. "I can't believe I'm going to tell you this. I've never uttered the words out loud. Not even to myself."

I squeeze her hand. "You can trust me, Kamryn."

She nods. "I know. I don't know why I feel like I can, but I know I can." She lets out a breath. "I'm in law school."

I sit up as my eyes widen in shock. Of all the things she could have said, that wasn't what I expected in the slightest. "What? Where? When?"

She smiles. "It's an online program. Obviously I can't take a full course load, so it will take a while, but I've been doing it for over five years. I have less than two left. I don't sleep so it's not hard to make time to watch the lectures and read all the cases. I have a photographic memory. The tests are easy for me. I have straight A's. I got a perfect score on the entrance exam which entitled me to a full scholarship. The program allows me to participate at my own pace. It's been working for me."

I grab her hand again. "Kam, that's amazing."

"You think?"

I nod enthusiastically. "Absolutely. Do you know what you want to do with your law degree?"

She shakes her head. "Just something that matters. That's all I care about. I'll graduate ahead of the Olympics. It's kind of my post-Olympics career plan."

"Why don't you tell people? You should be proud."

She blows out a long breath, "People see me as the goofy, crazy, outrageous one. I have a rep to protect."

I smile. "I certainly understand that. Well, I think it's awesome. I have no idea what I'm going to do after baseball. It's assumed that I'll move home, start a family, and probably end up being a high school baseball coach. It's not enticing to me at all."

"You could easily play another ten years, but you could do commentary when you're done. You certainly have the personality for it, and obviously you have a face for television."

I shrug my shoulders as I lay back down. "Maybe. I never considered that before."

"You should."

"How do you get into it?"

"You have natural charisma and game knowledge. I think those are probably the two most important things. You could take some classes to learn how to properly channel it all."

Hmm.

I look at the pile of candy, marshmallows, and crackers. "Want me to make you a s'more?"

She shakes her head. "No. I'm good."

"I have some pineapples. Do you want those?"

She narrows her eyes at me. "How do you know that I eat pineapples?"

"I didn't. I eat them because it's supposed to make my spunk taste sweeter. Want to test that theory?"

She giggles. "I eat them because it's supposed to make my honey pot taste good."

"It's working. I *love* the taste of your honey pot."

She yawns and nuzzles into me. "The fire is nice. It's soothing. I've never lived anywhere with a fireplace before. Thanks for staying up with me."

"There's nowhere else I'd rather be."

We talk for another two hours about nothing and everything. We both must drift off at some point because when I wake a few hours later, Kam is fast asleep on my chest with my arm wrapped around her. I'm happy she's at peace enough to sleep with me. On me.

Like a psycho stalker, I lay there awake for another hour with her on top of me, stroking her hair. I wonder what haunts her. I'm not sure why, but I have this need to help her. To take care of her.

She eventually blinks her eyes open. Her big brown eyes look up at me. "Sorry."

"Why are you sorry? I love that you were comfortable enough to sleep on me. It's the best compliment in the world."

Her face falls as she whispers, "Don't fall for me, Cruz."

Too late.

I answer, "I'll try my best. Can we hang out? I want to spend more time with you."

"Can you do casual? I'm not built for anything more."

I nod. "I don't see why not. I've never done anything else."

She sighs. "I want you to see other people and I need you to be cool with me doing the same. This is not a relationship. It's a...flingationship."

I chuckle. "I've never heard that term."

"I heard Nelly Furtado use it once in an interview. I loved it."

"Nelly Furtado? I haven't heard that name in forever."

"She just released a new album. I love her. She's funny as hell in her interviews. Just another in a long line of underrated women."

I squeeze her tight. "I can live with a flingationship, Kam bam."

She nods. "Okay. I think I'd like that."

KAMRYN

I'm a little dazed as I walk into our apartment at around noon. I can't seem to get rid of this big grin on my face. My fingertips move all over my body reliving everything we did. I think last night was one of the best of my life.

It wasn't just the sex. It was the time spent in the fort too. We talked and laughed for hours. I've never spent an intimate night like that with a partner in my entire life.

As I walk through the door, I see Bailey on our sofa with Ripley sobbing in her arms. I suck in a breath. "What's wrong?"

Ripley turns her face toward me. It looks like she's been crying for hours. Her eyes are red rimmed and nearly swollen shut. She stutters, "I'm...I'm...I'm pregnant."

I can't imagine my face masking my complete and total shock. As far as I know, she hasn't slept with anyone since we moved here. I know she went on one date with some random guy from the gym, but I haven't heard of anything else. Then I remember her weird demeanor with Quincy last night, and I realize what's going on.

"Is it Quincy's?"

She steels her face. "It's mine. I'll be raising the baby alone." Then she starts sobbing again. Wailing.

Bailey nods toward her open laptop. I glance at the screen long enough to see a headline about Quincy partying at a bar with some woman last night. It looks like he's doing shots off her body. Asshole.

I internally laugh. For about ten hours my faith in men was restored. Easy come, easy go.

"Let's go slash his tires. Maybe cut his curls in his sleep. No one will know it's us. I have three black masks in a drawer. Don't ask me why."

Ripley lets out a giggle through her tears before shaking her head. "Thank you but I'll pass. I just need to get through the next two weeks. I promised Arizona I would spend Thanksgiving with Layton so he's not alone. After that, I think I'm going to move home."

Arizona is on the other side of the world. With Layton massively depressed without her, she asked us all to stay in town to spend Thanksgiving with him. Quincy is hosting. Should be interesting.

"Home as in California?" I ask.

She nods. "My mom knows what I'm going through more than anyone else. I need her right now."

June raised Ripley as a single mother. I don't think Ripley even knows the name of her father. She's definitely never met him. June loves Ripley so deeply that it's almost palpable when you're around the two of them.

Like Ripley, June is a tall, gorgeous redhead. Mama June, as I call her, was here a few weeks ago visiting. I think she banged the Cougars' sexy coach, Dutton Steel, when she was in town. While Ripley is often embarrassed by some of her mother's provocative antics, I know they're extremely close and have always relied on each other. She's lucky to have a mom like June. I would kill for that.

Suddenly panicked, I ask, "How long do you plan to stay with her?"

Ripley sighs as her face falls. "Indefinitely, Kam. I need her. I can't do this alone."

I swallow down the lump in my throat. "Does Arizona know?"

She shakes her head. "I want to tell her in person. I owe her that much after sneaking around with her brother for so long. She'll be back toward the end of next month. I'll fly in to have this conversation with her face to face."

I sit down on the sofa and pull her into a hug. "I love you and I'm here for you. Whatever you need."

She hugs me back. "Thank you. I love you too. For now, I need to spend the day crying. Tomorrow, I'll need help starting to pack everything."

I nod. "How about ice cream and *Top Gun*?" *Top Gun* is Ripley's favorite movie.

She happily agrees, and we give her the fun, girly afternoon she desperately needs.

CHAPTER TWELVE

KAMRYN

I smile at Evan as I approach Cheetah's building. I've been here a lot over the past few weeks, and Evan has become my buddy. He's the sweetest man. He kind of reminds me of my father. With the holidays approaching, I'm really missing my dad. If our mother wasn't in the picture, Bailey and I would get to spend the holidays with him, but the thought of spending time with her is triggering for me and, for reasons I will never understand, he won't leave her alone.

I stop when I get to Evan. "Hey, buddy. How's it hanging?"

In a polite tone, he answers, "A little to the left tonight, Ms. Hart. Thanks for asking."

I love that Evan indulges my inappropriate questions. I think his years around Cheetah have desensitized him.

"Fantastic. I've heard that the right side is much trickier. Any big plans for Thanksgiving tomorrow?"

He nods. "I get off work at six. Then my wife and I will go to our daughter's house for dinner with her and her family. Of course, we'll also be watching the Camels game."

"Oh right, they play tomorrow night." That's why Vance and Daylen couldn't come to Thanksgiving dinner.

"And your plans?" he asks.

"We're all going to a friend's house." We're going to Quincy's. We're only doing it for Arizona. He's persona non-grata with our crew right now. "Have you seen the birthday boy today?"

Evan lifts his eyebrow. "He's been wearing a crown and pink birthday girl sash all day, telling everyone he passes that it's his birthday."

I let out a laugh. "That sounds like him. He likes being the center of attention."

Evan fights a smile. "I've indulged him by calling him Sir Cruz Gonzales, Knight of South Philly, all day. It's the one day each year I call him that."

"You're so good to him. I'm sure he loved it."

We hear Cheetah shout, "I sure did. I need to get more people to call me that."

I feign shock. "Don't you love it more when I call you kitten?"

He blows me a kiss. "Only when you make me purr like one."

Evan smiles at our interaction. "Where are you two kids off to tonight?"

I clap my hands in excitement. "Our first stop will be for dinner."

Cheetah's eyes widen. "Is it Indian food? That's my favorite."

I make a look of disgust. "Ew. No. I'm introducing you to the greatest way to eat dinner ever. Fondue. I can't believe you've never been to a fondue restaurant."

Cheetah asks, "What's our second stop?"

I wink. "It's not PG enough for Evan's virgin ears."

Cheetah grins. "Let's skip to stop two."

I bop his nose. "All good things to those little boys who wait."

I wrap my arms around his neck and softly kiss his big lips. "Happy birthday, Sir Cruz Gonzales, Knight of South Philly."

He dips me and kisses me hard in return. When he pulls me

back up, he says, "If you play your cards right, you could be the Dame of South Philly."

"Why would I want to be dame when I'm already a queen?"

He shivers before adjusting himself. "Fuck, that made me hard."

Evan shakes his head and points down the block. "Be gone before you scare your royal subjects, sir."

We laugh as Cheetah takes my hand, and we begin our walk toward the restaurant.

He smiles down at me. "Can I get a hint about stop two?"

I shake my head. "Nope, kitten. It's your present. Can't open it too early. It's one of those things you have to *see* to believe."

I look at him for a reaction to the clue I just gave him, but he's oblivious.

We arrive at the restaurant and are seated immediately. I had requested a dark corner because he's often recognized and people hound him for photographs and autographs. It happens to me now and then too, though not nearly as often as it does to him.

We make it through the first course, cheese, and the second course, shrimp and steak, which we cook in a vegetable broth. I'm pretty sure he doesn't love this, but he's pretending to for my sake.

When it comes time for dessert, I naturally order dark chocolate. He smiles when it arrives along with a big plate of fruit and cakes for us to dip into the chocolate. "Does stop two entail me rubbing this chocolate all over your body and eating it off you?"

"No, but that's not a terrible idea." I sigh. "You don't like this place, do you?"

"I like the company. And I'd like it more if you were to spread that chocolate across your lips and kiss me."

"Hmm. I can do that for you."

And I do.

When we messily break apart, he takes my hand. "I have to ask you something. You're going to be reluctant at first, but listen all the way through because I'm throwing in a big incentive at the end."

I narrow my eyes at him. "I'm listening."

"I told you that I go home for Christmas every year, right?"

"Yes."

"And that my mother is relentless about me marrying that woman from my hometown."

"I remember. Mariana, the hot yet boring woman."

He nods. "That's right. My younger brother mentioned that our mother has been looking for an engagement ring for Mariana, as if I would ever let her buy one for my future wife. As if I'm ever going to propose to Mariana."

I cross my arms. I'm not sure what he wants from me. "Where is this going?"

He fidgets nervously. "Is there any chance you'd be willing to come home with me and *pretend* to be my full-fledged girlfriend?" He holds up his hands. "It's just pretend. I know we're only in a flingationship. We would fly there on Christmas Eve morning and we'd be there for about five nights."

My shoulders fall. "I want to help you, I really do, but I can't just leave my sister for Christmas. It's not like we have other family in the area. Arizona is gone and Ripley is leaving in two days. We have no idea when she's coming back."

"What about Tanner?"

"What about him?"

"I'm pretty sure your sister is secretly banging him."

I raise an eyebrow. "How do you know about that?"

"Tanner is my agent and my friend."

"He talks about my sister with you?" I find that hard to believe.

"Umm, no. Tanner could have twenty-five children in an apartment nearby and we wouldn't know. He doesn't share at all, but we may have given him the nudge he needed to seal the deal with Bailey. He was pining after her for a long time. It was obvious."

"Hmm, we'll get back to that." I shake my head. "I'm sorry. I won't leave her alone on Christmas."

"She can spend it with Tanner and Harper. I *know* Tanner wouldn't mind."

I take a few deep breaths as anxiety begins to kick in. "Cruz, I've never been away from her for more than one night. And I've certainly never been in a different state than her."

His eyes widen in shock. "For real?"

I nod.

He thinks for a moment before placing his napkin on the table. "I'm not done. I was prepared for some resistance. I have a counteroffer."

I smile. "I didn't realize that this was a negotiation. Let's hear it."

"We'll spend a few days with my family with you being the doting girlfriend, and then I'll take you on an all-expenses paid trip to Jamaica for the New Year. Four days and nights in paradise. You and me. Beautiful scenery, perfect weather, great food, new adventures, and lots of fucking. All the fucking you want, any way you want it."

I steeple my fingers. "You drive a hard bargain, counselor. I understand why you want me to come home with you. Can you give me a few days to talk to my sister about it? I need to make sure she's taken care of, and I need to wrap my mind around being apart from her for that long."

I chew my lip, and he notices. "What else? What am I missing?" he asks.

"Well...I'm a nervous flyer. Like crazy, pacing, doomsday, disruptive-to-the-flight kind of nervous. My sister has to calm me on every plane ride. I've never flown without her."

He lets out a laugh. "You fly for your job. All the time."

I blow out a breath. "I know. I hate it. My poor teammates suffer through it every damn time."

"It's kind of ironic that you chose a college across the country from your hometown. One where you had to fly far away."

"That should show you how much I needed to get away from my mother."

"Got it. I appreciate you considering it. I may have already told my mother that my girlfriend was coming home with me, but I can always call one of my regulars if you can't make it."

I'm calling his bluff. "Give me the name of one of your regulars."

"Umm...Tami."

"Tami who?"

"Tami Maida."

I let out a laugh. "You're the worst liar ever. That's Gemma's pen name."

"Shit. How do you know that?"

"My sister reads her books. And you have them all on your bookshelf, dipshit."

He twists his lips. "Okay, I'll wait for your answer." His lower lip protrudes out. "Please come with me."

"Just give me a few days. In the meantime, are you ready for your birthday gift?"

CHEETAH

We have to take a cab to the address Kam gave the driver. It's in an area of town I've never been to. I wouldn't call it the high-rent district.

She's wearing her signature mischievous look throughout the entire ride. I can't imagine what we're doing.

The past few weeks with Kamryn have been amazing. She's let her carefully constructed walls come down a bit. Not a lot, but I get tidbits of the real her now and then in the forts she's come to love. And the sex? It's mind-blowing. We've been going at it like rabbits. I've never had this kind of connection with a woman before.

We arrive at a building with no signage and minimal lighting. "Are you planning to murder me, Kam bam?"

Her lips curl in amusement. "No, but a little choking might be involved."

"Color me intrigued."

She lets out a laugh. "I bet."

She knocks on the big metal front door of the building. A giant muscular man in a suit opens it and she gives him her name. He scrolls through his iPad until he seems satisfied, after which he allows us to enter.

Once in the small lobby, there's a sign leading into a better-lit area. It reads *Club Yeur*. "We're going to a club? Not what I was expecting but I do love dancing with you."

She shakes her head. "It's not that kind of club, and I can't believe you've never been here. It's right up your twisted alley."

"What kind of club is it?"

We emerge from the darkness into the lights. They're not bright, but brighter than the dark area of the entryway. There's music, but it's not loud. It's in the background and very sultry. There's a giant bar, several sofas, and a handful of tables and chairs. There are also multiple hallways that look like they lead to other rooms. The patrons, all dressed unusually nicely, aren't just talking. Several of them are full-blown getting it on. More so than what you'd expect at a bar that looks like this.

I look at her. "What is this place?"

"Club Yeur as in vo*yeur*. For lack of a better term, it's a sex club. It's about making your fantasies come true."

My mouth starts to water. Holy fuck. How do I not know about this place?

A different man approaches us with an iPad. "Ms. Hart?"

She nods. "Yes."

"Everything is set up for you and your friend. Follow me."

I turn to her. "What does Kamryn Hart have up her sexy sleeve?"

She takes my hand, and we follow the man to what appears to be a private room. Before we go in, he gives her a few safety instructions that I don't listen to because the throb in my dick has suddenly become so damn loud.

When we eventually walk into the room, we see a huge wooden bed along with a sitting area set up as though whoever is sitting will be watching whatever is going on in the bed. The room's colors are darker reds and greens, like a Ralph Lauren vibe. The lights are low, but not low enough that you can't see everything.

Kam instructs the man to give her two minutes to explain before showtime. What is showtime? Dear god, I feel like I'm at Disneyland.

He leaves, and Kam tells me to sit on the sofa before asking me, "Have you ever read one of those choose-your-own-adventure books?"

I nod. "When I was a kid."

"This is a little like that. You get to choose what you want tonight. In a minute, a blonde woman and a brunette woman are going to walk in here. You, birthday boy, get to choose what goes down."

Fucking hell. I have to rub my cock through my pants. "What are my options? Be very specific."

"Anything you want except you can only pick one of them to stay. I already blew my budget on this evening. I know you prefer brunettes, and you know I prefer blonde women. What you choose will determine which will stay. I can sit and watch you with the brunette. You can sit and watch me with the blonde." She visibly swallows. "Or you can pick one and the three of us can do whatever you want. I met both girls earlier today when I came down to deal with all the paperwork and make a few selections. They're both beautiful and sexy."

"I feel like this is a test."

She lets out a laugh. "I promise it's not. I genuinely want you to have a good time. I want you to get whatever it is that you want. A little fantasy fulfillment. It's my gift to you...and me."

The thing is, I don't actually want another woman. I know she wants me to want other women to prove that we're not headed for anything real, but I don't. I haven't since I met her. Why would I ever want sardines when caviar is on the menu?

Watching her with a woman is a whole other story though. I can't imagine anything hotter.

Without any hesitation, I respond, "I want to watch you."

She tilts her head to the side. "Are you sure you don't want to join?"

I shake my head. "I want to sit here and touch myself while I watch you do your thing."

She slowly nods. "Okay, but you're still in charge. You get to direct us."

I let out a moan. "Fuck, Kam. I might come before this even starts."

She points at me and commands, "Don't you dare. My only request is that you wait until I'm done and then blow in my mouth and only my mouth. Are you good with that?"

My cock leaks but I rasp out, "Yes, ma'am."

Kam opens the door and whispers into the hallway while I take my spot on the couch. A sexy blonde walks in wearing lingerie in a cheetah pattern. I wonder if it's a coincidence. She's got bright blue eyes and full tits. She resembles Tanner's ex-wife, Fallon, who's even more beautiful than the blonde woman in here with us.

But I'm not interested in the blonde. It's the brunette I want to watch.

"Kitten, this is Bambi." Kam and I both smirk, knowing that it's not her real name. At least I hope it's not. "You tell us what you want us to do. We're entirely at your command. Every single movement. Every single touch."

I lick my lips as I rub my cock through my pants again. This is stupid hot. "Position yourselves so I can see both of you. I want you to simply kiss for a bit."

Standing next to the bed, Kam runs her fingers through the woman's hair. As their lips are about to meet, I yell out, "Stop. Bambi, take Kamryn's clothes off first. Strip her to her bra and panties like you."

Bambi nods before lifting Kam's tight little sweater over her head. Kam is wearing the same cheetah print bra as Bambi. She planned the undergarments. She's a goddess. This might be every fantasy I've ever had rolled into one.

Bambi then gets on her knees and pulls down Kam's skirt until it pools on the floor. Fuuuuck. She's wearing a matching silk thong.

Kam is tall, probably about five feet, eight inches. Her legs are toned and go on for miles. They might be my favorite thing about her, but it's hard to pick one because she's so damn beautiful.

She's a professional athlete and built like one with defined muscles everywhere, but none more perfect than her ass. She's got an ass that women undoubtedly pay for or spend thousands of dollars at the gym to try to earn but can never quite get there. Her arms are sculpted but not bulky. And her tits? They fit perfectly in my hands and practically melt in my mouth.

Kam clears her throat, bringing me back to the present. Yep, I was busted ogling her.

"Now I want you two to kiss at your own pace. Let your hands roam free, but make sure they roam."

Bambi's eyes happily take in Kam's body. "You're beautiful."

Bambi is shorter and curvier than Kam. Sexy in a totally different kind of way. She's softer, with bigger hips and less muscle.

Bambi's hands run up Kam's body while Kam's fingers thread through Bambi's hair again as their lips meet for the first time. I swear to god, I almost come in my pants for the first time since I was thirteen.

I've watched more than my fair share of woman-on-woman porn, but watching someone you know, someone you're into, kiss another woman? It's off-the-charts hot.

I can't help but let out a moan. This might be over before it even starts.

Kam is definitely in charge of the kiss. Her tongue is very clearly moving around Bambi's mouth while Bambi simply follows suit. It's very different from our kisses. I suppose it makes sense for Kam to be the more dominant partner in her same-sex encounters, but she likes to be dominated when she's with me.

"Touch her tits, Kam."

Kam's hands immediately move down to Bambi's massive tits that are overflowing out of her bra. Unlike Kam's, Bambi's tits are obviously fake. Such a turnoff for me, but Kamryn doesn't seem to mind in the least as she pulls the cups of the flimsy bra down and runs her fingers over Bambi's nipples.

"Bambi, take Kam's bra off."

Bambi does as I instructed. I watch Kam's full tits bounce free from the confines of her bra as if it's in slow motion. Unlike Bambi's, they move in a natural way. She's objectively the sexiest woman in existence.

Their kiss turns even more passionate. Kam's hands

move down to Bambi's panties as if she's preparing to remove them. "No, no, no. I'm in charge, Kam bam. Leave those in place." I don't want to see Bambi. I want to see Kam. "Bambi, remove Kamryn's panties. Slowly. *Very* slowly. Kiss down her body as you do."

Kam smiles as the kiss breaks. Bambi slowly runs her lips down Kam's chest and stomach. Her fingertips surround Kam's waist before reaching the sides of her panties. She achingly slowly draws them down her long legs while her tongue glides down Kam's leg.

My pants can no longer contain my dick. I unbutton and unzip them before pulling my boxer briefs down enough for my cock to spring free. I squeeze it, needing some amount of relief. I don't think I've ever been this hard in my life. I can feel every vein in my dick pulsating against my hand.

Bambi runs her eyes and fingertips back up Kamryn's entire body. I can tell how turned on she is by Kam. Who wouldn't be?

Kam looks at me waiting for instruction. "Lie down on the bed, Kam. Spread your legs so I can see your pussy."

Kam does as I said, before again waiting for more instructions. How did this become my life? Best. Birthday. Ever.

"Touch yourself. Bambi, play with Kam's tits while I watch her touch herself. Take note of how she likes it. Her g-spot is shallow on the front left side."

Bambi's panties are still on. So is her bra, but the cups are pulled down. I'm half tempted to tell her to pull them up, but I don't. I'm not even paying attention to her anyway.

With her eyes locked on mine, Kam's hand slowly runs down her own body. She puts on a show for me by starting at her tits, running through her cleavage, down her muscular belly, over her pelvic bone, and eventually her fingers run through her slit. I can hear how wet she is.

I start to stroke myself, unable to wait any longer. I tried to slow-play it, but a man can only handle so much.

Kam's eyes move down to my cock as she first dips two fingers inside herself and then rubs her wetness all over her pussy.

"Taste yourself, Kam."

She lifts her fingers and slides them into her mouth, letting out a small moan.

"Tastes good, right?"

She nods.

"Now move them back down and touch your clit."

She begins to circle her clit as her half-lidded eyes fixate on me stroking my cock. It's turning her on. I love seeing her so turned on.

I think Bambi is pinching Kam's nipples, but I don't care. I'm watching the sexiest woman alive touch herself for *my* pleasure.

I have no idea how long we're there, but I know I need to move this along or I'm going to come. "Bambi, make Kamryn come with your mouth. Angle yourself so I can see what you're doing to her."

Kam pinches her eyebrows together. She clearly expected me to want the opposite. Kam loves to boast about how quickly she can make a woman come. She probably assumed I'd want to see it in action. Bambi's pleasure is inconsequential to me. It's Kam's I treasure.

Bambi crawls onto the bed and kisses her way down Kam's body until her face is buried between Kam's legs. Bambi's tongue takes its first sweep through her and I watch the bliss rush over Kam's face. That's the money shot for me.

"Kamryn, use your words. Big words. Tell me what you're feeling."

"It feels sublime."

I smile. "Give me more."

She fists the sheets as her breathing picks up, but still manages to say, "I'm enraptured by Bambi tonguing my fandango."

I can't help but chuckle. I love her mind.

For a bit, my eyes toggle between what Bambi is doing and Kam's face. Surprisingly, I prefer her face. It's hard for me to see her face when my tongue is in her pussy. I love having the opportunity to see what it does to her from a different angle.

With mine and Kam's eyes locked on each other, I watch until Bambi makes her come undone. Kam's back arches, and she bites her lip. I ache to be that lip. Her hands squeeze her own breasts in a way that I wonder if it's hurting her.

I have to stop stroking myself and squeeze my dick to the point of pain to make sure I don't come. Having a bird's eye view of Kam's explosive orgasm will now forever be my Roman Empire.

"Thanks, Bambi. Can you please head out?"

A moment of shock and then clear disappointment splashes across Bambi's face before she fixes her bra and walks out of the room.

Kam is still on the bed breathing heavily. With labored breaths, she asks, "You don't want more than that?"

"*That* was the best thing I've ever seen in my life. There's no topping it. And if I don't come in the next minute, I might actually die."

Realization hits her as she immediately pops out of the bed and stalks toward me like the naked goddess she is. She immediately drops to her knees between my legs and runs her hands up my thighs before pulling my pants and boxer briefs down to my ankles. My whole fucking body shivers at her touch.

Her delicate pink tongue slips out of her mouth, and she licks her way up my thigh, all over my length, and eventually to my balls which are feeling particularly heavy right about now. She's learned quickly how sensitive my balls are and how much I enjoy her giving them attention.

She sucks them into her mouth and twirls her tongue in circles as she pumps my shaft with her hand. I grit out, "Joder, Kam, no puedo durar. Estas demasiado caliente." *Fuck, Kam, I can't last. You're too hot.*

She moans with a mouth full of my balls. She fucking loves the Spanish dirty talk even though she doesn't know what I'm saying.

While gripping my balls, her tongue glides up my already slickened length, where she laps against the severely engorged veins. Kam savors sucking my dick like no one I've ever met. She gets off on giving me pleasure nearly as much as I get off giving her pleasure.

She moans as she licks through the moisture pooling at my tip. I'm gripping the sofa for dear life. I'm about to go off like a geyser, but I want to enjoy this a little longer. She hasn't even put my full dick into her hot little mouth yet.

After what feels like the slowest seduction to ever take place, she finally feeds my cock into her mouth until my tip hits the back of her throat. "Fuuuuuck."

I grip her hair because I know how much she loves when I do. I can pull her hair as hard as I want. It only serves to turn her on that much more.

She mumbles, "Harder," around my cock. Yep, she loves when I roughly fuck her mouth. *Did I mention that she's the perfect woman?*

With her hair in my hand, I begin to thrust up into her mouth and push her head down at the same time. She takes it all. The woman has no gag reflex.

One hand works my shaft and with the other she scratches her fingernails over my balls. That's it for me. I swear I partially black out as I come harder than I've ever come before in my life. And long. It keeps going and going until I see some dripping down her chin. That's an image that will forever live in my mind.

She sits up on her knees and licks around her lips until it's clean of my semen. "That was like another full fondue course, kitten."

I chuckle. "Did it taste good?"

She looks down at her finger which has a few drops on it and then feeds it into my mouth. I've never tasted my semen before. As soon as it hits my tongue, I harden again, and she notices. She shakes her head. "I told you that you were bi."

I tickle her and she giggles. I make a show of licking around my mouth. "Hmm. I think the pineapples are working. I'm delicious." Pulling her to sit across my lap, I hold her naked body in my arms. "Thanks for my present. Do you have a receipt in case I want to exchange it?"

"Are you already looking to trade me in?"

"Maybe I'll take Barbie home with me."

She playfully smacks my chest. "It's Bambi, not Barbie."

"Ahh, right. I'm sure that was her birth name," I sarcastically quip.

"No doubt." She runs her fingers through my hair as her smile fades a bit. "Why didn't you want me to do anything to her? I was hoping to show off my mad skills." She flicks her tongue suggestively.

I glance down at my cock. "You *did* show off your mad skills."

"You know what I mean."

"I do. I don't know. I like your face when you come. That does it for me more than anything. Fuck, just watching you kiss her was the hottest thing I've ever seen. So hot that I'm ready to put my sour cream in your burrito." I thrust my boner against her for added effect.

She wiggles her eyebrows. "Will this gland-to-gland combat be happening here or back at one of our places? They have private rooms where you can watch other people have sex. You can caulk the tub while we do that. We'll call it birthday gift number two."

I aimlessly rub her nipples with my fingers just because I can. "Tempting, and I'd like to come back here one day soon, but I want to get you home and have my wicked way with you all night." I tap my head. "What happened here tonight will forever live rent-free in my mind. Besides, Evan will worry if we're out too late."

She lets out a laugh. "I think we've scarred Evan for life."

I nod. Kam loves pushing his buttons as much as I do.

I grab her chin. "Thanks for tonight. It's the best birthday I've ever had."

"Watching Bambi go down on me made it your best birthday?" she asks.

I blow out a breath. "No. Being with you and you unashamedly feeding my inner freak made it my best birthday."

"Takes one to know one."

That's why we're perfect together. It's now my mission to get her to see that too.

CHAPTER THIRTEEN

KAMRYN

Thanksgiving dinner last night was potentially the most awkward dinner of my life. We were pissed at Quincy, yet he was hosting it. The guys are all a little protective of him, so it was tense between all of us. Quincy was pissed at his parents for some unknown reason. They seemed oblivious to all of it. Ripley was on the verge of tears the whole time. June, who's usually laid back, was hovering over Ripley, clearly worried about her daughter.

Bailey and I just sat back, drinking as much wine as humanly possible to get through the evening. I was stuffing my face senselessly until it hit me that I must be getting my period, which came as soon as I got home. My form of PMS is eating everything in sight.

As we were walking into our apartment, Justin appeared. He said that he thought we were his food. The poor guy was ordering takeout on Thanksgiving. We invited him to hang out in our apartment while he ate his meal...and I ended up eating my second of the night.

We're now in Ripley's apartment as June finishes packing the last of Ripley's things.

I hug June. "Take care of our girl."

She nods before pulling back and giving me a forced smile. "The St. James women are strong." She turns to Ripley. "We'll be just fine, right baby?"

Ripley stoically nods. "Umm hmm."

It's been a long two weeks for her, full of tears and self-doubt. I hate him for what he's putting her through. I honestly don't see how we will possibly be around him ever again.

Our groups hang out so much. I have no clue what it will mean for that, but that's the least of my concerns. Ripley's mental health is more important than anything right now. I hope June can give her the help she needs.

Ripley sighs as she pulls Bailey and me into an embrace. "I'm sorry to throw a wrench into our plans. I'll miss you guys. So much."

Bailey and I hug her. I croak out, "We'll miss you too."

Bailey adds, "We'll come and visit as soon as the baby is born."

Ripley pulls away and rubs her nonexistent belly. "I'd like that. Love you guys."

We help them to the car and return to our apartment with a huge sense of sadness and uncertainty. Will Ripley ever play again? Will we achieve our dream of playing in the Olympics together? Most importantly, will she be okay? She's not okay right now. I've never seen Ripley like this.

Bailey and Ripley are the caregivers of our foursome. Arizona and I are the ones they care for. Seeing Ripley so vulnerable is heartbreaking.

Bailey makes me a bunch of snacks, knowing I need them this week, before we plop onto our sofa and turn on a movie.

I notice her fidgeting before she finally mentions that Tanner invited her to go skiing in Colorado for the holiday.

Well, that kind of worked out well. I tell her about what

Cheetah asked and how torn I am about it since we've never been apart like this before.

She pulls me close. "You should definitely go, and so should I. This could be good for us, Kam. We're too old to have never spent time apart. We're eventually going to have to learn how to do that."

My eyes fill with tears. "You're my soulmate, Bails. You jump, I jump." The thought of being on a plane without her swirls around in my head. "I'm sweating just thinking about it."

She squeezes me back. "I know. You're my soulmate too, and I'm equally nervous, but we need this. We both know it's time. It's probably way past time."

We're both sobbing when Bailey's phone pings with a notification of a FaceTime call.

She looks at it and pinches her eyebrows together. "It's Daddy."

Weird. We talked to him for a long time last night before we left for dinner.

I wiggle my eyebrows. "Which daddy?"

She rolls her eyes at me and accepts the call. "Hey, Daddy. Is everything okay?"

I hear his shakier-than-normal voice respond, "Is your sister with you?"

I move until he can see me on the small screen. "Your favorite daughter is here, Daddy." I smile but he doesn't return it like he usually does. My face immediately falls. "What's wrong?"

Tears fill his eyes. "Girls, I've run your mother back and forth to the doctors a bunch over the past few months." He pinches his lips together. "We just received some news. It's not good. Her liver is beyond repair. It's failing her, and we can't do anything about it."

Without any expression, I ask, "How long does she have?"

His shoulders fall. He's starting to look so much older than his fifty years. I suddenly realize just how much his dark hair is graying. The wrinkles around his eyes are deepening.

He answers, "About a year."

Bailey starts sobbing. "We...we...we should come down. Right away."

I'm about to interrupt to say that there's no fucking chance of me going when he sadly admits, "She...umm...doesn't want to see you. She said you never cared about her in life, and it would be disingenuous if you came to her now."

Once a piece of shit, always a piece of shit.

He continues, "She'll change her mind. I know she will. Give it a little time. I think she's in shock about her prognosis."

Bailey is crying. I swore I'd never allow another tear to drop for that woman and I won't. Wrapping my arm around Bailey, I say, "Thanks for letting us know. Why don't we talk later after we've had the chance to digest this?"

He nods with a solemn expression on his once-handsome face. "I'm sorry, girls."

We end the call, and Bailey cries into my chest. I simply stroke her hair. Part of me needs to get out of here to get some fresh air, and part of me wants to be here for my sister.

"It's not like anything changes for us, Bails. She's not in our life."

She looks up at me with her tear-stained face. "Didn't you always think we'd eventually reconcile one day?"

I shake my head. "No. I didn't."

Suddenly I'm feeling light-headed. I need to stand.

I do, but it doesn't help. My mind is racing. I can't let her see me like this. I can't be here while she mourns a woman who doesn't deserve it, a woman who was prepared to throw her to the wolves.

"Bails, I've got plans. I need to go."

Her face scrunches. "What? Where are you going?"

"Umm, friends. Out." I grab my jacket. "Go see Tanner. I'll check in on you later."

I practically sprint out of our building. I'm the worst sister ever, but I can't sit there and watch her shed tears for that woman.

I know she'll go to Tanner's, and he'll console her the way she needs it. I can't give that to her right now.

For over an hour, I walk aimlessly around the city in the cold of the night. Without even realizing I was walking his way, I wind up at Cheetah's building. Evan smiles as I approach. "Did you have a good holiday, Ms. Hart?"

I plaster on my best fake smile and lie. "I did. How about you?"

"I most definitely did. I got to see my grandson take his first steps."

I give a genuine smile. "That's awesome. I hope you got it on video."

He taps his head. "I got it up here. That's even better. Your generation likes to run to the camera. Mine prefers the memories to be stored the old-fashioned way."

I nod. "I suppose you're right. I'm going to head up to Cruz's place."

His face falls. "Mr. Gonzales is out for the evening." He places his hand on my shoulder. "Are you alright? You look upset."

"I just received some...concerning news. I didn't realize he had plans. I'll head out." After the weirdness of last night and dealing with Ripley today, I haven't spoken to him all day. I didn't know he had plans.

I start to turn away, but Evan wraps his arm around me. "Nonsense. I know Mr. Gonzales would insist that I let you into his apartment to wait for him. I'll have the concierge fetch you some hot chocolate. Dark chocolate, right?"

I pinch my eyebrows together. "How do you know that?"

He gives me a small smile. "Mr. Gonzales has had a steady stream of dark chocolate deliveries made to his place since you've been in the picture."

"Maybe one of his other women likes dark chocolate."

Evan tilts his head to the side in a bit of bewilderment. "He's never brought a woman here until you."

What?

CHEETAH

"Hey, Daylen, how does a Camel find a sheep in long grass?" I ask.

Daylen twists his lips. "How?"

"Rather enjoyable."

Daylen lets out one of his house-shaking laughs as he folds his hand of poker by tossing them on the table. "Oh shit, that's funny, Cheetah. You're the second funniest person I know."

I'm sitting in Tanner's basement man cave with Layton, Vance, and Daylen. Tanner constantly runs upstairs for unknown reasons. Vance asks, "Where does he keep going?"

I shrug and joke, "He's probably got Bailey tied up to his bed."

Vance chuckles. "Maybe you're right." He stares at the big pile of chips in the center of the table. "How much is the pot right now?"

I shake my head in disbelief. "Fuck. You're dumb for a QB. I thought it was supposed to be the smartest position on the field. You can't even do simple math."

He gives me his trademark scowl. "I know math. What's sixty-nine and sixty-nine?"

"One thirty-eight," I answer quickly.

The corner of his mouth raises slightly. "No. Dinner for four."

My mouth widens in shock. "Vance McCaffrey, did you just make a joke?"

His scowl falls back in place. "Don't tell anyone. I have a rep to protect."

Layton smiles. "Do you know what comes after sixty-nine?"

I twist my lips. "Seventy suddenly seems like the wrong answer."

He smirks. "Mouthwash."

We all laugh as Tanner returns from whatever it is he was doing upstairs. Again.

We all lift our beers and offer our cheers to Daylen, who just signed a huge contract extension. I'm happy for my friend and certainly ecstatic that he'll continue playing in Philly for the foreseeable future. Daylen is such a genuinely good guy.

I say to him, "With all that money, think of all the hookers you can now afford."

He nods enthusiastically. "I know, right? What's the best part of having a hooker die on you?"

"What?"

He bites back his smile. "The second hour is free."

We all burst out laughing. "Oh fuck, that's a good one." I pull out my phone. "I need to text it to Gemma. She'll want to use that one in a book."

I look down at my phone and realize that I have no service. I forgot that there's none in the man cave.

As I head upstairs in search of better service so I can send Gemma the text, I suddenly receive a bunch of notifications on my phone. All my messages from the past few hours come flooding through all at once.

I ignore most until I see three from my doorman. That's odd. He doesn't reach out to me unless it's important. I click on our text chain.

> Evan: Sorry to bother you, but Ms. Hart stopped by.

A few seconds later, he sent:

An hour later there's another text from him.

Technically they're not allowed to let anyone in. He could be fired for doing so but I'm obviously happy he did. Especially if she's upset.

I immediately leave and head home. After Evan nervously fills me in that she was practically shaking when she arrived, I again assure him that she's always welcome. He also informs me that she asked him to make a fire, which he did. She loves fires. She has me make one every time she stays over. She sits in front of them and works on her laptop while I'm asleep.

I walk into my apartment and see a makeshift fort. It's not as good as mine, but she clearly tried hard to craft a good one.

I poke my head into the fort opening and see her in panties and a small midriff-baring T-shirt, lying on a bed of pillows. "Want to play haunted house? I'll scream when I'm inside you."

She sleepily smiles and stretches her arms. "You're back."

"I am. And I'm not happy with your wardrobe. My adult forts are nudist forts. You know the rules."

She sighs. "It's shark week for me. I tried to respect your rules, but this is as naked as I'm getting."

Ah, she has her period. Maybe she's just hormonal and that's why she's upset.

I wiggle my eyebrows. "I happen to love sharks. I'm an expert fisherman." I flick my tongue suggestively at her. "I'm all for a rainbow kiss."

She holds up her hand. "Not happening. My inner shark is a Great White and she's a ruthless bitch. We're talking *Texas Chainsaw Massacre*-level shit going on down there."

I chuckle. "That was bizarrely and disturbingly illustrative." I nod toward her cotton panties, not as sexy as her normal thongs, but still adorable. "I like the cute little bow on the front of your panties."

She looks down at them. "A bow on women's panties is a memorial to all the faces that have been buried there."

I can't help but laugh. She's so damn funny.

I start to unzip my jeans. "I'll match your wardrobe choice then, but I don't have a bow. I'll look into it though. I'm sure boxer briefs with bows on the front are all the rage."

I strip down to my undershirt and boxers before crawling in and lying down next to her. Rubbing her leg, I ask, "What's ailing you, Kam bam? Tell Dr. Gonzales. He's the master fixer."

Staring into the fire, and without an ounce of emotion, she says, "My mother is dying. They gave her a year to live. Before you ask, she doesn't want to see us. She's dying and hasn't spoken to her daughters in ten years. You would think she'd gain a little perspective, but not Beverly Hart. She specifically requested that we *not* come see her."

I maneuver her so her head is resting on my chest. "I'm sorry, babe. That sucks."

"I don't care for me. She's been dead to me for eighteen years. I feel bad for my sister. I think she's always hoped for a reconciliation and now she'll never get it."

I run my fingers up and down her arm, hoping to soothe

her. "A year is a long time. Maybe she'll change her mind about seeing you guys."

"Maybe. For my sister's sake, I hope so. I don't think I could go back there, but Bailey should go."

I think Kam might need it too but isn't ready to admit it.

She traces her finger along my chest and looks up at me. "I'm sorry that I broke into your place like a psycho stalker."

"Have I told you about the romance book I'm reading right now?"

She shakes her head. "No."

"She stalks him and," I bite my lip, "it's so fucking hot."

She giggles. "No way that's true."

"Okay, he stalks her, but it sounded more thematic the other way around. The stalker trope is huge. People love it. I think I'm turned on that you're stalking me."

"You get turned on when the wind blows."

"If it blows your scent my way, I most certainly do."

She sighs. "Honestly, I didn't set out to come here. I couldn't sit there and watch my sister shed tears over that woman. I was walking around aimlessly and just kind of ended up at your front door."

"It's fine. I'm glad you came. I'm sorry I wasn't here."

"Were you on a hot date?"

"You wish. I was with the boys. We were celebrating Daylen's big contract with a little poker."

"I want to come to your poker game one day and kick everyone's ass. I *never* lose. Counting cards is second nature to me."

"Hmm. I need to test this theory." And I want to help distract her.

I carefully place her on the pillows and sit up. "I'll be right back."

I gather a bunch of candy and a deck of playing cards

before returning to the fort. "Let's see what you've got, Hart."

She smiles as she makes a grab for the candy. We sit up and cross our legs, facing each other, as I shuffle the deck and she unwraps the dark chocolate Reese's Peanut Butter Cups I now keep on hand.

I quickly throw out about forty cards, one at a time. She can see them as I throw them out, but only for a second as the next card covers the last very quickly. I'm now holding twelve cards in my hand. Looking up at her, I ask, "What am I holding?"

She takes a bite of her Peanut Butter Cup. With a mouthful, she happily answers, "An ace, two queens, two tens, a nine, and six lower-numbered cards."

I turn them over and examine the twelve cards. She was dead accurate. I breathe, "What the fuck?"

She chews the chocolate with a huge smile. "Told ya so."

"Let's do that again."

I shuffle the cards, and we go through the same process with the same exact result. I run my fingers through my hair. "What in the actual fuck? You're *Rain Man*."

"I'm fucking smart. That's what I am. It's not that hard to do. I can teach you. In the most simplistic form, you can assign values to certain cards like plus one, minus one, and zero. Then you keep track as you see them. The way I do it is a little more complicated than that because of my photographic memory, but almost anyone can learn what I just explained."

She tries to teach me for an hour. I improve a little, but I am nowhere near accurate, and certainly nowhere near as good as her.

I shake my head in disbelief. "Let's go to Vegas."

She twists her lips. "I've been banned from Vegas. Long story."

"What about Atlantic City? It's only, like, an hour away."

She nods "I would do that sometime. Just know that as soon as I start winning, they'll kick me out. Every casino does."

I fall back onto the pillows. "I need to figure out how to harness your powers to my benefit."

She lets out a laugh. "I'm sure we'll come up with something." She looks down. "I..umm...spoke with Bails. Before we found out about my mom. If you still want me after the whole stalking thing, I'll go home with you for Christmas."

I sit back up in a bit of shock. "Really?"

She nods. "Tanner invited her to come to Colorado with them for the same week. Harper is bringing a friend, and he allegedly *needs* the extra help." She air quotes needs. "The timing works out perfectly."

Not only did I already tell my mother that Kamryn was coming with me, but I told her that we recently got engaged. I don't think I'll tell Kamryn that tidbit until I've already got her in Texas, but my mother is now freaking out about meeting her and welcoming her to the family properly.

Frankly, I assumed Kam wouldn't come and I'd just tell my family that my fiancée was with her own family.

This should make for a fun Christmas.

CHAPTER FOURTEEN

CHEETAH

It's been a weird few weeks. Quincy has disappeared. No one knows where he is. He simply sent us all a text that he was going off the grid for the foreseeable future. Arizona is about to come home, so Layton has been acting like a madman anticipating her arrival. He's still in his cast, but it comes off soon and he can't wait.

He mentioned a few weeks ago that he bought her an engagement ring. I wonder if he'll propose the second he sees her. He's whipped beyond comprehension, but I'm thrilled for my friend. Arizona is awesome, and he deserves this after a bit of a tragic upbringing.

Kam had her finals for this semester of law school, so she's been tied up in that. I wonder what Bailey thinks Kam does all night. She knows Kam doesn't sleep. Though I suppose Kam is the queen of deflection.

Kam and I get together a few times a week. She continues to refer to us as casual and loves to encourage me to meet other women, but I'm not. I don't want anyone but her. I have no idea if she's seeing anyone else. I'm not sure when she'd have time for it, but who knows?

Unbelievably, I bought an engagement ring. I assumed I'd freak out at the notion of buying it, but the thought of her wearing my ring was shockingly satisfying. I know it will be short-lived, if it happens at all, but I'm still a little hopeful. Kam is probably going to kick me in the balls when I place it on her finger.

It's early morning on Christmas Eve. I'm about to go to Kam's to pick her up so we can head to the airport together. My text tone rings.

> Gemma: Put a ring on it yet?

Gemma is the only person who knows my plan. For some reason, I always feel like I can confide in her.

> Me: Ha. No. I need to wait until we're past the point of no return. If I do it before we leave, she won't get on that plane.

> Gemma: Take careful notes. I might have to write a book about this. Fake fiancée for the holidays? That's ripe for an epic romance book.

> Me: Don't think this one will have a happy ending.

> Gemma: You never know.

> Me: Are you at Grammy Jane's?

Gemma, Trey, and Fletcher spend the holidays down in Florida at her grandmother's community.

> Gemma: Yep. Happy is in rare form.

Happy is the nickname of Grammy Jane's best friend, Harriet. She's full of dirty jokes. I get the biggest kick out of her.

> Me: Tell me. Tell me.

> Gemma: Yesterday at the pool she asked me 'what has 90 balls and fucks old ladies?'

> Me: What?

> Gemma: Bingo.

> Me: LOL. I love Happy. Tell her that I'll see her in February.

When we have Spring Training in Florida, we're not far from Grammy Jane. We always make time to visit her. Grammy Jane has a fun setup with a house on the bay.

> Gemma: Will do. Merry Christmas. Fingers crossed that all goes well.

> Me: Same to you. Thanks.

AN HOUR LATER, I'm walking off the elevator at Kam and Bailey's apartment building. As I exit, the door across the hallway swings open, and the messy bright-orange hair of her neighbor pops out.

His face turns from a smile into something akin to violent in seconds. "Oh. It's...*you.*"

I wiggle my fingers. "Hey...you." I don't remember his name. "Merry Christmas."

He narrows his eyes at me. "Why are you here?"

"I'm picking up Kamryn. She's coming home with me for the week to celebrate the holidays."

His face falls in horror. "Oh. I didn't realize she'd be gone."

"Yep. Have a Merry Christmas. I hope Santa is good to you."

He closes his door without returning any holiday sentiments. What a strange dude.

Kam's luggage is already by the door when I walk in, which means she's awake. She's *always* awake. I honestly don't know how she functions.

I yell out, "It's time, Kam bam. Get your hot ass up and ready to board the Cheetah kidney-buster."

I hear her voice coming from Bailey's room. This is going to be a very long goodbye for the two of them. They're as close as two siblings can be.

I notice a big pot on the stove with steam coming out. That's weird. What are they making at this early hour?

I walk into Bailey's bedroom and see them cuddled up together. Fuck, I swear my heart skips a beat every time I see Kam's face. She's so beautiful. Her smile lights up my universe every damn time.

The two of them cry for nearly an hour. When Kam goes to the bathroom, Bailey pulls me aside and hands me a few pills. I look down at them. "What are these?"

"Emergency pills. I'm worried about how she's going to be on the flight. If all else fails, slip the sleeping pills into her water. I've had to do it two or three times. She doesn't know about it."

I let out a laugh. "I'm not drugging her. I've put a lot of thought into this." Bailey warned me about Kam's airplane behavior. "I've got a little something special in mind for her. Something I know for a fact she'll enjoy." I wink at her.

She gives me a knowing nod. "Ooh. Mile-high club. That's a great idea. She'll love it."

"I know she will."

She looks up at me. Even though they're technically identical twins, their eyes are so different. Not physically. An outsider would struggle to see the differences. It's what they convey. Bailey is much softer than Kam. She has eyes that practically ooze sugar and kindness. Kam's eyes tell a million stories, most of which promise mischief. I think they're my favorite thing about her. Well, that and her ass.

Bailey bites her lip nervously before she quietly says, "I don't know exactly what you two are."

I let out a laugh. "You and me both, Bails. If she tips her hat, be sure to let me know."

She gives me a knowing nod. "Kam puts up this hard exterior. It's what she wants the world to see. But that's not who she really is. She's the best person I know even though she doesn't believe that about herself. She's fiercely loyal and protective of those she loves. She's a little damaged from our upbringing and some high school heartbreak, but her heart is the biggest one I've ever seen."

I swallow down my emotions as I nod. "I know, Bails. I've been able to break down a few walls. I know there are more to go, but I'm not going anywhere. I care about her. A lot."

"She's going to test your patience."

I wiggle my eyebrows. "I dig that. She keeps me on my toes."

"She keeps us all on our toes."

Kam returns and looks at our close proximity before joking, "Keep your hands off my fake boyfriend, Bails. He's too young for you. He's not collecting social security yet."

Bailey rolls her eyes, as she often does at Kamryn.

Kam continues, "Bails, you don't even need Santa this Christmas. You already sit on an old man's lap."

Bailey lets out a laugh as they hug one last time. She looks up at me. "I'd be forever grateful if you could bend her over and fuck the crazy out of her."

Kam nods. "I'm game for that."

Bailey simply sighs. "And watch your carry-on bag, Cheetah. She's known to plant things causing high levels of embarrassment."

I cross my arms in satisfaction. "I locked it."

Kam scoffs. "Oh please. There's zero chance your code isn't some combination of sixty-nine."

I scrunch my face and mutter, "Fuck. I need to change it."

She and Bailey both giggle.

We're now in the cab on the way to the airport. I look at her. "Did you sleep at all last night?"

She shakes her head. "Not a wink. I'll sleep some tonight with you. *After* the flight. Plus, it helps when you're wrapped around me."

I love that she sleeps a little better when she's with me. Never through the night, but she says it's more than her normal.

"Your finals are over, and the new semester hasn't begun yet. What did you do all night?"

Her face lights up. "I learned a few fun facts."

"I figured. Hit me with a good one."

With zero concern for her volume and the fact that the cab driver can hear her, she says, "Eating pussy decreases your chances of depression by nearly three hundred percent."

"Ooh. That explains why I'm so happy all the time."

She smiles. "I feel like you could be happier."

I chuckle. "Challenge accepted."

She rubs the now smooth skin of my face that I shaved for my mother's benefit. "I do like seeing your handsome face, but I think I like it better when there's scruff rubbing between my legs."

I raise an eyebrow. "Would you consider my normal facial hair to be a saddle beard?"

She lets out a laugh. "Holy shit. I've never heard that term."

I shrug. "Can't claim it as mine. I got it from a Jade Dollston book. She's one of my favorite romance authors. She's a dirty bitch and I'm here for it."

"Maybe I should start reading books instead of Google."

I nod in agreement. "What else did you learn last night?"

"Ashton Kutcher has webbed feet."

I chuckle. "What? For real?"

She nods. "Yep. I saw a picture. It was nasty but I bet he's an awesome swimmer."

AFTER A SEXUALLY EVENTFUL AIRPLANE RIDE, we land about an hour from my hometown and grab an Uber. My family offered to pick us up, but I still need time to tell Kam that we're supposed to be engaged so I told them not to worry about it.

I'm a fucking nervous wreck. It's been on the tip of my tongue since takeoff, but I haven't had the balls to tell her. This ring has been burning a hole in my pocket all day.

"Are you listening?" she asks.

I snap my head. "Sorry. I'm feeling...nostalgic for my hometown. I'm excited to show you a bunch of my favorite places. Obviously today and tomorrow will be about Christmas, but then we'll go out and see some of the sights of Galveston. It's a great town."

She smiles. "Cool. I love seeing new places."

After we arrive, I grab both of our suitcases from the trunk of the Uber. My knees are practically shaking as we approach the front door. It's now or never, Gonzales.

I reach into my pocket for the ring. There's a really good chance she throws it in my face and then gets on the first flight home.

I take her left hand in mine and kiss the backs of her knuckles. "Thanks for doing this. I really appreciate it."

She gives me a warm smile, one that will likely fade in about five seconds. "My pleasure. You're a good guy, kitten. I'd do anything for you."

I nod. "I'm glad you feel that way, because—"

Suddenly the door begins to open. Oh fuck. I have no choice but to quickly slide the ring onto her ring finger.

She looks down at it and her eyes practically pop out of her head. As I see my mother appear, I wrap my arm around Kam and smile widely. "Hola, Mamá. Te presento a mi prometida, Kamryn Hart." *Hi, Mom. Meet my fiancée, Kamryn Hart.*

My mother looks like she's going to burst with happiness. Kam turns a shade of green and looks like she might puke, but she doesn't out me. She simply takes a deep breath and holds out her hand to my mother. "It's a pleasure to meet you, Mrs. Gonzales. Thank you for having me. Merry Christmas."

I didn't know which way this was going to go. Whether she'd go along with it or slit my throat. One thing I knew for sure was if I asked her beforehand, she would have said no. She's going to be mad, but this was my only chance at her playing along.

My mother pulls her into a hug. "No handshaking. You're going to be my daughter. We hug in this family." She squeezes Kam tightly. "We're so happy to finally meet you. Cruz has told me so much about you."

Kam is tentative at first before gingerly hugging my

mother back. I know she wasn't given much motherly affection growing up, so this must be weird for her. That, and the fact that I told my mother Kam is my fiancée.

My mother pulls away and looks Kam up and down. "You are stunning, though I would expect nothing less from my handsome Cruz." She looks at me and mumbles, "No hay ni una pizca de latina en ella." *There's not a single ounce of Latina in her.*

I roll my eyes, but Kam is blissfully ignorant and does nothing but smile. "He really overachieved with me though, right, Mrs. Gonzales?"

Mamá laughs. "Ah, I suppose I see the compatibility now. Don't call me Mrs. Gonzales, mi hija. Call me Mamá. All my children do."

I see Kam stiffen immediately. She remains that way as my mother and I embrace. She touches my face. "Such a good boy, shaving for your mother."

I nod. "I'm always a good boy."

Kam shakes her head and narrows her eyes at me. "Nope, he most definitely is *not* always a good boy."

Mamá laughs before eventually walking ahead, leading us through the house.

Running my hand down Kam's back, I whisper, "Relax."

She whispers back, "I'm going to fucking kill you."

I lean over and say into her ear, "I'll give you oral every day for a year if you don't out us for not being engaged and just go along with it."

She stops short, looks up at me, and runs her tongue across her teeth. "Whenever I want it?"

I nod. "Yep."

"Anywhere I want it?"

"Absolutely."

"Hmm. I might be able to live with those terms. I'm not calling her Mamá though."

I shrug. "Suit yourself. She'll be relentless about it. She has a way of always getting what she wants."

"So do I."

Mamá turns around. "Your brothers and sisters will be here in a little bit. Your father won't be home until dinnertime. Why don't you two get settled in? Bring your bags upstairs so they're not in the way."

I nod. "Okay. Which room do you want Kam to sleep in?" I'm assuming she won't allow us to sleep together. She's never allowed anyone to sleep with their significant other until marriage.

Mamá smiles. "You're thirty and you're my seventh child to get married. You two can stay in your room. I want Kamryn pregnant as soon as possible. 'Tis the season."

Kam starts choking and coughing. I quickly lead her away from my mother before she has the chance to respond.

I carry our bags up the stairs and push our way into my bedroom. She's frozen in shock. Dropping the bags, I grab her shoulders. "Relax. Deep breaths. Just take a few deep breaths."

Her chest rises and falls a few times before she eventually collects herself. "What the hell is going on?"

I shuffle nervously. "I'm sorry I didn't tell you. After your reaction when I asked, I didn't think you'd come. When I spoke with her on Thanksgiving morning, I told her I was engaged to try to avoid Mariana being shoved down my throat. Then you said you'd come, and I was stuck in the lie. I couldn't exactly backtrack at that point."

"Fuck, Cheetah. Fake girlfriend is bad enough, but fiancée? I know your balls are big, but this is next level big."

I run my fingers through my hair. "I just wanted to enjoy my time with my family without constantly being pressured about marriage and my future. I don't get to see them often. Especially all together like this. It's the one week of the year I get with all of them. It's not even a full week. It's five days. I want happy times. Last year, my mother had Mariana come by every single day. She made us go to a house that was for sale around the corner to see if we liked it. It's uncomfortable. She probably wouldn't have stopped if I told her that you were just a girlfriend." I get down on my knees in front of her and give her my best puppy dog eyes. "Please. Five days. That's all I'm asking. Think of all the orgasms."

She's quiet for a few moments before she starts pulling her pants down her legs. I look up at her. "Umm, what are you doing?"

"You said you'd go down on me every day for a year, at any time I want it. I want it right now." She looks at me in challenge.

"I'm about to go kiss, like, forty members of my family. You want me to do it with your pussy all over my face?"

She shrugs. "Doesn't bother me in the slightest."

I pick her up and toss her on the bed as she lets out a screech. "Spread those legs, Kam bam. Let's get day one in the books."

She gives me her trademark smile. "If Santa eats my cookie, I'll drink his milk." She mimics my mother's accent, "'Tis the season."

KAMRYN

After making good on day one of his promise, and then me making good on mine, we walk back downstairs hand in hand to a very noisy house. Everyone is talking and laughing.

I turn to him, but he simply smiles warmly. "Welcome to the

crazy Gonzales household. There's a drawer of earplugs in my room if you need a set."

I've never had this before. Our holidays growing up were quiet and cold. Our first ten years included my parents bickering behind closed doors. The next eight years were full of my father managing my mother's excessive alcohol intake. The past ten have mostly been Bails and me alone, though some years were spent with the Abbotts. The Abbotts aren't exactly a ringing endorsement for a big, happy family either. Given all this, I don't equate Christmas with happy cheer and fun family times.

The reality suddenly hits me that this is the first Christmas Eve in my entire life without Bailey. I wonder how she's doing. She's going to Tanner's ex-wife's house tonight ahead of leaving for Colorado tomorrow. It must be awkward to spend time with his ex, though Bailey says she's awesome and that they get along really well. I met her briefly at one of Harper's softball games this fall.

I can't believe I'm going to wake up on Christmas morning without my sister. Breathing is suddenly not so easy for me. Tears sting my eyes.

Cheetah notices me getting emotional and rubs my back. "Are you okay?"

"Just missing my sister. It's weird to spend a holiday without her."

He gently grabs the sides of my neck and softly runs his thumbs along my face. "We can leave if you need to. I don't want you to be uncomfortable."

I reach up and squeeze his hand. He has a way of always knowing what I'm feeling and responding in a kind, compassionate manner. He's a good man, and no one has ever treated me better than he has. I want to give him all I can for the next five days to make sure he has a great time with his family. He deserves it.

I get on my tippy toes, wrap my arms around his neck, and softly kiss his lips. "I'm ready to be a good fiancée. Of course I'll have a little fun with it, I'm not a damn Stepford wife, but I'll try my best."

Obviously payback for springing this on me is in order, but I'll mostly behave. *Mostly.*

He smiles down at me and kisses me back. "Thank you. I see lots of orgasms in your future."

I wiggle my eyebrows. "Ahh, now you're talking my language."

He winks as we separate and walk into their crowded family room. I studied his social media and some of the pictures in his condo, so I think I know who everyone is by sight. Cheetah places his arm around me and proudly announces, "Family, this is Kamryn Hart, the love of my life. Kam, this is—"

Before he can finish, I go around and acknowledge every single person by name. Every sibling, spouse, niece, and nephew. They're all dumbfounded.

Cheetah shrugs. "My girl is smart. She's not only a professional ballplayer, but she's a lawyer too." I had given him permission to share my budding legal career with his family. It's not like they know me in my real life.

I shake my head. "I'm not a lawyer quite yet; I'm just studying, but I'm confident I can get you off."

His oldest brother, Alejandro, smirks at me. "You two make a lot of sense together."

Everyone is full of cheer as I take them all in. They're an attractive family, though he was right that he's the only one with blue eyes. His skin is a little lighter than the rest too. He explained to me that they have some paternal ancestors from Spain, which is where the lighter skin and blue eyes come from. All his siblings have brown eyes and darker skin, apparently getting that from their Mexican side.

His three sisters are all attractive, but the youngest, Camila, looks like she could be a model. She's stunning, with long, thick hair and curves in all the right places. She's like a younger Salma Hayek. Her smile matches Cheetah's mischievous, larger-than-life, one. Alejandro, Santiago, and Ruben are all cute in different ways with their dark hair and big brown eyes. Cheetah is significantly more handsome than all of them, though Santiago is attractive in a more rugged way. They're all less fit than Cheetah, but Alejandro looks more than a little out of shape.

They're dressed casually and appear to be comfortable around one another.

Cheetah's mother calls the grandkids into the kitchen with her. Apparently it's their tradition that she teaches them all to cook the famous Gonzales Christmas Eve meal. Cheetah has mentioned it a few times. I'm looking forward to that.

We sit down on one of the oversized chairs together. "I like that your mom teaches both the boys and the girls to cook. That's how it should be. I guess I expected more traditional roles in your house. Glad to see you come from a more modern family."

His sister, Luna, nods. "Yes, she teaches everyone, girls *and* boys, to cook. I think she makes sure each has their specialty though."

"What's yours?" I ask her.

Everyone chuckles, and Luna has a sheepish look. "I'm the worst cook in the family. Our mother no longer allows me in her kitchen. She thinks I'm cursed. My specialty is black quesadillas, as in I burn them."

I smirk. "Mine is black-bottom pancakes. We're a match made in heaven."

Her husband, Armando, a wiry-built guy with a man bun, rubs his nonexistent belly. "I think you're a great cook, cariño."

She smiles lovingly at him, but everyone else moans in malcontent. Cheetah leans over and whispers, "They've been married fifteen years, and he still dotes on her. They do *everything* together. Work, play, everything. Oddly enough, they have a catering business, but he does the cooking and she runs the actual business. She went to business school. She's super smart."

That's awesome. They're not what I expected at all.

I ask the group, "Who's the best cook of all the siblings?"

Luna pinches her eyebrows at me in confusion. "I can't imagine chefs get better than Cruz. He must cook for you all the time."

What? Maybe a few simple breakfasts, but nothing more than that. I suppose I had dinner at his place once, but I thought it was takeout.

Cheetah shrugs. "We go out a lot or order in. I don't cook much anymore."

Alejandro nods. "I guess you were just in season. It's probably hard to find time to cook."

Cheetah nods though I'm running through our meal at his place and starting to think he may have made it himself. I assumed it was takeout because it was so delicious.

I turn to him, and he seems to read my mind and whispers. "I made that meal."

Wow.

Alejandro asks, "How did you two meet? I don't think I've ever heard the story."

I smile. "Quincy Abbott is the brother of one of my best friends. Our groups started hanging out as soon as we moved to Philly this past summer. Cruz began using cheesy pickup lines on me from the first minute I met him. The creativity drew me in."

Alejandro chuckles. "He's been doing that for years. Which one got you?"

I twist my lips. "Hmm. There are a lot. I think I was partial to *did you wash your pants with Windex because I can see myself in them.*"

They all laugh, and I continue, "But what really got me were those blue eyes. So unusual for a Latino man. And I see none of you share those same eyes."

I smirk at Cheetah, knowing I'm poking the bear. He narrows his eyes and whispers, "Bitch."

Ruben deadpans, "Ah, Cruz's blue eyes. One day he'll find out who his real father is. Some gringo, no doubt."

Cheetah gives a fake smile. "You're a riot. My baby blues

attract all the ladies. Kam bam came right up to me and said she liked my eyes, and that they matched my shorts. I said, *Really? Do they also bulge when looking at you?*"

I giggle while everyone else seems unamused. His sisters scrunch their faces in disgust.

Adriana's husband, Santos, who had walked out a few minutes ago, walks back in with a huge pile of gifts in his hands and places them under the tree. He shakes his head. "My wife orders so much from Amazon that if I got a job there, they'd let me work from home."

Adriana winks at me. "A woman should be so expensive that a man can't afford a second one."

I'm about to respond to that sexist comment when Camila does it for me. "Adriana, a woman should be able to take care of herself. Kamryn strikes me as the type of woman who can and will."

And...Camila is officially my favorite sibling.

Adriana scoffs. "Don't be a bully, Cami. Not all of us are charity cases willing to spend Cruz's hard-earned money on medical school."

Cheetah holds up his hands. "Ladies, back to your corners. No name-calling. The only B-word you should ever call a woman is beautiful. Bitches love when you call them that."

That momentarily breaks the tension as everyone starts laughing, though Adriana and Camila exchange nasty glances.

We drink and laugh for hours. They're such a tight-knit, fun family. At some point, I excuse myself to go to the bathroom. When I walk out, I see his brother, Ruben, and brother-in-law, Santos, standing in the hallway. They both smile, and Ruben says, "I hope you're not too overwhelmed. I know we can come on kind of strong."

Santos nods. "That's the understatement of the year. I have a much smaller family. When I started dating Adriana, I was like a deer in headlights. At least you know names. It took me months to get that down."

I let out a laugh. "Yep. I studied hard before we came. I wanted to make sure I knew everyone by sight."

Ruben turns to Santos and says, "No sólo tiene un gran trasero, sino que también tiene cerebro." *Not only does she have a great ass, but she's got brains too.*

Santos chuckles.

Of course they assume I don't understand what they're saying. I respond, in perfect Spanish, "Si te gusta mi culo deberías ver mis tetas." *If you like my ass, you should see my tits.*

They both widen their eyes in shock, but I simply smirk. "Estan arrestado." *Busted.*

They both apologize profusely, but I don't care. That's the precise thing I was hoping would happen when I secretly learned Spanish. Cheetah still doesn't know. I can't wait for the big reveal.

Knowing what he's been saying while we have sex for the past few weeks has been amazing. It's so fucking hot.

Two hours later we're at one of two large tables. The siblings, spouses, and their parents are at one very long table, and all the grandkids are at another. There are so many people in this family. It's nuts.

His father came home shortly before dinner. I would say Cheetah resembles him more than anyone. Cheetah has his height, build, and charismatic warmth. He too embraced me like a daughter.

I didn't get to talk to him for long because he ran upstairs to take a quick shower before dinner. He looked like he had a lot of car grease on him when he arrived.

The amount of chatter at this table is like a crowded restaurant. It's full of smiles, laughter, and warmth. Such a stark contrast to the quiet, uncomfortable family meals of my youth.

No one asks me questions about my family. I'm guessing that Cheetah has something to do with that. He definitely warned them that it's a sore topic for me.

I look at Cheetah's mother. "Mrs. Gonzales, this food is

incredible. It's the best Christmas Eve meal I've ever had in my life. The pozole and tamales are to die for."

She gives me a bit of a forced smile. "Thank you, Kamryn. Esta gringa probablemente nunca haya probado la auténtica comida mexicana en toda su vida. Se imagina que Cruz encontraría a una mujer que no sabe cómo moverse en la cocina." She mumbles. "Mariana sabe cocinar." *This foreigner has probably never had authentic Mexican food in her entire life. It figures Cruz would find a woman who doesn't know her way around the kitchen. Mariana can cook.*

I see both Ruben and Santos smirk in amusement while Cheetah's lips tighten in anger. "Mamá, necesitas mostrarle algo de respeto a mi prometida." *Mom, you need to show my fiancée some respect.*

I grab his arm to stop him, ready for my big moment. The one I've been hoping would come. Calmly and confidently looking at her, I say, "Está bien. El respeto se gana. Solo dame un poco de tiempo y no tengo dudas de que lo ganaré. Después de todo, pronto seré parte de la familia." *It's okay. Respect is earned. Just give me a little time, and I have no doubt that I'll earn it. After all, I'll be family soon.*

You could hear a pin drop at the adult table for a solid fifteen seconds until every single person bursts out into laughter. His mother smiles at me and winks. "I think you and I will get along after all, mi hija."

She happily goes around and announces which grandkids helped make which dishes. While they're all fairly young, and I'm sure she did all the heavy lifting, her pride and love for her family practically ooze out of her. This is what a mother is supposed to look like. How did I get such a shit hand dealt to me in this regard?

My mind begins to drift. I know my parents are alone in their rundown house tonight. She's either staring out the window with a bottle of booze or already passed out cold. He's in front of the television, eating a microwave meal. My heart breaks for him. He's a good man and doesn't deserve his shitty life. Maybe it's merciful for her to have less than a year to live. It's not a nice thing to think, but I hate this life for my father.

I suddenly have a feeling of emptiness. I excuse myself to the bathroom and pull out my phone to text my sister.

Me: Miss you.

Bailey: Missing you too. How's it going?

Me: It's a big, happy family. How about you?

Bailey: Really nice. Fallon's Christmas décor looks like it should be featured in a magazine.

She sends me a few pictures. It looks like a movie set.

Me: Wow. Amazing. Glad you're having a nice Christmas Eve.

Bailey: It's different.

Me: Sure is.

Bailey: Tanner, Fallon, and Harper got me Coldplay tickets with backstage passes as a gift. Two tickets. Know anyone who might want to join me?

Me: Holy shit! That's amazing. Chris Martin is on my to-do list.

Bailey: LOL. Of course he is. I think he's dating the actress from Fifty Shades. I forget her name.

Me: She's on my to-do list too.

I hear a knock at the bathroom door, followed by Cheetah's voice. "Are you okay?"

I reply, "Be right out."

> Me: Gotta run. I hope Daddy Tanner fills you with a white Christmas. I'll talk to you in the morning. Love you, big sis.

> Bailey: Love you too, crazy little sis.

I open the door and smile. "Sorry. I was just checking in with my sister."

His face softens. "You miss her?"

I wordlessly nod.

"It's enviable how close you two are."

"*My* family is enviable? Ha. Look at what's happening in there." I point toward the loud chatter. "I hope you realize how fortunate you are."

He gives me a sheepish look. "You're right. It doesn't mean you're not lucky to be as close as you are with Bailey. You two can read each other's minds. It's cool."

"It is."

His dimples come out as he shakes his head. "I can't believe you speak Spanish. You've been fucking with me this whole time?"

"Nope. I taught myself after you asked me to come here. I knew they'd talk shit about me."

He stands there completely dumbfounded. "You taught yourself Spanish in a month?"

I start to open my mouth to respond but he holds up his hands. "Yeah, yeah. You're a genius. I forgot."

I nod enthusiastically. "I sure am." I grab his hand. "Come on, fiancé, we don't want to be rude."

As we walk back in, I hear Ruben say, "That's girl math, Lola."

Cheetah asks, "What's girl math?"

Ruben harrumphs. "My *beautiful* wife thinks that if she purchases something in cash, it's free." He turns to her and grits out, "I'm trying to explain that it's not the case, mi amor."

Everyone bites back their smiles.

Lola crosses her arms and narrows her eyes at him. "Well, *Ruben*, let's discuss boy math. I heard you complaining to your brothers that it's been weeks since we last made love. It's been two days. I guess we all have different interpretations of math, *mi amor*. And shall we discuss boy math when it comes to... measuring?" She bats her eyelashes at him.

I laugh. I think I like Lola too. In fact, I like everyone.

CHAPTER FIFTEEN

CHEETAH

I wake in the morning and reach my hand over to the other side of the bed, wanting to feel the warmth of Kam's naked body but knowing that I won't. As expected, it's cold and empty.

I blink my eyes a few times and see her curled up, sitting on a chair staring out the window with nothing but a blanket wrapped around her. She's so breathtakingly beautiful.

"Morning, Kam bam."

She turns her head and forces out a smile. It's clear from the redness and puffiness of her eyes that she was crying.

"What's wrong?"

She shakes her head. "Nothing."

"Did you sleep?"

She nods. "A few hours. Merry Christmas." She masks her sadness and gives me her special smile that I love. "I'm hoping to get into the spirit. Do you have a candy cane for me under there?"

I chuckle as I open the blankets to encourage her to

rejoin me. "I do. You're more than welcome to deck the balls and empty Santa's sack."

Her eyes light up as she stands, drops her blanket, and crawls back into bed. She nuzzles into me and my exposed morning wood.

I kiss along her jawline. "Merry Christmas morning."

She lets out a soft moan. "I'm hoping for a not-so-silent night. Want to fill me up with some holiday spirit?"

I smile into her face. She always makes me smile. Reluctantly pulling away, I reach down and grab an envelope from the bag on the floor next to the bed, excited to hand it to her. "Merry Christmas, Kam bam."

She raises an eyebrow before shaking the envelope like it's a regular present. "Hmm. This feels like a gift certificate for a threesome."

I shake my head. "Nope. Guess again."

"A gift certificate for anal."

"No, but that's not a bad idea."

"Batting lessons."

"Kam bam, you led your league in batting last year. I don't think you need lessons from me."

"Lessons *for* you, kitten."

I laugh. "Not that either. Just open it."

She tears it open and begins reading. Tears fill her eyes. She whispers, "You remembered?"

"I remember everything you've ever said."

"Is it for both of us?"

I nod. "Once we get back, we'll have a little over six weeks until I leave for Spring Training in Florida. I found a ballroom dancing class that's offered twice a week for six weeks. It's perfect. You can finally take the dance class you always wanted to take."

She blows out a long breath. "This is really thoughtful. Thank you."

"It's a selfish gift. I get to fondle you twice a week, and

we can show off our moves on the field this summer during the seventh-inning stretches. We'll shock the fans with our badass moves. Maybe we can choreograph a routine."

She giggles. "You'll probably replace me with a younger and hotter model by then."

"Maybe. She won't suck dick as good as you do though. No one makes my South Pole go north like you."

"So romantic." She kisses her way down my body. "I'll give you a reminder of that right now."

KAMRYN

"Whose deep voice is that?" I ask after hearing a cackle that practically makes the entire house shake.

Cheetah lets out a laugh as we make our way downstairs. "That's my Aunt Maria. My father's sister."

"That's the voice of a woman?"

"An out-of-shape woman who smokes two packs of cigarettes a day, severely down from the four packs she used to smoke."

I scrunch my face in disgust. "Ugh. Do people still smoke cigarettes? That's so twenty-five years ago."

He nods. "Totally. She's a fucking character, but at least she has blue eyes. Proof I'm not the bastard child my brothers like to claim I am."

"Ah, proof you're a real Gonzales."

"Yep. I do have a cousin with blue eyes too, but he lives in New York. My mother said he might make an appearance sometime this week. I think he's dealing with the sale of his mother's house. Hopefully you'll get to meet Cruz."

"Cruz?"

He smirks. "Yep. His name is Cruz too. It's like our mothers share a brain sometimes. They're cousins, but they're very close. More like sisters."

We arrive downstairs to what sounds like a stadium.

The living room in the Gonzales house can best be described as complete and total mayhem. There are at least forty people chatting and sipping their morning coffee, with all the little ones tearing into their gifts. The floor is covered in discarded wrapping paper, bows, and ribbons.

He looks down at the big bag I'm holding full of gifts. "I told you not to buy anything. I sent all the gifts in advance and wrote that they were from both of us."

I shrug. "I got small trinkets for your nieces and nephews. Kids should get tons of gifts on Christmas." I was lucky to get one gift each year. I would have killed to have a Christmas like these kids do, surrounded by dozens of family members and piles of gifts.

"What did you get them? You don't know what they like."

"When you're awake as many hours as I am, stalking social media to see what kids are into isn't that hard. I know which kids like sports, which like art, which like dance, and which like music."

He rubs my back. "That was nice of you. Thanks."

I twirl my diamond ring which feels very heavy on my finger. "I'm a great fiancée. I can't wait to trade this sucker in five days from now. I'm gonna get a new car with the funds," I joke.

He laughs. "It's yours. Do with it as you please."

My chin drops. "I'm just fucking with you. I'm not keeping this Queen of England ring."

He shrugs. "Suit yourself. I got it from a bubblegum machine."

No he didn't. It's the real deal. I can tell.

We walk through the living room to an absolute sea of hugs, kisses, and well-wishes. It's awesome. I quietly add the presents to the pile under the tree.

Cheetah's mom serves everyone a tray of what appears to be

hot chocolate. He smiles at it. "It's called Abuelita. It's a Mexican hot chocolate. No one makes it better than Mamá. Best drink you'll ever have in your life."

All the mugs are one color except the one she hands me. I raise my eyebrow as she encourages me to take it. "Did you poison mine?"

She smiles. "Cruz said you prefer dark chocolate to milk chocolate. I made you a special one."

Of course he told her. He thinks of everything. I rub his arm and whisper my thanks for always considering me.

Cheetah's parents and siblings were all kind enough to get me gifts. Shoes, purses, dresses, and a designer wallet. I'm totally overwhelmed by their generosity. I'm a stranger and yet every single one of them thought to buy me a gift. I think I might need to buy an extra suitcase to take all this stuff home with me.

Aunt Maria is a piece of work. Her boobs must each weigh more than me, and I think she cracked one of my ribs when she hugged me, but she's as happy as can be watching the Christmas morning magic of the Gonzales household unfold. Apparently she never married or had kids, so her brother's family is her only family. It occurs to me that she may very well be me in forty years, sitting in a chair watching Bailey's family in action.

As the morning roars on, Cheetah's mother grabs a can of Diet Coke away from his father. "Ay, dios mio. I told you. No more diet soda. Nunca."

I bite back my smile, but Cheetah asks, "Why can't he have soda? He always drinks Diet Coke in the mornings. It's been his choice of caffeine for as long as I can remember."

His mother winks at me. "My daughter-in-law-to-be and I couldn't sleep last night. Apparently, she's a bit of an insomniac like me. While I usually cook, she likes to spend that time learning new things on the internet. We learned things together. Right, mi hija."

I grin. "Right, Mamá."

Cheetah looks at me skeptically and mouths, "Mamá?"

I shrug. "We bonded. Turns out we have more in common than I thought."

Like that she's a dirty bitch. We were up half the night laughing as she discovered just how many things you can find on the internet.

Mamá nods emphatically. "I learned that diet soda kills testosterone, which kills erections. Your father is no longer permitted to have diet soda. I thought I threw it all away."

Cheetah and his siblings all start dry-heaving while his mother and I laugh.

She continues, "And raw eggs have the opposite effect. Raw eggs will now be part of your daily diet, mi amor."

Cheetah narrows his eyes at me. "What did you do to my sweet, innocent mother?"

I whisper back, "You didn't think you were coming out of this whole fake fiancée thing unscathed, did you?"

He shakes his head at me, but I can tell he's amused. He mumbles, "You're going to pay for that, Kam bam."

I wink at him. "Can't wait, kitten."

As more gifts are opened, I notice he's constantly checking his phone. It's very unlike him. I ask, "What's going on? You can't watch porn on Christmas morning."

He lets out a laugh. "It's not porn, you degenerate. My father's gift is running late. It was supposed to be here an hour ago. They're going to text when it arrives."

"What is it?" I ask.

"My mother is going to kill me, but if you can't spoil the people you love, what's the point in all this? It's—"

Before he can continue, his phone vibrates, and he looks at it. His eyes move to mine, and he bites his lip nervously. "It's here. I'm going out to deal with the delivery guy. Will you bring everyone outside in five minutes?"

I nod. "Sure."

He kisses my cheek as his dimples come out. "I'm so excited. See you in a few."

He really is very cute, especially when he's excited.

He practically skips out the front door, and I'm hit with yet another wave of emotion at how truly happy he is to give his father a nice gift. At least, I'm assuming it's nice.

Exactly five minutes later, I manage to wrangle everyone and get them to make their way toward the door, with his parents leading the curious charge. His mother is already mumbling about hoping Cheetah didn't go overboard.

Everyone steps outside, and his mother gasps. His father has tears pooling in his eyes. There's a giant, and I mean giant, brand-new shiny black pickup truck with an oversized red and green bow.

His mother croaks out, "Ay, Cruz, what have you done? It's too much."

Cheetah has a huge smile as he waves his hand dismissively at her. "It's not for you. It's for him. He works his cojones off. He deserves something nice."

She pinches her eyebrows together. "But he already has a truck."

Cheetah shrugs. "Give his truck to your church. They can use it to deliver food to shelters."

His mother, clearly overcome with emotion, nods. His father practically skips over to Cheetah and pulls him into a bear hug. "Thank you, mi hijo. It's the most beautiful thing these old eyes have ever seen."

With a tremendous amount of pride, Cheetah shows his father the inside of the truck and teaches him all the bells and whistles, half of which I imagine he'll never use but Cheetah just wanted him to have.

I would love to be able to do something like this for my father one day. He's had such a tough life, one that I can't imagine he wanted. To give him a moment of pure joy like this would be truly incredible.

CHAPTER SIXTEEN

CHEETAH

We've had the best few days visiting my family. I can't remember ever having so much fun during a visit home, at least not in a very long time. It's been relaxed with no pressure from my mother, aside from a few comments about poking holes in my condoms, which Kam now carefully inspects before we have sex.

I showed her all the best spots in Galveston, including Pleasure Pier, the Strand, and Galveston State Park. We did a rope course adventure with my siblings and their families.

Kam finished the course first, much to the shock of everyone there. I don't think they appreciated her athleticism until they saw it in person. I proudly threw my arm around her and announced to them all that she was a four-time All-American. She reminded me that if you include high school, she was an eight-time All-American.

We then had a wiffle ball game with all the kids. Kam is totally uncomfortable around kids and doesn't even attempt to censor herself, but the game was fun and turned into a pissing contest between her and me. We traded home runs back and forth, doing our best to one-up the other with our outrageous celebratory trots. She won everyone's vote when she got on the ground and did the worm all the way around our makeshift bases.

She also wildly amused herself by finding the most inopportune times to call in the promised daily oral satisfaction, but I never back down from a good challenge. I've now gone down on her in multiple public bathrooms, the woods, the back of my father's new truck, and under a table one night.

She's crazy in the best way possible.

On our last night here, we went line dancing at a bar. We hung out with my cousin Cruz and his girl, Lehra. They were dressed as a cowboy and cowgirl. When I asked him about it, he simply smirked and said that they like to do a little role-play now and then. Kam made me give her the full cowboy treatment when we got into bed that night.

Unfortunately, we also ran into Mariana while there. She was visibly upset by seeing me with my alleged fiancée. I felt terrible, but Kam was extremely kind to her. By the end of the night, I think Mariana fell for Kam as much as my family has.

My entire family is completely and totally besotted with her. Everyone except my mother has separately pulled me aside to convey that Kam may, in fact, be the perfect match for me. If only I could get Kam to realize the same.

We're leaving for Jamaica later this afternoon. Kam is out shopping with my sisters and sisters-in-law. She said she needs another suitcase to house all the gifts that my family generously gave her. I'm packing our bags when there's a knock at the door. I turn and smile when I see my mother entering the bedroom. "I was waiting for this talk."

She walks in and sits on the bed. "Yes, let's talk." She pats the bed next to her. "Siéntate." *Sit.*

I do as I'm told. She rubs my arm. "Kamryn is a special woman."

I nod. "I agree."

She briefly hesitates. "Most engaged women talk about their weddings. In fact, it's usually all they talk about. When Gabriela was engaged to Santiago, you couldn't have a single conversation with her without wedding planning being mentioned. Remember it was a bit of a family drinking game? Shots every time she mentioned the wedding. Everyone was drunk within an hour."

I chuckle at the memory. "I remember."

"Mi hijo, Kamryn hasn't mentioned one word about the wedding all week. Honestly, I was hoping you two would house shop while you were in town. What's going on?"

Ugh. I truly hate lying. "I think we'll have a long engagement. She's in law school, and she plans to play in the Olympics in a few years. We're in no rush."

"And what does her mother have to say about it? She must want to throw her daughter a wedding. There's no greater joy."

I exhale a long breath. "I told you before I came down, she doesn't talk to her mother. Her mom isn't like you. She's not a good person. Kam cut her out of her life. While they're close with their father, he's had to handle their mother for most of their lives. Kam and her twin basically raised each other."

"She's got some baggage." It's not a question. It's a statement.

"She does, but I've never met anyone like her. She's the most amazing woman in the world."

Mamá smiles. "I can see the love you have for her." She grabs my hand. "I realize now that Mariana isn't a match for you. I just want to see you settled."

"What if being settled isn't what I want?"

Her eyebrows pinch together before she taps my thigh.

"You've always been a little different from your brothers and sisters. My special boy, always with a smile, always making everyone else happy. I want you to be happy too."

"I'm trying to figure that out, Mamá, and I don't know if it's what you think it is, but I do know that Kamryn makes me happier than anyone I've ever been around."

She nods. "Well, then I can't ask for anything else."

She stares at me like she's waiting for me to say more, but I'm quiet.

I'm considering telling her the truth when we hear the front door open and the voices of all the girls returning. My mother reaches over and hugs me. "It's been good having you home and seeing you full of joy. Whatever she's doing, it's working for you. I love you."

"I love you too."

We say our goodbyes to everyone and leave for Jamaica. The second we step onto the plane, Kam hands me back the diamond engagement ring. I'm a little surprised by the tinge of disappointment I'm feeling. I liked seeing her in my ring all week.

She quickly distracts me by whispering, "There are twenty-seven bones in my hand. Want to make it twenty-eight?"

IT'S NEARING the evening when we land in Jamaica. Kam is bouncing in her seat with excitement as she stares out the window while we taxi to our gate. I'm happy to be able to give this to her. I take for granted that I have the finances to do whatever I want whenever I want to do it. Sometimes I lose touch with the fact that extravagant trips aren't something most people can afford. I'm suddenly patting myself on the back for the fact that I booked five-star accommodations for us. I want her to have an amazing experience.

She looks at me. "It's all-inclusive, right? That means *all* our food and drink are included? Anything? Everything? Like, if I want a margarita and nachos in the middle of the night, I can just have it?"

I chuckle. "Yes. Why is this a foreign concept to you?"

"I'm cynical by nature."

"I'm aware."

She grabs my hand. "Thank you for bringing me here. I've never done anything like this in my life."

I shrug like it's not a big deal, even though I know it is for her. "We had a deal. You lived up to your end of the bargain as the doting girlfriend."

"Fiancée," she corrects.

"Right. Fiancée. I promised you a nice trip, and I'm going to deliver."

She bites her lip nervously. "I would have done it for you without the trip. The agreement to give me oral every day on demand for a year stands, but you didn't have to spend all this money on a trip. I would have helped you out regardless."

I rub her leg and joke, "You couldn't have mentioned this a few weeks ago? It would have saved me a bundle."

She smacks my arm, and I chuckle. "Just kidding. I'm genuinely excited to bring you here. We're gonna have a blast over the next four days. There's no one else I'd rather bring here than you."

She leans over and softly kisses my lips before returning her gaze out the window.

We deboard the plane, and there's a man standing at the gate with a sign that reads *Anita Handjobe*. Kam lets out a laugh. "That's you, isn't it?"

I nod as I offer my hand to the man. "I'm Anita Handjobe. The E is silent. But you can call me Cheetah. The stunning woman on my left is the one and only mega-slugger, superstar shortstop, Kamryn Hart. Future Olympian with a great rack."

He gives me a gigantic smile as he shakes my hand before taking Kam's and kissing it. With a jovial Jamaican accent, he lifts his hands in the air and responds, "I'm Odean. Welcome home."

Kam lifts her eyebrow at me. "Is there something I don't know? Are you secretly from Jamaica, kitten?"

Odean lets out a laugh. "We say that to everyone, my queen. We want you to feel comfortable in our country, like you're at home." He grabs our backpacks for us. "I have a man gathering your suitcases now. I've already taken care of immigration and customs, per your request. We can get you out of here right away to enjoy the enchantment of Jamaica." He motions his hand. "Follow me to paradise, my friends."

Kam looks giddy with excitement as she grabs my arm, and we walk behind Odean through the airport. We're able to skip the long lines of both immigration and customs. Yep, sometimes having a lot of money has perks.

As we exit the airport, there's a man already standing there with our suitcases. Odean asks, "Would you prefer a luxury SUV with air conditioning or a Jeep with no top? It will be a bit hotter, but you can enjoy the beauty of the island so much more in the Jeep."

I turn to Kam, and she immediately points toward the old, beat-up Jeep. "Definitely that."

They Tetris our suitcases into the small trunk and front seat while Kam and I climb into the back. As we begin our journey, Odean gives us a bit of a history lesson on the island and the various sites as we pass them. Kam listens intently. She has this innate thirst for knowledge. I've never met anyone like her. She's a sponge, constantly absorbing new information. And once it's in her brain, it never leaves. She's probably the most intelligent person I've ever met.

She's been FaceTiming with Bailey and Harper every morning. Harper learns a new vocabulary word every day. She tries to stump Kam, but Kam always knows what the words mean. For someone who uses the word *fuck* in nearly every sentence she utters, she has a huge vocabulary.

Harper's word this morning was athwart. Harper fell on the floor laughing when I suggested it might be ass warts. Kam simply smiled as she shook her head. "No, it generally means in opposition to the right or expected course."

I guess Kamryn Hart is athwart to every other woman I've ever met in my entire life...in the best way possible.

As we approach a marina-looking area, Odean says, "This is the most spellbinding place in all of Jamaica. It's called the Glistening Waters Marina, where they take you by boat out to the famous Luminous Lagoon."

Kam gasps. "Is this the place where you touch the water and it lights up? I read about it when I was researching the island."

Because of course she did research.

Odean nods, looking very impressed. "Yes, it is. I see you did your homework, my queen."

Kam smiles. "Yep. I learned that the lagoon is full of unique, small organisms that, when disturbed, emit a flash of neon light. It glows like a powerful flashlight as you swim through them."

Odean adds, "It's *truly* magical. It should be a wonder of the world. It's where the freshwater river and the salty ocean meet to create something you can't see anywhere else. And there are legends about those special micro-organisms. For women, they make you appear ten years younger. And for men," he winks at me in the rearview mirror, "they give you an extra two inches. You should go one night when the sun is setting as it is now."

Suddenly, Kam removes her shirt. She's not in a bathing suit, just a bra. I look at her. "Umm, what are you doing?"

She yells out, "Stop the car, Odean. I want to go in the water. I want to see Cheetah with two more inches."

Odean lets out a laugh. "You're supposed to take a boat to the lagoon, my queen, but I know a private access point that only we locals know about. Give me a few minutes, and I'll take you there."

I turn to Kam and motion toward her see-through lace bra. "Maybe you should cover up while we drive there."

She rolls her eyes. "You've seen my nipples before. They were in your mouth just a few hours ago."

I discreetly nod toward Odean.

She rolls her eyes again. "Odean, you've seen nipples before too, right?"

He lets out a laugh. "I have, queen, but none as magnificent as yours." He smiles widely.

She returns his smile. "Thanks, Odean. Just wait until you see my ass in a few minutes."

Odean laughs again as our eyes meet in the rearview mirror. "You've got your hands full with this one, don't you, mon?"

I sigh. "You have no idea, Odean. No idea at all."

We drive through what appears to be a secluded area. I'm either about to see the eighth wonder of the world or am going to be murdered. It could go either way.

Eventually, we reach a clearing and Odean parks the Jeep in what appears to be an empty beach area. He points toward the water and wiggles his thin eyebrows. "Enjoy nature's Viagra."

Kam practically leaps out of the Jeep and immediately discards her shorts, leaving her in a flimsy thong. Her perfect ass is on display. Odean is staring at her the whole time. I clear my throat, but he doesn't budge. "Sorry, mon. She might be the *ninth* wonder of the world."

Truer words have never been spoken.

She starts running toward the water, screaming, "Last one in has to motorboat your Aunt Maria."

I jump out of the Jeep like a stuntman, removing my shirt and running after her as my shorts quickly fall down my legs and land on the sand, leaving me in my boxer briefs.

I assume we'll swim in our underwear, but that's the thing I like most about Kamryn Hart. You should always expect the unexpected. Before she reaches the water, her bra and panties are discarded on top of the sand, leaving me with a view of her luscious ass as she dives headfirst into the ocean.

When in Rome.

I manage to pull down my boxer briefs and discard them just before I dive in behind her into the warm, refreshing ocean water. We both emerge with huge smiles and eyes wide open in wonderment. It looks like little stars are falling into the ocean with each of our movements. It's something you have to see to believe it is real.

As if on cue, we both swing our arms around so the water sparkles around us. It comes and goes like the light of a firefly on a warm summer night. I've never in my life seen anything like this. It's spectacular.

Her mouth is wide open at the magic of what's taking place before our eyes. "This is probably the most beautiful, perfect thing I've ever seen in my life."

I stare at her face, which is covered in droplets of water illuminated by both the moonlight and the lights sparkling beneath us. Her eyes take in the beauty of our surroundings. *My thoughts exactly.*

It can't be more than five feet deep here, so my feet are on the ground. In perfect unison, we reach for the other. She wraps her arms and legs around me. "Too bad we don't have a condom. I kind of want to feel if this is truly nature's Viagra. I can't say I've ever had eleven inches before."

I rub my hard dick through her warm center. "Does it feel like eleven inches?"

She giggles softly as her lips move toward mine. She whispers, "Something like that," just before her lips meet mine for what may be my favorite kiss of all time. It's full of passion, lust, gratitude, and...magic.

My heart is physically fluttering in a way I've never before experienced. It hits me like a Mack truck at that moment. I would never in a million years want to do this with anyone else. For the first time in my thirty years, I'm in love. I love Kamryn Hart.

Shit.

KAMRYN

"Have a jamazing evening, my queen," my masseuse says to me as he exits our suite. Calling it a suite doesn't do it justice. It's the whole fucking top floor of the massive hotel. I can only imagine what Cheetah spent on this short little getaway. Everything has been over-the-top luxurious, from the ridiculous room to the butler service to the top-shelf liquor and bottomless lobster we dined on last night after we arrived.

We've had the best time. Last night in the Glistening Waters was undoubtedly the most incredible, sensuous moment of my life. We both wanted to have sex in there, but we didn't have a condom. Regardless, being close to him and kissing him in that special place was unforgettable. I can't imagine experiencing it with anyone else but him.

We were lazy and sat by the pool drinking and listening to music all day. I won the trivia contest. The DJ assumed he was stumping everyone with random Jamaican facts, but I knew the answer to each question. Add every guest at this resort to the long list of people who assumed I was an airhead.

We just had an in-room couples' massage. We're both in robes as the masseuses leave our suite in the late afternoon. I've never felt more relaxed in my life.

Cheetah is sitting on the sofa with his eyes closed and his head resting on the back, looking like he might fall asleep. I walk over to straddle him. He doesn't open his eyes, but his dimples slowly form as he wraps his arms around me. "Feel good, baby?"

"Juan gave me the best happy ending. The most explosive orgasm I've had in months. Too bad Sofia didn't give you one too."

He tickles me, and I giggle before running my fingers through his sexy, messy hair and saying, "It was jamazing. Thank you."

He rests his hands on my hips. "For the thousandth time, please stop thanking me. This trip is more for me than it is for you."

I know he's just saying that to make me feel less guilty about the ungodly sums of money he's undoubtedly spending. The people here might be calling me queen, but it's Cheetah who's treating me like one.

Opening the top of his robe, I rub my hands all over his slippery, broad chest, and breathe, "It would be wasteful not to make use of all this oil." We're both covered in it from our massages.

He lifts his head, and his eyes open. I can feel him immediately harden under me. "I dream about your ass every time I close my eyes."

"Me too."

He pinches his eyebrows together. "You dream about my ass?"

"No, mine. It's incredible." I smile.

He chuckles. "You're not wrong. When you play ball, all I can think about is holding onto your Princess Leia hair handles and pounding that ass. I swear I get hard every time you take the field."

I immediately take the hair ties off my wrist and fix my hair as close as I can to the way I wear it for games. Standing, I slowly remove my robe and let it fall to the ground. "I'm here to make all your fantasies come true, Luke Skywalker. Or do you prefer to be Chewbacca? I haven't seen *Star Wars*, but I can play along."

He gasps. "You haven't seen *Star Wars*?"

I shake my head. "Nope."

"It's my favorite movie, like *Titanic* is for you."

I scrunch my face. "It's a boy movie."

"It's an *everyone* movie. It's the highest-grossing franchise of all time."

"*Titanic* is literally the highest-grossing movie of all time." I sigh. "Which is it? Luke Skywalker or Chewbacca?"

His face lights up with mischief. "I think I prefer Han Solo. Want to see my lightsaber?"

I nod. "Always."

Before I can take another breath, he's standing with his robe on the ground, lifting me up, and running toward the bed.

I laugh as he throws me on it. Immediately flipping me over onto all fours, I wiggle my ass, turn my head around, and say, "Be gentle, Han. Your lightsaber is bigger than most." I haven't had anything nearly as big as him in my ass before.

He wiggles his eyebrows. "Just be happy we're not in nature's Viagra. My lightsaber would have two more inches."

"Oh god. Then it would come out my throat. But your balls might still reach my clit."

I laugh at my own joke before he spanks me hard and asks, "How much lube do you need?"

"Duh. A buttload."

He rolls his eyes. "For real."

"What's on my body should suffice."

He does his best to gather as much of the oil covering my body and his as possible. He first rubs it all over his dick. There's something incredibly erotic about seeing him do that. I start touching myself as I watch him stroke himself. He's so hot.

As soon as he notices me rubbing my clit, he lets out a groan. "Shit, Kam bam. You're so fucking sexy."

"I know." I look his body up and down. "So are you."

His eyes bore into mine. "I guess we're a perfect match."

Too perfect.

I take a deep breath. "Stop jerking off. My ass is only on the table for another few minutes."

He looks out toward the balcony area. "Any chance I can talk you into doing it out there? I've dreamed of bending you over a balcony since I met you."

"Can people see us?"

He shrugs. "Do you care?"

I twist my lips. "Hmm...nope. Let's do it."

I pop up off the bed and open the sliding glass door. We have a huge balcony overlooking the ocean. We're very high up, and it's getting dark out. It would likely be hard for people on the ground to see us, but I suppose you never know with cameras and zooming abilities. Whatever. We'll put on a show.

I bend over and place my hands on the top railing of the glass balustrade. He lets out a loud moan. "Fuck, Kam bam." In a Jamaican accent, he adds, "You slay me, queen."

I turn my head and, also in a Jamaican accent, reply, "Just make sure I have a jamazing time, mon."

He gathers a handful of oil from my legs and rubs it over and then into my back entrance with two fingers. Then he moves them in and out of me. His other hand reaches around and starts rubbing my clit.

"Hmm. That feels good."

He pushes in to the knuckles. "It's about to feel even better."

"Ahh. Keep going. Me gusta eso." *I like that.*

"Voy a hacer que te corras muy fuerte." *I'm going to make you come so hard.*

Withdrawing his fingers, he runs his tip over and then just

barely into my puckered hole. He whispers, "Don't worry, I'll go slow."

"I'm not an ass virgin, kitten. Give me your best. Bang the balloon knot like you mean it."

He chuckles as he pushes deeper into me, all while continuing his strokes over my clit. "Oh fuck, Kam. That feels good. Are you okay?"

I roll my eyes. Men will fuck you until they break you on the front end but treat you like you're a piece of glass on the back end. "This Chunnel to France has been traveled before. I want the full-speed train. Tom Cruise in *Mission Impossible*-level speed."

Admittedly, I drop in comments about how experienced I am anytime I can. I'm not ashamed or embarrassed about my active sex life. A lot of people, mostly men, can't handle it. They feel threatened. But not Cheetah. He likes me exactly as I am. In fact, he gets a kick out of my mouth, and I think he gets off on my past experiences. He's never once tried to make me anything other than what I am. In turn, I would never want him any other way than exactly how he is.

At that, he begins long, hard, deep strokes inside me. Once he establishes a rhythm that's got me forgetting that he's fucking my ass in plain view, I'm able to push back and give as much as he is. He now has one hand on one of the Princess Leia buns and the other still on my clit, all while pounding my ass like he owns it.

"Tu culo está tan jodidamente apretado." *Your ass is so fucking tight.*

"Fóllame el culo tan fuerte como puedas, gatito." *Fuck my ass as hard as you can, kitten.* "Te siento por todo mi cuerpo." *I feel you all over my body.*

"Fuck me, I love that you can talk dirty to me in Spanish."

"You could fuck Mariana in the ass. I bet she would talk dirty in Spanish."

He spanks me, and I giggle. That girl doesn't have a dirty word in her vocabulary. I'm not sure what Cheetah's mother could possibly have been thinking. She's not the right girl for him.

He needs someone who makes him laugh. Someone who challenges him. Someone who's as dirty as he is.

Fuck. Is that me?

Two orgasms and two hours later, we're having a private dinner on the beach. It's nothing short of spectacular. The immaculately set table covered in candles is only a few feet from the ocean. The moonlight is reflecting off the ocean surface in a scene that looks like it belongs in a movie. There's a canopy over us with sparkling lights. A red carpet was rolled out so we could walk from the patio area to the table without sinking into the sand.

We have a private band playing for us and a five-person, dedicated catering staff bringing us amazing food and drinks like we're feasting for fifty people, not two. I've never been treated like this in my life, but it's not the luxury that's making me smile. It's Cheetah. He brings a perma-smile to my face.

I'm wearing a long, sleeveless, casual dress with a huge slit up the side. It's white with large red flowers and hugs my body well. He was practically drooling when I walked out of the bathroom wearing it. I'll have to thank Gemma for the suggestion. She's always dressed well, so I asked her where she shops for the vacations she and Trey go on. I went there and bought a few things just before we left.

Cheetah looks sexy as sin in his white linen pants and matching short-sleeved, button-down shirt that's tight in the arms due to his bulging biceps. It contrasts beautifully with his darker skin and blue eyes. He's a gorgeous man. Even better, he's been smiling from ear to ear the entire time.

I joke, "Cheez, if I knew anal would make you so damn happy, I'd offer it up more often."

He chuckles. "I'm smiling because of you, Kam bam. I'm

having the best time. I never want to leave." He takes my hand and kisses it. "Have I told you how beautiful you look tonight?"

I nod. "About a thousand times."

A man interrupts and says in a thick Jamaican accent, "He's right, my queen. Prettiest lady at the resort. Good evening to you both. My name is Akein. It rhymes with bacon, which works out because I'm Jamaican. But," he wiggles his eyebrows, "I look and dance like *Magic Mike*." He shakes his hips.

Cheetah and I both laugh. This guy is a character.

Akein continues, "I will be your sommelier this evening. I hope you've enjoyed your cocktails. Now it's time for the wine Mr. Gonzales and I selected earlier. May I say, he has excellent taste in *both* wine *and* women."

I look at Cheetah. "Is that where you disappeared earlier?"

He simply winks.

Akein pours the wine into our glasses, and we both taste it. Cheetah grins at Akein. "Thanks, buddy. It's perfect."

Akein nods. "Very well. I'll leave you to enjoy it."

He places the bottle on a wine stand before he walks away. I look up at Cheetah. "The people here are so freakin' friendly."

"It's only because you're hot."

"Or because you have a lot of money."

He shrugs nonchalantly. "Maybe that too. You're too perceptive. Tell me one of the fun facts that overflow in the enigmatic brain of Kamryn Hart. Dazzle me."

He really is attracted to my mind. He asks me stuff like this all the time.

I think for a brief moment until I remember a good one. "What's a woman's biggest sexual organ?"

"Biggest as in size?" he asks, appearing perplexed.

I nod. "Yep. Biggest."

I see him moving his eyes up and down my body before they land on my chest. He perks up like he knows this answer. "I got it. The heart."

I shake my head. "Nope. Any other guesses?"

"Hmm. Ass?"

I let out a laugh. "Ha! Not even close. It's the right side of the brain."

"The brain is a sexual organ?"

"Yep. It controls your senses, which is why great dirty talk is so effective."

"Do you like my dirty talk, bombón?" *Hottie.*

"You know I do. It's not over the top like it's forced. A lot of guys try to force it, and they fail. You don't do it because you think it's what a woman wants to hear. You do it because it's what is organically on your mind at the given moment. It's so much more of a turn-on that way. And the fact that it's in Spanish is next level." I flutter my eyelids. "I didn't know I had that kink until you unlocked it."

"Bueno, porque no puedo esperar para quitarte ese vestido más tarde." *Good, because I can't wait to take that dress off you later.*

I smile as I hold up my glass to clink with his. "A la salud, la felicidad y los orgasmos." *To health, happiness, and orgasms.*

He smiles as he clinks his glass with mine.

"Speaking of happiness, tomorrow we're jumping off that waterfall. It's *really* high up. Are you sure you're still game?" he asks. "It's a little dangerous."

I nod. I've been dying to do this. "Hell yes, kitten. I can't —"

As if on cue because my life sucks sometimes, my phone rings. I quickly glance down at it and notice that it's my sister, the only person whose call I would take right now. I look up at Cheetah. "It's Bails. She knows what we're doing, and she's supposed to be at dinner with Tanner, Fallon, and the girls right now. It must be important. Do you mind?"

He motions toward my phone. "Of course not. Take it."

I accept the call on speaker. "Shouldn't you be getting tied up by Daddy Tanner right about now?"

She sniffles. I know immediately that something is wrong. If

Tanner Montgomery broke her heart, I will get on a plane to Colorado tonight to kick his ass. Fuck, I knew this was coming.

"What's wrong?"

Bailey croaks out, "She's gone, Kam."

"Who's gone?"

"Mom."

"They finally split up? Good. Now he can have a normal life."

She sniffles again. "No, Kam. She's *gone*. She died."

Cheetah immediately takes my hand as I stoically respond. "Okay, well, it's not like it impacts our life. We haven't seen her in ten years. The world is better without her. Should we have a party to celebrate when I get back to Philly?"

She sighs. "I'm flying down to Florida tomorrow morning. Tanner is coming with me. Fallon is here with Harper and Dylan. The funeral is the next morning. Kam, please come."

"What? No way. Tomorrow is New Year's Eve. Cheetah and I have plans. I'm in freakin' Jamaica. That bitch isn't ruining my good time. I don't owe her shit."

I see Cheetah fiddling on his phone, undoubtedly texting with Tanner.

Bailey pleads, "Please, Kam. If not for her, do it for me and Daddy. Come home. We need you there. Maybe saying goodbye will be good for you."

I shake my head. "Bails, I don't know. I swore I'd never step foot in that town again."

CHEETAH

I'm holding her hand while her face remains expressionless. Completely and totally expressionless.

I feel my phone vibrate in my pocket and pull it out to see that it's a text from Tanner. I swipe to open it.

Tanner: No matter what you have to do, get her to that funeral.

I look back up at Kam. She's still not giving anything away. I'm honestly not sure if she's happy or sad, and I really don't think she'll want to go.

Looking back down at my phone, I type a response.

Me: She's not emoting over this. It's weird. I'll try.

Tanner: I told Shannon to book us two suites at a nearby hotel. One will be in your name. If you need her to take care of anything else, just text her.

Shannon is his longtime secretary.

Me: Thanks, man. How's Bailey?

Tanner: Worried about Kamryn.

Me: Sounds about right.

Tanner: Our flight arrives in the late afternoon. Get. Kamryn. There.

I hear Kam saying goodbye.

Me: I'll do my best. Let me run. They're getting off the phone. I'll keep you updated.

I tuck my phone away and look at Kam. She takes a sip of her drink and calmly says, "Anyway, like I was saying, I'm looking forward to going to the waterfall. It's supposed to be a huge high. We'll need lots of pics."

I blink my eyes a few times. Am I in a bizzarro universe? "Babe, your mom just died. I think we need to fly out tomorrow morning so you can be there."

She shakes her head. "No, we need to enjoy our vacation. Funerals are about paying respects to someone who has passed. I have no respect for her whatsoever. And I won't go back to my hometown. I can't step foot in that house."

"Tanner got us a hotel. You don't have to go to the house if you don't want to, but I think you should attend the service."

"Why would I go to her funeral? I had nothing to do with her in life. Why would I mourn her death?"

"Because of your father and Bailey. You love them. You need to go for them. You'll regret it if you don't."

She's silent.

I take her hand again. "How about we make a deal? Your sister and Tanner are coming from across the country. They won't get there until later in the day."

"I can't believe Tanner's coming. It seems excessive."

"I'm sure he wants to be there for Bailey. The same reason you should go. It's a shorter flight for us. I'll book us on a late afternoon flight. We'll do the waterfall thing in the morning. I know you were looking forward to it. Then we'll fly out."

Her face falls. "It's New Year's Eve tomorrow night. I'm not going to ask you to miss out on partying here."

I squeeze her hand. "You're the party, Kam bam. Wherever you are, that's where I want to be."

Her eyes finally fill with tears, but I have no idea whether it's for her mother or something else.

CHAPTER SEVENTEEN

CHEETAH

"This is fucking nuts. We're way too high."

Kam lets out a laugh. "Don't be a pussy cat, kitten."

Odean lets out a big laugh. "God, I love you Kamryn. Marry me."

She smiles at him, looking gorgeous in her pink and white striped bikini. "I'm not the marrying type, Odean, but if I were, you'd be number one on my list."

Odean grins and elbows me. "You hear that, mon? The queen is picking me to be her king."

"It's because you're an enabler." I look down at the waterfall. We must be thirty-five feet in the air. I thought this was going to be ten feet up. "I'm pretty sure making this jump is an act of unnecessary danger, against both our contracts."

Kam shrugs. "Suit yourself. I'm jumping." She turns to Odean. "If my top falls off, will you help me?"

Odean nods enthusiastically.

I sigh. "Is there anything I can say right now to change your mind?"

"Hmm. That you'll cancel our flight tonight so we can stay here instead of going to Amityville."

I'm silent. I believe she'll eventually regret it if she doesn't go. She needs to be there.

"Cheetah, grab those elephant-sized balls of yours, and let's do this together." She holds out her hand in invitation of me taking it.

I simply stare at the craziest woman on the planet.

She sighs. "Why are you looking at me like that?"

I answer, "My doctor told me to watch what I eat."

She cracks a smile before whining, "Come on, kitten. Let's do this. I *really* want to do this *with* you." She playfully pouts. "I've been waiting for this since the day you invited me. *Please.*"

She reaches her hand out for mine again and this time I take it as I grab my balls with my other hand and begin praying in Spanish.

She pulls me until our toes dangle over the rocky ledge. "Uno, dos—"

Before she gets to tres, she pulls me and we're flying through the air. Not really flying. More like plummeting to a certain death.

We're both screaming. I might be screaming louder and at a higher pitch.

With a loud smack, our feet break through the surface and our bodies are immediately pulled under the water. We sink down a few feet before it's time to swim back up to the surface. I try to pull her with me, but she lets go of my hand.

The water is clear, so I open my eyes. She's looking at me as she sinks toward the bottom, making no attempt to move toward the surface. It must be at least fifteen feet down.

I quickly kick my arms and legs as I swim to her, grab

her waist, and pull her with me to the surface until we both break through and audibly gasp for air.

With labored breaths, I eventually breathe out, "What were you trying to do?"

With an equally labored breath, she responds, "I wanted to touch the bottom, cockblocker. Now we have to do it again."

"Fuck. No."

Yep, we do it again.

KAMRYN

We're in the rental car with Cheetah driving because I probably would have driven in the opposite direction. My anxiety skyrockets when I see the sign for my hometown approach. My breathing becomes labored. What the fuck am I doing here?

Bailey and Daddy. I'm here for them.

Cheetah turns to me. "Do you want to go see your father, or do you want to go straight to the hotel?"

"Go to the hotel. I told you, I'm not stepping foot in that house. Let's see if Bailey and Tanner want to go out. It's New Year's Eve for fuck's sake. We need to party."

"We're here for a funeral."

"Whatever. It's not like it's a normal, sad funeral. It's a celebration. I already signed my dad up for Tinder. He's gotten a few hits. He's a good-looking guy."

He shakes his head. "He's burying his wife of nearly thirty years tomorrow."

"Meh. It's a party. And parties have music. I started a playlist for this one." I click on my music app and hold up my phone as the song "Another One Bites the Dust" plays, followed by "Ding Dong the Witch is Dead."

He shakes his head again before cracking a smile. "What's the worst thing you can do at a funeral?"

Now he's talking my language. "What?"

"The corpse."

I let out a laugh. "That's a good one. At my funeral, I want Bailey to send everyone a text from my phone that reads *OMG it's dark in here.*"

He chuckles. "You're deranged."

I smile. "Thank you."

We pull into the hotel, drop our bags in our suite, and then head straight to Bailey's room. Tanner informs us that she's been at my father's house for a few hours, but a minute later, I feel her comforting arms wrap around me from behind. She whispers into my back, "Thanks for coming."

I close my eyes. God, I missed her. I turn around and hug her back, taking in her familiar, comforting scent. I mumble into her, "I'm here for you and Daddy, not her."

She nods into my neck. "I know. I'm still happy you're here. I missed you."

"I missed you too. How's Daddy?"

Bailey lifts her head and looks me in the eyes. "He's surprisingly calm. He's all business about it. It's weird."

Well duh. "He's probably relieved to be rid of the witch."

We chat about our father for a bit and then about my trip. At some point, Bailey yawns and stretches her arms. "I'm beat. I'm headed to bed."

I place my hands on my hips. "What? It's New Year's Eve. Let's go party. We can celebrate the new year and the end of an error."

"An era?" she asks.

"An error. Beverly Hart's existence was an error of grand proportions."

She reminds me to behave tomorrow before she shoves us out of her suite and tells us not to stay out too late.

Once we're in the hallway, I turn my head to Cheetah. "They're probably gonna stay up and fuck all night."

He nods. "Totally. We should do the same. Let's see who gets the first noise complaint. We can bring in the new year with a bang. Literally."

I look at my watch. "Tempting. We can still do that, but it's New Year's Eve. Let's go get a drink or two first. I know it's not the big party we were planning to attend in Jamaica, but let's have a little fun. The locals here are morons. We can fuck with them."

He takes me into his arms. "We can get drinks, we can go streaking, or we can get into bed and eat ice cream. Know that I'm here for you, and I'm up for whatever puts a smile on your pretty face."

"What if it were to make me smile if I let you fuck me in the ass on my mother's grave tomorrow?"

He sucks in a breath. "I read a dark romance once where they did something like that. It was shockingly hot, but I'm not sure I'm into it in real life. Fucking your ass I'll happily do again though."

I bite my lip. "Hmm. It's kind of a fitting send-off for my mother. A little sodomy funeral foreplay before the big goodbye. Drinks first, ass later."

He squeezes my behind. "Deal. Where should we go?"

My shoulders fall. "There's only one bar in this shithole town. It's called Fisherman's Reef."

He raises an unimpressed eyebrow. "So unoriginal."

I nod. "Right? I haven't lived here in over ten years. Hopefully I won't see anyone I know."

An hour later, we're two beers in and slow dancing to the beat of the same old jukebox that was here when I was a kid. Bailey and I used to love slipping quarters in and making our selections. I don't think the music in it has changed since then.

My father used to bring Bailey and me to eat here every month when we were little kids. He told our mother that he needed one date a month with his little girls. It was sacred time away from her when the three of us were temporarily free of the black cloud we lived under. It was consistent from the time we were five or six through high school graduation.

We'd have dinner, and then our father's friends would come for a game of poker. For years, Bailey and I simply watched them while messing with the jukebox. That was when I learned to count cards. I have no clue how I did it, but I just started a system, and it worked for me. I taught Bailey how to do the same. She's not quite as proficient at it as me, but she's an amazing poker player.

At some point, I started whispering in his ear when to go all in and when to fold. I was *always* right. When we were roughly eight or nine, his friends indulged us by letting Bailey and I play a few hands. At first, we'd sandbag until the stakes got higher. Then we'd take those grown men for every dime they brought until they stopped letting us play.

Bailey and I hustled many high school and college boys out of their paychecks. Since our family came from very little, this was how Bailey and I made some of our living expenses in college.

While looking at the jukebox offerings, I selected the theme song from *Titanic* in honor of my sister, which we're dancing to now. We've watched that movie no less than a thousand times.

Cheetah runs his hands up and down my back as we put on a little dirty dancing show for the local nimrods. He asks, "Are you going to behave at the funeral tomorrow?"

"No."

"Why not? Can't you just pay your final respects?"

"As I've said before, respect is earned. Beverly Hart was a piece of shit. She's burning in hell right now, and I want to celebrate that fact."

He nods. "I know you said she was a terrible mother, an alcoholic, and did all kinds of bad shit, but why do you hate her more than Bailey does? What happened to you specifically that didn't happen to her?"

I'm not in the mood for an inquisition. I look up at him. "Why do you care?"

He stops dancing but continues to keep ahold of me. "Kamryn, in case it's not clear, I care about you. A lot."

I shake my head. "I very specifically told you not to fall for me. I'll never truly be what I was this past week with your family. I was your *fake* fiancée, Cruz. It will *never* be real."

He sighs. "Humor me as some random guy who will someday be one of your many nameless and faceless bedfellows. What happened to you that didn't happen to Bailey? Does it have something to do with the fact that you don't sleep well?"

My eyes widen. How does he see me better than anyone else?

Despite my attempt to hold them back, tears immediately blur my vision. Why am I suddenly so emotional? It's unlike me. I've learned to mask my pain throughout the years. It's probably this damn town making the emotions all bubble at the surface.

He immediately notices and grabs my hand, pulling me out the front door and around the corner until we're out of sight of any intruding eyes.

He rubs his hand along my face. "Baby, talk to me. Let me in. Let me take some of the pain. I see you, Kamryn Hart. You bottle things up. You don't always have to play the tough guy. Sometimes it helps to unload. You can trust me. I promise. I'll never betray your confidence, no matter where we end up."

"I...I've never talked about it before."

"Not even with Bailey?"

I shake my head and croak out, "I don't want her to know. Then she'll be as fucked as me."

"Know what?"

I don't know why, but for the first time in my entire life, I unload what I heard that night in the production studio and what I'm confident it meant. How it made me irrevocably hate my mother. How that moment basically ended my childhood. How it's made me so protective of my sister that it's become nearly debilitating.

He holds me and lets me cry into his chest. I haven't sobbed about that night in over a decade. I can't believe how good it feels to both tell someone and to emote over it. It's like some of the toxicity is leaving me.

We must stand out there for over half an hour. He simply consoles me and whispers assurances to me. Obviously my sister has always been a bit of a caretaker to me, but that's different. Cheetah is giving me support that I've never considered letting anyone give me.

I eventually pull my head away and look into his face for some reaction. "Do you believe me? Do you think I'm crazy?"

He lovingly rubs my tears from my face. "I think you're the strongest person I've ever met. You're amazing, Kamryn Hart. Don't ever consider otherwise."

"Everyone thinks I have a screw loose, me included."

"I don't agree. I think you're perfect just the way you are."

I wipe a few of my tears, not wanting to ruin his New Year's Eve more than I already have. "We should go inside."

"We don't have to do anything you don't want to do."

"I don't want to be sad. I want to be happy. The ball is going to drop soon."

He winks at me. "I'd rather watch your pants drop."

I giggle as I clear away the last of my tears and grab his hand. "Let's go back inside. It's almost midnight. I might make you go down on me at midnight in the middle of the bar. I haven't called in your debt to me yet today."

CHEETAH

That was a big moment for Kamryn. I understand her damage a lot better now. I certainly understand her constant need to protect Bailey. I used to think it was overbearing, but now I think it's endearing. I'm also better grasping her deep-rooted hatred for her mother. It's hard to imagine a mother acting like hers. I'm suddenly feeling grateful for my over-intrusive mother who does it because she loves and cares about me so much.

I send her a quick text to wish her a happy new year and to tell her how much I love and appreciate her.

Before Kam's moment outside, she and I were having a pretty chill night. We've had a few drinks, a few laughs, and a few dances. There were two men at the bar earlier who Kam apparently hustled in poker when she was just a kid. That doesn't surprise me in the least. They were happy to see her but didn't mention her mother's passing. I wonder if it's because they don't know she passed or know how Kam feels about her. I suspect it's the latter.

As soon as we walk back into the bar, Kam stops short. An attractive blonde woman's eyes widen when she turns from her seat at the bar and sees us walk in. "Kamryn Hart. Wow. I never thought I'd see you back in this town."

Kam swallows. "Dakota Briggs. I'm here against my will. My mother died. I'm only in town out of respect for my father and sister."

Dakota gives a knowing nod. I guess she knew Kam's mom. "I'd say I'm sorry for your loss, but I'm guessing those aren't the words you want to hear right now."

Kam shakes her head before threading her fingers through mine. "Dak, this is my...fiancé, Cruz Gonzales."

And...I'm back to being her fiancé.

Dak. I remember hearing that name. Ahh. Kamryn's high school sweetheart. The one who broke her heart. I guess I always assumed it was a man, but it most definitely is not.

I mumble into Kam's ear, "This will cost you oral every day for a year."

The corner of her mouth raises slightly as she gives me a subtle nod.

Dakota briefly acknowledges me and then points to a brunette who could be Kam's doppelgänger, albeit not nearly as attractive as Kam. "This is my wife, Kelly."

Kam holds out her hand. "It's nice to meet you, Kelly."

Kelly nods as she shakes Kam's hand. "You as well, Kamryn. I've heard a lot about you."

Dakota gives me a once-over before turning back to Kam. "I'm not surprised you ended up with a man. I'm pretty sure I told you that would happen."

Kam squeezes my hand hard before plastering on a big, fake smile. "Cruz is confident enough in our relationship to allow me to be me. It's a refreshing change. Anyway, we were just about to grab a drink before celebrating the new year. Have a good night."

We walk to a corner booth, and Kam takes a few deep, long breaths before sitting and hiding in the corner. In the six months I've known Kamryn Hart, I've never once seen her cower from anything or anyone. This town is opening wounds for her.

I slide into the same side as her so I'm shielding her from anyone possibly seeing her break down. "Are you okay?"

Her chest moves up and down at a rapid pace. "This is why I didn't want to come back here. So much baggage. It's overwhelming." She runs her fingers through her hair. "I'm so sorry. I'm fucking up your New Year's Eve."

I shake my head. "You know, I'm not feeling this place." I look at my watch. "If we leave now, we can ring in the new year in that huge jacuzzi tub in our suite. That's way more appealing to me."

She looks up at me. "But you're a party guy."

"Your naked body next to my naked body sounds like a party to me."

THIRTY MINUTES LATER, Kam is laughing hysterically. "Do it again. Do it again."

I'm standing naked outside of the jacuzzi tub while she's in it. I have a cowboy hat hanging on my dick as I flex it up and down. For some reason, she's wildly amused by it, and I'm happy to do anything that makes her laugh after such an emotional night for her.

"Last time, then I'm getting in."

I flex my dick, and the hat moves up and then down. She starts cackling again. I have no idea why this is so funny to her.

I leap into the tub of bubbles, sinking down into the warm water. I then pull her legs until they surround me, and our chests are flush together. "My dick is very strong. I can't believe you didn't realize that men have to work out that muscle like they do all others."

She wraps her soft, wet hand around it. "That explains a lot, though I still don't think it's true."

I chuckle. "It's true for me."

She runs her thumb over my tip. "Do you know why a penis has a hole at the tip?"

"Umm, so I can pee and come."

She shakes her head. "Nope. It's so a man can be open-minded."

I smile. "That pretty head of yours is full of useful information. What's going on in it right now?"

She twists her lips. "Hmm. I was regretting not peeing in the Glistening Waters."

"Why is that?"

"Would it have glowed? I want my pee to glow."

"I've known some guys who had that issue, but it had nothing to do with Glistening Waters, and it wasn't a good thing."

She giggles. "No doubt. I can only imagine how many women baseball players get to bang. How crazy are road trips for you guys? We have strict curfews and bed checks. We can't party at all. I feel like you guys are partying all night."

"We don't have hall monitors. We technically have curfews, but it's mostly self-enforced. No one checks. It's split into groups. The younger, single guys like to party and bang all kinds of women, and the older, married guys might have a drink or two before they go to their rooms to have phone sex with their wives."

"You single guys must have POD."

"What's that?"

"Pussy on demand."

I let out a laugh. "Something like that. I guess I fall in the middle. I can no longer party all night and play the next day like the young guys, but I've never had anyone worth running back to my room for phone sex with."

"So you watch porn and jerk off?"

"I turn on porn to fuck with whoever my roommate is. I've been pigeonholed into a certain character, and I just play into it." I squeeze her ass. "None of them are as hot as you anyway. You've forever ruined all porn for me."

She rolls her eyes. "Umm hmm."

I rub my thumb across her plush lower lip. "Feeling more relaxed now?"

She simply nods as her eyes momentarily drift closed.

I ask, "Will you tell me what upset you earlier with your ex?"

She aimlessly traces the veins on my arms and quietly

admits, "She broke my heart. It's a tale as old as time. I loved her, and she shattered me. It was bad enough to make me swear off love forever."

"Did it have something to do with your sexuality?" Dakota made that comment about it figuring Kam would end up with a man.

She nods. "It did. She said I'd always have this desire for a man, and she could never compete with that. She's only into women and didn't understand my attraction to both. She also accused me of only wanting a woman because it pissed my mother off. Honestly, I think bisexual people are the most misunderstood of all."

I rub circles on her hips with my fingertips. "How so?"

"We accept attraction to the opposite sex, and even though some ignorant assholes are morally opposed, we generally accept attraction to the same sex. But an attraction to both? No one gets it. I'm always asked a million questions that my heterosexual and homosexual friends and teammates never get. It's baffling to people. I don't know why."

I've never thought of it that way, but she's right. People don't question as much when you're attracted to one sex or the other. It's both that throw them off kilter. I'm as guilty as everyone else.

I look her in the eyes. "I'm sorry if my jokes and comments about your sexuality have ever offended or hurt you."

She shakes her head. "They don't. They're funny. They're half the reason I was attracted to you."

"They are?"

She nods. "Yep. Your sense of humor, Cruz. It's my absolute favorite thing about you."

It suddenly occurs to me that we must have hit midnight. I look over at my phone and see that it's a few minutes past. "It's a new year. We didn't ring it in, though your hand is still on my dick, so I won't complain."

She looks down and giggles. "I suppose it is." She looks back up and brings her lips close to mine. "Happy New Year, Cruz."

Just before I kiss her, I whisper, "Happy New Year, Kamryn."

CHAPTER EIGHTEEN

CHEETAH

The last of the dirt is thrown on top of the grave. Kamryn simply stands there and stoically stares at the men completing their jobs and clearing out their equipment.

She insisted on wearing a hot pink dress and heels, calling today a celebration, but she's otherwise been respectful. In fact, she hasn't said more than two words since we arrived at the cemetery.

In fairness, Bailey has been quiet too, and their father, Chris, only said a few words at the funeral along the lines of hoping Beverly is now at peace. There were only a sprinkling of people in attendance. I think I recognized half of them from the bar last night. Kam and Bailey didn't appear to know the other half. I guess they've been gone for a long time.

I was briefly introduced to Chris Hart, but I otherwise simply stood behind Kamryn, offering her whatever support she needed. Tanner did the same for Bailey as he and I exchanged frequent glances throughout the most awkward funeral in the history of the world. I've never been to a funeral where not one positive thing was said about the deceased. Even the officiant kept it to general prayers, nothing overly individualized.

Bailey and Chris aren't hysterical but are clearly emotional as they begin to move away from the grave. Chris silently walks to his car. A man who was in attendance, who I assume is a friend, walks with him and appears to console him. Tanner has his arm wrapped around Bailey as they make their way toward their rental car.

I see Bailey's shoulders begin to shake as they approach the street, no doubt reality finally setting in. I wonder if it will be the same for Kam at some point.

She hasn't moved from the graveside. She's still hovering over the fresh pile of dirt, staring at it without any expression on her face.

I move to stand behind her. She turns only her head to me. "You should go. I have a few things to say to Beverly. Some parting words."

I rub her arms and pull her back to my front. "I'm not leaving you alone. Say what you need to say and then lean on me when you need that. I'm here for you, Kamryn."

"It's not going to be pretty, Cruz. You might not like what you hear."

"I share a locker room with thirty men. I can handle it. Do your worst."

She nods before she turns her head back to the grave. She takes a few long breaths before practically gritting out, "Beverly Hart, you are the biggest piece of shit to ever walk this planet. I know what you did. I see you. I always saw you. How could you throw your child to the wolves? What kind of human being does that? What kind of mother does that to her child?"

She spits on the grave before she continues, "You never should have had kids. Why? Why did you get pregnant? I know you did it to trap him, but you weren't capable of mothering. How fucking dare you bring children into this world. How fucking dare you consider doing to Bailey what you and I both know you were prepared to do."

I can't see her face, but I know she's crying. Her voice cracks. "Bailey is perfect. She's kind, sweet, compassionate, and thoughtful. I'm not sure how that's possible with half your genes, but she is. I guess she got Daddy's genes. I got all your shit genes." She falls to her knees and yells out, "I'm no good because of you."

I see both Chris and Bailey snap their heads our way at the sudden increase in the volume of Kam's voice.

I hold up my hand and shake my head at them, letting them know to stay away. Kam needs this. She needs to finally let it all out.

She cries out, "You made me this way. I'll never be normal because of you. I fucking hate you. I loathe everything about you. I hope you burn in hell where you belong."

She sniffs and then wipes her nose before she spits on the grave again. Finally, she begins sobbing. Heavily. I expected the yelling and screaming, but I didn't expect this. I'm happy for her that she's letting go this much.

I drop down to one knee behind her and wrap my arms around her, whispering, "Let it all out." She tries to fight me, but I don't release her. "Let me in. Let me hold you. Lean on me."

She shakes her head. "Why? You should get as far away from me as possible. You're too good for me. I'm no good. Look at who my mother is."

I squeeze her tightly. "Don't say that about yourself. You *are* good. You're great. You're the way you are despite her, not because of her. You're not Beverly Hart. You're so much better. A million times better. She made people sad. You make them happy. You have a gift for brightening the lives and lifting the spirits of everyone around you. You're loved by all who know you. You're the most loyal and loving person who exists. She was incapable of any of those qualities."

"I'm not capable of love."

"Are you kidding me? Look at how much you love your sister. I've never in my life seen someone love so completely the way you love her. I have no doubts that you would take a bullet for her without a moment of hesitation."

I pull her to stand so I can turn her around and take her into my arms. She wraps her arms around my waist and sobs into my chest. "I hate the way I am. I don't want to be like this. I'm going to end up an old maid like your Aunt Maria, with my tits hanging by my toes and a man voice."

I inwardly laugh at the description before kissing her head. "I happen to love the way you are. I wouldn't change a thing about you."

She lifts her head. Her sad eyes meet mine. "You wouldn't?"

I tuck her hair behind her ear and whisper, "No. Brains, beauty, and the best sense of humor. You sound pretty perfect to me. You *are* perfect, Kamryn. Don't ever think otherwise."

A small smile finds her lips. "What about my boobs? Do you think they'll end up at my toes?"

I shake my head. "Not a chance. Your nipple holsters are too good for that."

She sighs. "Can we leave today? Right away. I don't ever want to come back to this town again. There's nothing but sadness here. I don't want to be sad. It's not a good look on me."

I nod. I had assumed she'd want to leave today, and I made a call that I think will be good for her. "Of course. We were supposed to be in Jamaica for a few more days. We don't need to go home to the cold weather yet. Are you up for something a little out of the box?"

"Anywhere but here."

"Okay." I rub her back. "What can I do for you right now? I'll do anything to make you happy."

"You're already doing it." She rests her head on my chest for several long beats until she randomly says, "I wish I had a penis."

"Well...that's not what I expected you to say. May I ask why?"

"So I could whip it out and piss on her grave."

I can't help but smile. "I just so happen to have a very large penis. I also happened to have had a lot of water before we came here."

She looks up at me in question, and I nod. Her trademark mischievous smile finds her face. "I'll block you from view."

We both look around. The only people still in sight are Bailey and Tanner, standing by their rental car on the street. Their backs are to us. Kam positions herself so that her body blocks mine from their possible view.

Because I'm a bit of a goner for this girl, I unzip my pants, whip out my dick, and piss all over her mother's grave.

I mumble, "Don't develop a grave pissing fetish. This is a one-time thing."

She giggles, and it's music to my ears.

CHAPTER NINETEEN

KAMRYN

We're driving north up the Florida coastline in our rental car. I have absolutely no clue where our final destination is. I turn to him from the passenger seat. "Where are we going?"

Cheetah smirks as he casually changes lanes. "You'll see." He winks at me. "It's an unexpected treasure I found in Florida a few years ago. That's the only clue you're getting."

Clue? That's no clue. He's being elusive on purpose. Ugh. I hate uncertainty.

It's nearly midnight when we eventually pull into some sort of large community with a gate. Cheetah stops the car as a security guard approaches and asks, "Who are you here to visit?"

"Cruz Gonzales here to shower love and affection onto the one and only goddess of West Coast Florida, Jane Rockefeller. She's expecting us."

Why does that name sound vaguely familiar? Damn. I can't place her.

The guard looks at his clipboard and nods. "Yes, sir. She left your name." He presses a button and the gate opens. "You can go through. Do you know which house is hers?"

Cheetah nods. "I sure do."

"Have a good night."

"You too."

We drive through the gate to the expansive community of homes. There must be hundreds of them, all in varying sizes from one-level smaller homes to large mansions. It's hard to tell at night, but it looks like there's both coastal water and a golf course. That's kind of common for Florida communities. Though they're usually for older people. I'm not sure what we're doing here. I don't think Cheetah has grandparents in the area.

He navigates us through the streets of the community as though he's been here before. Finally, we pull up to a decent-sized one-story home. Probably the biggest one-story home I've seen yet. Before I can ask any more questions, the front door opens. Trey, Gemma, and an older woman walk out. Jane Rockefeller. Oh. Gemma's grandmother. I briefly met her one time, and I know Cheetah adores her, but they call her Grammy Jane. I don't think I've ever heard her last name until tonight. That's why I couldn't place her.

Other than recommending the clothing boutique and a few short conversations at Screwballs, I haven't spent a ton of time with Gemma. She doesn't come out often because they have a baby boy whose name I can't remember. Bailey is closer to her, and Cheetah considers her one of his best friends. I know they have monthly lunches to discuss their mutual love of romance novels.

"That's Gemma's grandmother, right?" I ask. "The one who visited a few months ago."

He nods. "Yes. We call her Grammy Jane. She's the best. I sometimes hang out here during Spring Training. She and her friends are a riot. This place gives you perspective. Luckily, Gemma and Trey are visiting this week for the holiday season. They come down here anytime they can."

"Remind me of their baby's name."

"Fletcher. He's almost one. He's a cutie."

We park in the driveway and get out of the car. Gemma immediately pulls me into a hug. "Sorry for your loss, Kam."

I tentatively hug her back. "It's cool. We weren't close. The world is a better place without her in it."

She pinches her lips together as she pulls away and nods. "I'm not terribly close with my mother either. Just my grandmother."

Cheetah and Grammy Jane embrace. It's so warm and familiar. He lifts and spins her. She simply giggles. "Put me down, you big feline."

"Takes one to know one, you sassy cougar," he replies.

Grammy Jane giggles again while Gemma leans over and whispers to me that her grandmother's boyfriend is much younger than her.

Damn. Good for Grammy Jane. She must be around eighty years old.

Trey kisses my cheek while Cheetah continues to pour love on Grammy Jane. Their mutual affection is clear.

Once he places her feet on the ground, she reaches over and hugs me. "Welcome to my home. We're so happy to have you both here."

I like that her expression isn't one of pity and that she doesn't offer her condolences. I don't want either.

I hug her back. "Thanks for having us." At least I assume she's having us.

She warmly squeezes my arm. "I'm sure it's been a difficult time for you. Did you know that life is like a penis?"

Gemma moans in exasperation. "Grammy Jane. She just got here. Behave yourself."

Grammy Jane shakes her head. "Never, my beautiful Gemma Morgan."

I smile. "Don't stop her, Gemma. I'd love to know how life is like a penis."

Grammy Jane nods emphatically. "Because when life is soft it's hard to beat, but when it's hard you get screwed."

I start laughing hysterically. I think I love this woman. Now I know why Cheetah adores her so much. He watches on with a huge smile covering his face while Gemma and Trey shake their heads like they've heard it a million times before.

She rubs my arm. "Happy to have you. We'll have a little fun for a few days. And all the ladies in this community love Cruz walking around the pool area topless. They sometimes try to get him to go bottomless."

This woman is a riot, and she's giving me exactly what I need right now. I'm suddenly *very* happy to be here.

Cheetah and Trey carry our bags into the house. I look around. It's a nice place. It's shockingly modern and well-decorated. Not what you'd expect from a grandmother. My grandparents had floral couches covered in plastic when I was growing up.

Grammy Jane looks around. "Please feel free to help yourself to anything you want. Don't ask, just take." She points to a door in the hallway. "That's my bedroom." She points to another. "That's Trey and Gemma's." She points to one more. "And that will be yours. Each bedroom has its own bathroom."

Cheetah looks at Gemma and Trey. "Are you guys sure it's okay for Fletcher to sleep in your room? I feel bad about taking his room."

Grammy Jane answers. "We moved his crib to my room, not theirs. I don't want to prevent Gemma and Trey from playing bam-bam with the ham. I want another great-grandbaby as soon as possible."

I can't help but laugh out loud. Cheetah laughs too while Gemma and Trey simply roll their eyes.

Gemma says, "You're a crazy old lady. I should have you committed." Before smiling and adding, "But Trey's ham says thank you, as does my bam-bam."

Grammy Jane winks before she waves. "I'm off to get my beauty sleep while Fletcher is still sleeping. Like I said, help yourselves to anything you want. I'll see you all in the morning."

After we say goodnight to her, Gemma asks if we want to go

out back and have a drink. I agree, and she retrieves four beers from the refrigerator. We make our way through the sliding glass door into an unexpectedly expansive backyard. The property overlooks the intracoastal waters. It's beautiful. There's a dock with a speedboat and two jet skis.

As we get seated in the large Adirondack chairs, I nod toward the boat and jet skis. "Are those Grammy Jane's?"

Cheetah nods. "Yep. The boys and I all come here a ton during our Spring Training. We go out on the boat, hang out at the community pool, and ride the jet skis. Grammy Jane's friends are hell on wheels. We all love them."

I narrow my eyes at him. "You're telling me that a bunch of single, attractive, professional baseball players, who could basically bang anyone they want, come *here* to hang with a bunch of old people?"

Gemma giggles. "I know. I find it hard to believe myself. They eat it up."

Cheetah agrees. "The young guys don't come with us. It's just me, Trey, Layton, and Ezra. Quincy came last year too. We're not here every day, but maybe three or four times during the course of the five weeks we spend down here for Spring Training."

I ask Gemma, "Do you visit often?"

She nods. "Whenever I can. I'm unusually close with my grandmother. I told you I have a bit of a strained relationship with my mother. Grammy Jane is my closest family member. I'm just happy that she and Trey have always gotten along well."

Gemma is so normal. She seems at peace with her apparent mommy issues. Why can't I be like her?

As if sensing my inner turmoil, she continues, "It's not our fault that we got dealt a bad hand of cards when it comes to mothers. I don't know the details of your situation, and I don't need to. But choosing to live your life differently is how we overcome it. Find your happy place and reside there. Don't reside in the past because no matter what, you can't change it. Before I met Trey, this was my happy place when I needed a moment. I'd come here and watch these people live their best lives with an *I don't give a fuck what anyone thinks* attitude. You have no idea how crazy the residents are here. The universe then blessed me with Trey. Lucky for me, my two happy places meshed so well into one big super happy place."

Trey smiles lovingly at her as he lifts her hand and kisses it. The handful of times I've been around them, he's completely doted on her. I've never seen a man love a woman harder than he outwardly and unapologetically loves Gemma.

"How did you two meet?" I ask.

She smiles at Cheetah, and he raises his hand. "It was all me. I'm taking full credit."

Trey moans in annoyance.

Cheetah continues, "I was a fan of Gemma's writing and was fangirling over a funny drunken video she posted with some of her author friends. I showed it to Trey. He then became a psycho in pursuing her. Legit stalker, crazy, lunatic psycho."

Trey rolls his eyes. "I wasn't that bad."

Gemma and Cheetah both laugh. She grabs his hand. "It's okay. It was hot." She turns back to me. "Despite a few hurdles, it all worked out. I believe it always does. I love my life. Whatever your mother did is on her, not you. My mother is still alive, and we see her now and then, but we're a lot closer to my grandmother because that's who we choose to be around. It's who we choose to have our son around. It's who makes us happy. I might share genes with her, but I'm not my mother, and I never will be. Something I'm more than proud of."

I take a long sip of my beer as I let all her words sink in. *Find your happy place and reside there.*

Gemma stands and grabs for Trey. "I know it's been a long day for you. We'll leave you guys to talk and see you in the morning. Prepare for poolside morning margaritas."

I raise my eyebrows. "They morning drink here?"

She smiles. "They all-day drink here. Honestly, it's hard to keep up."

I shake my head in disbelief. "I can't wait to see it. Thanks again for having us."

She nods before Trey wraps his arm around her, and they walk back inside.

I look at Cheetah. "I've never spent that much time talking to Gemma. She's very sweet."

He nods. "She's one of my favorite people in the world." He briefly pinches his lips together. "I thought she was a true unicorn until I met you. You guys are a lot alike."

"How so?"

"Beautiful, smart, loyal, funny, dirty. You both have this inner glow that draws people to you. You innately make everyone around you happy."

"Me?"

"Yes, you. I wish you saw yourself like I see you."

He swallows hard before he pulls a folded piece of paper from his pocket and tentatively hands it to me.

I look down at the handwritten name Chastity Pearl with an email address and a telephone number. I pinch my eyebrows together in confusion. "Did you get me a stripper?"

He lets out a laugh. "No, but Chastity *is* kind of a stripper name." He bites his lip nervously. "I...umm...asked around, and she's a psychologist who specializes in helping people with parental issues. I thought it might help to talk to a professional."

My shoulders fall. "You think I'm fucked up."

He shakes his head. "Getting help doesn't mean you're fucked up. It means you're strong enough to take steps to overcome demons that were not of your making. Your mother was fucked up, not you. Maybe talking to Dr. Pearl will help you realize that."

I fight back the tears. I thought he was the one person who *didn't* think I was crazy. He told me as much.

Tossing the paper aside and feeling defensive, I bark out, "I didn't ask for help."

"But you tell me you're not normal and will never be normal. I love that you're not like everyone else. You're the one who seems to have a problem with it. I think you should talk to someone who can help you overcome whatever it is *you* think you need to overcome."

"So I sit on a stranger's couch and tell her that I've spent the past fifteen years of my life fucking a ton of people to numb the pain caused by having a monster of a mother?"

His eyes widen, followed shortly thereafter by mine. I think I might have gasped. I've never admitted anything like that. Not even to myself.

Holy shit. Is that what I've been doing?

He moves down to his knees in front of me and places his hands on my thighs. "I think you're the most special person in the world. I just want you to realize that too. If Dr. Pearl can help you get there, I'm all for it. It's obviously up to you. You need to want it for it to work."

I cup his handsome face as I'm hit with a wave of emotion for this man, the likes of which I've never before experienced.

Suddenly I'm finding it hard to breathe. This is too intense. I can't have this conversation with him.

I stand and begin to remove my shirt.

"Whatcha doing Kam bam?"

I smile as I unbutton my jeans and pull them down along with my panties. I nod toward the darkened water, illuminated only by a few exterior lights of the houses that run along the shoreline. "You didn't think there was any chance I wasn't going skinny dipping tonight, did you?"

I start running toward the dock and yell back, "Last one in has to smell Aunt Maria's bra."

He sucks in a breath as he stands and immediately begins removing his clothes too. "It won't be me."

I drop my bra along the way before running straight down the dock and cannonballing into the ocean. The cool, calm water feels good as my overheated body is completely submerged in the quiet ocean.

My head pops back up just in time to see a naked Cheetah

yelling out, "Yeehaw," while doing a full flip over my head into the water, the resulting waves pulling me back under.

We both pop up with smiles on our faces. I ask, "Are you able to stay afloat? Or are your balls like anchors, pulling you down?"

He reaches over and tickles me, causing me to giggle.

"You think you're so funny. I'm going to drop those balls into your mouth while you sleep tonight."

"You don't even need to squat to teabag me."

He smiles as we tread water, and asks, "What happened to the guy who got fired from the teabag company?"

I twist my lips. "Hmm. What?"

"He got sacked."

I stick out my tongue in disgust. "Yuck. That was lame. Where's your trademark creativity?"

"Do you have a better one?"

I wiggle my eyebrows. "You know I do."

"Have at it, princess."

"If you teabag someone with a nut allergy, is it attempted murder?"

He starts laughing as he pulls me into his arms, his very hard dick sliding between my thighs. I wrap my legs around him, and he maneuvers us until my back is to the dock and his hands grip it, holding us in place.

He flashes his dimples before rubbing his nose along mine. "I adore you, Kam bam."

"I adore your stamina, kitten."

He rolls his hips until his tip runs through my wetness. "How about I show you my stamina right now?"

I pat up and down my bare waist and hips like I'm looking for something. "Ooh, sorry, but this outfit doesn't have pockets. No condom."

He kisses along my neck as his cock continues to move through me. "How about we go bare? The sun isn't out right now. Perhaps you could use a little boost of Vitamin D."

"Umm, no. Absolutely not. You could be a walking STD for all I know."

He chuckles. "I haven't been with anyone else since you moved to town."

I jerk my head back in surprise. "For real? Why not?"

He nods. "As soon as I met you, I stopped noticing others. It's kind of annoying, but no one stirs my dick, brain, and funny bone like you."

I shrug. "Too bad I can't say the same. Maybe I'm the one who isn't clean." I know I am, but I can't do this. I never have. It's too intimate.

He narrows his eyes at me. "Have you been with another man since the night of the *Sports Illustrated* party?"

I squeeze my eyes shut. I can't lie to him, not after all he's done for me over the past few days. With a long sigh, I open my eyes and admit, "I didn't go home with that guy. No man has buzzed the Brillo besides you since I moved to Philly. Only women and none since your birthday."

"What about—"

"None, Cruz."

His dimples come out in full force, and I roll my eyes. "Don't get all starry-eyed on me. It doesn't mean anything. I wasn't actively choosing not to go home with someone. None were of interest to me. If they were, I would have happily let them check my oil."

He raises one of his dark eyebrows. "Don't bullshit a bullshitter. It means everything. You're more into me than you're admitting, even to yourself."

I'm quiet. He's not wrong.

He swivels his hips again so his tip breaches my entrance. He moves it in and out a few times. Just the tip. No further.

He whispers. "Did you know that whales have the second largest dick in the ocean?"

Trying to pretend like his unsheathed tip isn't moving in and out of me, I respond, "No, they're not second, they're first."

He smiles. "Let me clarify. They're second when *I'm* swimming in the ocean."

I let out a small laugh before things take a serious turn. We simply stare at each other. His blue eyes are filled with so much emotion. This might be the most intimate moment of my life. I'm taking deep breaths, trying to remain calm.

His lips brush across mine before latching on. The kiss is soft and sweet with his tongue grazing across my inner lip, immediately relaxing me. When did his taste start to have a calming effect on my inner crazy?

I wrap my legs tighter around him and roll my hips forward, causing his dick to move further and further inside me. Oh fuck, that feels good. It's like I can feel every ridge and vein of him inside me.

He smiles into my mouth when he's eventually seated to the hilt. I can't help but let out a moan.

My breathing becomes labored to the point where I need to pull out of the kiss. But then I do what I should never do. I begin to think. My head starts spinning. What am I doing? I can't let this happen. It's too much.

I pull away and let him slip out of me before exhaling and dipping below the surface until I reach the bottom of the ocean floor.

We're in the bay, so it's only a few feet down, but I can feel the soft sand hit my feet. I don't want to go up and face him. I should never have let that happen.

Within seconds, I feel a big arm around my waist, pulling me up. I remain lifeless as I let him use his free arm to help us back up to the surface.

We're both breathless when we break through.

With labored breaths, I frantically say, "I'm sorry. I can't be with you like this. I'll suck your dick. Just give me a second."

He pulls me into a hug. "Relax. It's okay. I'm sorry I pushed. It's my fault."

"You didn't. I just...I can't. I'm not the person for you."

He's quiet for a moment before calmly saying, "It's been a long, emotional few days. Let's get some sleep."

I go to say something, but he simply gives me a soft kiss and then a small smile. "We're fine. Don't stress. I brought you here to put a smile on your face. That's my only plan for the next two days."

Why is this man so good to me? I don't deserve him. More importantly, he deserves someone so much better than me.

I look around. "Umm, I guess we don't have towels. Grammy Jane's neighborhood is about to get a view of the goods."

He motions his head back toward the house. "She keeps a bunch in a cabinet by the outdoor shower. I'll get out first and then shield you from any possible nosey neighbors as we walk back toward the house. Or I can run back and bring you a towel if you'd like."

I raise my eyebrow. "Do you honestly think I care if some old dude wants to get his kicks by seeing me naked?"

He smiles. "Well then, let's give them a show and dance our way to the shower."

And we do.

CHAPTER TWENTY

CHEETAH

I wake in the morning to the greatest sensation known to mankind. Without opening my eyes, I grab Kamryn's hair and feel her bob her head up and down between my legs. I croak out, "Hmm, Daylen, that feels good. No one does this better than you. Nothing like a big tight end sucking my cock in the morning."

I hear her giggle around me as she continues sucking the life out of me and tickling my balls until I explode into her mouth. Fuck, she sucks a good dick.

As she kisses her way back up my body, I blink my eyes open and smile at her naked body pressed to mine. "What did I do to deserve to wake up getting my love pump licked?"

She raises an unimpressed eyebrow. "Licked? I more than licked it. I sucked every ounce of the filling out of your Twinkie."

"I stand corrected. Thank you for swallowing down nature's breath mint with such vigor. Please come again soon."

She gives me a small smile before she bites her lip nervously and runs her hand over my chest. "Thanks for being so understanding last night. Sorry I was a crazy woman."

I run my hand down her sexy bare back before giving her equally sexy bare ass a little squeeze. "No apology needed. You know I dig your crazy, Kam bam. How about I take a turn and give you some moral support without the M?"

She lets out a laugh. "Maybe later. I can smell breakfast, and it's making my mouth water. It's probably why the blow job was so lubricated."

I act offended and gasp in horror. "What? I just gave you breakfast. Are you complaining about the food at this establishment?"

She shakes her head as her face turns more serious and tender than normal for her. "It's my favorite restaurant in the world, kitten."

We stare at each other as a rare moment of emotion passes between us. I think the past few days have her feeling vulnerable. In some ways, I think it's good for her to let her carefully constructed walls down for a bit, but I know Kamryn Hart. Laughter and silliness are her medicine. Today is about both of those, and I'll do everything in my power to make sure her face hurts from all the smiling and her belly hurts from all the laughter by the end of the day.

I feign disappointment and blow out a breath. "Fine. Should we go see if they need help buttering the morning biscuits?" I mumble, "Since you won't let me butter yours."

She nods. "Yep. I'm starving."

As we roll out of bed, I instruct, "Put on your bathing suit. The pool shenanigans start early at the geezer ghetto."

She lets out another laugh as we both dress in our bathing suits. I add a T-shirt, and Kam adds a sexy little sundress. She's going to give these old men a heart attack.

She lifts the back of her dress and takes in her skimpy bikini in the mirror before scrunching her face. "I thought it was just going to be you and me in Jamaica. I only have thongs. Too much?"

I shake my head. "Hell no. Thanks to you, they won't need Viagra today. The people here are hornier than you could ever imagine, and you're playing right into their fantasies. I'm telling you, they're a hoot. You'll love it. There's a reason I brought you here."

I grab her hand, and we walk out of the bedroom and into the kitchen area. Gemma is sitting on the counter next to the stove with Fletcher on her lap, both still in pajamas. Trey is at the stove flipping french toast while alternating between feeding Gemma and Fletcher fruit, followed by kisses to them both. Gemma and Fletcher are both giggling uncontrollably. They may be the cutest family ever created.

Fletcher is a true combination of his parents. He inherited Gemma's unique emerald-green eyes that she shares with Grammy Jane, but he otherwise looks like Trey with wavy dark hair and a chin dimple we used to love to make fun of.

I catch Kam staring at me staring at the DePauls. She releases my hand and exhales a long breath.

We hear Grammy Jane's voice. "Good morning, you two. I hope you slept well, and I hope you have a big appetite. Trey makes the absolute most divine french toast in existence."

Kam pinches her eyebrows together. "I didn't realize that Trey is a gourmet chef."

Trey shrugs. "Mostly just breakfast foods. My sister is a professional chef. She's taught me a few recipes throughout the years."

Gemma nods enthusiastically. "She's an amazing chef. She and her wife own a restaurant in Connecticut. It's the best food you can imagine."

Kam offers, "Can we do anything to help?"

Grammy Jane, who's sitting at the kitchen table with a mug of coffee, motions toward the chairs at the square, modern, dark gray stone table. "He doesn't like anyone besides Gemma in his kitchen. And he only lets her in to fondle her. He doesn't actually let her cook anything. *Thankfully*. There's fresh coffee in the pot. Have a seat and relax."

Gemma lets out a laugh. "Yep, he's all about the fondle."

I pour us two coffees, making Kamryn's just as she likes it, and we sit at the table. I ask, "What's today's theme at the pool?" I turn to Kam. "They always have themes. On the fifth of each month, it's always cinco de whatever month it is. There are margaritas and other Cinco de Mayo decor. On the last day of the month, it's always a New Year's Eve theme. On the twenty-fifth of each month, it's always Christmas. You get the point."

Kam smiles. "That's fun." She holds up her hand to Grammy Jane. "Don't tell me. I want to try to figure out what today could be. January second...hmm...what famous things happen on the second of a month." She's quiet for only a few seconds before she perks up. "Groundhog Day is the second of February."

Grammy Jane gives an impressed nod. "You got it. Since no one has a groundhog and the weather here doesn't get cold, it's morphed into the one day each month we're allowed to bring our pets to the pool."

Kamryn's face lights up, and I chuckle. "Now you're speaking Kam's language. She loves dogs."

Gemma asks, "Do you have a dog, Kam?"

She shakes her head. "No, I can't with our travel schedule. The second I retire, it's the first thing I'm doing. I want, like, ten dogs."

Gemma smiles. "Did you have one growing up?"

Kam's face immediately falls. "For a few weeks until my

mother killed him. One of the millions of reasons she's currently suffering eternal damnation in the fiery pits of hell."

Well...that's an oxygen sucker.

Everyone is silent as Kam stares off into space. She shakes her head. "I didn't grow up with Christmases like you all. My house wasn't full of happiness and cheer. My sister and I weren't showered with love and gifts. Honestly, being with Cheetah's family last week was the best Christmas I've ever had."

I see concerned looks spread across both Gemma and Grammy Jane's faces.

Kam continues. "But one year, I think my father felt particularly bad. It was the year my mother's alcoholism hit new heights. I won't bore you with the details of the things she'd do when she was trashed, but it was extreme. Worse than you can imagine." She cracks a small smile. "On Christmas morning, I was awakened by a lick across my face. I opened my eyes, and the cutest golden retriever puppy was sitting on me. I named him Gilmore after the show *Gilmore Girls,* which my sister and I were obsessed with at the time. We called him Gilly. We had a very small backyard, but it was fenced in. I came home from school every day at lunchtime to let him out. One day, I had detention, and Bailey had a teacher meeting. We asked my mother to let him out that one time. *One* time." Tears fill her eyes. "She was blitzed and mistakenly let him out the front door instead of the back. A car hit him, and he died immediately."

Gemma and I exchange looks. She knows I brought Kam here to brighten this difficult week.

Gemma slides down from the counter and hands Fletcher off to Grammy Jane before rubbing Kam's back. "I'm so sorry, Kamryn. That must have been devastating for you."

Kam wordlessly nods, in another world right now. She then shakes her head a few times. "Shit. Sorry to put a damper on the morning. I haven't thought about that day in a while." She cracks a smile. "One day I'll get my dog. Anyway, I'm excited for this french toast, Trey. Did you know that french toast didn't even originate in France?"

Trey shakes his head. "I didn't."

She nods. "It was ancient Rome. And it was how they found a use for stale bread. Instead of throwing it out, they soaked it in eggs and butter to soften it. It was served as a dessert with honey and sugar. It was called something else. It only evolved into french toast when it came to America, and that's because it's made like other French dishes."

Grammy Jane asks, "How did you know that?"

Kam gives her a mischievous smile. "I'm a wealth of useless information. Ask Cheetah. He knows."

I nod. "True. It's endless." I wink at Grammy Jane. "Kam told me that over sixty percent of seniors are still sexually active."

Grammy Jane grabs right onto the easy setup I gave her. "In this community, it's one hundred percent. Proud of it."

I chuckle while Kam asks, "Is it all senior citizens in this community?"

Grammy Jane answers, "Not all, but most."

Kam questions, "How often do you make it up to Philly?"

Grammy Jane scrunches her face. "Not too often. I don't go anywhere that the temperature is less than my age, which somehow manages to go up every damn year. I only visit in the summer. I watch a few of Trey's games and usually get in a dance with Cheetah." She blows me a kiss.

I nod. "Ooh, you can certainly move, old girl, but now you're my number two favorite dance partner."

I've got a new number one girl, and her name is Kamryn Hart.

KAMRYN

I'm folded over, belly laughing. Grammy Jane and her friends are officially the funniest people on the planet.

We're sitting at the pool with Grammy Jane, her much younger boyfriend, Marvin, married couple Millie and Mortimer, both well into their eighties, and a hilarious woman named Happy. Happy's boyfriend, Samuel, had to go home for a nap after drinking too much too quickly. She told him not to spank the monkey when he got home, and then, in what was possibly the biggest overshare of all time, whispered to me that he can only come once a day, and she wants him to save it for her.

I'm madly in love with these people. Now I know why Cheetah loves it here. And there are so many dogs. As terrible as I am with kids, that's how good I am with dogs. I think it's because I'm allowed to curse in front of them. Every single dog here has spent time on my lap today, regardless of size. It's like I died and went to dog heaven.

Grammy Jane looks exactly like what Gemma will look like in fifty years. They share the same gorgeous green eyes and darker hair, though Grammy Jane's is mostly gray now. Happy has a gray bob, Millie has a dark bun that she likely colors, and Mortimer is bald with a belly that Millie loves to rub.

We're all at least three or four drinks in while the music plays, dogs run free, and everyone is having a great time. It's one big party, and apparently they do it every day. I sort of want to live here.

They're talking about a man Happy used to date, who she says was good in the sack but not otherwise very good for her. Grammy Jane has not hidden her contempt for him and said, "He was a Floridiot. Just because it's good for your hole doesn't mean it's good for your soul."

Cheetah and I spit our drinks in laughter. Gemma smiles as she rolls her eyes. "Grammy Jane, you are truly one of a kind." She turns to me. "I swear, half the one-liners in my books come from her." She pulls out her phone and starts typing. "In fact, that line will slot nicely into my next book. As will her made-up word, Floridiot, which happens to accurately describe a lot of people down here." She lifts her eyes until they meet mine. "Grammy Jane gets the biggest kick out of seeing her lines in my books. I think she plans out when to drop them on me to best ensure they'll be used."

"Your grandmother reads your books?" I ask in complete shock. I haven't read them, but my sister is obsessed with her books and has shared that there are a lot of dirty scenes. I know Cheetah has read all of them too.

He nods. "I can totally tell which lines are yours when I read the books, Grammy Jane. You have a brilliant, dirty mind. I want to be like you when I grow up."

She smiles and winks at him.

Just then, a man who must be younger than this group by at least twenty years comes by. He's got a full head of dark, perfectly combed hair. He places his hands on Grammy Jane's shoulders and smiles. "How are the cool kids doing on this beautiful day?"

Without giving it a second thought, Grammy Jane removes his hands. "Jack, we've discussed this. You should only touch a woman when invited."

"I'm just waiting for you to invite me to sit with you."

She waves her hand like she's shooing him away. "That's not likely to happen. Move along."

His shoulders fall, and he walks away while Gemma's eyes widen. "What the hell? That was so rude, Grammy Jane. That's not like you at all."

Grammy Jane scrunches her face. "I don't like him. He's a

creep. I've asked him for years to stop touching me. A woman, even one as flexible as me, can only bend so far before she breaks."

Happy nods enthusiastically. "He's been hitting on Jane for years. Won't take no for an answer. And he truly does always find ways to touch her." She makes a look of disgust.

I get that. It drives me nuts too. Why do men think they can do that?

Grammy Jane shrugs. "What can I say? I'm a magnet for younger men."

Marvin places his arm around her shoulders. "Beautiful women attract men of all ages. None more beautiful than you." He kisses her cheek. So cute.

Grammy Jane smiles. "I don't need much at my age, but I do need a gentleman. Being one isn't that hard. Hold her hand while you're out, and hold her hair while you're in."

Our whole table erupts in laughter. I think Grammy Jane is secretly my grandmother. At least I wish she was.

Gemma happily types away on her phone. "That one is going in a book too. I don't know where you come up with this shit. There's no one else like you in the world, though Christian had a bunch of one-liners for me this week."

I ask, "Who's Christian?"

Happy throws her shoulders back and proudly replies, "My grandson, the bisexual."

I smile. "I'm bisexual too, Happy."

She claps her hands together and gasps. "How exciting. I have questions. Christian rolls his eyes at me when I try to ask anything. He told me a few years ago that he's bisexual. Jane had to explain to me what it was. Now he says pansexual. What's the difference? They sound the same to me."

I let out a giggle. "They're similar. Pansexual is like bisexual but less horny."

Gemma shakes her head at me in disapproval. "Oh, stop it. That's not true. You'll confuse her even more. I've been trying to educate them for years." She looks at Happy. "Bisexual is when you're attracted to both men and women. Pansexual is when you don't see gender. You're attracted to the person."

Happy sits there dumbfounded. "Still don't see the difference."

I nod. "Yep, my definition is much easier to understand."

"Yet wrong," Gemma corrects. "I love that Happy is supportive and wants to understand Christian's sexuality, but let's give her real facts. While I appreciate that older generations are confused by some relatively newer terminology, it's our job to help educate them, not make light of it. I feel very strongly about this. How will we progress as a society without giving real facts?"

I suppose she's right. I get annoyed when people misunderstand my sexuality, yet I only add to that by cracking jokes and giving misinformation. Nodding at her, I say, "You're absolutely right." I turn back to Happy. "I do see gender, but I'm physically attracted to both men and women."

Millie asks, "How do you know who to marry, Kamryn?"

I answer, "Not everyone wants to get married, but it's no different from you. You had all these men to choose from, and you chose Mortimer."

Mortimer nods. "Damn straight she did. I'm the luckiest man alive. I don't know how this beautiful woman picked me from the long line of suitors. I practically had to beat them all away with a stick."

Millie rubs his arm lovingly. The cuteness is almost unbearable.

I continue, "You had all these men interested in you, your long line of suitors, and you chose one. You no longer consider other men. A bisexual person just has a bigger pool of candidates, both men and women, but it doesn't mean he or she can't choose one to spend his or her life with. If that's what they want."

Happy contemplates my words. "Sounds good. As long as he's happy, I'm happy." She hiccups and giggles. "Happy is happy." She then starts giggling uncontrollably.

Happy is trashed. That's what Happy is.

Suddenly I'm taken back in time to fourteen years earlier. I wish my mother had felt like Happy when I told my parents that I'm bisexual. My mother berated me and tried to shame me. Support from my father and Bailey got me through that first year when I was fifteen. I know Bailey lost any lingering feelings of affection for our mother when she treated me the way she did when I came out. I know that's why Bailey thinks I hate her so much. While it's one of the many reasons, the night at the studio remains the day I stopped seeing Beverly Hart as my mother.

My mind drifts back to the first and only time I walked into our house with Dakota. My mother immediately kicked her out. She started quoting the Bible and acting belligerent. It was one big nightmare, one that caused me to never again bring a friend or anyone else into our home.

Parents and grandparents should support their kids no matter what. I hope Christian knows how lucky he is to have a grandmother like Happy.

Happy rubs my arm. "You know, Kamryn, when I was your age, I was quite the sexpot. My maiden name is Silver. They called me Swivel Hips Silver for a reason."

She starts thrusting her hips uncontrollably until Grammy Jane grabs her arm. "Stop all the thrusting. Do I have to remind you about what you and Samuel were up to on the seventeenth hole of the golf course last year? You'll break your hip again."

Happy leans over and whispers in my ear, "It was totally worth it if you know what I mean."

AFTER ONE OF the best days of my life, we head back to the house to shower for dinner. I'm so thankful to Cruz for bringing me here and giving me the day full of laughter and joy that I desperately needed.

So much so, that we have amazing sex in the shower. He loves shower sex, and I happily indulge him whenever I can. I love how strong he is. I'm not a huge woman, but I'm not small, and I have muscles. Not every man can lift me and fuck me against a wall like he can.

I've never had sex with one person as much as I've had sex with him. I get lost in the familiarity and pleasure at times. It terrifies me.

We're both now in towels, standing in front of the vanity as I brush my wet hair and then apply my face lotion. As I pick up my body lotion, his eyes meet mine in the mirror, and he asks, "Can I rub that on your body for you?"

My face scrunches in disgust. "What? That's serial killer weird. Why?"

"Because I fucking love the way you smell. It's something between a peach and a tropical flower. I've never smelled anything like it. It's so damn good."

I hold up the bottle as he reads the scent aloud, "Tropical Peach. Well, my sniffing abilities are top-notch."

"I originally bought it because it's basically an oxymoron. No peaches can grow in the tropics. They need a dry climate. There's no such thing as a tropical peach. That's why this is the only company that makes this scent. Whoever came up with the name lies somewhere between idiot and innovator, therefore it amuses me."

"Whatever, brainiac. It's fucking hot. I love it. I want to rub it all over your body. Hell, I want to rub it all over mine."

Handing it to him, I say, "Knock your socks off, killer."

He smiles as he lifts me onto the vanity and pulls open my towel, leaving me naked and exposed. He squirts a healthy amount onto his palm and rubs his hands together, spreading the lotion all over them. "I don't want it to be too cold for you."

I bite back my smile. "I'll be okay."

He bends and rubs my lotion over every square inch of one leg and then the other with extreme precision. Kneading it into my skin. His thumbs and fingers press into my muscles, soothing them. It's like a massage.

Taking his time, he leaves no inch of my legs untouched. It's much more sensual than I would have expected.

He then does the same to my arms before landing on my body and breasts. This is shockingly nice and extremely erotic. I could let him do this to me all day long.

He's savoring it as much as I am. We just had sex, yet I can see by the large tent in his towel that he's hard again.

"A little lotion turns you on, kitten."

"*You* turn me on." He brings his hand to his nose and inhales deeply. "And your smell. Fuck, now my cock is leaking." I think I'm leaking too.

"I'll need visual confirmation," I challenge.

He immediately and happily rips off his towel. His cock is, in fact, leaking. Rivulets of water drip down his chest while his giant cock, oozing pre-ejaculate, is staring right at me. He's so hot.

My eyes roam his body until they land between his legs. "It's a good thing you don't have to lotion your balls. You'd go through a bottle a day."

He chuckles, though he doesn't break stride as he continues to rub the lotion into my breasts, which are now more than adequately moisturized.

I wrap my legs around his waist and my arms around his neck before softly kissing his lips. "Thanks for today. It was just what I needed."

His handsome face lights up. "I'm glad. I brought you here to see how these people live their best lives. Some have lost spouses, some have lost children, and I'm sure there are countless other losses and other life downturns they've dealt with in their seventy-plus years of life, yet they wake up every morning and do nothing but have the best time. There's something inspiring about it, don't you think?"

I nod as I consider his words. "There is."

He tucks a strand of my hair behind my ear. "You can't

change the past, especially the things that were never in your control. You can control your future though. You can choose to move forward and appreciate life like they do."

I swallow down the large knot forming in my throat. "I can try. I'm sorry we missed out on our full stay in Jamaica, but I'm kind of happy we ended up here."

What I don't say out loud is that I think I'd be happy anywhere as long as I'm with him.

CHAPTER TWENTY-ONE

KAMRYN

"Honey, I'm home," I shout as I walk into our apartment.

Bailey sprints from the kitchen and jumps into my waiting arms, wrapping herself around me like a monkey. "I missed you, little sis."

I squeeze her tight. "Daddy Tanner wasn't fulfilling you?"

She places her feet back on the ground and gives me an uncharacteristically spicy smile. "He more than fills me."

"How about some details?"

"Nope." She pops the P. "Not happening."

So weird that she won't tell me anything.

She randomly starts searching my body. She lifts the bottom of my sweater and inspects my bare stomach and back. She then pulls up my sleeves to continue her meticulous inspection.

"What are you looking for? I didn't smuggle any diamonds if that's what you're after."

"I thought for sure that your first time away from me, you'd get a tattoo."

"Ha! I only say that I want one sometimes to fuck with you.

In the words of the super famous attorney, Kim Kardashian, *you don't put a bumper sticker on a Bentley.*"

Bailey giggles. "That's a good one. Wait, she's an attorney?"

I nod. "Allegedly. She takes time out of her busy spray tanning and club-promoting schedule to help a few prisoners now and then. I don't believe she passed the bar though. No way."

"Truth." She rubs my back as her face softens. "I understand why you left right after the funeral. I'm really proud of you for being there. Thanks for coming."

I do my best to act unaffected. "I just wanted to make sure she's truly worm food. Her soul is burning for all of eternity, but her body has already begun the decomposition process. Her teeth and nails will rot as her cells begin to liquefy—"

She holds up her hands. "Enough. I get it."

I let out a laugh as she continues, "Well, Daddy and I appreciated the effort. He's visiting soon. He said he needs to talk to us."

"Good. Maybe he'll visit more often now that the witch is gone."

"Maybe."

I look at the mess in our kitchen. There are dirty bowls everywhere. "What in the world are you up to?"

"I'm making a cake for Harper's laser tag birthday party this weekend. She loves my baking skills and begged me to make one for her."

"How old is she turning, thirty?" Harper is arguably more intelligent than any adult I know.

"Eight."

My chin drops. "Seriously? She's only eight? That's nuts. Can I come to the party?"

She raises an eyebrow. "You want to come to an eight-year-old birthday party? You hate kids."

"I'm awesome at laser tag though. Those little bitches won't see me coming."

She giggles. "Your maturity matches theirs. Arizona will be

back in town from LA tomorrow." She was there for some promotional thing. "She's coming too. And Tanner's father will be there. I'm looking forward to meeting him."

"The OG Daddy Tanner? The Mac Zaddy Daddy? Now I'm definitely coming."

Her face falls. "You need to behave around the children."

I smile. "No problem, big sis."

I HAD a blast at Harper's party today. I crushed all the kids at laser tag, winning every round until Bailey pulled me away and wouldn't let me participate anymore.

Tanner's father, who I happily called Daddy Stanley all day, is a flat-out handsy deviant. Between him and Grammy Jane, I have a new appreciation for that generation. They certainly put the boom in baby boomers. How did I not know that all old people are horny?

While Tanner and his ex-wife, Fallon, got along well, Daddy Stanley and Fallon's parents most definitely did not. They were fighting for the whole party. I even had to protect my new bestie, Daddy Stanley, a few times. Mostly because they were making comments about Bailey and Tanner's *inappropriate* relationship. No one trashes my sister and gets away with it.

Bailey was blissfully unaware, and that's how it will stay. She was too busy playing Mary Poppins to all the kids. It's truly amazing how good she is with them. I hope she has ten kids one day. Then I'll fulfill my destiny of being the fun aunt. Hopefully one who's in better shape than Aunt Maria.

In good news, Arizona shocked us all by telling us that she and Layton secretly got married a few weeks ago. They're planning a big reception later this year, but they eloped last month. I can't believe they're married. They've only known each other for six months.

Ripley greeted Arizona at the airport to fill her in about the baby and Ripley's moving back to California. Arizona was shocked, as were all of us. She's been trying to get in touch with Quincy, but he's still off the grid. No one knows where he is or what he's doing. He has to report to Spring Training next month, so I imagine things will come to a head then, but as expected, Arizona supported Ripley wholeheartedly. They have a sisterly bond that nothing and no one will ever break.

We're all going out to Screwballs tonight to celebrate Arizona and Layton. Even Vance and Daylen are coming. They prefer clubs to the more laid back Screwballs, but they're making an exception for Layton and Arizona.

We eventually make our way to the bar. Everyone has arrived except for Daylen. He walks in last, and all the guys start catcalling him. His face falls. "Shit, I don't play your stupid game. I don't spend my nights jerking off on Google searching for random facts like you guys do."

Layton smiles as he shakes his head. "You're on our turf now. You've got to play by our rules. Give us something. There must be a few random facts floating around that giant head of yours."

He scratches his messy blond hair as he sits down and takes up half the booth. Fucking hell, Daylen is a big man.

His face lights up like something has occurred to him. "What two things in the air get a woman pregnant?"

Like a nerd, I start thinking of specific scents and things along those lines.

After downing an entire beer in one gulp, Daylen smirks and answers, "Their legs."

We all laugh. Typical Daylen joke. That's not exactly a fun fact, but it's Daylen, and no one seems to mind.

I wasn't sure how Cheetah would act with me. We're obviously casual, but we spent every second together for nearly two weeks. An *intense* two weeks.

He grinned when he saw me and immediately sat next to me

before softly kissing my lips and telling me how much he missed me.

The truth is that I've missed him too. It's only been a few days, but I got very used to spending all my time with him. We start our dance lessons next week, so I know we'll be together at least twice a week for that.

At some point, he leans over and whispers, "Want to come over and eat what my mom made."

I gasp. "Mamá sent food? What did she make?"

"Me."

I giggle. I should have known where that question was headed. "Sure. I've been dieting all week. You can be my cheat meat."

His dimples make an appearance as he threads his fingers through mine. "Perfect."

Our attention turns back to Arizona and Layton as the drinks arrive. Cheetah asks everyone to hold up their glasses. "Let's toast Arizona and Layton." He looks at Layton. "Not everyone can say they have a loyal, trustworthy, talented, smart, and handsome best friend. But you, Layton Lancaster...can say that about me."

We all laugh as he smiles and continues, "Layton, they say you should never meet your heroes, but you met me roughly ten years ago."

After the laughter again subsides, Cheetah pulls a note from his pocket. "There's a special person who isn't here today." He must mean Quincy. "I have a note though." He unfolds it. *"Layton, thank you for the years of support and love. I'm sorry I can't be there, but I'm thinking of you. With love, Crystal from the Viper Den."*

The guys all burst into hysterics. I suppose stripper jokes are always funny. I imagine there's a good story or two there.

Cheetah's eyes move between Layton and Arizona. "In all seriousness, I knew the second Layton met Arizona that he was a done deal. He was immediately besotted with the blonde beauty. So besotted that Trey and I had to delay a few games because

Layton would sport wood in the middle of an inning after looking at Arizona eating a hot dog." He wiggles his eyebrows. "Admittedly, it was hot. I may have had a little wood too."

Arizona appears confused, but I see Layton and Trey hiding their smiles. I think that may have happened.

"Some might say your union is quick, but when you told me months ago that you bought a ring, I wasn't surprised. She's clearly your other half. *Definitely* the better half, but you two couldn't possibly be more perfect together. I'm not a married man, but in doing *extensive* research on the topic," he mumbles, "in the cab on the way here," he winks, "I've found that there are two things you should be mindful of as you begin your journey. One: if at first you don't succeed, try doing it the way your wife told you. Two: never stop laughing. Arizona, I know Layton makes lame jokes, but always laugh together, not apart." He holds up his beer. "Cheers to the happy couple."

We all clink our glasses, but I feel like someone should speak on behalf of Arizona. While I know Ripley is her best friend, she's not here tonight, so I'll step up. I re-raise my mug. "I'd like to say a few short words. Arizona and Layton, please look at each other in the eyes." They do, with dreamy looks on their faces. "Know that the person you're staring at right now is the person who is statistically most likely to be your murderer."

They smile into each other's lips as they meet for a sweet kiss.

"We all know that Arizona had a poster of Layton on her ceiling as a kid. Wow, how incredibly special and romantic is it to end up marrying the man who you undoubtedly surfed the slit to countless times as a horny teen?"

Arizona giggles and mumbles, "Truth."

"Layton, you're a lucky man. Arizona is one of a kind, and you two have a seamless love. Just remember, love is like a fart. If you have to force it, it's probably shit. The good thing about you two is that nothing is forced at all. You're as natural as Arizona's blonde hair. Don't worry, I've seen her naked countless times. I promise the curtains match the drapes."

Everyone laughs. Cheetah whispers, "Fuck, that's so hot."

I elbow him and mouth back, "Pervert."

He nods. "Takes one to know one."

I wink at him before continuing. "I know you two are the real deal. At a minimum, you'll make it to your reception in a few months, but more likely, it will last forever. I love you both. Wishing you a lifetime of blinding happiness and explosive orgasms. Cheers."

Everyone clinks their glasses, and we spend a fun night celebrating our friends.

CHEETAH

"You're in love with her."

I turn to Gemma at the lunch table and exhale a long breath. "I am."

She grabs my hand as tears fill her eyes. "I'm so happy for you. No one deserves their happily ever after more than you."

I shake my head. "I don't think that's what I'm getting with her. She continues to say that we're casual. Hell, she encourages me to sleep with other women. She claims she'll never want more with me or anyone. I feel like I'm always waiting for the other shoe to drop. Why am I doing this to myself?"

Gemma considers my words. "I think she loves you too. Maybe she doesn't realize it, but I see it in the way she looks at you."

"This isn't a romance book, Gem. It's real life. We're not going to gaze lovingly at each other and all our shit melts away. She's got some real issues. I gave her the name of the therapist you emailed me, but she tossed it aside and took offense that I thought something was wrong with her. She's kind of a dichotomy. She purposefully acts crazy but fears people thinking of her as crazy."

She nods. "It's a self-defense mechanism."

I sigh. "This is all new for me. Sometimes I'm not sure if I'm giving her what she needs. I'm pathetically thirty and have never had a real girlfriend. Not one I truly cared about."

"I think you handle her beautifully. We had some tension that first morning but then you made her happy all afternoon. You guys were very loved up at dinner and the following day."

I twist my lips. "I suppose. We were in a bubble though. Now that we're home, it's back to keeping me at arm's length. I have no experience and certainly no success with this. I don't know what to do. She's basically my first non-Twitter Bang."

"What's a Twitter Bang?" she asks.

"Having sex with someone before the two of you have exchanged a hundred and forty words."

Gemma bursts out laughing and then starts typing on her phone. "Love it. I'm using that." She places her phone back on the table and looks at me. "Does anyone have success until they find *the one*? I had zero relationship success until Trey. They were all a bunch of disasters on varying levels. I was about your age when Trey and I got together."

I run my fingers through my hair. "I'm nervous, Gem. I think I'm going to get hurt. It's like I know what's coming, but I can't seem to help myself. Maybe I need to hold back a little for my own sanity."

She rubs my back. "If you protect your heart, you can never truly give it away."

I raise my eyebrow. "That was very romance book author of you."

She giggles. "I suppose. You know I'm a romantic at heart."

"I don't think I know how to be romantic."

Her mouth widens. "Are you crazy? I think you setting up those dance classes because she always wanted to do that as a kid is one of the most romantic things I've ever heard in my life."

"Really? I never thought of it that way. I just remembered her saying that once."

"What do you think romance is, Cruz? Understanding the needs of your partner and giving it to them is the very definition."

"I do it because it makes me happy to make her happy."

She clutches her heart. "So fucking sweet. I'm swooning. I'm sure she is too."

I shake my head. "I don't think so."

"Maybe it's time to be an adult and have an adult conversation with her. About what you are right now. Not what you were when you started."

She's not wrong.

The problem is, I'm afraid of the answer.

CHAPTER TWENTY-TWO

CHEETAH

It turns out that I can't get through dance classes with Kamryn without massive boners taking form. Wearing sweatpants for the first lesson was a colossal and embarrassing mistake. I've worn tight jeans since, which hold him at bay but happen to be incredibly painful for me.

Kam, on the other hand, is wildly amused by it and finds subtle ways to touch him when the teacher isn't looking or does other things she knows will drive me crazy. She wears spandex shorts, tight midriff-baring tank tops, and high heels. Her shapely legs look a mile long. How is a man expected to function with Miss Sex on a Stick grinding up against him for an hour? The struggle is real.

That being said, we've been having an absolute blast. In addition to our normal dose of laughs, we basically rub up against each other for an hour and then hurry out to head to my place for more amazing sex. We're both so worked up by the time we finish the lesson that we barely make it through the front door. Poor Evan has seen more than he bargained for. And our instructor is undoubtedly scarred for life.

Kam doesn't care though. She never does. Fuck, I love that about her.

She's getting good at dancing. She's a natural athlete with a great work ethic. I know she's practicing in between sessions. It shows. While the ballroom dances are fun, it's the Latin dances we love. I can't wait to do one in front of our entire stadium this summer. Their minds will be blown. We decided to wait until mid-summer, just ahead of her season. It will be good PR for the Anacondas.

Our instructor, Ms. Rylee, claps her hands at us. "Focus, you two. We're almost done. Then you can do...whatever it is you two do when you leave here. Hold your posture, Kamryn." Kam immediately straightens her back. "Step back with your right foot for the salsa, but then only shift your weight to your left, don't step." Kam has been messing that up all night. It's very unlike her.

I whisper, "Is something wrong?"

She shakes her head. "No, my dad is in the air on the way here right now. You know how much I hate airplanes. I'm nervous. I'll feel better when he lands."

"He's fine, babe. I forgot he was coming tonight." I look down at my cock straining against my jeans. I guess he isn't getting taken care of after this session.

As if reading my mind, her lips curl in amusement. "Don't worry. I have time to take care of that before he arrives. Bailey is picking him up at the airport."

I let out a groan. "Thank god."

"She put me in charge of dinner."

I raise an eyebrow. I wouldn't trust Kam to make a piece of toast, let alone an entire dinner.

She smiles. "I already ordered Chinese food to be delivered at the time they're expected home. It gives us a little under an hour for you to make me come at least twice."

I salute her. "Yes, ma'am. Ladies first. Always."

She whispers in my ear. "By the way, I'm wearing a butt plug right now."

My eyes widen as I look behind her back as if I could see it. I run my hand down the middle of her ass. Sure enough, there's something hard there.

I breathe, "Holy shit."

She nods and whispers, "I only wore it to fuck with you, but it's making my clit throb. I need you to place your thigh between my legs. I'm so worked up. I might be able to come from it."

The problem is that the salsa doesn't call for that. It's a sensual dance, but not the most sensual one we've done.

"Focus, Kamryn." We snap our heads to Ms. Rylee as she barks out the order. "We're almost done." She's very clearly at her wit's end with us tonight.

I can't worry about her though. I've got an erection that feels like the product of the Luminous Lagoon.

I swallow, willing my dick not to break through my jeans. I turn to the instructor and give her my often panty-melting smile. "Ms. Rylee, can we return to last week's Bachata? I think that's our favorite dance, and we want to perfect it."

She narrows her eyes at me, and I can feel Kam silently laugh. The Bachata is the most sensual dance and calls for my thigh to be between her legs at times.

Ms. Rylee taps her lip. "Very well. If that's what you want."

When she turns to change the music, I grab Kam into the Bachata frame and push my leg between her thighs. She lets out a small moan as her eyes flutter.

She breathes, "Yes, that could do it for me. Just rub a little."

I want her to come from this so badly. An orgasm mid-dance? How fucking hot would that be?

Moving my leg as much as I reasonably can, I sway our hips together but grind my leg between hers. Her grip on me immediately tightens.

The music begins playing. The Bachata is a very side-to-side dance, so I continue to sway us. Unfortunately, there are turns, and Kam practically snarls each time I have to remove my leg from between hers to turn her.

I don't know how, but she stays in the movements. Her hips are doing an extra sway, but I think that's more about gaining the friction than anything else.

"*Very* good, Kamryn," we hear Ms. Rylee say. "Your hips look excellent in this dance. It's like making love on the dance floor."

Something like that.

After the next turn, I push my thigh even harder to her pussy. She moans out, "Oh god, don't pull away again. Rub me. I'm almost there."

I manage to discreetly twirl and then pull a lock of her hair before whispering into her ear, "Puedo sentir tu humedad en mi muslo. Me encanta hacer bailar tu coño para mí. Córrete. Ahora." *I can feel your wetness on my thigh. I love making your pussy dance for me. Come. Now.*

She sinks her teeth into my neck and bites down hard as her body shakes. I can feel her fluids seep through my jeans and onto my thigh.

Oh fuck. The whole scene is too hot, and I'm too turned on. Feeling her come on my leg is my tipping point. My spine starts tingling, and I come too. In my fucking pants.

I'm in shock. I've never done that as an adult. A teen? Yes. Adult? No. This woman drives me crazy.

We're both panting, a little out of it. I think I blacked out for a second or two. The same goes for Kam.

As her eyes blink open, she looks down at the now-saturated crotch of my pants. Her lips curl in amusement.

A throat clearing brings us back to the present. We look at Ms. Rylee. Turns out we weren't as discreet as I thought. Her fingers are rubbing her temples. "Get the fuck out of here. Both of you."

Twenty minutes later, we're crashing through Kam's apartment door with our lips locked. I think I saw the weird ginger neighbor scowling at me when Kam and I got off the elevator with her wrapped around me. I swear he's going to kill me in my sleep one night.

I place her down on the kitchen table, and she breaks the kiss. "I'm going to be eating here with my father in less than an hour."

"Be sure to think of me when you do. I'm not fucking you on that waterbed. I have PTSD from that thing."

She giggles as she removes her tight top and her tits fall free.

"Fuuuuck. You weren't wearing a bra all night?"

She shakes her head. "Nope. I can't believe you didn't notice. You usually have a radar for that. I kept waiting."

Huh. That's very unlike me. I must be slipping. I've been very focused on her legs lately. When she's in small spandex shorts and those heels, it's her legs that make my dick hard. I imagine them wrapped around my body, my face, anywhere.

And then there was the butt plug. How was I supposed to focus on her tits with that going on?

By the time my daydreaming is over, she's completely naked. Fuck, she's so sexy. Her tropical peach smell is invading my senses. I have to squeeze my dick for a little relief. Yep, he was hard again before we left the studio.

Without another thought, I flip her around so she's bent over the table with that luscious ass in the air. I fall to my knees and see the end of the butt plug staring at me. Holy hell.

I bury my face in her ass, running my tongue over and around the plug. She wiggles her ass in delight.

Put simply, Kam loves ass play. I've never been with a woman so open and exploratory with it. She lets me do anything I want and always gets off on it. It's so fucking hot.

I slowly slide my tongue down her slit until I reach her clit. It's completely swollen and practically pulsating. Her juices cover my face. All women should walk around with butt plugs. It's like a direct line to their clits. It certainly makes my job easy.

Slipping my fingers inside her, I curl them into the spot I've come to know like the back of my own hand. I've gone down on her quite a lot since Christmas. If we don't see each other on a given day, I always make up for it by muff diving multiple times the next.

With my fingers still applying pressure inside her, I flick my tongue over her sensitive bundle over and over.

She's yelling and cursing. She's going to come in less than a minute. Maybe the fastest I've ever gotten her there.

As soon as I apply some pressure to her butt plug, she screams out, "Oh fuck, Cruz. Yessssss."

She grips the table as her entire body convulses into one of the most explosive orgasms I've ever seen or felt. My face and fingers are gloriously drenched in her fluids.

I stand, and she lies there lifelessly. She breathes out, "Give me a second. I have no feeling in any of my limbs."

I chuckle. "That's how I like you. Just spread your legs and lift that pretty ass in the air. I'll take care of the rest."

Kam doesn't like to be a passive bystander in our sex life. She gives as much as she takes. She gets off on my pleasure, just like I get off on hers. But she's come twice in the last thirty minutes. I think she's spent.

I pull my dick out, sheath myself in a condom, and slam into her hard and deep. She lets out a loud scream of pleasure.

"Hold onto the end of that table like your life depends on it."

She immediately obliges, reaching for and then tightening her grip on the far end of her kitchen table.

I then push her legs together and spread my legs wide. I love the added tightness of doing that, and she loves it when I do different things to her.

Running my fingers up the back of her hair, I grab as much as I can, as hard as I can. It forces her body to arch up. She gets off on a hard hair pull.

I know we only have a few more minutes before the food, her father, and Bailey arrive. "This is going to be fast. I've been dying for you. My cock is engorged. I might not be sitting in nature's Viagra, but you make me so fucking hard, Kam bam. So. Fucking. Hard."

She grits out, "Give it to me. Joderme." *Fuck me.* "I want it all."

With one hand in her hair and the other gripping her hip with bruising strength, I fuck her like a man possessed. I don't think my cock has ever been this ravenous. She must feel every full vein in me begging for release.

"Me encanta ver ese tapón en tu culo. La próxima vez voy a follarlo." *I love seeing that plug in your ass. Next time I'm going to fuck it.*

"Oh god. Yes. Yes!"

I move my hand from her hip to her plug and apply pressure to it.

She screams at the top of her lungs. "Fuck! Yes!"

After just a few more thrusts, we both come violently and *very* loudly. The whole building might have heard our joint moans of ecstasy.

My body shakes uncontrollably at the impact of the

orgasm. Hers does too. She whimpers as she comes down from the orgasm high.

It's silent except for our mutual loud breathing. I'm sweating through my clothes. I need to go home and shower.

After pulling out, I slowly remove the plug and toss it into the sink. "Do you make butt plug stew in addition to dildo stew?"

She giggles. "It's my second-best recipe."

KAMRYN

Cheetah is in the bathroom disposing of the condom while I slip back into my clothes after the mind-altering sex we just had. The whole evening was incredible, from dancing with a butt plug in, to the mid-dance orgasm, to him fucking me blind on my kitchen table. I don't think it gets better than this.

I take a deep inhale. Shit, I need to spray something in here. It reeks of sex.

As I'm searching for some Febreze, there's a loud knock at the door. It's more of a banging than a knock.

I have a moment of panic that it's my father and Bailey until I realize that they wouldn't knock. It must be the food.

I open the door to see a scowling Justin. What's his problem? "Hey. I'm a little busy. What's up?"

He hands me a big plastic bag. "Your Chinese food was delivered to my apartment because the delivery man thought someone was being murdered in yours. Is everything okay?"

I inwardly laugh before I simply smile and reply, "Yes, Justin. Cruz was fucking me. That's what it's supposed to sound like when a woman is being fucked properly."

He chokes on his saliva. Sometimes it's truly fun to shock people with brutal honesty.

I hold up the bag. "Thanks for delivering it. Catch you later."

I close the door just as Cheetah reemerges. He's tucking in his shirt. "Who was that?"

"The ginger delivering my food since our noises of ecstasy scared away the delivery man."

"Should I not fuck you as well next time?"

I twist my lips. "Hmm, no. Keep up the good work. I mean that both literally and figuratively." I nod toward the door. "You should head out. They'll be back any minute, and I have a few things to sanitize."

He stands there for a moment. I think he wants me to ask him to stay. There's no chance of that happening.

He shuffles nervously on his feet. "Will I see you tomorrow night?"

I shake my head. "No. We're having dinner at Daddy Tanner's. Bailey is cooking in his allegedly giant, gourmet kitchen." She practically orgasms when she talks about his kitchen. "Harper is smart. I was thinking that I might teach her how to play poker."

He lets out a laugh. "She's a cool kid."

"I don't usually do the whole kids thing, but she's a sharp one. I can handle her. I'll see you at our next lesson."

He hesitates for a moment before kissing my cheek and then leaving.

I'm just finishing sanitizing the kitchen table and laying out the food when the front door opens and Bailey and my father walk through.

After I hug him, Bailey complains that I got takeout instead of cooking. Is she joking? I never cook.

We chat for a bit about the apartment and life. My father appears nervous. He very clearly has something on his mind, but Bailey seems blissfully unaware.

He notices me staring and visibly swallows. "Listen, girls, I want to talk to you about something. I've wanted to talk to you about it for a long time. There were a few things about your mother you never knew. Before you jump down my throat, I am *not* condoning her behavior. She was a shitty mother, plain and simple."

Bailey and I exchange glances. He's never uttered those words out loud before.

He exhales a long breath. "She was sick. She suffered from mental illness, depression, abuse of pain meds, and alcoholism. The booze only made her depression worse. It was a vicious cycle with no end. She wasn't the woman I knew when we were kids. The one I fell for. Her diseases and demons overtook her until she was unrecognizable, even to me."

I can't keep quiet anymore. "Why didn't you leave her, Daddy? You could have found someone else. You could have had more kids."

His eyes fill with tears. It's more than sadness. It's fear. What is he hiding from us?

He places his napkin on the table. "I did find someone else. After you girls left for college, I started seeing someone. Your mother knew about this person. I stayed with your mom as a caretaker, not a husband. I've been with a wonderful companion for about ten years now. I hope you don't think less of me."

I look at Bailey as his words set in. She has tears trickling out of her eyes. I think I'm in too much shock to emote.

She says, "We would never think less of you. Honestly, we're relieved. We want you to be happy. You deserve a woman who can give you that."

Dad flinches. "That's the thing. It's not a...woman."

What the fuck? My father has been in the closet his whole life? "You're into men?" I ask.

He simply nods with a dash of trepidation in his eyes. Why would he be afraid to tell me of all people?

I don't know why, but he needs our approval. He needs me to

tell him it's okay, that there's nothing wrong with him. He did the same for me all those years ago.

I grin from ear to ear as I sing, "I'm a chip off the old block. Best day ever. Let your freak flag fly, Daddy. I'm with you."

He rolls his eyes at me before nervously looking at Bailey for her response. She slowly nods. "It actually makes a lot of sense. If you found someone who you love and you're happy, I personally don't care if it's a man, woman, or anything else. But, Daddy, why after all this time? How long have you known?"

She's right. How long has he realized that he's gay? Or bi. Whatever. That he's into men. I hate the notion of him feeling like he had to hide his true self.

His shoulders slump a bit. "I grew up in a different era. I think I always knew but didn't always accept it. Your mother was beautiful back in the day. You girls look so much like her."

I wince. "Ugh. She looked like a saddlebag with eyes." Her looks declined rapidly once she began hitting the bottle hard. I hadn't seen her in person in ten years, but the handful of times she flashed by the screen on our calls with him, I could see that her once-good looks were completely gone.

He sighs. "The years of alcohol abuse took their toll on her. You know full well that when she was younger, she was stunning like you two. We were high school sweethearts. She followed me to college. I experimented a bit while there but always maintained a relationship with her. When she fell pregnant with you two, I did the right thing. I married her. I don't regret any of it because it gave me the two most precious gems in the world, but when you two left for college, I decided that I would no longer hide myself. That's when I met Ray. I spend most of my free time with him, but I couldn't leave your mother to fend for herself. She had no other family, and I couldn't afford a hospital. I took care of her and spent time with Ray. He's been understanding, but now I'm going to officially move in with him. I'm selling the house. The bags I brought are a lot of our belongings and some of your awards and trophies from over the years. Take what you want and do as you please with the rest. Ray's house is beautiful. I don't need to bring anything but my clothes."

I'm practically bouncing up and down with excitement for him. "Is he hot? Can we see pictures? When can we meet him? I need to meet the man who makes my father happy. Maybe a little interrogation too. I need to make sure his intentions are honorable."

Dad replies, "Perhaps I'll bring him with me on my next visit, or perhaps you two will actually come home now that...things are different."

Bailey stands and hugs him. "I'm so happy for you. I love you."

"I love you too."

I then stand and join their hug before whispering, "Want to get matching rainbow flag tattoos?"

He chuckles before we pull apart and sit back down. He looks at me. "I'm sorry for how your mother acted toward you when you came out. I should have done more. She knew my... preferences and blamed me for you. It was a dark time for us."

I let this all register. I don't care about me at this point, I care about him. "She knew about you before Ray?"

He nods. "Yes. She always knew I preferred men."

I shake my head. "Why did she want to marry you?"

"There's a reason you only had my parents as your grandparents before they passed."

Bailey looks at him. "Because hers were already gone."

He shakes his head. "No, they weren't. Not until you were five or six. People like your mother aren't born that way. No one is born filled with hatred and bigotry. They're made into that by their surroundings. If you think she was bad, you should have seen her parents. She wanted to get away from them. She saw me as that opportunity. For me, she was *my* opportunity to hide my true self. It was almost a business arrangement in which we both benefited. I know you think she got pregnant on purpose, to trap me, but she didn't. She wanted me to play professional ball and support us." Our father was a college basketball player but had to stop playing when my mother became pregnant with us during their senior year. "She was doing a little modeling at the time. When she became pregnant, I had to get a job to make us money. She couldn't model anymore. You two arrived, and everyone oohed and aahed over how gorgeous you were. She saw you as her new meal ticket and...lost her way."

I cross my arms. "It was more than that."

He nods. "I know. Once you made it clear how much you hated modeling, I fought her on the issue. I know it took longer than it should have. I tried to make all three of you happy. In the end, I failed her the most. The misery consumed her until she turned into someone I didn't recognize. My guilt over that is the reason I chose to take care of her all these years. But when I see how you two turned out, the amazing women you've become, I know I did something right." Tears fill his eyes. "You both have such pure, kind, and caring hearts."

I shake my head. "Bailey does. I don't."

"No, Kamryn, you do," he says more sternly than normal for him. "Just because you're more abrasive and a bit of a button-pusher doesn't mean all those attributes aren't there."

Bailey nods her head. "Of course you're all those things, Kam."

I'm not going to sit here and argue with them. I know what I am.

He grabs both of our hands. "I'm closing the chapter on my past and looking forward to the future. In the words of the artist Henri Matisse, 'There are always flowers for those who want to see them.' I'm choosing to see only flowers moving forward. Let's start off by you telling me all the good things going on in your lives.

I can't believe my babies are going to be Olympians. My mother will dance in her grave when you guys are on the podium."

Our grandmother was an Olympic champion swimmer. We

were about fourteen when she passed. She left my father her gold medal, which my mother sold to support her habits. I've never seen my father as angry as the day he found out.

Bailey shrugs. "I'm not sure I'll be on the team, Daddy. Ripley, Arizona, and Kam will for sure."

I shake my head. "Don't put yourself down. You're just as good as us. We're *all* going. That's the plan. It always has been."

Our father nods in agreement and then turns his attention to me. "What about you, Kamryn? Are you serious with the baseball player you brought to the funeral?"

I shake my head. "No, he's my fuck buddy."

He sighs. "Can you please not talk like that in front of me?"

"Okay. He's my sex friend."

He shakes his head. "That's not any better. It was nice of him to come to the funeral."

"We were away. I was...umm...helping him out with something."

"Like what?"

"It's better you don't know."

Bailey wiggles her eyebrows. "They're taking dance lessons together."

I sigh. "That was my Christmas present from him."

Dad's face lights up. "Dance lessons? That's wonderful. I remember you begging to take them as a little girl, but your mother felt like you didn't have time with all your modeling commitments." He winces. "I should have signed you up myself."

I don't want him to feel bad. "You're forgetting to see your flowers, Daddy. Yes, we're enjoying the dance lessons. Better late than never, right?"

He smiles, but it doesn't quite reach his eyes. He's feeling guilty, and I don't want that for him. I ask, "Now that you're not housebound, do you and Ray have any plans?"

I see a small smile form on his lips. "I don't have much saved, your mother drained what we had for her...habits, but I'd love to save for the next few years and then do some traveling. I've never been anywhere. Hell, until today, I hadn't left the state of Florida since your college graduation. What I wouldn't give to see the world. My time is coming."

I rub his hand. "That's awesome. I can't wait to follow your new adventures."

Bailey begins to clear the dishes, but I hear a gasp as she approaches the sink. I look at her, and she mouths, "I'm going to kill you."

It takes me a moment before I realize why. With the kitchen table cleanup, the search for Febreze, and the food delivery issues, I forgot all about the butt plug Cheetah threw into the sink. I can't help but let out a laugh as I encourage my father to bring his bags into Bailey's room so I can clean up the sink.

CHAPTER TWENTY-THREE

CHEETAH

It's been a weird week. Ripley went into severely premature labor out in California. It was touch and go for a while. We were all freaking out.

Coincidentally, Quincy had just arrived in Florida for pitchers and catchers to begin Spring Training. He was with Arizona and Layton when the call about Ripley came in. They all flew out to California to be with her and the baby, who's currently in the NICU.

Kam and Bailey wanted to fly out right away, but Arizona told them not to come. She told them that only family members were allowed around Ripley and the baby for the next several weeks. She encouraged them to visit once both were completely out of the woods. Kam and Bailey have been a mess about it. I did my best to distract Kam, and I know Tanner has been doing the same for Bailey.

Tonight was our last dance class. I leave tomorrow to go to Florida for five weeks of Spring Training.

Kam and I are in bed, breathing heavily after an amazing round of animalistic sex. I'm going to miss her.

The thoughts of hotel-room phone sex are running through my mind when she turns to me. "I guess that was our grand finale. It's been a good run, kitten."

She pats my legs in an almost condescending manner.

"What do you mean?" I ask.

"Our dance classes are over. You'll be in Florida for over a month, and then your crazy season begins. I know there will be women all over you. Pussy on a platter. We've had fun this off-season, but things will change once you're in season. At some point, my season will begin too."

"It doesn't mean we have to stop seeing each other."

She shakes her head. "I know what hot, single professional baseball players do on the road, kitten. It's cool. I have needs too. We can hook up now and then when we're both around and feel like it. We can still be friends with benefits."

Friends with benefits? We're more than that. We've been in a real relationship for months, and she knows it. How can she be so cavalier, like what we've shared means nothing?

I look at her in disbelief. "Why are you doing this? We have a good thing going."

"Doing what? It's a flingationship, remember?"

It's not like I don't know that Kamryn Hart is damaged, but I thought we broke through some barriers. I thought she knew we were more than ordinary. On one hand, I knew this was coming, but on the other, I'm finding it hard to believe that she can be so fucking cold.

I simply turn my head and stoically respond, "Right. My bad. I knew what we were."

I can feel her get out of bed and hear her starting to get dressed. I snap my head. "What are you doing?"

"You have an early flight, and I've got a test to study for. I'm going to head out." She leans over and kisses my cheek. "Thanks for a fun few months. This was my favorite off-season ever."

KAMRYN

Yep, I was a fucking asshole last night. He deserved more than the cool send-off I gave him. I did it for him. He should fuck whoever he wants, and I knew he wouldn't if I asked for more. I'm not sure I'm ready to give more, so how can I ask that of him? I'm too fucked up. He's such a great guy. I truly want him to find someone who can give him all the things I'm incapable of giving him or anyone else.

I've thought a lot about our conversations over the past few months. It felt good to open up to someone for the first time in my life. It was like some of the burdens I've carried lightened.

It took several weeks for me to finally work up the courage to set up this appointment, but I did. I decided to wait until Cheetah was gone for Spring Training. I'm not sure how I'm going to feel about it, and I don't want him around asking questions and pushing me to talk about things I'm not sure I want to talk about.

Yes, I understand that it's because he cares, but I need to do this on my own. I need to fix myself before I can ever consider making myself available to anyone. The fact that it's even crossing my mind is progress for me.

The last thing I want is to string him along. If he finds someone else in the meantime, so be it.

My sister is tied up in all things Tanner Montgomery right now. She finally started giving me details about their relationship.

She's in love with him, and I'm terrified of what that means. She told me he doesn't ever want to get married again or have more kids. She assured me that she can handle casual if that's truly what he wants, but she thinks he wants more, and I'm scared for her. This is headed toward heartbreak. I can feel it.

I've done a few modeling shoots this off-season, but nothing too crazy. With my sister out of the house so much, Cheetah now gone, and Ripley and Arizona in California, it's leaving me time for school and to focus on myself.

My sister is at Tanner's house when I open my laptop and click on the Zoom link at the allocated time. A woman in her fifties immediately appears. She's well put together in nice caramel-colored slacks and a cream-colored cardigan sweater. She's wearing pearl earrings and a matching pearl necklace. It looks like she raided Barbara Bush's wardrobe, but she's attractive, with short dark hair that has a sprinkling of gray interspersed throughout.

It appears as though she's sitting at a big desk with a bunch of framed degrees hanging in the background. I googled her after Cheetah gave me her name and number. She's widely considered the best in her field with regard to the specialty of parental abandonment. Her reviews were off the charts. Cheetah researched this thoroughly when finding her for me.

She smiles. "Hi, Kamryn. I'm Dr. Chastity Pearl. Most patients call me Dr. Pearl, but you can call me whatever you want as long as it's something nice."

I let out a small laugh. Dr. Pearl has a little personality. I like that. "Hi, Dr. Pearl. I'm Kamryn Hart." My hands fidget a bit. "I'm...umm...a little nervous about this."

She gives me a reassuring smile. "That's perfectly okay. Everyone feels that way at the beginning. I just want to get to know you today and for you to get to know me. Have you ever spoken with a therapist before?"

I shake my head. "No. Never."

"Well, you've taken a very brave step in being here. I commend you for that. I understand that you're a professional athlete?"

I nod. "Yes, I play softball for the Philly Anacondas."

Her face lights up. "I did a little research. You're quite an impressive young lady. Many personal and team accomplishments. Everything I read says you're a shoo-in for the next Olympic team. That must be fulfilling."

"It is. Softball has always been my happy place."

"Have you played your whole life?"

I can't help but shiver at the memories of what it took to finally be allowed to play softball. "No, I didn't start until middle school." I tell her everything about how our mother forced us into modeling and how it left little time for the things we wanted to do.

She listens intently before placing a file down and picking up a notepad and pen. "I read through all your intake forms, but why don't you tell me in your own words why we're here and what you hope to gain."

I exhale a long breath as I consider an answer. "You know from my answers that I had a severely strained relationship with my mother." I mumble, "More than strained."

"She's now passed, right?"

"Yes. It's been a little over a month."

"And it had been ten years since you last saw her, correct?"

"Yes. I want to be clear. I'm not here questioning my feelings about her. She was a disgusting person, and I have no remorse over removing her from my life. As far as I'm concerned, that's the best decision I've ever made, and I don't regret it at all. Even after her death, I don't regret not mending fences. Those fences fucking blew away in the storm and were beyond repair."

She pinches her eyebrows together before flipping open a file as if she's looking for something. "Yet I see here that you're an insomniac. Do you think there's some part of you that wishes you had made peace with her before she passed?"

I shake my head. "No. I don't sleep because I have nightmares about something she did, not because I longed to have my mother back in my life or was sad that she wasn't a part of it. I'm damaged by the things she did to me and my sister. That's what I'd love to one day get past so I can consider a more normal life."

Figuring I'm here for one reason, I go on to tell her about that day when I was ten. She attempts to mask her shock and disgust, but I see it. It's there. How could it not be?

"And you're sure that you overheard things as you mentioned?"

"Yes. I've questioned it a lot throughout the years because sometimes my nightmares take on a different form, a different version of that night, but the core events happened as I stated. I'm absolutely certain that I heard those parts of the conversation just as I relayed them to you. I went back and found that man about to go into my sister's dressing room. There's no good reason for a grown man to be alone in a dressing room with a ten-year-old girl."

"And you've never shared what happened that night with your sister, father, or anyone else, even after all these years?"

"My father and sister don't know. I never told them."

"Why?" She looks down at the folder. "You've indicated that you're close with both, particularly your sister. Why haven't you confided in them?"

I twist my lips. "I didn't tell my sister to protect her. Why should she suffer the same fate as me? The same nightmares and anxiety. As for my father...I guess I'm not sure why I never told him. I suppose I was afraid he wouldn't believe me."

"Is that an issue? Him not believing you?"

I shake my head. "No."

"In all these years, you haven't told another living soul? That's a lot to bear."

I blow out a breath as Cheetah's face pops into my mind. "The only person before today that I've ever spoken to about it is the man I occasionally spend time with, and that was recently. He's the one who found you and suggested I reach out."

"Is he your boyfriend?"

Isn't that a loaded question.

I pinch my lips together. "I don't do boyfriends or girlfriends. Not in over a decade. I want to shoot straight with you, Dr. Pearl. That's why I'm here. I've always lived a promiscuous lifestyle. I sleep around with men and women. A lot. Interpersonal connections are not something I'm interested in. I struggle with them."

"Do you have friends?"

I nod. "Yes. I have an amazing circle of friends, and as you know, my sister is my best friend in the world."

"So you don't struggle across the board with interpersonal connections. You struggle with intimate connections."

I'm not sure if that's a statement or a question. "I suppose that's a better word choice. Intimacy is hard for me. I don't like to let people in, and I don't want to disappoint anyone since I don't think a normal, traditional family is in my future."

"Yet this man cares enough to have searched for me, and you heeded his advice by contacting me?"

I kind of like that she's challenging me. I'm not sure what I was expecting from today, but this isn't it.

I nod in agreement. "I know. He's my friend too. Yes, I've seen him more than most, but I've always been clear about what we can and can't be. He understands my inner turmoil more than anyone. It's not like I have this strong desire to be fucked up."

"We're all fucked up in our own ways, Kamryn. Me included."

Hearing someone who appears prim and proper curse strikes me as funny.

The corners of her mouth turn up in obvious amusement. "See, you assumed that someone who looks like me would never curse, yet I just did."

I smile and nod.

She scribbles something on her pad before looking back up at me. "Let's save our chat about him for another day. I want to know why you're here. In your own words, not why someone else thinks you need to be here. What do you hope to gain?"

I take another deep breath. "Honestly? I'm not sure I know the answer myself. He got me to admit something recently that I had never considered. He was pushing and pushing until I blurted out that I sleep around to numb the pain. Until that moment, in my mind, I'd always felt I do it because I like the freedom it brings. I don't see myself with a normal future. I never have."

"That's the third time you've used that word. What is it you think *normal* entails?"

"Marriage. Kids. The whole fucking princess fairy tale that's been shoved down our throats by society for all of time."

She gives a slow, knowing smile. "I have a lot of opinions on fairy tales, Kamryn, and none of them are good. I agree. Society has us trained to believe there's only one happily ever after, but that's not true."

I shrug, "I think Sleeping Beauty and all the Disney princesses would disagree."

She places her pen down and looks me right in the eyes with extreme conviction. "Let's discuss what your princesses all *really* wanted. Cinderella wanted to get away from a shitty family situation and go to a party. It was the prince who wanted marriage. Ariel wanted to travel the world and see new things. It was the prince who wanted to get married. Belle wanted to study. Books and education were her dream. It was the beast who wanted marriage. None of these women ever mentioned wanting your," she air quotes, "*normal* marriage. Yet it's considered a happy ending?" She tsks. "I don't think any of those stories have happy endings. None of the women got what they actually wanted. If they were stronger, like you, perhaps they would have gotten a real happily ever after. Real meaning what *they* wanted, not what someone else wanted."

My mouth drops and I breathe out, "What in the actual fuck?"

She continues, "In the words of Coco Chanel, '*A woman should be who and what she wants*'. Don't let anyone tell you what you're supposed to want, Kamryn. If you want marriage and a family, good for you. You should have that. If you don't, that's okay too. Do what makes you happy. I think you need to figure out what it is, but your version of happy is the *real* happily ever after for Kamryn Hart."

I can only blink, completely flabbergasted by her insights. I'm at a total loss for words.

"I've shocked you."

I nod. "You have. And I promise you that it's not an easy thing to do. I'm usually the one shocking people, not the other way around."

She smiles in satisfaction. "I'm glad I have your attention. Now that we've established that individuals have different definitions of fairy tales, can you tell me what your ideal future would look like?"

"Being the best aunt ever to my sister's future kids. She's the most maternal woman I know. She's destined to have a dozen kids. I'll be the fun spinster aunt. I'll probably be living above her garage with my fifteen dogs and cats. Hopefully I won't have droopy boobs."

"Is that what you *think* your future entails or what you *want* it to entail?"

I chew my lower lip as I contemplate her words before answering honestly. "I suppose I don't know."

She nods. "That was an honest answer. Thank you for giving it to me."

"I have nothing to gain by not being honest with you."

"You'd be surprised how many sessions it takes people to realize that." She looks at her watch. "Unfortunately, our time is up for today."

I look at the clock on my computer. How the hell did an hour already pass? It felt like five minutes.

"Oh. Okay. Well, thank you for your time."

"Thank you for opening up to me. I'd love to see you again. You have my online scheduler. I don't like to push. The ball is in your court."

It takes me all of five seconds after we end the call to set up weekly appointments with her for the next two months.

CHAPTER TWENTY-FOUR

CHEETAH

I plop down on my bed at the hotel. I sucked today. I've sucked every day this first week of Spring Training. My mind isn't here. I need to get it together.

Trey, my roommate, walks in a few minutes later. He's our third baseman and a truly great ballplayer. He always has been.

He used to play for the New York Bombers but demanded a trade to Philly after he met Gemma. It was a whole big, public thing. Gemma can't step foot anywhere near the Bombers' stadium anymore. The fans blame her for losing Trey.

Although he's a few years older than I am, I've known him throughout my entire career, considering we share Tanner as our agent. Even when he lived in New York City, we were close.

He walks over and sits on the foot of my bed. "What the fuck is wrong with you?"

I can't help but let out a laugh. "Don't pussyfoot around me, Trey. Say what you mean."

A small smile forms on his face. "Sorry. You're uncharacteristically off. What's happening?"

I sigh. "Kamryn Hart is happening."

"Ahh. What's the deal with you two?"

"I thought we were something special, but she basically told me to fuck off the night before we left."

He scrunches his face. "I'm sorry. That sucks. This isn't really my area of expertise. Should we call Gemma?"

"My future wife? Sure. I'll tell her all the things I plan to do to her one day."

He gives me the finger as he pulls out his phone. Within seconds, his FaceTime is ringing, and Gemma quickly answers. "Hey, baby. I miss you so fucking much."

Trey smiles in triumph as he gives me the finger again and answers, "I miss you too. How's Fletch?"

"Sleeping. Finally. He still has a fever. The bedtime routine is rough when he's cranky."

Trey's face falls. "I hate that I'm not there."

She sighs. "Me too. Anyway, I just sat down to write. I want to get in at least a few thousand words before I masturbate and go to bed."

I can't help but let out a laugh.

She yells out, "Trey! I've told you a million times to tell me if there are other people around when you call me."

He scrunches his face. "Sorry. I have Cheetah with me. He's having girl issues and needs to ask your advice."

I lean toward the phone to see her gorgeous face. Even tired and disheveled, she's beautiful. "Hey, sexy. Do you need me to talk you through your masturbation? I can dirty talk like a boss."

She rolls her eyes. "Trey's dirty talk lives rent-free in my brain. Now tell me what Kamryn Hart advice you need today."

"What I really need to know is what has one hundred and twenty-two teeth and holds back a monster?"

She asks, "Hmm. What?"

"My zipper. You should check him out one day."

Her big green eyes light up as she giggles. "I like that joke. I'm writing it down for future use."

I wiggle my eyebrows. "Excellent."

Her face turns more serious. "Is something up with you and Kam?"

I shrug. "I thought we were doing great, but the night before I left, she wished me well and kicked me to the curb. She said she knows there are lots of girls on the road and encouraged me to imbibe. She was very casual about it like she wasn't breaking my heart or hers. I told you it was probably coming. Maybe she truly doesn't give a shit about me."

Gemma shakes her head. "That's very contradictory to the way she acts around you."

"Contradiction? Do you want a contradiction? George Washington had wooden teeth. Wouldn't that make it a contradiction when he ate beaver?"

She lets out a laugh. "That's funny, but you're deflecting. You do it all the time. Stop using humor to deflect having real conversations with people. Perhaps this is why you and Kam are having a communication issue."

Trey bites back his smile. "Damn. She has your number. It's so fucking hot when she calls people out on their shit."

She's right. I always do that. I nod. "Okay. I promise to be mature...ish."

Gemma winks at me. "Maturing is realizing that disagreements are better solved with gagging not nagging."

I chuckle. "I love you, Gemma. Marry me."

She simply shakes her head, and Trey punches me in the arm. Hard.

Her eyes meet mine. "Back to the subject at hand. It's difficult to watch the person you care about head out on the road where you know there will be a bevy of willing pussy at every turn."

Trey and I exchange glances. She's not wrong.

She continues, "It might have just been a self-defense mechanism. You guys are new and undefined. Did you talk to her about what you would and wouldn't be doing on the road before then? Did you have the conversation I encouraged you to have with her?"

I shake my head. "No, I didn't. Maybe I should have. But," I run my fingers through my hair, "she's not like most women. She's kind of like a dude."

"But she's not one, Cruz."

Gemma means business. She *rarely* calls me Cruz.

"I don't know, Gem, she was so casual about it. So unaffected. She simply got dressed after we had sex, told me to have a good time, and walked out my door in the middle of the night. I was practically in the fetal position sucking my thumb when she left."

"She's kind of a badass. I think I want to base a character on her."

I nod enthusiastically. "She most definitely is, and you should."

"She's totally flipped the tables on you, but I saw you two together in Florida. I think there's more going on. Have you reached out?"

I shake my head. "No. She didn't indicate that she wanted me to contact her."

Gemma rolls her eyes. "Oh, young cub, you still have so much to learn about women. Do me a favor, before you get any weepier, reach out to her. Test the waters and get back to me. I'll be up for a few more hours."

I twist my lips. "Okay. I will. Thanks, Gem."

"My pleasure. Can I ask you for a favor?"

"Anything."

"Leave the room so my husband and I can have phone sex without you jerking off in the corner."

I chuckle as I nod. "Yes, ma'am."

I step out of the room and into the hallway. Sliding down the wall until I'm seated on the carpeted hallway floor, I pull up my text string with Kamryn and start typing.

> Me: Miss me this week?

> Kam: New phone. Who 'dis?

She always makes me smile.

> Me: It's a thesaurus salesman. I heard you're in the market.

> Kam: I am! Perfect timing. Not only was my last thesaurus terrible, but it was also terrible.

I laugh out loud at that one. She's so damn funny. I'm realizing it might be the first time I've smiled in a week.

> Me: Whatcha up to, Kam bam?

> Kam: I'm setting up my new legal research software. I splurged and bought the fancy kind. I need a password for it. Got anything good?

> Me: How about mypenis? I use that as my password for everything.

> Kam: Just tried it. The program says that it's not long enough.

I chuckle. She's always on.

Me: Good one.

Kam: How's life on the road?

Me: Lonely. I miss you. No one here appreciates my forts.

Kam: Your forts are my happy place.

That makes me feel good.

Me: You're mine.

Kam: Can I call you?

Me: Of course.

My FaceTime immediately rings, and I answer. I get a knot in my throat from simply seeing her face. Tears immediately well in her eyes. Maybe Gemma was right.

I try to smile through my emotions. "Hey, beautiful."

She studies the screen. "Where are you?"

"I'm in the hallway of our hotel. Trey and Gemma are having phone sex in our room and I'm giving them privacy."

"It's probably hot. I would totally listen while flicking Fiona."

I fan my face. "It's *extremely* hot, and I've most definitely cuffed the carrot to them going at it, but she begged me to leave them alone tonight, and I wanted to reach out to you anyway."

She smiles before her face turns serious. "Kitten?"

"Yep."

"I'm sorry for how I was on our last night together."

I simply nod. I can't tell her that it's alright. It's not.

She blows out a breath. "I want to shoot straight with you. I'm trying to work on me a little bit. I won't ask you to wait for me. I'm not sure I'll ever be cured. I care about you too much to hold you back."

"Hold me back from what?"

"Women, sex," she mumbles, "marriage, family."

I think I'm starting to understand why she acted the way she did. "What are you doing to work on yourself?"

She twists her lips. "Don't get all girly on me about it, but I met with Dr. Pearl. In fact, we've now had two sessions. You'll be happy to know that in our second session, she substantiated the fact that I mistreated you. I hope you know it's only because I care."

I swallow down my emotions. "I'm so fucking proud of you."

"You are?"

"I am."

She bites her lip. "I think I'm proud of myself too. She's really opened my eyes to a few things. I'm excited to keep talking to her."

I think I know what Kam needs to hear. "Take your time, babe. I'll be here. I'm not going anywhere."

Tears fill her eyes again and she barely croaks out, "You don't have to wait."

I trace her face on the screen with my fingers. I wish I could touch her. "Maybe I want to wait." *Because I love you.*

"Just know that you don't have to. I have zero expectations."

I nod. "Okay. I'll do my best to bang random chicks when all I really want is to be one of the guys sitting in my room having phone sex with their special girl back home."

She smiles softly as she stands and appears to prop the phone on something. She then stands in front of the camera and pulls down her sweatpants and panties.

I quickly look around as if someone else can see my

phone screen. As if there's anyone else in the hallway. "What are you doing?"

"You said you wanted phone sex. I'm giving it to you."

She's now naked from the waist down. I immediately harden. Grabbing onto myself, I moan, "Fuck, now I have a pink cigar situation."

She licks her lips suggestively. "Hmm. I wish I could smoke that cigar right now."

I moan, "Kammm."

"This is what you wanted."

"I'm in the hallway, not my room."

She raises an eyebrow. "I let you fuck me in the ass on a balcony overlooking an entire resort of people in Jamaica. You can stick your hand down your pants in an empty hallway."

Well...when she puts it like that.

Sliding my hand into my shorts, I instruct, "Toca tu coño rosado. Quiero verte correrte." *Touch your pink pussy. I want to watch you come.*

CHAPTER TWENTY-FIVE

KAMRYN

I hear my sister's alarm go off, so I walk into her room and slip into bed with her. She stretches as she turns to me and sleepily croaks out, "Good morning."

"Good morning. What are you up to today?"

She yawns as she considers my question. "Oh, I have a meeting with Reagan Daulton and then I'm spending the afternoon with Tanner."

"Ooh. Tapping Daddy in the afternoon. How modern-day romance of you. Are you going to give the hot poultice to the Irish toothache?"

She shakes her head. "I honestly have no idea what that means."

I let out a laugh. "Cheetah would know."

She rubs my arm. "Are you two together?"

I shake my head. "Have you seen me *together* with anyone since Dakota? As I've told you before, we're casual fuck buddies. The sex is incredible. I'm not in a rush for it to end."

"Have you *casually* fucked anyone since he's been gone all month?"

It's been a *long* month without him.

I'm silent, and she sighs. "It's okay to admit that you have real feelings for him. I know he has real feelings for you."

I roll my eyes. "Whatever."

"When you're ready to admit it to yourself, you can admit it to me too. There's no shame in it, Kam."

I don't want to talk about this with her. "Are you going to admit how often Daddy Tanner ties you up?"

She winks at me. "All the fudging time, and I love every second of it."

I smile. "It's funny how adults told us growing up not to bite, lick, slap, or pull hair, and now it's all we want to do."

She giggles. "Truth."

A FEW HOURS LATER, I'm sitting on my couch, staring at my phone in complete and total shock.

An intruding voice asks, "Kamryn, are you with me?"

I snap my head back up toward Dr. Pearl on my computer screen. "Sorry, my sister just sent me photos of her and her boyfriend skydiving. I didn't know she was going. I'm flipping out."

"If she's sending photos, they've probably safely landed."

"Hmm, valid point. You're a smart woman, Dr. Pearl."

She points toward her wall of degrees. "I didn't order these in the mail, Kamryn. Let's get back into things."

I place my phone down. "Sorry."

"I had something else planned for today, but since your sister and her safety are on your mind, let's chat more about her."

I shrug. "We've been through this. I told you I'm a selfish bitch. I've manipulated her life to keep her close."

"She allows it. On some level, she must want it too."

I shake my head. "She's too sweet to say otherwise." I swallow the knot in my throat. "She feels like I need her to mother me, and I've allowed her to think that. The reality is, I need to protect her."

"You'll have to let go at some point."

I nod, knowing she's right. "I will. When I know she's safe from all the monsters out there. They come in different forms, but they're there."

"What makes her unsafe right now?"

"She's dating a man fifteen years older than her who has told her he doesn't want marriage or any more kids. She's admitted to me that she's in love with him. Her heart isn't safe, and it's eventually going to blow up in her face."

"What about your heart?"

I steel my face. "It's stone."

"It's anything but, Kamryn." She taps her pen on her notepad. "We're a few sessions in now. You always manage to steer the conversation away from the man who caused you to come talk to me. We had one brief conversation about how you coldly sent him off, but nothing else. Can we talk about him today?"

"You're the bosswoman."

She smirks. "Yes, I am."

Over the past month, I've come to adore Dr. Pearl. We've developed a fun relationship. She has an unusually dry sense of humor, which is probably why we click. She's not uptight like I expected. She pushes me in a way no one else ever has. Each time we meet, I feel like the weight I carry gets just a pound or two lighter.

She asks, "What's your current status with him?"

"He's in Florida at Spring Training. I haven't seen him in a few weeks. He'll be home by the end of the week."

And I'm fucking nervous as hell to see him.

"We've talked about your more promiscuous lifestyle. Have you seen anyone else since he's been gone?"

I reluctantly admit, "I haven't."

"Did you discuss exclusivity with him?"

I shake my head. "We're absolutely not exclusive. I just...I haven't met anyone of interest."

"Is that *normal* for you? I know how much you love that word."

"I haven't gone this long without sex since I started having sex at fifteen."

"What about him?" she asks.

"He knows he's welcome to fuck whoever he wants. I would never hold him back that way."

"Do you think he is?"

I shrug. "Not my business."

She raises her eyebrows, and I sigh. "Look, all I know is that before he left, he said he hadn't touched anyone since he met me. That no one stirs his mind, dick, and funny bone like me. What has he been up to in Florida? I don't know. I don't ask."

"Do you speak to him?"

I slowly nod. "He calls me every day. And...he said he'd wait for me to work through my issues." I run my fingers through my hair. "But I don't expect anything. He should do whatever makes him happy. I've told him as much."

She gives a small, knowing smile. "Tell me about him."

I can't help the thrill that runs through me when I think about him. "He's funny, hot, and sweet, but that's honestly not what attracts me to him. Maybe it was at first, but that's not why I've hung around him longer than I have for anyone since I was a teen. God help him, but he likes me exactly as I am. No matter how you slice it, I'm not normal and never will be. It doesn't bother him. In fact, the weirdo gets off on it. I'm probably closer to him than I've been to a bedfellow in my entire life." I mutter, "Definitely closer to him."

"Then why are you reluctant?"

"Because I'm toxic. He's a genuinely good man. Maybe the best I've ever met. He deserves better than me, but for some reason, he wants me. For now. One day he'll want what all the princes want, and I'm not the princess who will ever do something she doesn't want to do for a partner, man or woman."

She thinks for a moment. "Have you ever taken the love language test?"

I let out a laugh at the memory. "Oddly enough, yes. Last year, my friends were all taking it and I did too."

"Often our most *toxic*, as you called it, trait is the exact opposite of your love language."

"How so?"

"Those who avoid intimacy are the ones who crave physical touch."

I think about that. Physical touch was Arizona's love language. Before Layton, she avoided men for over a year. Maybe Dr. Pearl is on to something.

She continues, "Those who have insecurities often like words of affirmation."

Yep. That's Ripley.

"What do you think my love language is?" I ask.

She taps her lower lip. "Hmm. I'm not a gambler, but if I were a betting woman, knowing how you like to handle things on your own and hate asking people for help, I'd wager that you crave simple acts of kindness. You've spent so much of your life taking care of your sister and yourself. And while she's also taken care of you, you missed that in your mother. I imagine you'd be most attracted to someone who fills that role. Someone who cares enough and knows enough about you to give you what you need. I believe the test calls it acts of service."

She's one smart bitch.

She smiles in satisfaction. "I take it by your face that I'm right?"

I nod. "Yep. I can't believe it."

"Is that what this man gives you? Acts of service?"

I think about Cheetah and our past few months together. Suddenly it's the easiest answer on the planet. "In every single thing he says and does."

"He sounds like a keeper. It's obvious you care about him."

"I care enough to know that I won't ever hold him back from anything. Ever."

I'M STUDYING a case on my computer when I hear the front door open. Without looking up, I say, "Are you fucking kidding me, sending me those photos and then going radio silent? Did you jump out of a fucking airplane? Are you insane?"

I smile as I lift my head, expecting a little sass from Bailey, but am shocked to see her in tears. I leap from the sofa and take her into my arms. "What's wrong? Are you hurt?"

She collapses into me. "He had a vasectomy. He strung me along, making me feel hopeful about a future when there is none."

Oh my god. "Oh, Bails. I'm so fucking sorry."

She's practically hyperventilating in tears. "I...I thought he loved me too."

She can barely stand. She's so brokenhearted. I knew she couldn't be casual with him. It goes against her grain. I rub her back. "I know you're hurting, but didn't he tell you from the beginning that you guys weren't long-term? That he didn't want marriage and more kids?"

Just like I said to Cheetah before I went and fell for him.

She nods and sobs, "Yes, but the way he acts with me didn't match those words. Other things he's said to me don't line up with that. No man has ever treated me with more love, compassion, and tenderness. Everything he did told me he was falling the same way I was."

She's not wrong. I've seen them together. He was at the funeral acting like the doting boyfriend. And every time since, I watch him watch her. I was starting to think he was falling in love with her too, and I've only been around them together a small handful of times. She's with him nearly every day.

Suddenly I'm realizing that I'm like Tanner in this situation. I told Cheetah we were nothing, but we became something, and I knew it. Then I tossed him away like Tanner is doing to my sister.

I nod. "You're right. Want me to burn down his house? I'll do it and not think twice about it."

She manages a small laugh. "No, but thanks for offering."

"I'd do anything for you. *Anything*."

She knows I mean it. I would burn down the world for my sister. In some ways, I have.

She leans her head on my shoulder. "Right now, I need to spend a weekend crying and figuring out my life."

"You don't need to figure out your life this weekend, but we can eat gallons of ice cream and watch *Titanic* on repeat if you'd like."

Fuck, I have a big test tonight, but she needs me. I can't abandon my sister in her time of need. I'll email my professor. Hopefully she'll be understanding.

AFTER A LONG WEEKEND OF CRYING, my strong sister wipes the theoretical dust from her shoulders and tells me that she has to go coach Harper's softball team. I beg her to quit her job with Tanner, but because she's the best human being I know, she refuses, saying she intends to honor her commitments.

There's not a fucking chance of me letting her coach without me during her time of need. Even though the thought of working with twelve eight-year-old girls terrifies the living shit out of me, I tell her that I'll be her assistant coach. Apparently, the season runs for about two more months. I can handle two months of sticky, whiny kids. Hell, I like Harper. She's like a mini adult.

Admittedly, the girls' eyes when we both arrive at practice are priceless. Sometimes I forget that little girls look up to us as role models. Me, a role model. What a joke.

We're huddled up as I'm introduced, and Bailey encourages me to say a few words. "Hey, bitches." They all giggle, and Bailey elbows me to remind me not to curse in front of them. Fat chance of that happening.

I continue. "I'm Kamryn Hart. You can call me Kam or Queen Kam, whichever you prefer."

Bailey interrupts. "You can call her Coach Kam."

I roll my eyes. "Or that. Unlike my sister, I'm shit at working with kids, so I'm going to treat you like adults. Hell, Harper is smarter than most fucking adults I know."

The girls all laugh, and Harper's face lights up. Harper Montgomery is a pretty little girl with light brown hair and unique blue eyes that stand out. She's always happy and thinks the world revolves around my sister, which means she has excellent taste.

"I recognize a few of you from Harper's birthday and our games." I tap my lip as I study their faces carefully. "You, with the dark curly hair. You're Andie, right?"

She smiles and nods. Her father is one of the team owners of the Anacondas. She's always at our home games. I think she's Harper's best friend.

I narrow my eyes at her. "I see you wearing an Abbott jersey all the time. Where's the love for me?"

Her eyes widen in fear, but my sister simply shakes her head. "She's just kidding, Andie. Wear whoever's jersey you want. We appreciate the support. Why don't each of you say your name and position? My sister has a very good memory. You only need to say it once."

The girls all give me their names and positions. The shortstop is a little girl named Sapphire. I mumble to Bailey, "Did her parents put a pole in her crib when they gave her that name?"

She simply shakes her head at me as practice begins. The girls aren't bad. Harper is by far the best player on the team. She apparently moved from shortstop to second base to be like Bailey, but she should be the shortstop. She's got an amazing arm, and her softball IQ is off the charts.

Sapphire, the future exotic dancer, plays shortstop. She's not good enough. I whisper to Bailey. "We should move Andie from third to short. The stripper can't handle it."

She scrunches her face. "At this age, I'm trying to let them play where they want to. Andie likes third. They should move around some anyway. We'll rotate them as the season progresses. It's all about them learning."

"And winning," I add.

"That's much less important."

"Champions or bust, sis."

She simply sighs at me like she's done millions of times throughout the years.

Watching my sister work with the girls brings a lot of emotions to the surface. This is so clearly her passion. What she's meant to do. She's so fucking good at it. I'm the asshole who's kept her from it because I couldn't bear the thought of not being with her all the time.

When practice is over, I see her talking to Fallon, Tanner's ex-wife. She's fucking hot, even in scrubs with messy hair and no makeup. Maybe she's a doctor. A sexy-as-sin doctor.

When we get into the car, I ask her what Fallon said. She responds, "She thought my wounds would be a little too fresh to see Tanner tonight, so she came to pick up Harper even though I was supposed to drop her at Tanner's. It was thoughtful, but I'm going to have to see him at some point."

"You could quit."

She exhales a long breath. "Kam, I love Harper. I'm not losing her too. I need you to understand and respect that."

I nod, knowing it's true. "Okay, but don't feel obligated. Do what feels best for you."

Yes, I'm a hypocrite.

I try to lighten the mood. "Did you hear the word Harper busted out today?"

She shakes her head. "No. What was it?"

"When Stacey was talking in the middle of the drill, she told her to stop confabulating."

Bailey lets out a laugh. "That was on her word-of-the-day toilet paper a few weeks ago. She's been using it in lieu of the word chatting ever since. Isn't it amazing how she remembers all these words and uses them appropriately? She's such a special kid."

I'm not sure what I'm more worried about, her love for Tanner or her love for Harper. But there's one thing I know for sure. All roads lead to heartbreak for Bailey Hart.

CHAPTER TWENTY-SIX

I've somehow convinced my sister to go to a club with me tonight. It was nothing short of a miracle. She was shaken after leaving Tanner's house for the first time since the breakup, but I threw her in the shower, put her in some sexy clothes, and made her take two shots of vodka to loosen her up. I wouldn't take no for an answer. She can't stay home and cry every night.

We're meeting Vance, Daylen, and a few of the other guys from the Camels. They have a new teammate, Champ Williamson, who was just traded to Philly. They want to introduce him to new people. I've seen pictures of him. He's gorgeous. He looks sort of like Odell Beckham, Jr. It's unlikely that Bailey is ready for a hookup, but I'm still holding out hope.

As we walk out of our apartment for the evening, we hear loud moaning coming from Justin's apartment. I snap my head to Bailey. "Do men moan loudly when they're jerking off?"

She narrows her eyes at me. "Why do you assume he's jerking off? Maybe he's in there with a woman."

"A woman? He never leaves his apartment. Do you know why gingers burn so easily?"

She shakes her head. "I don't, but I'm sure you'll tell me why."

"It's nature's way of telling them they should remain indoors."

She giggles, but it's interrupted by the loud moan of a woman coming from his apartment.

I gasp. "Maybe he's murdering her. He's sweet, but lots of serial killers were sweet in their real lives."

As if on cue, we hear Justin groaning, "Right there, Trisha. So good."

My chin practically falls to the floor as I point to myself. "I set them up. I didn't know they hit it off. He was tight-lipped about it. I assumed that meant nothing came of it."

I've achieved one of the greatest miracles of the century. I got ginger Justin Bieber laid. I can't help the big grin on my face.

Bailey wraps her arm around me. "You did good, little sis."

"Do you know why gingers—"

"Quit while you're ahead, Kam," she interrupts.

I laugh. "Will do."

We're in the Uber on our way to the club when she says, "I forgot to tell you about my meeting with Reagan Daulton the other day."

The morning before she went skydiving and then the big breakup, she was summoned to Reagan's office without any explanation. With the emotions of her breakup, I forgot all about the meeting.

"Oh, right. What did she want?" I ask.

She nods toward the driver before leaning over and quietly saying, "She asked me not to tell anyone," a rule which has never applied to us, "but she's thinking about bringing a new basketball franchise to Philly."

"Oh cool. More women's sports. That's awesome."

She claps her hands excitedly. "I know. It will be great. It sounds like she'd rather wait another year to do it, but if she does it now, she automatically gets the first pick in the upcoming draft."

I nod in realization. "Sulley O'Shea?"

She smiles. "Yep."

Sulley O'Shea is what the social media world would call a femininomenon. Kind of a superstar female phenom. She's a college basketball player who's breaking all kinds of records, bringing never-before-seen attention to the sport. Women's college basketball is beating men's college basketball in television ratings thanks to her. She's become a media darling and the face of the sport. It seems like people are hopeful that when she enters professional basketball, it will boost the women's league tremendously. She's basically a marketing goldmine, and I'm sure every single team is dying to draft her. I understand Reagan wanting to change her timeline just to draft Sulley.

"That would put the team on the map right away. Why did she confide in you?"

"She's concerned that Sulley is a small-town girl and Philly will be intimidating for her. She's coming to visit in a few weeks. She thought with my basketball background and the fact that I'm a new athlete in Philly, I should be the one to show her around."

I smile. "That's a nice compliment to you, Bails. She's putting a lot of faith in you."

Bailey's face beams. "I know. She offered to pay me, but I declined."

"Why the hell would you decline money?"

She scrunches her face. "What if Sulley found out I was paid to spend time with her? She'd be hurt. Isn't showing someone new around town simply the right thing to do?"

Have I mentioned that my sister is the best person I know?

I wrap my arm around her and pull her close. "You're right. I learn how to be a better person from you every day. I love you."

She giggles. "I learn from you every day too. For example, this morning you taught me the super useful fact that farts travel at seven miles per hour. I can honestly say I had never given any thought to how fast farts can travel."

We both laugh. I offer, "Want another lesson?"

She nods.

"Female dragonflies are known to often fake their own death to avoid sex with male dragonflies." In a squeaky voice, I say, "Oh no, here comes Chad, I need to play dead." I close my eyes and let my head fall to the side with my tongue hanging out of the corner, feigning death.

Bails laughs uncontrollably as the Uber pulls up to the club. I'm so happy to see her smiling.

I'm looking forward to seeing the guys. It's been a few weeks. I'm both excited and nervous for Cheetah to get home tomorrow, so a few drinks and a good time tonight will hopefully settle my nerves. We talk all the time, but I'm not sure where we stand. I know that I missed him more than I thought would be possible.

Despite the long line out front, the rope is lifted for us and we're shown right into the club. Bailey and I have never once waited in line at a club or bar in our entire lives. We stopped getting carded at sixteen. The simple fact is that clubs like having attractive women in them. Being twins only ups the ante. Men are always fascinated with twins. I think it plays into some weird fantasies. We unashamedly take advantage of it.

We walk in and head straight to their normal booth. It's always flanked by security, but all those guys know me by now and allow us to pass straight through.

I hear Daylen's booming voice before I see him. The man has no volume control. He loudly says, "When a woman looks at you and puts her hair in a ponytail, there's only one of two things about to happen. If you're not sure which one it is, run."

I hear all the guys laughing as they notice us approaching. I smile as I nod in agreement. "That's a true statement."

Daylen winks. "It's Cheetah's Kam. Happy you made it."

"I'm no one's Kam." I look at Vance. "How's grumpy pants tonight?"

Daylen answers, "I think he has his man period. He's *man*struating."

I laugh while Vance gives him the finger. The two of them are like the odd couple, though I never see one without the other.

We're introduced to Champ, who is even more attractive in person. Bailey sits next to him, and they start chatting right away. At least ten girls approach him, but he doesn't give them the time of day, seemingly engrossed in all things Bailey. Initially, I think all hope for her isn't lost, but it doesn't take long for me to realize that Champ is gay. I don't know why, but my gaydar is always spot on. I'm never wrong.

So much for Bailey getting action tonight. She's blissfully ignorant though, seeming to enjoy her conversation with him. Her being social is a win, so I'm saying nothing.

Some skanky girl starts throwing herself at Vance. I can tell he's not interested so I purposely spill my drink on her. I never see him with women. The other guys indulge and bask in the adoration of the woman throwing themselves at them, but Vance never does. He's not gay, I can tell. He's an interesting dude. I wonder what his story is.

Bailey and Champ leave the table to dance. He's putting a smile on her face. That's all I care about. They're laughing and dancing up a storm on the dance floor. It warms my heart to see her like this after the week she's had.

My Bailey stalking is interrupted by Vance, who asks, "Have you been watching the Spring Training games? Your boy toy got off to a slow start, but he's ramping it up just in time for the season."

It's true. Cheetah was terrible for their first few games but is doing well now. "I have. They're going to have a good season. I can feel it."

Daylen scratches his head. "Speaking of feeling, I have a lesbian question for you."

I roll my eyes. This routine from men is getting old. "I'm not a lesbian, André the Giant."

The guys all laugh hysterically. Even Vance smiles. "Holy shit, I'm calling you André the Giant from now on. Ha! It's perfect."

André the Giant was a famous wrestler in the eighties, though most women know him as the giant from the movie *Princess Bride*. The man stood at over seven feet tall, weighed more than five hundred pounds, and could barely string together two sentences.

Daylen bites back his smile. "That's a good one. Seriously, I have a question about beaver bumping."

The corners of my mouth raise in amusement. "Ask away, André. I'm here for your education and amusement."

He wiggles his big, meaty fingers. "Would you consider lesbians with fat fingers to be well hung?"

The guys all laugh again. They're idiots. I'm over this scene. I miss Cheetah and his clever sense of humor.

Bailey and Champ eventually return. I see the drinks are getting low, and the waitress is nowhere to be found. I need a break from them, so I offer to go buy a round. It will give me fifteen minutes to breathe.

I manage to talk the bartender into giving me a tray. I'm carefully placing it on our table when a familiar scent invades my nostrils. Warmth, familiarity, and a sense of calm blanket me. I know he's here before he whispers into my ear, "Want to play *Titanic*?"

I have to bite back my smile and calm myself from the fact that I'm so fucking happy right now. I answer, "Fine, but I'm going be the iceberg this time, and you're going to be the ship that goes down."

I feel him silently laughing as I turn around in his arms and look into his gorgeous blue eyes. I have to hold back my tears. I've missed him so damn much.

He's in jeans and a blue button-down shirt. His skin is sun-kissed from being in Florida for the past month. His scruff is more overgrown than how he normally keeps it. He looks edible.

He grabs my ass and pulls my body flush to his before

explaining that their final game for tomorrow was rained out, so he hightailed it to the airport to come home early.

I narrow my eyes at him. "How did you know where I was?"

He runs his tongue along his lower lip. "Find My iPhone."

"Stalker." I may have made him add me to his Find My iPhone when we went to Jamaica. It was my first time out of the country, and I was reading too many articles on sex trafficking.

He winks at me. "Don't lie to yourself. You get off on me stalking you."

True. I totally do.

We engage in a little of our normal banter, but my head is spinning with just how happy I am that he's back. Dr. Pearl thinks I'm more into him than I'm allowing myself to admit. At this moment, I'm thinking she may be right.

Finally, after five long weeks, his lips meet mine. A sense of contentment I've never known floods through my body.

Uncaring where we are and who's watching, I thread my fingers through his silky hair and deepen the kiss. Our tongues meet, and I can't contain my moan.

I want him. No, it's more than want. I *need* him.

Completely absorbed in the moment and forgetting where I am, my hands begin to undo his belt buckle. I'm about to unzip his jeans when everyone at the table starts whistling and making all kinds of noises.

Whoops.

We reluctantly break our lips apart but don't otherwise move away from each other. I need his body on mine. In mine.

I smile into his mouth. "I think you were the last to arrive tonight, kitten. You know what that means."

His smile matches mine. "I've got a good one for you. The clitoris is made up of the same tissue as a penis. It expands and engorges when aroused, so technically women get erections too."

I nod in acknowledgment of the throb currently taking place between my legs. "That makes sense for what I'm feeling right now."

His lips and nose tickle my cheek as he breathes, "Let's get out of here, Kam bam." I can feel the desire pouring from him. He's been missing me as much as I've missed him.

I want to leave with him, but I'm not sure I can abandon my sister in her time of need. All the guys at this table are good ones and will look out for her, but I still feel bad.

I turn my head around. Daylen mouths, "It's okay. We've got her. Go."

I look at Bailey. "We're going to take off. Are you okay to get home?" I silently communicate that I'll stay if she needs me.

She happily encourages me to leave while Champ offers to see her home.

Cheetah grabs my hand and pulls me through the hordes of people while growling, "I need you naked. Stat."

"I can get on board with that plan." I smile. "Should I take my clothes off here?"

He chuckles as we finally make our way out to the street. The air of the unseasonably warm spring night hits me. Or maybe it's the heat of my desire for him currently causing my body temperature to rise.

Fuck, we need a cab or an Uber. We can't walk to either of our places from here. It's too far. Ugh. It's going to delay things. I can't wait any longer. Maybe we should go back inside and fuck in the bathroom. Or maybe we'll just fuck in the cab.

As I'm scanning the street for cabs, I notice a giant boat with wheels parked right in front of the club. The side of it reads Ride the Ducks, and there's a huge smiling duck painted on it and he looks like he's swimming.

The driver nods at Cheetah. "Your chariot awaits, sir."

I look at him. "What in the fuck is this?"

"It's the Ride the Ducks vehicle. It's a car and a boat all in one. They used to tour people around Philly in these until about eight years ago when they shut down. A guy I knew bought one of the boats. I called him before my plane took off and rented it for the evening. It goes on land and sea. We'll create our own Luminous Lagoon."

I wiggle my eyebrows. "I do like the motion of your ocean. Is your vessel full of seamen?"

He laughs. "No, but I am. *A lot* of it. Let's get you to the water so I can make you all wet."

I run my nails across his scruff. "Oh, kitten, I'm most definitely already wet."

I grab his hand and run it under my short skirt until he feels my drenched panties.

He moans out, "Fuuuck."

I nod. "Fucking sounds good. Let's do that."

I giggle as he quickly scoops me into his arms, and we board the weird truck/boat. This thing is wild. I've never seen anything like it. It looks like it would have fit about twenty people in its heyday, which is long past.

His friend disappears into the front, which is in a makeshift cabin. I don't think he can see us back here since we can't see him, but I don't really care one way or the other. We're gonna fuck on this thing whether it's in front of an audience or not.

As we ascend the steps, I notice there are piles and piles of blankets and pillows. In fact, it's a fort. I look at him. "I recognize this handiwork. Is this a Gonzales nudist fort native to Galveston, Texas?"

His dimples make an appearance as he sets me on my feet. You can barely see them through his scruff, but they're there. Fuck, I've missed those dimples. "It sure is. You know the rules. You can't go in until you drop your clothes onto the floor. All of them."

"No problem." Uncaring that there may be a few prying eyes as the boat on wheels begins its journey down the street, I make very quick work of my skirt, top, and undergarments until I'm completely naked.

Cheetah simply watches as I do so while the bulge in his jeans gets bigger and bigger. He shakes his head. "My spank bank does not do you justice. You. Are. Perfection." He very obviously and purposefully adjusts himself. "My weapon of mass titillation is about to reach its intended target."

I make a bit of a show of crawling into the fort, wiggling my ass along the way. "If you want me to ride your sturdy stallion, you better take off your clothes too."

Once I reach the middle of the fort, I sit, leaning back on my hands, as I wait for him. He reaches into his pocket and throws at least ten condoms into the fort. I look up at him. "How long did you rent this for?"

He chuckles as he removes his clothes. "Just making sure we're covered. Unless you don't want to use condoms. I'd be game for that."

I mouth, "Never." He knows I'll never have sex without a condom.

He nods in understanding of my hard line in the sand. "I have it through sunrise. I thought it would be cool to sleep out here and watch the sunrise on the water." He points to the side of the fort. "This fort has windows."

Hmm. Look at that. The sides have small openings so we can see out. He put real thought into the design.

He smiles as he crawls naked into our fort. He's so hot. I'm aching to feel his bare body on mine.

In five more seconds, I get what I want as he falls on top of me between my legs. I nearly weep, I'm so happy right now. Just the skin-to-skin contact is the breath of fresh air I didn't know I needed.

It suddenly occurs to me that the last time we were like this, I was an asshole. He senses where my head is. "It's in the past, Kam bam. Let it go. I have." He groans as his cock runs through my center. "Fuck, I've missed intimacy."

"You didn't..."

His eyes meet mine as he shakes his head. "No, Kamryn, I didn't. You're the only one I want. It's okay if you did. We made no promises to each other. I made my choice for me. I had no expectations—"

"There was no one," I interrupt. I tilt my chin toward the sky and blow out a breath. "I...umm...couldn't. I didn't want to." My eyes meet his again. "Well, I wanted to, but not with anyone but you."

He smiles as his lips meet mine. I happily welcome his tongue into my mouth, savoring the taste I've missed for five long weeks.

The kiss escalates quickly as our weeks of frustration reach a boiling point. I roll us over so I'm on top. I want to take in our scenery when I bounce on top of him all night.

I reach down and run my hand up and down his velvety length. His hands freely roam my body before landing on my breasts. He loves playing with my nipples. It's an erogenous zone for me, so I more than welcome it.

My body is overheated, but the truck/boat has begun to move, causing a cool breeze to whip through our fort. There's something so erotic about the hot and cold dichotomy.

He lifts his head and takes my hardened nipple into his warm, wet mouth. His bare cock runs through my pussy again. I think we both moan at the same time.

He breathes, "Fuck, Kam bam, I love how wet you get for me."

In the most desperate sound that has ever escaped my mouth, I say, "My pussy is weeping for you. I need to sit on your beard. Please. I want it."

He lays back down and motions his fingers in a come-hither manner. "Siéntate en mi cara." *Sit on my face.* He licks his lips. "Este gatito necesita probar tu dulce coño." *This kitten needs to taste your sweet pussy.*

Grabbing my hips to help me, he pulls me until I'm situated on his mouth. His beard scratches along my most intimate region. Oh god, that's good. He takes it a step further by rubbing his beard all around, covering himself in my juices.

So. Fucking. Hot.

His tongue slides in and out of me as he mumbles, "I missed your taste."

"I missed your tongue."

He teases me, knowing my body so well. I'm kind of sitting there enjoying what he's doing to me when he loudly mumbles into me, "Rebota en mi cara." *Bounce on my face.*

I don't need much more of an invitation than that. I move up and down on his tongue while his thumb finds my clit, knowing exactly how I like to be touched. He gives me everything I need, as always. He's so in tune with my body. He's a maestro, and I'm his instrument.

I'm practically fucking his face, so desperate for a non-self-induced orgasm. It's not long before I explode all over him. He licks around and savors every last drop.

I immediately slide down his body and lick all over his beard. I love tasting me on him. There's something so sensual about it.

He sits up and begins to kiss me again. It's hungry. We're all tongues and teeth. Neither of us can get enough of the other.

His hands run up my body as the kiss breaks, and he looks into my eyes with an intensity that's almost too much, but I don't pull away.

He breathes, "Tell me what you need. Use your words."

I search for something sassy to say, but only honesty meets my lips. "You, kitten. I just need you."

I reach for a condom. I experience a brief moment of wanting to feel him inside me with nothing between us, but I think better of it. It's not something I do. This is already more intense than I've ever felt before. I can't give any more than I already am.

I open it and then roll it down his perfect cock. I ache for him on a level I'm having a hard time understanding, but I'm trying not to get too much in my head. Neither of us have had sex in a month. We're horny. Plain and simple. At least that's what I'm telling myself so I don't jump out of this weird-as-fuck vehicle.

He lifts my hips and places his tip at my entrance before pulling me all the way down onto him.

It knocks the breath from my lungs. Holy shit. Did I revirginize after five weeks of no sex? Is that a thing? He feels so fucking big. I'm so fucking full of him.

He stills inside me. Our mouths are nearly touching. Our ragged breath becomes one. He visibly swallows as his blue eyes practically stare into my soul. "It's like I can't get close enough to you."

I feel down to the spot where our bodies join. "We're as close as two people can be."

"And yet it's still not close enough."

Feeling the same way, I whisper, "Cruz."

He whispers back, "Kamryn."

I'm teetering on the edge of freaking out and letting myself go when the vehicle makes some kind of loud mechanical noise and then drops a few feet. It causes his dick to push hard inside me. I think my eyes momentarily roll to the back of my head as my stomach clenches, and I let out a loud moan.

We turn and look out our makeshift fort windows to realize that we're now on the water. "Holy shit."

He smiles. "I told you it was also a boat."

"My below deck is feeling pretty good and wet right now."

"So is my hull." He squeezes my tits while asking, "Do you want me on your bow?" He then squeezes my ass. "Or your stern?"

"Why choose? But I know I need to start moving to both the port," I move my hips to the left, "and starboard," I move my hips to the right, "sides to enter the rough seas that I like."

He wiggles his eyebrows. "Here's to not-so-smooth sailing."

I smile. "Anchor's away."

I begin my slow movements as I rock on top of him. It's only been a minute, and I can already feel my insides coiling with uncontrollable pleasure.

My fingernails dig into his broad shoulders as his big hands cover my back. This isn't just physical for me. There are so many emotions flowing through me right now.

He then slides his fingers through mine as we continue to stare at each other. It seems so simple, yet I don't think I've ever held a man's hands while I'm riding him.

He encourages me to lean all the way back. It feels like I'm falling, yet I completely trust that he won't let me do so.

I arch my back as his hands move to the spot between my wrists and forearms. Gripping me tightly while holding me in place, he thrusts into me over and over. He keeps my back hovering just above his legs.

I might be on top, but I'm totally at his mercy. As always, he doesn't let me down.

"Alguien te ha follado así alguna vez?" *Has anyone ever fucked you like this?*

I shake my head and whimper, "No."

For the first time while on top, I completely give up control. I couldn't stop my orgasm if I wanted to.

"Está bien romperse. Choca por mí. Déjalo ir." *It's okay to break. Crash for me. Let go.*

And I do.

I'M AWAKENED by the sounds of multiple female voices, but my eyes are still closed, not wanting to open them to the bright morning lights. I can feel and smell that I'm wrapped in Cheetah's arms. If I dreamed last night, I don't want to wake up.

It was amazing. We kept going at it over and over. I swear the man has endless boners and stamina.

"You two have been a very *nauti* buoy and a *nauti* gull."

I hear the females all giggling. I finally peel my eyes open to see Reagan Daulton's smiling face standing over us. Next to her is an attractive blonde woman who resembles Reagan but with huge green eyes, and a shorter brunette with the same green eyes.

I look around. The pillows of our fort have collapsed so I can see where we are. We're still on the truck/boat under a bevy of blankets, but we appear to be parked in a lot next to the river.

I elbow Cheetah. "Wake up. We've been busted by the sex police."

The women laugh again while Cheetah blinks his eyes open and looks at the three of them. "Did we do a fivesome that I forgot about?"

I giggle. "You wish." I take in Reagan and the two women with her and mumble, "Actually, *I* wish."

Reagan shakes her head. "You guys are lucky that the port authority officer recognized Cruz and called me. Otherwise, you'd be in deep ship." She points to the blonde woman next to her. "This is my sister, Skylar." She points to the brunette. "And this is my other sister, Harley. We were having coffee this morning on our way to work when I received a lovely call about one of my players being naked in public. How exciting for me to arrive and learn that it's *two* of my players," she says sarcastically.

Skylar is dressed in a fancy business suit like Reagan, but Harley is in scrubs.

I shrug as I yawn. "He's been gone for a month. My porthole was in need of servicing."

They all smile, and Reagan shakes her head. "You've got a lot of big deck energy, Cruz."

Harley adds, "Tell us the hull truth."

I roll my eyes. "Your family is full of cheesy puns. I've got one for you. Kiss my aft. It's no one's business but ours."

Cheetah nods. "Yeah. Ship happens. Get over it. We're not bothering anybody."

Reagan holds up her hands. "No judgment, but they were about to call the cops, so I said I'd handle it."

Cheetah looks at Harley more closely. "I feel like we've met."

I nod. "You probably slept with her." I hold up my hand for a high five. "She's hot. Nicely done."

Harley shakes her head. "I was one of the doctors treating Layton Lancaster when he broke his leg. I met you that night."

Cheetah slowly nods. "Oh right, the hot doc who was Reagan's sister. I remember." He turns his head to me and unashamedly announces, "We thought someone ordered him a stripper."

I look Harley's gorgeous body up and down. "I get that."

Reagan sighs. "Just get dressed and get out of here before the press gets wind of this. I've got a lot of shit going on. The last thing I need is bad press from my players."

CHAPTER TWENTY-SEVEN

TWO MONTHS LATER

KAMRYN

"Who got wet first?" Cheetah asks while trying to hold in his laughter as we sit naked in his living room fort, eating dark chocolate-covered pineapples, our new favorite treat. It's our compromise since I got him to admit he hates the fondue restaurant that I love. He said if he wanted to cook, he'd stay home and do it himself. Given that we both like pineapples and I like dark chocolate, we made our own fondue treats for our middle-of-the-night forts.

I smile as I lick my fingers clean of the chocolate. "Bridget. I felt a little bad for her. She was so embarrassed."

Cheetah is well into his season. He's having a great year. His speed is better than it's been in a few years, and he leads the league in stolen bases. I go to as many games as I can. I get the honor of his seventh-inning stretch dances every few weeks, but we're waiting a little longer to do our choreographed dance so that it's perfected.

After much begging, Ms. Rylee agreed to be our teacher for this specific dance. We had to promise no more mid-session orgasms. It hasn't been easy. For some reason, the dance lessons get us both worked up.

Our Anacondas team practices are well underway, and our season is about to start. The team looks good, and because Ripley gave birth early, she hopes she'll be ready for opening day. We initially assumed we wouldn't have her until mid-season, if at all.

She moved back to town with Quincy and their daughter, Kaya, who has red hair and blue eyes just like her mom. Everyone fawns all over her. Everyone except me.

June moved back with them so she can help care for Kaya and train Ripley. I *love* having Mama June in town. She's a constant source of amusement. I'm headed over to Quincy's house later this week for a girls' day by the pool while the guys head out of town for a road trip.

When I'm not with Bailey or at softball, I'm with Cheetah. I wish it was more often, but I can tell that my sister's defenses are breaking when it comes to Tanner Montgomery, so I try not to leave her side very often.

They practically stare at each other with googly eyes at Harper's games. It's only a matter of time before she starts fucking him again. I think it's time for me to educate her on the real rules of casual sex, though I'm not doing a good job of it myself these days.

The beginning of our practices is my favorite time of year because they mean one thing. Rookie hazing.

As it turns out, the guys do it too, but they're totally different from us. Cheetah and I are trading hazing war stories in the comforting confines of his nudist fort after an evening of crazy fucking, something we've been doing a lot since his return from Spring Training.

Cheetah nods. "Which one is Bridget?"

"The tall brunette. She plays first base for us."

"Oh right." He shakes his head. "I can't believe you make the rookies sit naked on running washing machines and wait to see who gets wet first. How can you tell if they're wet, other than the obvious touch test?"

I smile. "Paper towels. You can see them start to saturate. It's classic," I giggle.

"Did you have to do it your rookie year?" he asks.

I nod. "Yep. I was wet before they even turned on the machines and proudly admitted as much."

He chuckles. "Was it seeing the other women naked?"

I wiggle my eyebrows. "Sure was."

"We do something similar. We make the guys stand naked and watch weird porn to see who gets hard first. Like bestiality or some crazy shit like that."

I giggle. "Classic. What else?"

He twists his lips. "There's the always-present elephant walk."

"Obviously." That's when the rookies all have to walk in a circle for a certain amount of time, holding each other's dicks. That's a longtime legend, and everyone knows it's done.

His eyes widen with excitement. "We did a new one this year in Florida. We dumped several jars of rainbow jimmies on the ground. Then we covered all the rookies' hands in maple syrup and told them they had to sort the jimmies by color." He lets out a laugh. "It took them all fucking night."

"Ooh, that's a good one. Maybe we'll use that. Give me another."

"Hmm. They have to attend their first practice of the season with a potato in their asses. Not all the way in but sitting nestled between their cheeks. All the veterans walk around spanking them and watch them wince."

I scrunch my face. "Ouch. It must be hard to play with a potato in their ass."

The corners of his mouth raise in amusement. "Some handle it better than others."

I let out a laugh. "I bet."

"Oh, you'll like this one. We tell the guys it's an ice cream speed-eating contest. They each have to gobble down a full gallon. When it's over, we tell them that we first melted the gallons, jerked off into them, and then refroze them. We don't actually do that, but they think we do." He starts hysterically laughing. "Most of them puke." He grabs his stomach in laughter. "Shit, it's so funny when you see their faces as realization hits them."

"Oh my god. Okay, guys are way worse than girls."

We finish the last of our chocolate-covered pineapples and lay down. Middle-of-the-night fort time has quickly become my favorite thing in the world. We talk and laugh for hours. It's a level of intimacy I've never shared with another person, Bailey included. Cheetah knows all my secrets, and he isn't running the other way. Just the opposite. We're getting closer and closer every day. It both terrifies and excites me.

TONIGHT IS the semi-final game for Harper's softball team. If we win, the championship is in a few days.

Admittedly, I've had fun doing this with my sister...once she stopped trying to censor me. I've always been afraid of kids because I don't know how to talk to them and can't relate to them, so I simply started talking to them like adults, and they seem to like it.

Bailey fielded a few parent complaints about it at the beginning, but I've learned that softball parents care about one thing. Winning. And we do a shit ton of that, so the complaints ended pretty quickly.

As I had predicted on the first day of practice, Sapphire, the future ass-shaker, couldn't hack it at shortstop. We moved Andie over, and she's done a great job. In my opinion, Harper is still the slightly better option, but she's obsessed with my sister and wants to play the same position as her. Andie is a little bigger and stronger than Harper, so it's not all bad. She's by far the best shortstop in the league.

Tanner pokes his head into the dugout, and I narrow my eyes at him. "If you're here to stare at my sister's ass, she's not wearing tight shorts today."

He subtly gives me the finger while scratching his nose as he hands me a water bottle. "Harper left this in the car. Can you give it to her?"

I shake my head. "Don't enable her forgetfulness. If she forgets her water, she shouldn't get any. That's the only way to teach her a lesson."

He rolls his eyes. "Please let me take in your pearls of wisdom from your years of parenting. She's eight, and it's over eighty degrees today. Her getting dehydrated isn't the lesson I care to teach."

"You're a shit father."

"You're simply a little shit. I can't believe none of these parents have called the cops on you with how you talk to the girls."

Yep, there's no love lost between Tanner and me. I don't like the way he treated my sister, and I've been extremely vocal about it. In return, I very clearly and happily get on his nerves.

I place my hand on my hips. "Parents like winning teams. We're a well-oiled machine. You have to admit we're good coaches."

He raises one of his thick, annoyingly sexy eyebrows. "*Bailey* is a good coach. You're riding her coattails. You've probably done it your whole life."

I cross my arms, and he sighs in defeat as he admits, "Fine, you happen to be decent at coaching. It's kind of shocking, given your lack of interpersonal skills."

"Did you throw up a little in your mouth when you said that?"

He nods. "A lot actually."

Bailey walks into the dugout and pulls the back of my shirt.

"Back to your corners, kids. I swear, you two are less mature than the players on this team."

Tanner mumbles, "She started it."

I'm about to say something back when the girls all enter the dugout. Harper looks at Tanner. "Why are you here, Daddy?"

I give a big, fake smile. "Yes, *Daddy*, you shouldn't be in here. No parents allowed in the dugout."

He scowls at me before smiling at Harper. "You forgot your water, bug. I thought you might be thirsty."

"Why do you call her bug?" I ask. "Did she play with bugs when she was younger?"

He shakes his head. "When she was born, she was all eyes. They covered half her face. Fallon and I joked that she looked like a bug, and I've called her that ever since."

I shrug. "It's babyish. Don't call her that. I'm sure it embarrasses her."

Harper crosses her arms. "Yeah, Daddy, don't call me bug anymore. It's babyish like Kam said."

Tanner pinches the bridge of his nose. "God help me. I'm going back to the stands."

He walks away and I pull Harper aside. "You know what all daddies hate being called?"

"What?"

"Dad. It drives them nuts. It means you're all grown up. Start calling him Dad until he stops calling you bug. That will teach him."

She smiles as she nods enthusiastically. "Good idea. I will."

I inwardly laugh, remembering how much our father hated the brief period of time we called him Dad. I love fucking with Tanner Montgomery. It's my new favorite hobby.

My sister shakes her head as she mumbles to me, "You're the biggest shit-stirrer of all time."

"Thank you."

"Not a compliment."

I shrug. "Sounded like one to me."

The game is finally underway, and we're about to take the field. I have a highly specific individual handshake with each girl on the team. They didn't think I could remember all twelve, but I showed them.

We win handily and are on to the championship game. As always, Harper puts on both an offensive and defensive display, the likes of which no one her age can match. I love her love of the game. Her mind is always in motion like mine was at her age.

She's officially the first kid I've ever liked. Hmm...maybe Andie too.

CHEETAH

"If she can take getting a tattoo, she can definitely take it up the backdoor," Daylen mutters as he complains about the woman he hooked up with last night.

I chuckle as I throw my cards on Tanner's poker table and announce, "I fold. I think I might head out for the night."

Daylen wiggles his eyebrows as he holds his cards. "Is that code for banging Kam? She's definitely into backdoor action. She likes the freaky shit, no doubt. You can see it in her eyes. She's got those crazy eyes." He raises his hands in the air like he's preaching. "When doth have crazy eyes, doth is a freak in the sheets. I think that was written in the Bible. The First Sluttippians, verse sixty-nine."

I give him the finger. "Your proverbs are about as useful as a knitted condom."

He laughs loudly while Tanner simply shakes his head. "You're still with that batch of crazy? I don't know how you stand her. All I want to do is muzzle her."

My jaw tics. I hate it when he trashes Kam. I know they don't get along, but he knows I care about her.

It's on the tip of my tongue to say something, but I don't want to put a damper on an otherwise fun evening.

He looks at his watch. "Maybe we should call it a night. I have an early morning meeting with Sulley O'Shea."

I notice Vance shift uncomfortably in his seat before Tanner continues, "I'm hoping to sign her even though I still don't have anyone to lead my damn women's division. I can't have the biggest star on the planet come to play in Philly and not sign her as my client, but I really don't have the bandwidth."

I shrug. "Hire someone."

"It's easier said than done. I won't hire just anyone. It's a big dick job. I want a female attorney who understands sports at a high level, who also happens to not take shit from anyone. It's a lot harder to find than you'd think."

"Have you interviewed anyone?" I ask.

He nods. "Over a dozen women. None were right for the job, and I won't settle. I met one the other night who spent the whole time asking me about Vance. I told her he's impotent and to steer clear."

Vance doesn't even flinch. He's a million miles away. I wave my fingers in front of his face. "Earth to Vance."

He snaps his head up. "Sorry, what was that? Did you say it was important?"

Tanner shakes his head. "I said you're impotent just to see if you were paying attention. Why did you wince when I said Sulley O'Shea's name? Is she going to be a problem? I don't need a problem client. No amount of money is worth that."

Vance visibly swallows. "I haven't spoken to her in years. We grew up in the same town. I was friends with her older brother, Finn."

Something passes between Vance, Tanner, and Daylen. Clearly they have some sort of secret that I'm not in on.

Tanner slowly nods. "I didn't realize the connection." He gives Vance a look to suggest that they'll talk about it later.

I think I need to lighten the mood. I look at Daylen, who just buzzed his hair short. He has a different hairstyle all the time. Sometimes it's long and sometimes it's short. It grows bizarrely fast. "Nice haircut, Forrest Gump. Did you lose weight with it? You did grow a little dad bod this off-season. Losing weight on the top could only help your slow ass."

I'm fucking with him. The guy doesn't have an ounce of body fat. He's built like a brick house.

He gives me his trademark crooked smile. He knows what I'm doing. "Actually, I lost fifteen pounds, ten from the haircut."

"Where did the other five come from?"

"I got circumcised."

We all laugh hysterically. Daylen is always full of funny jokes. I love the guy.

I KNOCK on Gemma's office door and look at her. I used to think there was no better woman on this planet than Gemma DePaul. While I'll always have deep affection for her as my friend, I know now that I was just waiting for Kam to come along. She's my perfect match. That won't prevent me from fucking with Trey though. I let out a whistle. "Hey, sexy. You ready for lunch?"

She smiles as she looks up from her computer. "Can you give me five minutes? I need to get this email out before we leave."

I nod. "Sure. Is your hot boss in today? Maybe I can get some lunchtime action like her husband."

"Good luck with that. Yes, she's here today."

"I'm gonna go say hi to her. Come get me when you're ready."

She wordlessly nods as I walk away and head toward Darian Knight's office and knock on her door. She looks up from her computer and smiles much like Gemma did. I swear they could be mother and daughter. "Cruz! What a nice surprise. Are you ladies lunching today?"

I let out a laugh. "We are. Then we're getting bikini waxes."

"Is that how you keep your speed? By being aerodynamic?"

My eyes widen. "No, but now that you say it, maybe I should consider waxing for real."

She lets out a laugh before inviting me in. I slowly walk around her office and look at the dozen or so picture frames scattered throughout her office. "Wow. You have a big family."

"I do. My three daughters are all married with kids, and Jackson's three sons are all married with kids. Our blended family is enormous. You should see the size of my dining room table."

I pinch my eyebrows together. "I didn't know Jackson wasn't the original Mr. Darian."

She somberly nods toward a photo of a blond man smiling with three little girls. "That was my first husband, Scott Lawrence. He passed about a decade ago."

"I'm sorry. I didn't realize—"

"It's okay. A lot of people don't know."

I point to one of the little kids in the photo. One who looks very familiar. "Is that Reagan?"

She smiles. "It is. She was a pistol then and she's a pistol now. My girls are all adults and in their thirties, but they all have the exact same personalities they had as kids. It's amazing. You don't have kids yet, do you?"

I shake my head. "I don't."

"Maybe one day."

I twist my lips. "I think I always assumed I wanted kids because it's what's expected, but the woman I'm seeing doesn't want kids."

"What do you want?"

I'm considering how to answer that when Gemma pokes her head in. "Knock, knock. Don't steal my lunch date, Darian."

"He's a cutie. If Jackson wasn't coming by in a few minutes I'd definitely steal this one."

Gemma grabs my arm and mumbles, "Trust me, we want to get away from this office for the next hour. It's going to get...loud."

Darian laughs as we say our goodbyes and head to lunch. All of four seconds after we sit down at the restaurant, she asks, "How's it going with Kam?"

I smile. "Good. Really good."

"Are you an official couple?"

I think for a moment before answering, "I'm not sure. We haven't talked about it. She doesn't like the word commitment. She prefers flingationship."

"What the hell is that?"

"Basically friends with benefits. It was supposed to be open, but neither of us are seeing anyone else. At least I'm not."

"Is that what you want?"

I think for a moment. "I wouldn't mind us being more, but she's always been clear that it's not what she wants. I respect her wishes."

Her green eyes soften. "What about your wishes, Cruz? What you want should matter as much as what she wants." She tilts her head to the side. "You can't do all the giving.

That's not how relationships work. It's supposed to be give-and-take on both sides. I know you're a pleaser by nature, but if she's not bending for you like you are for her, maybe it's not meant to be."

My head is spinning as I consider her words. "But I love her."

"Does she love you?"

I shrug. "She would never admit that even if she did."

She leans back in her chair and sighs. "I know you're already in deep with her. And I really like her for you. A lot. But you need to think about your needs and make sure they're being met. It can't only be about hers."

I shake my head. "It's only been a few months. I don't think it's right to put pressure on her when she's never been anything but upfront with me."

She takes my hand. "You're a grown man. Probably my second favorite grown man on the planet." She smiles. "Don't tell my besties I said that. I'll deny it."

Gemma's two longtime best friends are men. It was a whole fucking thing for Trey when they first started dating. I think it's cool. Gemma is a guy's girl through and through.

She continues, "You deserve to have everything you want. When you decide what you want, make sure your partner gives it to you."

I nod. "You're right."

Later that afternoon, I'm at Layton's penthouse. I suppose it's now Layton and Arizona's penthouse.

Layton makes bats in his woodshop. He texted to let me know that he had finished my new one, and I should come pick it up. I'm excited about it. He happens to be very talented.

I run my hand over the smooth contours. "This looks awesome, man. Thank you. I love it."

He pretends to blow a whistle. "Coach Layton reporting for duty."

Layton now helps out as a part-time assistant coach for both our team and the Anacondas.

"How's married life?"

He smiles. "Amazing. Can you keep a secret?"

I nod. "Of course."

"We're trying for a baby."

I practically gasp. "Really? What about her season?"

"We've talked about it. We want to have one kid before the Olympics. If she gets pregnant in the next month or two, she'll be able to play this season and will have the baby well enough ahead of next season to get back into shape for it. I'd be lying if I said I wasn't concerned about the possibility of her being pregnant and the physical demands of catching, but it's best for her career, and I want to support that. This is stuff male athletes don't ever have to consider."

I nod. "You're right. No one worries about timing and getting back into playing shape. I never thought about it until now."

"Yep. And we just met with Quincy's builder." Quincy built a giant mansion in the suburbs. "We bought the lot next to Quincy, and we're going to break ground as soon as possible."

I sit down, in a bit of shock. I was finally used to the fact that Layton is no longer a single man. But now he's also moving to the suburbs. Everything is changing.

I can't help but shake my head. "I can't say I ever saw you as a minivan dad in the 'burbs."

He chuckles. "No minivan...yet. I'm married. We're

starting a family. I want land for our kids to play on. You can't get that in the city. Isn't that what everyone wants?"

I hold out my hand for him and say, "Congrats, man. I'm happy for you," but my mind is a million miles away. Is that what everyone wants?

Is it what I want?

CHAPTER TWENTY-EIGHT

CHEETAH

The time Kam and I have been waiting for has arrived. Tonight, during the seventh-inning stretch of my game, she and I are performing the rumba. It's called the "dance of love" for a reason. Lots of hip movements and lots of sensuality.

The dance works well with my regular song, "Cheetah" by Chris Brown. We went back to Ms. Rylee to practice this specific dance a handful of times. There's not one second of our practice time I haven't loved. It's Kam and me with a heavy dose of fun, laughter, and the best foreplay in existence.

Kam isn't remotely nervous. She's so excited about the big performance.

We chose this game because it's the first Ripley will attend. They moved back a few weeks ago, but Ripley has been home with Kaya. With her being a preemie and them getting a little media attention, they didn't want to take her in public for a bit, but today is that day. All our friends are finally at a game together, and Kam and I have secretly been planning a big show for them. They have no idea it's coming.

When the time comes, she's escorted out to the field. She removes the jersey she's wearing to reveal a sexy suede outfit. It's got a Tarzan and Jane vibe, with a barely-there strip of material and beads across her generous chest, her abs on display, and a purposefully jaggedly cut, very short skirt, also clad with beading. It works well with the sensual movements of the dance, and her long, bare legs are capped with heels. I think everyone in the stadium is salivating, me included.

There's a loud sea of whistles coming from the stands and the dugouts. Kam pays them no attention. She's homed in on me with her giant smile. How did I get so lucky?

She approaches me with an excited bounce in her step. I take her hand and kiss it. "You're stunning."

Her smile widens as she turns my baseball cap backward. "Just don't drop me, kitten."

I wink. "Never."

She falls into my arms as we get into ready position. She smells so fucking good. I love it. It's become so familiar and soothing to me.

The music begins, as do the erotic synchronized movements of our hips. The fans are going crazy. They expect a little something extra from Kam and me at this point, but nothing as polished and professional as what we're giving them.

We're hitting every sexy movement with perfection, and we nail the first two lifts. Neither are as grand as the finale lift though.

We have huge grins on our faces as we twirl and sway around the field. The fans are getting into it. They're all on their feet, clapping their hands, singing the words to the song. I love bringing so much joy to everyone.

The end is nearing. For the finale, we do a spin move

that flows seamlessly into me lifting her into the air above my head with one hand. I'm basically supporting her entire weight with my hand on her hip. It took me forever to learn how to balance her properly like this, but we've nailed it at practice enough for me to feel confident to perform it today.

The song comes to an end with her hoisted above my head. After a pregnant pause for what I imagine is extreme shock at the professional-level routine and ending lift they just witnessed, every person in that stadium erupts in cheers. It may be the loudest I've ever heard this stadium, and we've been in the World Series before. The stunned faces in the dugout are priceless.

I gently pull Kam down until she falls into my arms like a bride. She's smiling like a loon before she cups my cheek and softly pecks my lips.

That's not enough for me. I'm too wired. I deepen the kiss, and the fans go wilder. I know they must feel like they're witnessing a real live love story. I know I do. It's like I'm living in one of Gemma's novels.

Once I set her feet on the ground, I watch her as she raises her hands in the air and then curtsies. I stare at her in awe. She's my everything. I'm so fucking in love with her.

While being overcome with my love and affection for this woman, I do the dumbest thing possible. In front of over forty thousand people, I drop down to one knee.

Kam doesn't notice at first, but the entire stadium collectively gasps in shock. I see her brief moment of confusion before her head turns to me, and her eyes widen in shock.

She breathes, "What are you doing?"

I beam at her. "Kam bam, I love you more than anything in this world and don't want to live another day of my life without you by my side. What do you say to a little long-term prostitution? Marry me."

Tears immediately well in her eyes. Her head swivels as if realizing just how many people are silently waiting for her answer. And waiting...and waiting...and waiting.

The silent pause is so long that people separately begin yelling out, "Do it!" before forty thousand people end up chanting it in unison.

I can tell she's struggling. The look on her face tells me that I'm not going to get the answer I had hoped for. Eventually, I stand, and my shoulders fall. "You're not going to say yes, are you?"

Tears spill down her cheeks. "I'm so sorry, Cruz. I can't. I told you I'm not the marrying type."

"Do you love me?" I pathetically ask.

She's again silent, simply staring at me, looking miserable.

The extreme awkwardness is broken only by the bevy of boos being leveled by the crowd as they begin to understand that I'm being rejected. They start shouting expletives at her. And then they start throwing things onto the field. Hot dogs, beer bottles, pretzels. All of it.

Shit. This is bad. *Really* bad.

Security rushes out. They have to shield and escort her to the underground, private area of the stadium. What the hell did I do?

Despite the warm weather, a chill suddenly works its way through my body. My hands are shaking.

As my team silently takes the field again, my teammates all slap my back and mumble things like, "Sorry man," and "That sucks."

Trey is the last to walk over to me. I look up at him. "I feel like such a loser. She doesn't love me like I love her."

He sighs as he hands me my baseball glove. "I don't know if that's true, but given her issues, it was an impossible spot to put her in. And now you've probably turned her into the most hated person in Philly. This is going to be a PR mess. I'm truly sorry, this sucks for you, but it's about to get really fucking bad for Kam."

I remove my baseball cap and run my fingers through my hair. "Shit. You're right. I didn't mean to do it to her. I was just feeling the moment."

He nods. "I know, buddy. We'll figure out a way to make it right. Let's focus on finishing this game for now, and we'll deal with this afterward."

KAMRYN

I'm pacing in front of the locker room. What in the fuck was he thinking proposing to me? He knows my feelings about marriage. And in a public setting? Is he on crack?

I don't know what to do. Should I go find my sister? Although she's not herself right now. She and Tanner started things back up again but are supposedly truly casual. She's pulling the purse strings this time around, keeping him at arm's length. But I know my sister. Casual sex isn't in her vocabulary. I'm fearful that she's going to get hurt all over again.

I can't think about her fucked relationship with Tanner Montgomery right now. It consumes too many of my thoughts. I've got my own fucked-up relationship to deal with.

Should I leave? Maybe this was for the best. We were never headed for his happily ever after. Maybe this will give us a clean break. I haven't wanted to let him go, but perhaps this is the push I needed. He obviously wants to get married. I don't think I'm capable of it.

But the thought of losing him hurts more. Is that what marriage is? When you'd rather be with a person than not? I can't imagine it's that simple. It's not exactly like I had an example of a happy marriage to watch growing up.

My head is spinning with a million thoughts. Maybe I should go call Dr. Pearl. I have an emergency number. Yes, I'll go home and do that. She'll tell me what to do. More likely, she'll push me to figure out what it is I want to do, but I think I need her thought-provoking questions to figure this out.

I hurriedly walk to the end of the hallway to the exit and place my hands on the large, heavy metal door. My eyes stare at my hands pressed against the cool metal. As hard as I try, I can't seem to make myself push that door and leave.

I'm hit with the sudden realization that I don't need Dr. Pearl for this because I know what I want to do. I don't want to walk away from him. For some reason, I know if I leave, it's truly over between us. I can't stomach that.

After a long, calming breath, I turn back around and head toward the locker room. This will probably be a press shitstorm, but that's not my concern. I don't give a crap about any of that. It's Cheetah I care about. The look of disappointment on his face is what will now haunt my nightmares. I need to figure out a way to make this right.

About thirty minutes go by with me practically wearing a hole in the ground. I can hear that the game is finally over. Within minutes, I see several members of the team making their way to the locker room.

None of the guys make eye contact with me. I don't blame them. I'm sure they all hate me, as does every fan in this stadium. Within a few hours, the entire city will despise me. By morning, the whole country will. Fuck 'em.

Cheetah eventually makes his way toward the locker room door. He's walking slowly, and his head is down, looking like someone shot his dog. I start to say, "I'm sorr—" but he looks at me and holds up his hands.

"Don't." He shakes his head. "I know I shouldn't have done it in this setting, but it still hurts. I don't want to be around you right now. Give me time."

Fuck, he looks so pained. It hurts me to see him hurting. My instinct is to wrap my arms around him and tell him that I care about him. I do. I just don't want to marry him.

"How much time?" I ask. "I'm not known for my patience."

He drops his eyes to the ground as he simply shrugs. "I don't know, Kamryn. I don't know when or if I'll ever be okay with this." He looks back up at me with tears filling his eyes. "You broke my fucking heart."

Fuck. Fuck. Fuck. This is always what I feared getting in too deep with him. Hurting him. It's the last thing in the world I want. He doesn't deserve it. Why does it feel like my heart is breaking too?

I whisper, "I'm so sorry."

His shoulders fall. "Just leave me alone." His normally happy blue eyes have tears now trickling from them. "I feel like I'm always the one giving in this *flingationship*. When is it my turn to receive? I'm always the one fighting for you. You know what,

Kamryn? I think I'm finally fresh out of fight. You win. Game over."

I swallow down my emotions and nod. "I just don't think I can give you what you want."

"What is it you think I want?"

"I saw the way you looked at Gemma, Trey, and Fletcher in Florida. You want the happy, married, family life."

He takes a few long breaths. "You think you know what I want, but you don't. I didn't ask for any of that." He looks down and then back up at me. "You know what would be nice? What I do want?"

"What?"

"I want you to care about my needs the way I care about yours. I've watched *Titanic* fifty times in the past year. How many times have you watched *Star Wars*? Let me answer that for you. None. I'm single handedly supporting the dark chocolate industry. I've gone to your fondue restaurant, the one you know I hate, three times. How many times have you been willing to eat Indian food with me? Let me answer that for you. None. I don't ask for much, Kamryn, but if you care, a little give now and then wouldn't hurt."

He wipes the tears streaming down his face and steels his face. "I'm sorry I broke your fucking rule and fell in love with you. You'll be extremely satisfied to know that it was the worst mistake of my life. Loving *you* is the worst mistake of my life."

I stand in stunned silence as he walks through the doors into his locker room.

CHAPTER TWENTY-NINE

KAMRYN

I haven't moved an inch since he walked away. He's right about everything. He gives, and I take. No matter what we are and aren't, that's not fair to him.

I can't manage to make myself leave, so I pace some more with my mind spinning on every axis possible. The past year plays in my head like a movie.

Every single thing we've been through together. Every tear. Every laugh. Every intimate moment. Every thoughtful thing he's done. There are too many to count.

He's right. He gives and gives to me. Pushes me. *Loves me.* What have I done for him? Nothing.

I've never hated myself more than I do at this very moment, and that's saying something because I've spent a good part of the past eighteen years hating myself.

Tears freefall down my face. What the fuck have I done? I feel like I'm losing my best friend. The agony is nearly unbearable. I feel it in my heart. I've never felt pain like this before. Real physical pain in my chest. This must have been what Bailey felt when Tanner hurt her all those months ago. What Ripley felt when she moved away.

I eventually get to the point where I realize the truth. It's been staring me in the face for a long time, but I didn't want to see it.

He's right about the fact that he's always the one fighting for me and for us. Maybe it's time for me to return the favor.

Fuck this, I'm going into the locker room. There's nothing in there I haven't seen before.

I push through the doors and see a handful of guys standing by their lockers in a half-dressed state. They're staring at me like I'm crazy. Maybe I am.

I walk through the massive space until I hear the sounds of the showers and loud chatter. I poke my head in and see almost the entire team in a huge communal shower. There must be twenty showerheads. Guys really use communal showers? I thought that was a movie-created thing. So fucking weird. Girls would never do that.

I see Cheetah at the very end, slightly removed from the group. They seem to be giving him a little space. His back is to me, and his hands are on the wall with his head down. The water runs down the strong muscles of his bare back.

I pace again for another minute or two as I wait for him. My hands are practically twitching. Once again, I think, fuck this. I'm not waiting for another second.

CHEETAH

I can hear all the guys engaging in their normal banter in the shower. At least they're trying to normalize things for me, but I'm a million miles away.

My hands rest on the far back tile wall as I let the

scalding hot water beat down on me. Have I been spinning my wheels for a year? On some level, I've always known I was, but the problem is that I love her, and I can't imagine being with anyone but her.

What do you do when your perfect match doesn't want you?

Where do we go from here? You don't just propose to someone, they say no, and you go back to what you were. You can't love someone who refuses to ever love you back. I don't ask for much, but I have enough self-respect to know I deserve at least that.

I'm running through a million different scenarios in my mind when the steady stream of voices suddenly goes silent. I hear a few people breathe, "What the fuck?" and a few others whistle and snicker.

Without even having to turn around I know that Kamryn has stepped into the showers. I can feel her presence. After taking a calming breath, and without turning around, I break the silence and grit out, "I swear to god, Kamryn, if you're naked, I will kill you, you crazy fucking bitch."

I hear her voice, "You're not the only one with big balls, kitten. A gang bang is on my bucket list."

The shower area is suddenly covered in a sea of deep laughter from all the guys. I hear Jimmy say, "Look at her jugs."

Another teammate replies, "You probably don't know the difference between jugs and balls."

Jimmy lets out a laugh. "Well, I know I wasn't touching your mom's balls last night."

There's another eruption of laughter and cheering. Fucking neanderthals. I'm too old for this shit.

I hear Kamryn's voice again. "Boys, relax. You've all seen a naked woman before. At least I hope so. It's good to see that none of you are hung like Justin Timberlake."

As the guys all cackle like a bunch of old ladies, I turn my head to Trey, who's next to me, and whisper, "Is she *completely* naked?"

The corner of his mouth raises slightly as he subtly nods.

I shout, "Everyone get the fuck out! Now!"

It quickly goes silent. After a brief moment of hesitation, I hear them all scramble to leave. Once I'm confident they have, I turn around. Sure enough, Kamryn Hart is standing in the communal shower of a professional baseball team, naked as the day she was born.

I cross my arms and stare at the lunatic standing before me. "You're one hundred percent certifiable. You. Are. Nuts."

She cracks a small smile. "Your nuts are huge."

I shake my head. "No, sweetheart, no one has bigger nuts than you."

She shrugs. "I needed your attention."

I exhale a long breath. "There are other ways to go about it. Better ways than being naked in front of twenty grown men."

She places her hands on her hips. "It was a bit of a community service. I felt like the two gingers on your team deserved to see their first naked woman."

I have to bite back my smile. She loves her ginger jokes.

I'm not sure how she could possibly make me smile given how I feel right now, but Kamryn Hart always makes me smile. It's one of the things I love most about her.

I ask, "What's the difference between a ginger and a calendar?"

She immediately answers, "A calendar has dates."

I can't help but let out a laugh. There's no ginger joke she doesn't know.

After a short stare-down, my face turns serious. "There's

nothing left to say. I have nothing left to give. What is it that you want, Kamryn?"

"You."

"You just rejected me in front of forty-thousand people. You don't want me."

Sincerity blankets her face. "I never said I didn't want you. You know my feelings on marriage. We should have had a conversation about it before you proposed, especially in a setting like that."

In fairness, she's not wrong. I know she's dead set against marriage. We've never discussed otherwise. Not only did I propose, but I did it publicly. On national television.

I throw my hands in the air. "What can I say? I love you and want to spend my life with you. You looked so happy and so beautiful. I was swept away in the moment."

"You know full well that I'm about to pay the price for that moment of yours."

I shamefully nod. She's right. She'll be crucified. Vilified. It will probably negatively impact her modeling career. "I'm truly sorry about that. You know it wasn't my intention. I have no excuse other than the fact that my heart was bursting with love for you. I know you told me not to, but I fell in love with you, Kamryn. I love you." I throw my hands up and let them fall. "There, I said it. I can't take it back. I'm madly in love with you."

She tentatively walks toward me as if I'll retreat from her touch, but I don't back away. "I don't care about the backlash, Cruz. I care about you." She moves within an inch or two of me and fidgets nervously. "I didn't get to answer your question on the field."

"I'm pretty sure your silence implied that you were rejecting my marriage proposal."

She shakes her head. "Not *that* question." She nervously chews on her lower lip. "You asked me if I love you." She takes my hands in hers as the shower water now pelts down onto her too.

Without flinching in the slightest, she says, "I do love you. I fell in love with you too. You aren't alone in your feelings. You know what a big deal it is for me to say that." Her eyes are wary, but she doesn't look away.

I nod.

She continues, "I'm just not the marrying type. I'm a work in progress, Cruz. But I'm trying. I am. I've changed so much over the past year. Being around you has changed me for the better. I'm working on me, but I'm just not comfortable with marriage. Maybe that day will come, and maybe it won't. If you can't live with it, then I'll let you go for your own sake. If you can be patient, I want to try to be with you. No more caveats. No *flingationship*. No more pretending that we're just fuck buddies. No more avoiding deep conversations about us. I want to be your girlfriend. I'm going to fuck up sometimes. I freak out. It's who I am. But for you, and only you, I want to try."

Now it's my turn to be silent as I absorb the enormity of her words. This is her way of giving.

She continues, "Tell me what you want, Cruz, and I'll try to give it to you without compromising myself."

I swallow down the large knot in my throat as I think about how to answer her. "I want to be your sounding board, and I want you to be mine. I want to build you fires, build you forts, talk for hours, and feed you dark chocolate in the middle of the night when you can't sleep. I want you to drag me to your terrible fondue restaurant when you need your comfort food, but I equally want you to go with me when I need mine. I want to watch the movies you love, but I need you to watch the movies I love too. I want to be the man who brings you coffee in bed in the morning because I'm the reason you can't walk there yourself."

After a few deep breaths, she nods. "I want all those things too."

I slowly take in both her words and her physical beauty. There's no denying it. She's my everything. My body floods with warmth for her.

Her eyes move down my body until they land between my legs. "I can't believe you're hard right now."

"Kamryn, if the day ever comes where your naked body doesn't make me hard, take me out to pasture with all the cows."

She looks back up at me. "Did you know that cows have a three-hundred-and-thirty-degree field of vision? Can you imagine how great that would be for playing ball? I wish I had that."

"No, Kamryn, I didn't know that super relevant piece of information. Thank you for shedding light on how cows see. I had been wondering about it my whole life."

A giggle bubbles in her throat. "You're welcome."

I slowly move the wet strands of her hair now stuck to her face. She simply stares at me through her thick, wet eyelashes. My heart beats for this woman. I can't be without her.

I look into her gorgeous face. "I love you, Kamryn. I just want to be with you. Whatever form it takes is fine by me; all I ask is that you consider my needs at times. I'm sorry I put you in that position today. We'll figure something out for the impending fallout."

She runs her hands over my chest and brushes her lips across mine before whispering, "I don't care about anything but you. Fuck everyone else and what they think. I want to be with you too."

Her hand moves down until it grips my cock, but I shake my head. "I'm not having sex with you in this shower with all the guys within listening distance. Hell, half are probably watching."

She begins to stroke me and peppers kisses along my jawline. "What if I told you that we don't have to use a condom? Would that change your mind?"

I suck in a breath. Shit. Shit. Shit. She knows how much I want this and what it means to me.

Her strokes over me get faster. I manage to breathe, "You're a crazy bitch."

She nods as her lips and hands continue to roam my body. "I know."

"I wouldn't want you any other way."

"I know."

"Where should I come?" Does she want me to pull out? Come inside her? I'm not sure why this is running through my mind at the moment, but it is. I've never had sex without a condom. I've never considered the logistics, but suddenly they're all I can think about.

She looks up at me with a bemused grin. "Now that we're officially going steady, we'll have to learn how to compromise. I'll pick dinner. You pick where you spew the goo."

I chuckle as I lift her into my arms and enter her completely bare while she wraps her legs tightly around me. We briefly did this once before in Florida, but I never got the chance to move inside her before she freaked out and pushed me away.

This time, I freely slide inside my woman and manage to make love to her in the communal shower of the Cougars' locker room. It's slow and sweet, full of intense eye contact and deep kissing.

As soon as she comes, I let go inside her. I love the feeling of possessiveness, but I love that she allowed it even more.

Your walls are crumbling down, Kamryn Hart. It might be slow, but it's happening.

CHAPTER THIRTY

KAMRYN

The next morning, Reagan looks up at the ceiling of her giant executive office and blows out a *very* long breath before barking out, "This is a fucking PR nightmare!"

I sit next to Cheetah in the chairs on the other side of her desk and throw my hands in the air in exasperation. "I don't want to get married. He shouldn't have asked, especially at the ballpark. What do you want from me?"

I'm not scared of anyone, but she's a little intimidating in her expensive red suit, sitting behind her massive executive desk on the top floor of the highest skyscraper in Philly.

She moves her head back down and stares at me. "You should have said yes in front of the crowd and then broken off the engagement afterward like a normal person would have."

"I would *never* do that to him."

Cheetah audibly groans. "Ugh. That would definitely have been worse."

She turns to him. "No, it would have been *much* better. We could have waited a few weeks or months until the press over the romantic engagement wore off and then quietly issued a press release that you've consciously uncoupled."

I scrunch my face. "I'm not plagiarizing Gwyneth Paltrow in the ending of my fake engagement. I definitely would have come up with something more creative. Maybe relationship ejection?"

Cheetah adds, "Cancelling the joint Netflix account. People would know what that means."

I nod. "Yes! Something original like that. Maybe that we've decided to take our relationship to the previous level."

Cheetah sits up straight. "Ooh! I've got one. Kam bam, you look like a snack. Unfortunately, I'm going on a diet."

I take his hand in mine. "You remind me of Halley's comet. I don't want to see you again for another seventy-six years."

He winks at me. "Are you a dollar bill? Because you're single."

I bite back my smile, but Reagan narrows her eyes at us. "I'm glad you two think this is so funny. Until today, do you know what video had the most internet views in history?"

Yay, I'm about to learn something new. I love it when that happens.

Cheetah and I both shake our heads.

Reagan replies, "That stupid, fucking Baby Shark video from a few years ago has nearly fourteen billion views."

My face scrunches. "Ugh. Now that song is going to be in my head for the rest of the day. Worst day ever."

She pinches her lips into a thin line before asking, "Do you know what video just eclipsed that one when it hit the fourteen billion views mark an hour ago?"

I shrug and smile. "I don't, but if I had to guess by the context of the question, I'd answer that the video of Cheetah and me is trending."

She briefly closes her eyes as she nods. "Correct."

I shrug my shoulders. "From my perspective, we did the world a favor. That shark video was arguably the most annoying thing in the history of the world."

She sighs. "Well then, congratulations. Your rejection of him has officially knocked off Baby Shark and won the internet. How happy you must be," she adds sarcastically.

I twist my lips. "Isn't there an old adage that no publicity is bad publicity?"

She smacks her hand on the table. "Except this. This, Kamryn, is bad. *Very* fucking bad. How can you be so calm? It could ruin your career."

I lean back in my chair and place my arms on the armrests. "Maybe my endorsements will go away, but I'm a great softball player. I hit fucking homeruns for breakfast. I make defensive plays that no other shortstop in the world can make. That's what people should focus on. This kind of meaningless, personal shit blows over. Remember when Kim Kardashian's sex tape leaked? I'm sure at the time she thought it was the worst thing to ever happen to her. You know what happened? She got her own reality show, makeup line, clothing line, and now has a billion-dollar empire. Most people don't even remember the sex tape, but that's the only reason she became famous."

Cheetah pinches his eyebrows together. "I don't even remember who the sex tape was with."

I nod. "Exactly. It was Ray J, Brandy's brother."

"Oh right."

Reagan scoffs. "You two are crazy. I can't believe we're having a conversation about Kim Kardashian's sex tape from nearly twenty years ago."

I widen my mouth in shock. "Wow. Twenty years? Time flies when you marry and divorce three people all while chronicling it for multiple reality shows."

Reagan practically pulls her hair as she groans in frustration. I've never seen her this worked up. Obviously I know the video went viral. More than viral. I needed an army of security just to leave my apartment this morning. But I'm hopeful the fickle public will have something else to watch in the near future.

Cheetah winks at me. "Maybe we should do a sex tape."

I perk up with excitement. "Yes, let's do that. We can put Kim and Ray J to shame with some of the shit we do. Maybe we can pop another waterbed. That will change the topic of conversation."

Cheetah tries to stifle his smile while Reagan is rubbing her eye sockets, clearly done with both of us.

There's a knock at the door, and she yells out, "Not now!"

The door opens slightly, and Reagan's cousin, Jade, pokes the top half of her body inside. I met her once at Quincy's house. Her boyfriend or husband, I'm not sure which he is, built Quincy's mansion, and she struck up a friendship with Ripley. She refers to the boyfriend/husband as her baby daddy, which is why I don't know whether or not they're married.

Jade looks sexy as hell in her well-fitted hot pink pantsuit. I know she works here, but I have no idea what she does. She's six feet tall with blonde hair, blue eyes, and a killer figure. She looks like a taller, younger Reagan. She's probably in her mid-to-late-twenties. Jade is so my type. I can't help but drink her in. Cheetah notices and simply smiles.

Jade says, "I've been thinking about this situation. I've come up with a plan that I think could work."

Reagan leans back again in her oversized leather chair. With a defeated tone, she says, "I guess I'll take anything right about now."

Jade walks all the way through the door before closing it behind her. As she approaches us, I notice she's holding a can of something. It can't be what it looks like. I must be misreading the name of the drink.

She smiles when she notices me staring at it. "It's Pussy Juice. It's a natural energy drink that I like." Her smile turns mischievous, and her eyes sparkle as she holds it out for me. "Would you like to taste my Pussy Juice, Kamryn?"

I'm sure she's expecting a flustered response. Button-pushers like her usually do. I guess she doesn't know me very well.

"I'm bisexual, Jade. And sexy blondes with big tits are exactly my type. So, if that's an invitation, yes, I would *love* to taste your

Pussy Juice. Cruz likes to watch. He'll be with me. I hope you don't mind."

I wink at Jade, and her face falls. I'm guessing she's never had that response before.

Reagan starts laughing hysterically. "Oh. My. God. After all these years, someone has finally rendered Jade speechless. You've totally redeemed yourself, Kamryn."

Jade sits down in one of the other chairs before scrunching her face. "Hmm. I'll admit, I've never had that response. Back to the topic at hand though. I think I know how to make this work in our favor."

Reagan leans forward. "I'm all ears."

Jade briefly pauses as if choosing her words carefully. "Instead of fighting it, lean into it."

I ask, "How so?"

She takes a slow, purposeful sip of her Pussy Juice before placing it on Reagan's desk, much to Reagan's clear disdain. "I called Francisco Lane this morning."

Reagan pinches her eyebrows together. "The famous jeweler?"

Jade nods. "Yes. I told him what I was thinking, and he said that he was one hundred percent onboard. He loved my plan." She reaches into her purse and places five ring boxes on Reagan's desk. "He just messengered these over. He'll get Cruz a new batch every week or so for the rest of the month until this hopefully blows over."

She then goes on to describe what might be the most brilliant plan I've ever heard. By the end, Reagan is grinning from ear to ear. "Fucking hell, Jade. That's perfect. A perfect fucking solution."

Jade looks at me and thumps her head with her index finger. "I'm not just a sexy blonde with big tits. I've got brains too."

I nod. "I'll be sure to consider your brains when I'm tasting your Pussy Juice."

CHEETAH

Okay, the plan is kind of genius. I never would have thought of something like this. The best part of it is that I know Kamryn and I will have an absolute blast with it.

We discussed a few details with Reagan and Jade for another hour before exiting her palace-office. I think my first apartment was smaller than that office.

As we descend to the lobby in the elevator, I look at Kam. "Mamá called last night. She's an unhappy camper."

Kam scrunches her face. "Shit. I hadn't thought about that. What did you tell her?"

"The truth. About everything from last Christmas. That I sprung the fake engagement on you just before she opened the door."

Her face falls. "You didn't have to do that. You could have thrown me under the bus."

"Nah. It was the right thing to do. I shouldn't have lied in the first place. She was already suspicious since there were no wedding plans in the works. I'm a grown man. It was time to own it. She can't hate me forever. She just wants me to be happy. I might get the silent treatment for a few weeks, and then we'll be back in business, but that's more about me lying than anything else."

We exit the elevator into the impressive lobby of Reagan's skyscraper. I ask Kam, "Do you think this will work?"

Her head toggles back and forth with the same uncertainty I'm feeling. "I think it's super creative and might work but just know that I'm okay if it doesn't. I truly believe this will eventually blow over."

In the past twenty-four hours, I've had moments of guilt and moments where I don't think I did anything wrong. Regardless, I hate that Kam has all the bad press for something I did. It was completely out of her control.

I currently have a small bag with four ring boxes, the fifth being in my front pocket. Nodding toward the glass doors, I say, "It looks like the press is waiting for us."

They followed Kam and me here this morning separately. Poor Evan was fighting them off in front of my building. It took an obscene amount of time for him to push me through and into a cab. Then it took the cab driver ten minutes to drive through the hordes of reporters blocking his car, trying to get my picture.

Reagan has indefinitely supplied Kam with security, who are all currently following closely behind us. We decided as a group that until this fizzles out, which it hopefully does soon, the security will stay with Kamryn at all times. I have one security guard, but that has to do with the million dollars of jewelry on me, not my personal safety. People feel sorry for me. They hate Kam.

As expected, the press appears to have set up camp outside this building, waiting to see if we'll exit together. It wasn't the initial plan for us to be seen together, but the new plan calls for something entirely different. As Jade said, we're leaning into this. *Really* leaning into it.

I look at my beautiful girl. "Are you sure about this?"

She shrugs. "Not really, but I suppose it's worth a shot." She leans her body into mine and kisses my lips sweetly. "Thanks for what you're about to do. I love you."

I kiss her back in the same fashion. "I'd do anything for you because I love you too."

Taking a deep breath, I grab her hand. "Let's do it."

We walk out of the revolving glass doors of the building to absolute and total mayhem. Layton Lancaster has been my best friend for over ten years. For a long time, he was the most popular player in all of baseball. I'm used to the press acting like animals to get photos. But this? This I've never seen before.

There are hundreds upon hundreds of flashes going off in our faces. They're lined up down the entire block. I see all the surrounding rooftops flanked with telephoto lenses. They're rapid firing questions at us about the status of our relationship.

It's madness, plain and simple.

I suppose it's now or never. I'll do my best to drown out the lights. Hopefully Kamryn can do the same.

As soon as we're both fully through the door in plain sight of everyone, I turn toward her and drop to one knee. The press all momentarily gasp before the flashes go even more berserk. It's like a machine gun of flashes in our faces.

I take Kam's hand in mine. "Kamryn Hart, you are the love of my life. I'll never stop wanting to marry you."

Her chin drops as though she's completely and totally shocked by my actions.

I pull the ring box out of my pocket. I open it in such a manner that the giant ring inside will be easily photographed, which it immediately is. "You are the peanut butter to my jelly. The salt to my pepper. The root beer to my float. The Mary Kate to my Ashley. The Bert to my Ernie. The Thelma to my Louise. The Cagney to my Lacey. The Joey to my Chandler. The Rose to my Jack. And the delicious cream in my morning coffee." She bites back her smile as I plead, "Please do me the honor of being my forever partner. Marry me."

She pretends to examine the ring and then yells out, "Is that a Francisco Lane ring?"

I loudly reply, "Why yes, it is. It's six-point-five carats. Perfect clarity. Princess cut. One of a kind."

She brings her lips into a tight O as she answers, "Ooh.

So tempting, only because of this spectacular ring. And I do love being the Cagney to your Lacey."

We both smile at each other before she continues, "But no. My answer is still no. I'm more of a loner, like Albert Einstein or Edward Scissorhands. Maybe try again... tomorrow."

And that's what happens for the next three months. Every single day that we're both in the same city, which is just about half the time, I find elaborate, outrageously worded ways to publicly propose to Kamryn. Always with a different Francisco Lane ring and always with an inevitable response of no from Kamryn.

It took less than a week for everyone to assume the first proposal was a huge publicity stunt to set up this marketing campaign for Francisco Lane Jewelry. Analysts are calling it the greatest marketing ploy of all time.

Kam and I have actually been having a blast coming up with crazy ways for me to propose. It's become a social media phenomenon for people to both catch videos of my multiple public proposals per week and for people to come up with even crazier proposals than the ones we come up with and tag us on their social media. It's always met by a clever denial from the woman. *#ProposeLikeCheetah* and *#DenyLikeKam* are the top two trending hashtags.

CHAPTER THIRTY-ONE

CHEETAH

I lift my head from between Kamryn's legs just before her orgasm is about to crest. With a face full of her juices, I ask, "Will you marry me?"

She groans out, "Ahhh. I hate you. Finish the job, dickhead."

I chuckle as she pushes my head down and get back to business.

What turned into a three-month contract with Francisco Lane Jewelry ended two weeks ago, but I keep asking her to marry me every single day. At least now I can do it in private. I try to find the most inopportune or random times just to drive her crazy.

The originally planned first month of our constant fake proposals was so outrageously successful that Francisco Lane Jewelry ended up paying Kam and me a small fortune to continue the charade. I'm not sure I would have wanted to accept their proposal, but it was huge money for Kam, and I didn't want her to miss out on the opportunity.

Unfortunately, softball players make a lot less money than baseball players.

The Cougars lost in the National League Championship Series. We were one win away from making it back to the World Series, but our bullpen buckled under the pressure. Not Quincy. He had two wins in the series and might very well win his first Cy Young Award this year, awarded to the best pitcher in each of the two leagues. It was our relief pitchers who let us down.

The silver lining was that I got to watch all of Kamryn's championship series games. The Anacondas swept the best-of-five series, winning in only three games. Kamryn hit seven home runs in that stretch and was awarded the championship's Most Valuable Player. I rewarded her by marching out onto the field and dropping to my knee for our final public proposal. By that point, the crowds simply laughed when I did it and then cheered her on as she rejected me in glorious fashion. They often encouraged her to reject me.

Somehow the whole marketing ploy not only helped the jeweler and Kam's momentarily damaged reputation, but it also helped the Anacondas and Kam from a marketing perspective. The Anacondas are getting more attention than ever. Kam is now the poster child for girl power. Daily rejections of a professional baseball player apparently make you a bit of a cult hero. Modeling and endorsement offers are pouring in for her. She's going to have a very busy off-season this year.

After she orgasms, I slide up her body and immediately enter her. I grab a pillow and shove it under her hips. The angle makes my tip hit directly into her G-spot. It drives her wild.

My mouth captures hers in a searing kiss as our tongues tangle with need. I grab her feet, spread her wide open, and run my fingers through her toes as I pound into her.

She breaks the kiss. "What in the fresh fuck is this move?"

I smile into her mouth. "It feels good, doesn't it? It's intimate."

"I swear to god, you have more tools in your tool bag than any man on this planet."

"Por eso tu coño me pertenece." *That is why your pussy belongs to me.*

Her eyes roll to the back of her head, her back arches, and she yells out, "Ahh, here I go again."

Once we both come, I fall back onto the bed. She moans out, "Fuck, that was good."

I nod in agreement. "It was. It always is." And I love coming inside her. I'm slightly obsessed with knowing she's full of my come. I've never considered myself to be an overly possessive man, but I suppose that's because there's never been anyone I wanted to possess until now. "I can't get enough of you."

She turns her head until our eyes meet. "I'll miss you tonight." That's her way of telling me she can't get enough of me either. I've learned to speak Kamrynese.

Our relationship isn't perfect, but we're navigating these unchartered waters together. I'm trying to better communicate my needs, and she's trying to give a little when she can. She indulges me in one Indian dinner a month. I know she hates it, but it makes me love her all the more for trying. And we've watched all the Star Wars movies. All twelve of them.

Tomorrow is Arizona and Layton's wedding. The girls are all staying in a hotel suite together tonight, meaning we won't sleep together, something we now do almost every night.

I've been thinking that I want to ask Kamryn to officially move in with me. I haven't broached the topic yet. Given the three straight months of public rejection I've endured, I'm a little trigger-shy on asking, but I'm going to do it at the wedding. I'm hoping she'll be a little swept up in the emotions of the day.

I've gradually made space for her in my bathroom and closet, but she hasn't noticed yet. But since Kam misses nothing, she's probably just ignoring it, which doesn't exactly inspire confidence in me.

It's also a touchy situation because of her sister. She's not going to want to leave her, but Kam is almost thirty. It's time for them to learn to live apart. She might disagree, but I'll make strong arguments and hope for the best. Despite a few bumps here and there, we've been pretty good at the whole boyfriend and girlfriend thing for the past three months.

I run my hand up her leg. "I'll miss you too. I could go on a panty raid and sneak into your hotel room in the middle of the night."

She shakes her head. "Absolutely not. Tonight and tomorrow are all about Arizona. I don't want to steal any thunder."

"I suppose you're right. We're taking Layton out tonight, but he said to keep it tame."

She rolls her eyes. "He's such a wet blanket."

I nod. "Totally."

Just then her phone rings. She rolls over to look at it. "It's Tanner."

"Answer it on FaceTime. I'm sure he'd love to see us Full Monty."

She smiles as she accepts the call and switches it to video before moving the phone so that both of our naked bodies are visible on the screen.

His face appears, and then he immediately turns away and groans in malcontent. "Oh, for fuck's sake. Cover up, you two."

We laugh as we slide under the blankets, and Kam says,

"You've been fucking my sister for most of the last year, except that time period where you shredded her heart into a million pieces like a ruthless piece of shit. We have the same body. I don't turn you on just a little bit?"

Tanner, who is in a business suit and sitting in his office, scrunches his face in disgust. "Not one drop. Not so much as a stirring happening for me right now. You two look nothing alike from my perspective. She's made of sugar and spice, and you're the bacteria that sits on the surface of an undisturbed pond."

I'm about to get angry and tear into him, but Kam lets out a laugh. "Holy shit. That was bizarrely descriptive. I feel like you've considered this before."

He deadpans. "All the fucking time. I can't believe I'm being saddled with managing your modeling career."

She shrugs. "You didn't have to say yes."

He looks at me and raises one of his dark eyebrows. "Cruz begged me."

I nod. "That's true. I did." He was occasionally helping Kam with endorsements over the past year, but when things exploded for her three months ago, she needed real representation. I told him he was the only person I trusted.

Despite the fact that Bailey and Tanner have been sleeping together once or twice a week for months as pure fuck buddies, things between Tanner and Kamryn remain ice-cold. Her outgoing personality annoys him, and his perceived treatment of her sister makes him public enemy number one to her, but they have an aligned interest in her career. She needs him to negotiate her contracts, and even though he doesn't care for her, she's bringing him a nice agent fee, though I think he's doing it because I asked and because Bailey wants him to represent Kam.

Tanner looks down and starts flipping through papers. "Between you, Arizona, and Sulley, I'm drowning in all this shit. I really need to find someone to head up my women's division."

My chin drops. "You still haven't found anyone?" I know he's been interviewing women for at least six months.

He sighs as he looks at me. "No. I'm steadfast on it being a woman. I just haven't found the right one. I won't hire the wrong one just to fill a spot. The job is too important for that." Looking back down, he says, "Kamryn, I've been reviewing your new offer from Hubba Bubba." Kam always chews grape Hubba Bubba gum on the field, and she did a small campaign for them last year. They now want her as their top spokesperson. "They want to photograph you at a vineyard."

She nods. "Okay. That sounds fun. What's the big deal?"

"The grape season in Napa Valley is basically over. You need to get out to California right away, as in next week, before all the grapes are gone."

She shrugs. "That's fine. Make sure you put in language to protect me in case of emergency. I want a termination clause completely at my discretion. You never know what could happen. You fucked over Arizona when you didn't put that in her contract last year, and she got stuck on a two-month shoot she didn't want to go to. You're a shitty agent."

He narrows his eyes at her. "I didn't negotiate that contract for her, Miss Know It All. In fact, I heavily advised her to get counsel because of that clause, and she didn't listen to me. And why do you know that term? Are you a fucking lawyer now?"

She doesn't even flinch at the fact that he inadvertently hit the nail on the head. "No, but I'm smarter than you." She mumbles, "It doesn't take much."

He pinches the bridge of his nose. "God help me. You're a nightmare." He grits out. "I will tighten up the wording in that paragraph. Anything else, princess?"

"Since you're asking, I'd love it if you were to break up with my sister. We can try to avoid you shattering her heart again, which we both know is inevitable."

"I'm not discussing my private relationship with Bailey with you. Ever. Period. End of discussion."

"Whatever, Daddy Tanner. You know my sister and I have no secrets. I know you like to tie her up and spank her with a paddle, you weird fucker."

I burst out laughing. "You're into BDSM, Tanner? I didn't know you were such a kinky bastard."

He blows out a breath. "I despise both of you. Goodbye."

He ends the call, and I look at Kam. "Does he really do all that?"

She nods. "He sure does. She loves it. And she calls him Daddy."

I pull the blankets down and roughly flip her over. Placing my palm on her ass, I ask, "Want me to spank you, bad girl? I'll be your daddy."

She wiggles her sexy backside. "I'd rather you fuck that ass instead of spanking it."

I jump on top of her on my knees so that my legs are spread over the backs of her thighs. With my fake lasso swinging in the air, I yell out, "Yeehaw! Saddle up, cowgirl. I'm about to ride this ass."

KAMRYN

"Kam, stop farting."

I kick Bailey while we're under the covers of the king-sized bed of the hotel room. "You know what milk chocolate does to me."

"Take a Lactaid pill like a normal person."

"I'm not lactose intolerant." I probably am, but I refuse to acknowledge it. It makes me feel like an eighty-year-old woman.

She pats her stomach. "We both know who has the stronger constitution. I could eat jalapeño peppers all night and be totally fine."

"Truth. I wish you could eat Indian food with Cheetah every month. It fucking kills my insides, but I have to muscle through it. You got Beverly's iron-clad stomach. Literally the only thing you got from her was her only positive trait. I got all her shit traits."

Bailey sighs in frustration. "Fake news. Not true. You're nothing like her. Stop saying that."

"Whatever. I spoke with your boyfriend this morning."

"He's not my boyfriend. He's my fuck buddy, remember?"

I roll my eyes. "If that's what you're telling yourself. Anyhow, he's finalizing my new deal with Hubba Bubba. I have a photo shoot out in Napa Valley next week. Come with me. We'll tour vineyards and drink wine. Maybe we can invite Daddy to join us. He's never been. I'll take care of everything."

She shakes her head. "I can't. I have Harper."

I scrunch my face. "Ugh. I hate your job. I have to be there for a week. I'm still mentally recovering from the last time we spent a week apart."

She takes my hand in hers. "It's time for us to learn how to spend time apart. We're going to be thirty in a few months. We're not kids anymore. We need to grow up."

As if on cue, Arizona and Ripley come running into our bedroom of the suite in pigtails, giggling uncontrollably. Ripley jokes, "Don't you think Arizona should wear her hair like this for the wedding tomorrow?"

I nod. "Absolutely. Guys love that look. Are you sure you want to go through with this wedding? Statistically speaking, one hundred percent of all divorces start with a wedding."

Bailey kicks me under the covers while Arizona giggles. "That

ship has sailed. We're already married, and I'm already pregnant."
We found out earlier in the season that Arizona was pregnant. She
and Layton are so excited about it.

Bailey twists her lips. "I wonder if this is technically a shotgun
wedding."

I shake my head. "It's not. They're legally married. This is just
an excuse to party."

I look at Arizona. "Didn't you say you were turning in? That
you need your beauty sleep? We said goodnight fifteen minutes
ago."

She shrugs as they both crawl into bed with us. "I'm too
excited. Let's cuddle and watch a movie. When will the four of us
be able to do that again?"

"Okay, but you know I like busty blonde women, and none
are hotter than you." I grab her leg. "I can't be held responsible
for my roaming hands."

Arizona laughs, but Bailey slaps my hand. "Leave her
alone."

I mock gasp. "Don't be a twat swat."

She pinches her eyebrows together. "What's that? Is it like a
cockblock, but the girl version?"

I nod. "It is."

The three of them start giggling. Ripley asks, "What are other
terms for it?"

"Hmm. Clam jam."

Now they're all hysterically laughing, and that's kind of how
the last night of just the four of us together goes. It's a sisterhood
that will never be broken.

THIS MUST BE the first wedding I've ever been to where I'm not
running doomsday scenarios through my head the whole time. I
believe to my core that Arizona and Layton are the real deal.

They're madly in love. It might also potentially have to do with my current status.

I'm a little loved up by Cruz Gonzales these days. Things have been going well for us since the disastrous proposal night. It's not all smooth sailing, but mostly great. Sometimes I'm a complete asshole and treat him terribly, but I'm learning to recognize when I'm being selfish and attempt to apologize.

He's endured a lot over the past few months. He's basically been publicly humiliated nearly every day. He does so willingly and happily, all for my benefit. Where does one go from Cruz Gonzales? I've never been happier than I am right now. I'm at the height of my career, and an amazing person loves me wholeheartedly. I fear it's the calm before the storm.

Arizona is full of excitement, not nerves, as she prepares to walk down the aisle. Ripley serves as the maid of honor, while Bailey, Gemma, and I all serve as bridesmaids. We're in long, strapless royal-blue gowns. They're well-fitted and have a long slit up one leg. I know Cheetah will see it as easy access and will have his hand up it all night. I can't wait. I missed him last night. I've gotten used to sleeping with him.

I know the day is coming soon when he mentions us moving in together. He's been slowly clearing space in his bathroom and closet for me. Being super mature, I'm pretending not to notice.

The music starts playing, and everyone is paired off. I'm excited to see Cheetah in a tuxedo. He's going to look hot as fuck.

He finally comes into view. My mouth starts watering. He looks even better than I imagined. As soon as he sees me, his dimples come out, and he fans his face, mouthing, "You're so hot."

It's about to be our turn to walk down the aisle together, and he offers me his arm. He leans over and whispers, "Is that slit for easy access?"

I inwardly laugh. Do I know my man or what?

I respond, "It is." I nod toward his bowtie. "I want you to do me only wearing that later."

"Deal."

We start walking down the aisle. He again whispers, "Will you marry me? I still have the original ring from Christmas. It's in my pocket." He wiggles his eyebrows up and down.

I simply roll my eyes at him, like I do every other day. He gets off on finding the most ridiculous moments to propose to me.

The ceremony and reception go off without a hitch. Arizona and Layton's love practically radiates from everywhere. It's kind of inspiring and has me all up in my feels.

Cheetah and I have been dancing up a storm, busting out all our Ms. Rylee moves. He's so much fun to be with.

I notice Tanner dancing with my sister. That's odd. I've never once seen him publicly touch her or acknowledge their fucked-up relationship.

The night is about to come to a close. Most people have left. I see Bailey leaving with Tanner. She told me earlier in the evening that she's going to end things with him once and for all but wanted one more night with him. We'll see if that actually happens. I hope it does. She needs to move on from a man who will never give her what she deserves.

Cheetah and I decide to have one more drink before leaving. We're sitting there laughing, and before we realize it, the entire place is empty except for the band. He motions toward them, and they start playing a slow Latin song.

Cheetah smiles as he stands and offers me his hand. "May I have the last dance, beautiful?"

I happily nod as I stand and take his hand. He gets into position, and we do one of our routines from Ms. Rylee's sessions. He's so romantic.

When it comes to an end, he gives me an uncharacteristically serious look. "Kam, I love you so much." He gets down on one knee and pulls out a ring box.

I'm about to turn him down as usual when it hits me that I'm not sure I want to. Why do I keep saying no? I love him. I want to be with him. I have no interest in anyone else. Isn't that what marriage is?

As he slowly opens the box, he says, "I want to go to sleep with you every night and wake up with you every morning—"

I don't know what comes over me, but I blurt out, "Yes."

The box opens fully, and I see a key. He grins widely. "Yes? You'll move in with me?

Move in with him? That's what he's asking?

I'm speechless, deep in my head, considering the fact that I was just about to agree to marry him when I feel a blinding pain in my lower back and stomach. So bad that I fall to my knees and yell out, "Ahh."

He reaches for me. "Kam, baby, what's wrong? Are you hurt?"

These are phantom pains. I've had them before when Bailey has gotten injured, but never this painful. I grit out, "Bailey. Something has happened to her."

He exhales an annoyed breath. "If you don't want to move in with me, fine, but why the hell did you say yes?"

"Cruz, get me my fucking phone. My purse is at the table. Something is wrong. I can feel it."

After a brief moment of hesitation, he stands, walks to our table, grabs my purse, and brings it to me.

I'm still feeling shooting pains down my back as I pull my phone out and dial Bailey's cell phone.

Tanner answers, "Hello, Kamryn," but he sounds off. His voice is shaky. Tanner oozes confidence and sophistication, but that's not what I'm getting from him right now. And I think I hear a siren and several other voices.

I blurt out, "Something happened to my sister. I can feel it. Is she with you?"

He takes a few breaths like it's hard for him to breathe. With a voice that sounds like he's on the verge of tears, he says, "Yes. We've been in a car accident. She's conscious but hurt. She...she can't feel her legs. We're in the ambulance. Meet us at Philly Hospital. She doesn't want you to tell Arizona."

Tears start streaming down my cheeks. My heart feels like it's beating a million times per minute. My hands begin shaking. "I swear to god, Montgomery, if this is as bad as it sounds, I will kill you with my bare hands."

Cheetah grabs my phone from my hand. He undoubtedly heard both sides of the conversation. He rubs my arm. "Calm down. Let's just get to the hospital."

My voice cracks, "I...I can't lose her. I can't live without her."

He visibly swallows. "She'll be okay. I know she will. Let's just get to the hospital."

I wordlessly nod. I think I'm officially in shock.

He speaks into the phone. "Sorry, man. She's hysterical. Just worried about her sister. We're on our way. Text me a room number when you get one."

Cheetah ends the call, and suddenly I feel like my world is ending.

I knew a storm was coming, but I didn't realize just how dark these clouds were going to be.

CHAPTER THIRTY-TWO

CHEETAH

I don't have my car here. We were drinking, so we were going to Uber home tonight. Fortunately, there's an Uber nearby, and the hospital isn't too far away.

With my jacket around Kam, I hold her in my arms in the backseat of the Uber as she shakes uncontrollably. I'm trying to whisper reassurances in her ear, but I have no idea what we're walking into.

If this goes badly, she'll be permanently wrecked for life. There will be no coming back from it for her. I pray for her sake and Bailey's that this has a happy ending. I'm terrified that it won't.

I managed to text Quincy. He and Ripley are now also on their way to the hospital. They were already halfway home, meaning they're about twenty minutes behind us.

The Uber drops us off at the emergency room door. Kam sprints inside with me hot on her heels. She starts screaming at every employee in sight. No one gives her any answers and she's freaking out. They keep promising that they'll look into it and that she should sit and wait, but that's not good enough for her.

It's mayhem. I'm trying to keep her calm, but it's an uphill battle.

Eventually, Reagan Daulton and her husband, Carter, walk in. They're still dressed as they were for the wedding. She immediately grabs a hysterical Kam by the shoulders. "Calm down. You're not going to get answers acting like this. My sister and brother-in-law work here. I called them as soon as I heard about the accident. He's a spinal surgeon. He's with her in imaging so they can pinpoint exactly what's wrong with her. He couldn't say much more without your permission, but I know he'll be down to talk with us in a few minutes. We'll get you answers, just be patient a little longer."

Kamryn nods and whisper-cries, "Okay, thank you."

Tears are pouring from her eyes. I hate seeing her like this.

I pull Kam into my arms as Reagan continues, "I know every single board member at this hospital. We're going to get her the best treatment available. I promise you that." She rubs Kam's arm. "The press is already on this. I need to issue a statement on behalf of the team. I won't give any health updates without your approval, but I need to say something. Do you know why she was with Tanner Montgomery?"

Kam stoically responds, "She's been fucking him for a year."

Reagan's eyes widen as she looks to me for confirmation. I nod. "She nannies for his daughter. They've quietly been dating for about a year."

Kam's voice cracks, "Like I said, she's been fucking him for a year."

Reagan's lips twist. "Perhaps something along the lines

of *she had a lot to drink, and he was making sure she safely got home* would be better."

Kam brings her hand to her mouth as if something is just now occurring to her. "I bet Tanner was drinking. I want the electric chair for him if he was." She looks around. "Where the hell is he? Did he drop her and leave?"

I sigh as I rub her back. "You know that's not the case. He cares deeply for her."

Reagan nods. "He passed out when they got to the hospital. He had refused treatment at the scene, wanting to stay with your sister. He's now getting imaging done too. Last I heard, he was still unconscious."

Shit. I hope he's not hurt too badly. I pull out my phone and text Fallon. I don't have Tanner's father's information. Maybe she can reach out to him.

Ripley and Quincy run in through the emergency room's automatic glass doors. As soon as they locate us, Ripley and Kam run toward each other and embrace in a pile of tears.

We all stand there quietly as the two of them sob in each other's arms. No words need to be spoken for us to know that we're all fearing the same thing.

Eventually, a tall blond man in a white lab coat walks toward us. He looks like he's about forty. He and Reagan exchange a familiar glance. He must be her brother-in-law.

Looking at Kamryn, he asks, "I suppose it's safe to assume you're Bailey Hart's sister?"

She immediately turns to him. "Y...yes. Is she okay?"

He holds out his hand for her. "I'm Dr. Brody Cooper. I'm the head of the neurosurgery department at this hospital. I'm married to Reagan's sister, and she asked me to take the lead on Bailey's case."

Kam shakily takes his hand. "Please tell me she'll be fine."

He swallows as he gently drops her hand. "I won't lie,

her injuries are severe." Kam starts getting hysterical. I take her back into my arms as I practically hold her upright. "The imaging showed two issues. Do you have a medical background?"

Kam shakes her head.

He nods. "Okay. I'll give it to you in layman's terms for now. Her first injury, which is not my area of expertise, was to her lower abdomen. I'm only involved because Reagan asked me to be. The trauma is severe enough that she'll need to have her right ovary removed."

Kam gasps before yelling out, "Will she be able to have children? That's all she fucking wants in this world."

"Women with one ovary can have children. If you'd like, as a backup, we can harvest any eggs we find in the right ovary when it's removed."

Kam nods. "Yes, harvest everything you can. I'll have her kid if it comes to that."

He presses a few buttons on an iPad before looking back up at her. "That surgery will take place right away. She's being prepped now. As for her other injury, she sustained a spinal fracture."

Kam nearly collapses, but I hold her tight. "Will...will she walk again?"

He pulls something up on his iPad and shows it to her. It's a three-dimensional illustration of a spine. "I've reviewed the imaging thoroughly, and I will operate on her tomorrow."

The illustration then runs like a video, displaying the fracture and exactly how he'll go about the surgery and what it will entail. The technology is amazing. He explains it in detail. "I'm optimistic that with a lot of physical and occupational therapy, she'll make nearly a full recovery."

Kam asks, "What does *nearly* mean?"

He answers, "It means that there are no certainties with the spine. I think she'll walk, but I also know she's a professional athlete. There may be certain things she can't ever do again. A numb finger, toe, or more. Areas where the nerve connections are never quite right again. Something along those lines. As you know, athletes require a bit more than regular people. I don't know if playing softball will be in her future, but I'm confident that living an otherwise normal life will be in her future. Like I said, no promises, but I think we can get her up and running."

Kam nods. "I understand. As long as she can live a normal life. And you don't know my sister. She can do whatever she sets her mind to. If she wants to play again, she will. What's the timeline for her recovery?"

He blows out a breath. "Assuming the surgery tomorrow goes as I expect it to, I'd say three to four months of intensive inpatient treatment followed by a few more months of outpatient treatment. She'll start her therapy here right away, and that will last for about two weeks. Then we'll transfer her to the facility of your choosing. We can get you a list of facilities covered by your health insurance."

Reagan shakes her head. "Give me only the name of the top facility. We'll cover it if her insurance doesn't. I want her to have the best care."

Dr. Cooper clicks something on his iPad and shows it to Reagan. "If she were my family member, this is where I'd want her."

Reagan takes down the information while I ask, "What about Tanner? How's he?"

Kam mumbles, "Who cares."

Brody types away on his iPad again before looking back up at me. "Are you family?"

I shake my head. "No. I'm a longtime friend and client though."

He winces. "Does he have any family here?"

I shake my head again. "His father lives in Florida. I

texted his ex-wife, but I haven't heard back from her. I'm as close as it gets. I've known him for a dozen years."

He looks around. "I'm breaking a few laws by telling you, but he sustained a very severe concussion. The CT showed no brain bleed, but he's unconscious right now and probably will be for a few more hours. He'll need to stay away from light for at least a week and will require a decent amount of rest."

Kam scoffs. "A concussion? That's it? My sister is losing an ovary and has a broken back, and all that asshole got was a headache for a few days. Was he drunk? I want to press charges if he was."

Dr. Cooper visibly swallows. "His bloodwork won't be back until tomorrow, but it's standard protocol to take it." He slides his iPad into his lab coat pocket. "I need to run. Your sister will remain sedated until after her second surgery. We'll know more when that's done. I'll come find you then. What she'll need most is support and positivity. She's got a long road ahead of her. She'll be shaken when she wakes up and discovers all that she's going to face in the coming months."

I feel my phone vibrate and peek down at it. It's Fallon. It looks like she was on an airplane when I texted but is now coming straight here from the airport. She asks for an update, and I give it to her.

I **TRIED** to get Kam to go home considering the fact that Bailey will be sedated for several more hours, but she refused to leave. Reagan and Carter left, promising to return when Bailey wakes. Along with Ripley and Quincy, we've awkwardly been sitting in a room with two beds. One has Tanner, who's still out cold. He's got a bandage around his head. Apparently, he hit it very hard. Hard enough to cause a big gash requiring stitches. Fallon has been on and off silently weeping, sitting at his bedside.

Fallon is a blonde-haired, blue-eyed bombshell. There's no other way to describe her. Even with red-rimmed eyes in the middle of the night, she's a beautiful woman. She and Tanner had an amicable divorce. I don't know the specifics of the breakup of their marriage because Tanner has always been tight-lipped about it, but I've never once heard him utter a bad word about her. All I know was that it was roughly five years ago, and they very peacefully co-parent Harper. Joint meals and full family vacations are the norm for them.

Fallon works in the physical therapy department of this hospital. Several of her coworkers have popped in to check on her. She's obviously well-liked.

The other bed in the room is open, waiting for Bailey to return from her surgeries. Kam has been sitting in it while bashing Tanner for hours. I can tell Fallon is getting annoyed but is keeping quiet, likely knowing that Kam is simply scared for her sister.

After a few hours, Tanner eventually wakes. Every time he attempts to gather information, Kam berates him and peppers him with questions about the details of the accident. Finally, Fallon reaches her breaking point and grits out, "E-fucking-nough. Just shut your mouth. I can't listen to you bitch and whine anymore. It doesn't help anyone, especially Bailey."

The three of us smile at each other. Kam had that coming. Ripley stands and takes Kamryn's hand. "She won't be out of surgery for a little while. Let's grab a snack. We'll give Fallon a chance to catch Tanner up on everything."

We leave and head to the cafeteria. I buy all the coffee and dark chocolate I can find before we all sit. I look at Kam. "You need to relax with Tanner."

"He—"

"They were in an accident. By definition, accidents are not on purpose. I was with him enough throughout the wedding to know he wasn't drunk, Kam. If, for some reason, the bloodwork shows that he was, then he'll have something worse than your verbal assaults to deal with. Tanner is not a bad man, and I know he cares about Bailey. It will be better for her if you work *with* him, not *against* him."

Ripley nods in agreement. "He's right, Kam. Bailey won't want you two at each other's throats. It won't help her."

Tears begin streaming out of Kam's eyes again. She croaks out, "I'm just so fucking scared for my sister."

I wrap my arm around her. "I know, babe. She's strong. You both are. Like the doctor said, let's stay positive. When she wakes up, make your usual Kam jokes. Bailey can give her standard eye roll at you. She's going to be scared out of her mind. I think you being yourself will be the most calming thing for her."

She slowly nods her head. "You're right. I'll try."

"Good. Have you heard from your dad?"

She shakes her head. "He must have already been asleep when I reached out. I left him a message to please call me as soon as he wakes, but I didn't want to just leave a voicemail as to why. I'm sure he'll fly up right away."

"What can I do to help?"

She reaches for my hand. "Just pray for her."

KAMRYN

"No. Fucking. Way."

Tanner clenches his jaw. "Yes. Fucking. Way. I've already made all the arrangements. I've purchased all the equipment she could possibly need. You know full well she'll be more comfortable recovering and doing her therapy at my house than at some cold hospital."

Is he stupid? There's a reason people need to be inpatient.

I pull my hair as I bark out, "Hospitals have professionals for this very reason. Who is going to work with her? You? The person who did this to her."

He exhales a few calming breaths. He's clearly at his wit's end with me, but I don't give a shit. "Fallon is moving in. She's taking a leave of absence from her job to be totally dedicated to Bailey for the next three months. I trust her and only her to do this. There's no one better and certainly no one who will care more."

"Maybe you hit your head harder than they thought. You're telling me that your former fuck buddy and your current fuck buddy are all going to live together as one big happy family?"

He sighs. "You are a child. Grow up. How are you possibly related to her?"

Cheetah pulls me into the hallway and grabs me by the shoulders. "Hey, relax."

I shake my head. I'm so fucking exhausted, but I refuse to leave or sleep until my sister is out of surgery and awake. Every inch of my body is running on caffeine and adrenaline right now. It feels like it could all give out at any moment.

I collapse my face into his chest and start sobbing. "Why did this happen to her? She doesn't deserve this. It should have been me."

He rubs his hands over me in a soothing manner. He's a godsend. I'd be institutionalized right now if he wasn't here.

He lifts my chin so our eyes meet. "Don't say that. Don't ever say that. I know your head is spinning, babe, but think about how much happier Bailey will be in his home than in some random hospital. Harper will be there. She loves Harper so much. You know that. She'll be in a real bed, not a hospital bed. She'll be surrounded by people who love her all the time. You won't have to deal with hospital hours and rules. You can come and go whenever you want."

I nod robotically and a bit reluctantly. He does make compelling points.

"Let's go back in and tell him that you're onboard. It's best for Bailey. When she wakes up, you two need to be a unified front. After we tell him, I want you to get some sleep."

I shake my head. "Not until I know she's out of surgery and her back is fixed."

"We'll sit in her room. You'll sleep on me. I'll stay awake. When she's out of surgery and conscious, I promise to wake you. Don't you want to be fresh for her? She can't see you freaking out. You need to pull a Kamryn Sarah Hart."

I pinch my eyebrows together. "What's that?"

He smiles as he rubs my face. "Making people laugh. Making everyone around you happy."

"I don't think I make Tanner happy."

He chuckles. "Definitely not."

"I think my mind is too tired to come up with jokes. Do you have one I can use?"

He thinks for a few seconds. "Hmm. Oh, I've got a thematic one. What do you call a nurse with dirty knees?

"What?"

"The head nurse."

I let out a laugh, and he winks at me. "I love that laugh. Bailey needs you at your best. You need sleep to be at your best."

"So do you."

"It's just like sex. You first."

I smile. I think it's my first smile since this nightmare started. Nodding, I say, "Okay. She should be out and awake before my dad gets here but wake me if he arrives first." Dad and his boyfriend are flying in tonight.

"You got it."

We go back into Bailey's room, and I must fall asleep in less than five seconds because I barely remember sitting down.

CHAPTER THIRTY-THREE

CHEETAH

She's been fast asleep on my chest for hours. I've dozed a few times, but I haven't allowed myself to get into a deep sleep.

Bailey is out of surgery. They think it went well. She's asleep in the room while we sit on the chairs by her bed. The two of them actually look more alike when they're sleeping. I guess that's because their eyes and smiles are so different to me, but neither are visible now.

Bailey isn't as outwardly battered as I would have thought. For some reason, I assumed her face would be bruised and swollen, but it isn't. I guess her back and stomach sustained the brunt of the trauma.

It's going to be a long few months, and it won't be easy on anyone. I'm glad it's my off-season so I'll be around to help out. This off-season is going to be unlike any other I've ever experienced.

A FEW HOURS LATER, things are already in motion. Bailey woke up and absorbed everything that has happened to her. Kam got it together for her sister, cracking jokes and making Bailey laugh despite the horrific circumstances. Tanner even agreed to give Kam one of his guest rooms so she could be there for every minute of Bailey's recovery. I know I need to shelve any thoughts of us moving in together. She'll never consider it until Bailey is back to normal, though I'm happy Kam was receptive to it before all hell broke loose. I keep replaying that moment over and over in my head, wondering if she thought I was asking something else.

Their father arrived with his boyfriend, Ray. Chris broke into tears when he saw Bailey, but Kam pulled him out of the room and told him to get his shit together for Bailey's sake.

I think the sleep did her good. She's rejuvenated and taking charge like the badass boss she is.

She's created a big group chat with all our extended friends letting them know in no uncertain terms that she wants things light and normal around Bailey. She also suggested a schedule for keeping Bailey company so she's never alone. I wonder if she realizes that she's a caregiver by nature.

With Bailey settled and Chris in tow, I get Kam to agree to let me take her home to shower and change clothes. Once there, she pulls me into the shower with her. It's like she needs me touching every inch of her and can't get enough. I'm happy to give it to her.

Once out, we sit on her bed. I swore I'd never go near this damn bed again, but I tentatively sit. She notices and cracks a smile. "Don't worry. It won't break."

I lift an eyebrow. "I know for a fact it can."

She lets out a laugh. "God, I love that story." Her face

turns serious. "It's going to be a hard few months. If you want to bail, I understand."

I shake my head. "For better or worse, right?"

"We're not married. You can jet due to the worse whenever you want. That's the benefit of not being married."

It occurs to me that I haven't proposed today. With my towel wrapped around my waist, I quickly drop to one knee. "Louise would never leave Thelma in her time of need. In fact, that was literally the whole plotline of the movie. For better or worse, will you marry me?"

She usually sighs or rolls her eyes when I do my daily proposals, but this time her eyes fill with tears. "Not like this, but thanks for asking."

THREE WEEKS LATER

KAMRYN

I shove his arm. "Get out, Tanner. She doesn't want your help, you fucking hairy gorilla."

He elbows me out of the way. "I'm stronger than you. She needs to be carried in and out of the shower. It should be *me*."

I'm at the end of my rope with this man. I grit out, "I will take care of my own sister. Sans the nine minutes she existed in this world without me, I've been doing it her whole life. *I* don't need you. *She* doesn't need you. *We* don't need you. Get. The. Fuck. Out."

After two long weeks at the hospital, with me sleeping on the most uncomfortable chair in existence, we're at Tanner's house.

We've only been here for a week, and it's already feeling claustrophobic...and this place is about ten thousand square feet.

In fairness to Tanner, his gym has been totally transformed into a rehab facility that likely rivals the top ones in the world. I'll never admit this to him, but I'm grateful for what he's doing for her. She'd be miserable at a hospital. Being surrounded by loved ones in a home is much better for her mental well-being as she faces this unimaginable uphill battle.

At first, I thought he did this out of guilt for the accident, but I've been watching him with my sister. He's in love with her. I have no idea what that means with him not wanting to get married again and having had a vasectomy, but he loves her. That much is clear to me.

She loves him too but has been keeping him at arm's length, which is driving him nuts. I'm enjoying watching him squirm like a teenage boy around her though. My new favorite hobby is making him feel insecure.

He was originally hanging around her all day, every day. However, because her intensive physical therapy is in the morning and with Arizona, Ripley, and I never missing a session, Bailey basically kicked Tanner out of his own house. She told him he had to go to his office at least in the mornings every day. He wasn't happy about it, but he now respects her wishes and just about everything else she asks for.

She has occupational therapy and sometimes meets with a psychologist in the afternoons. It's amazing how much it all exhausts her, but she's working her ass off. She seems to progress a little every single day.

Showering is the worst time of day for her. She despises how much she has to depend on us for help. She especially loathes the fact that she has to sit in an old-lady shower chair. I think it symbolizes her inability to do something as fundamental and simple as bathing without assistance from someone else.

Tanner crosses his arms. "*She* does need me. I'm not leaving."

Bailey starts crying. "Stop it! Both of you! I can't take the constant bickering. Tanner, wait outside. I want my sister."

I wave at him as I smile in satisfaction. "Bye. Have a good night. Don't let the door hit you on the ass on the way out."

He narrows his eyes at me. "I'll be right outside the door waiting. Let me know if I'm needed."

I happily shut the bathroom door in his face and turn back to my sister sitting in her wheelchair. "He's such a dick."

She leans her head back. "Please stop fighting with him. I can't take it anymore." Her eyes fill with tears again. "This is hard enough for me, Kam. I hate being dependent on you guys."

"I get that, but I also know you want me to help with bathing more than any other thing."

We don't need to say the reasons out loud for us both to understand the reasoning. She's got a big puffy wound on her back from the spinal surgery, another smaller one in the front from her ovary removal, and she's still a little bloated from all the meds she was on while in the hospital. She doesn't want him to see her body like this. I get it.

She simply nods.

I undress her and help her get situated in the shower. She doesn't like me to wash her hair though. She insists on doing that herself. As I wait just outside the stall, I text Cheetah.

> Me: Can you come over? He's driving me nuts. Orgasm therapy from Dr. Gonzales is best for me right now.

I need him tonight.

> Kitten: I'm here. I'm in the living room with Harper trying to distract her from the sounds of you and Tanner arguing.

A giant sense of relief washes over me. How did I get so dependent on him for my mental health?

> Me: Great. I'm showering her now. I'll be out when she's in bed.

I see three dots on the screen, but before he sends anything, I text,

> Me: No, you can't watch.

> Kitten: LOL. Busted. You know me well.

After getting her ready and then into bed, I quietly make my way to the living room, hoping to not run into Tanner. This mega mansion isn't big enough for the two of us.

I can't help but smile as I approach the living room. Cheetah has built a giant fort. I can hear him and Harper whispering in there.

Harper asks, "Uncle Cheetah, why are you suddenly here all the time?"

He replies, "Because of Kam. I love her."

"Why do you love her?"

"Because she makes me laugh. Oh, and because she's the smartest person I know. Don't tell your dad I said that."

Harper giggles. "Daddy's smart. He always knows my words of the day. Now that Kam lives here, she teaches me new words every day too, but she said I can't tell my daddy about them."

I bite back my smile. I'll admit that I truly enjoy my time with Harper. She's an articulate, smart, inquisitive little kid. I've never liked kids, but I've also never met one like her. She crawls into my bed when Bailey's asleep. In my new life's quest to fuck with Tanner, I'm teaching Harper as many offbeat, yet not dirty, words as I can think of.

I hear Cheetah chuckle. "Oh really? Tell me what word she taught you today."

"Do you promise not to tell my daddy?"

"I pinkie promise."

"Today's word was simp. It means a boy that is pathetically desperate for the attention of a woman."

Cheetah lets out a loud laugh. "That sounds like a Kam word."

"Do you think Kam is pretty?"

"The second prettiest girl in the world."

"Who's the prettiest?"

"You, of course."

I subtly peek into the fort opening and see Harper grinning. As I pull my head out, Fallon appears. She whispers, "It's past her bedtime, but it's too cute to interrupt."

I've spent the better part of the past three weeks with Fallon. I *really* like her. She's funny in both a straight-shooter and a self-deprecating kind of way. She's been amazing with Bailey. I suppose Bailey has always said that they get along well, but I didn't realize they had become close friends. They genuinely like each other. It's so weird to me, considering Bailey was banging Fallon's ex-husband, but if Fallon doesn't care, neither do I. As long as she's good to Bailey, I'm good with her.

I nod before whispering. "They're having a heart-to-heart."

We hear Harper's voice. "Uncle Cheetah?"

"Yes?"

"You're my favorite uncle. But you can't tell Uncle Layton."

He gasps. "Oh my god." He pretends to cry. "This is the best day of my life."

Fallon and I both silently laugh before I crouch down and crawl into the fort with them. "Can I join this party?"

Fallon bends down and sticks her face in. "It's your bedtime anyway, kiddo."

Harper's face falls. "Already?"

Fallon nods. "Yep. Sorry. Let's go brush your teeth. What's left of them."

Harper is missing a few teeth. It's kind of cute.

Before she exits the fort, Cheetah loudly mumbles, "Don't tell your mom about the Skittles I gave you." I've learned in my short time here that Harper is a Skittles addict.

Harper's eyes widen. "Shh. Snitches wind up in ditches."

I silently laugh as Fallon playfully narrows her eyes at me. I taught Harper that last week. The kid is a damn sponge. Just wait until they find out how good she's gotten at poker. And yesterday's *Kam word of the day* was hustle. Contextually, she learned that hustling involves hiding your skills in poker to lure someone into wagering more money. I can't wait for Tanner to see the fruits of my labor.

Fallon and Harper disappear while I rest my head on Cheetah's chest. He pulls out a bag of dark chocolate peanut butter cups.

I grab them. "You're a godsend."

"It's a bribe."

As I dig into my first peanut butter cup, I ask, "What are you bribing me to do?"

"To marry me, of course. How 'bout it?"

I smile as I roll my eyes. "Not today. Maybe tomorrow."

"One of these days—"

I blurt out, "I can't ever marry you because you want kids. You might say you don't care, but I know you do. Look at how you are with Harper."

I've spent a lot of time over the past three weeks thinking about the fact that I almost accepted his proposal just before the accident. I was obviously caught up in the wedding atmosphere. I didn't mean it.

I feel him stiffen. "Don't tell me what I want. I'm sick of people doing that. It's been happening my whole life. I'm not saying I need to have kids, but why are you dead set against it? You're very good with Harper too. She worships you."

"She's a unicorn." I rub my fingers over his chin as my face falls serious. "Cruz, I don't see myself as a mother. I never have. Crazy Aunt Kam will be my title one day. That's it."

His face turns serious too. "Then I can be Crazy Uncle Cheetah."

"I don't know if I believe that will be enough for you." I blow out a breath as I look up. "I want to be unselfish and tell you to go find some child-bearing woman, but I can't right now. I need you too much. You're my happy place."

He squeezes me tightly. "You're mine too. How was Bails today? Sorry I wasn't here at all. We had a few mandatory team meetings and then a team workout."

"Inch by inch, we're getting there. I know she wishes it was faster, but she's a hard worker." I sigh. "I need to work out too. I've never gone this long without breaking a sweat."

"You can bounce on top of me right now. Sweat away."

I giggle before looking around. "I've missed your forts. Too bad it's not a nudist fort."

He wiggles his eyebrows. "We can make it one."

Tanner yells out from somewhere nearby, "You better not."

This fucking guy is driving me nuts.

I smile into the camera on my computer. "Thank you, Dr. Pearl."

"You're a good sister, Kamryn. Make sure to carve out time for yourself. You'll go mad if you don't."

I nod. "I'll try." I hear a knock at my door and know it's time to shut down. "Have a good day, Dr. Pearl."

"You too."

I close my computer screen, unlock my door, and open it to see Fallon. She pokes her head in my room. "Who were you talking to?"

"My therapist. No one but Cheetah knows that I see her, so keep it under wraps."

"I will. Does it help?"

"Like you wouldn't believe. I started earlier this year to help me overcome my boatload of issues. Every session, I feel a little less fucked up. Maybe one day I'll get to the point where I'm only slightly fucked up. Unfortunately, some issues never truly leave you."

"Like what?"

"Like how much I hate your ex-husband."

She lets out a laugh as she holds up a folder. "Nice deflection. Speaking of him, he left this for you. He said you need to sign all the cancellations of your endorsement deals. You don't have to miss them all. I'm here for her."

I shake my head. "I'm not leaving my sister anytime soon. Plus, there's the added perk of Tanner not getting his agent fees." I smile.

She lets out a laugh. "You two are oil and water."

"That's because he's jerked my sister around for a long time. Speaking of which, is she awake?"

She naps nearly every afternoon. I think it's part exhaustion and part depression, though she perks up when Harper gets home from school. Harper has been amazing. She plays board games with Bailey every single day before dinner.

Fallon shakes her head. "Nope. I'm bored. Harper won't be home for a bit. Can I interest you in a glass of wine?" She wiggles her eyebrows up and down. "We can steal one of Tanner's expensive bottles."

"Now you're talking my language. Let's do it."

An hour later, we're giggling as we polish off the last of the bottle. She sighs. "This was nice." She looks around. "It's weird living in this house."

"Is this where you and Tanner lived when you were married?"

She shakes her head. "No, we lived in New York City. That's where Tanner built his company. When we got divorced, I wanted to move to Philly. This is where I grew up. My parents still live here. I was a mess for a long time and needed to come home.

Sometimes a girl needs her mom." She winces. "Sorry, I know yours passed last year."

"It's cool. I hadn't spoken to her in a decade. I most definitely didn't need her, but I understand needing family. That's how I feel about my sister. Sometimes I just need her to calm the voices in my head. How come Tanner didn't stay in New York? He couldn't have been happy to move his business. He must have fought you tooth and nail."

She leans back in her chair and tilts her head to the side. "He's not the monster you think he is. He didn't fight me at all."

"Divorce guilt?"

"The events leading up to the divorce were my fault, not his. He didn't fight because he knew it was best for Harper. He's a good man, Kamryn. He's not so bad when you get past the gruff exterior of his like your sister has. We both know he's in love with her. You should probably learn to get along. I don't think he's going anywhere."

I shake my head. "He can't give her what she deserves."

She gives me a knowing smile. "Maybe he'll change for her."

"Have you ever read the book on how to change a man?"

She shakes her head. "No."

"It's nine hundred blank pages. You can't change a man."

She smiles. "Can women change?"

"We...adapt."

She lets out a laugh. "We'll see. I have a feeling about them though."

"It doesn't bother you? You're practically rooting for it."

She shrugs. "Tanner and I are never getting back together. If you could pick a stepmom for your child, could you do better than Bailey Hart?"

I shake my head. "Nope. There's no better person on this planet."

She nods. "Exactly."

"What about you, Fallon? Do you date? You're fucking hot."

She shakes her head. I half-jokingly hit on her all the time. "I was a little damaged by the end of my marriage. It's taken me time to get back out into the dating pool."

"Tell me how it ended."

"Tell me what you discuss with your therapist," she challenges.

My lips curl in amusement. "Point taken."

"To answer your question, I haven't dated much, but for the first time since my divorce, I met someone who interests me. We're not dating, but I'm finally letting myself be attracted to someone. My life is on pause right now, and I would never ask him to wait. If he's still available, we'll see what happens in a few months when Bailey doesn't need me anymore."

"You're a little mysterious, Fallon."

She winks.

The front door opens, and Harper and Tanner both walk inside.

He raises an eyebrow while examining our empty bottle. "Help yourselves, ladies. Two-thousand-dollar one-of-a-kind bottles grow on trees."

My chin practically drops to the floor. I had no idea. Fallon simply smirks. She knew.

She shrugs her shoulders. "I took a hiatus from a job I love and put my life on hold because you asked." She bats her eyelashes. "It's the least you can do for me. And I'm sure you love nothing more than spoiling Kamryn."

She and I both try to bite back our smiles.

He sighs. "How's our girl?"

Fallon answers, "She had a good morning. She's putting more weight on her legs every day. We're getting there."

Harper throws her backpack on the kitchen counter and falls into Fallon's body.

Fallon wraps her in her arms and kisses her head. "How was your day, baby?"

Harper shrugs. "That girl Laura was being mean to Andie

again." Harper looks at me, "But I told Andie to just smitch at her like you said to, Kam."

Fallon pinches her eyebrows together. "What does smitch mean? Is it one of your morning words?"

Harper and I smile at each other as Harper answers, "No, it's one of the words Kam taught me." She looks around nervously. "Can I say a bad word?"

Fallon skeptically nods before Harper continues, "Smitching is smiling at a bitch without killing her. Kam said I should smitch at Laura. That it will annoy her more than getting a reaction from us."

Tanner groans in annoyance. "Kamryn! Stop teaching my kid fake words."

I start laughing. "It's not fake." I wiggle my eyebrows at Harper. "Right, girlfriend?"

She nods enthusiastically. "It's a real thing, Dad. Laura was so upset about it that she threw something and got a detention. It worked."

His face turns all red. Damn, I take joy in fucking with him.

CHAPTER THIRTY-FOUR

TWO MONTHS LATER

KAMRYN

It's the middle of the night, and I'm sitting on a kitchen stool, finishing up watching a replay of a lecture that I missed.

I'm not paying as close attention as I should be. My mind is drifting. The future feels uncertain, and I hate being out of control.

About two weeks ago, Bailey let Tanner back into her bed. He's in there with her every night. He sneaks out before Harper wakes, but I hear her moaning every damn night. Except around Harper, he's no longer bothering to hide their relationship anymore. He can't keep his hands off her. His hand was down her pants under a blanket when we all watched a movie the other night. He thought he was being discreet, but he wasn't.

I haven't said much about it to her because she's finally happy, and her recovery is moving along extremely well. She's walking and needs much less assistance from everyone. If rekindling things with him has aided in that, I'll swallow my words as much as I'm capable.

There's no denying that she's madly in love with him, and much to my surprise, he's madly in love with her. What happens when two people are in love and one wants marriage and children while the other doesn't? How does it get resolved without one of them, obviously my sister in this case, compromising herself? Is she going to be another in a long line of princesses who gives in to the prince and doesn't get her version of happily ever after, only his? I hate that for her, but I don't know how to save her this time.

We can't be more than a few weeks away from her switching to a much less intensive therapy program. That means it's time to move out. She's going to want to stay here with him. She hasn't said it, but I can feel it coming. I'm going to suggest we move back to our apartment together, but she won't. I know my sister.

That leaves me considering my own future. Our lease is up next month. I haven't re-signed in part because I know she'll want to stay here, and in part because I'm wondering if I should move in with Cheetah. We haven't had any deep conversations lately. He's just kind of been here for me, giving me what I need.

Always giving to me, never expecting anything in return. As soon as I'm out of here, I plan to rectify that. If me moving in with him will make him happy, I'll do it. If letting him go so he can find a more traditional woman will make him happy, I'll do that too. For the first time in our relationship, his needs are going to come first for me, whatever it costs me. I'm steadfast in this.

He leaves soon for Spring Training. A decision needs to be made on us before he goes.

As the lecture ends and I pull out my AirPods, I see Tanner appear from Bailey's room in nothing but flannel pants and a satisfied look on his face. I run my eyes up and down his imposing form. "You have a shockingly good body for an old fucker."

He rolls his eyes. "Do you ever sleep?"

I shrug. "Not really."

"Why not?"

"I like to sit here and plot ways to keep you away from my sister. Instead, I'm forced to put in my earphones to drown out the sounds of the nightly orgasms you give her."

He cracks a smile. "How about a drink, Kamryn? We can have a chat, man to man."

Color me intrigued. We've never once done this in the nearly three months we've been living together. "You're on. I can scratch my balls just as well as the rest of you."

He sighs, as he often does around me, before pouring us two glasses of whiskey. I notice that mine is double the size of his. Nodding at it, I ask, "Trying to get me drunk?"

He shakes his head. "Your sister doesn't like it when I drink too much. I've cut back significantly."

"I imagine it's because our biological mother was an alcoholic."

"I imagine you're right." He sits in the chair next to me and hands me my drink. Clinking his glass with mine, he says, "To the one and only thing we have in common. She's nothing short of a miracle."

I nod as I pick up my glass and take my first sip. Fuck, that burns going down. I don't know how people drink this shit, but I do my best to act like one of the guys. I even manspread.

He smiles as he notices my reaction, but I narrow my eyes at him. "Why is this happening? I can't imagine you want extra time with me. You must have an ulterior motive."

He takes a slow sip of his whiskey before placing the glass down on the kitchen counter with a small clank. "Something interesting came across my desk today."

I shake my head. "Nope. I'm not doing any modeling right now." I've cancelled everything I have this off-season. "Thank god I insisted on the cancellation clauses. My shitty agent would have had me locked in."

He lifts an eyebrow and sarcastically replies, "Yes, it would have been a true shame for you to have to leave us. We would have missed you terribly. My daughter wouldn't have told me that the bag of Doritos I packed her for lunch today was a chiptease."

I can't help but smile. I taught her that a chiptease is a bag of chips that looks full but is mostly air. I hate it when that happens.

He continues, "Or that when two boys at school were fighting the other day, they got a dudevorce."

I can't contain my laugh this time. "Ha. Admit that it's funny how she always uses these words in the right context. That's the genius."

He doesn't emote at all. "I will admit no such thing. Back to this tidbit that found me today."

He's up to something. "What do you have up your gray-haired sleeve, Montgomery?" He looks down at his arms, which only have dark hair. His beard and chest hair have a little gray though, and I enjoy playing on his insecurities.

He narrows his eyes at me again before reaching for his glass and taking another sip. He lets the silence fill the air for a good ten seconds before he continues, "As I believe you know, I'm growing my women's division. I've been searching for nearly a year, hoping to find the right woman to lead that division, but apparently female lawyers with deep knowledge of athletics and a steel constitution are harder to find than I imagined. I had a thought recently. Since the right lawyer doesn't seem to currently exist, I decided to reach out to an old law school professor of mine to see if he knew of any budding superstars. You might know him. His name is Byron Burke."

My eyes widen in realization. He was my contracts law professor.

He gives me a knowing smirk. "Why doesn't anyone know you're in law school, Kamryn?"

"It's no one's fucking business. And Cheetah knows."

"Why not Bailey?"

I gulp my whiskey, letting the amber fluid burn a hole in my throat. Anything to avoid having to answer. I've considered this a lot throughout the years. "Because I needed something for me, and I've never been quite sure what I want to do with my degree. Playing with my sister and two best friends in the Olympics is my priority. What happens after that remains in the air."

"Why law? You don't do anything without purpose. What is it you want to do?"

"Something that makes a difference. I honestly don't know what. I initially applied with an altruistic notion of representing kids with shitty parents. I can relate. But then I realized that I'd have to work with kids, and I suck at that."

He shakes his head. "You don't suck. You're just...different. Kids respond to the fact that you don't treat them like kids."

"Harper is the only kid on the planet that I like. I suppose I can also tolerate Andie and Dylan, but Harper is like a little adult. I don't see myself working with kids on a daily basis. I've also come to realize that it wouldn't be good for my mental health to continuously come across those terrible home life situations considering what I suffered throughout my childhood."

He looks like he wants to ask follow-up questions but holds back. "Byron tells me that you have the brightest legal mind he's come across since he had me as a student."

"Well, I'm pretty fucking smart. You know that. Honestly, law school has been easy for me. I have perfect grades, and I rarely need to break a sweat. What are you getting at, Tanner?"

"I think you know what I'm getting at, being so *fucking smart* and all."

"You can't possibly want to work with me. You hate me."

The corners of his mouth raise in amusement. "I wouldn't be working *with* you; you'd be working *for* me." He tilts his glass until he finishes the remaining contents before his eyes meet mine again. "Kamryn, I'm fighting the battle to get women equal pay in athletics. You're the best shortstop in the world and you make less than a hundred grand a year. The highest-paid shortstops in baseball make thirty-five million dollars per year, and none of them hit as well as you. Doesn't that injustice piss you off?"

"Of course it does."

He points his finger at me. "*That's* how you can make a difference. I need a smart woman who knows sports inside and out and who happens to be a real ball-buster. Does that description sound familiar to you?"

I let his words sink in for a few moments before responding. "What about when things go to shit with you and my sister?"

"What if they don't go to shit?"

"You can't give her what she deserves. Why are you spending time with her when you can't and won't give her what she needs?"

"Isn't that the pot calling the kettle black?"

I wince. "Fuck you, Tanner."

He smiles. "You certainly like to dish it out, Kamryn, but you don't like to take it. Can you give Cruz what he deserves? What he needs?"

I stand and place my glass in the sink. "Good night."

As I walk away, he says, "Think about my offer."

With my back to him, I simply hold up my middle finger as I round the corner toward my bedroom. I can hear the asshole chuckling as I do. What does my sister see in him *besides the whole sexy, domineering, older man thing?*

I walk into my room and see Cruz peacefully asleep. Am I a hypocrite? I want Tanner to set Bailey free so she can find someone willing to give her what she needs. Should I be doing that for Cruz?

How can things work out for two people when there's a clear divide in needs with little to no overlap? I don't want my sister to compromise. Why should she? I won't ask him to do the same.

I can't look at his innocent face right now. Walking back out into the house, I quickly make sure that Tanner went up to bed. When I see the coast is clear, I quietly tiptoe upstairs and into Fallon's room before closing her door behind me.

Her eyes blink open. "Kam? Is everything okay?"

"Can I sleep with you?"

"Sleep, sleep or sex sleep? I don't think I'm adventurous

enough to sex sleep with a woman at this point in my life. Maybe I should have done that in college at least once, but that ship has sailed for me."

I giggle. "I'd totally be up for sex sleep with you anytime, but I meant sleep, sleep. Maybe a little talk sleep now that you're awake."

She smiles as she opens her blankets, and I slip into bed. Fallon has become my friend in the past few months. She's only nine years older than us, but she has such a maternal, calming nature to her. Given that the only maternal figure in my life has been Bailey, and I haven't been willing to burden her the past few months, I've come to rely on Fallon for that. Our staying up late talking has become commonplace.

I take in her skimpy sleep shorts and tank top. Her nipples are poking through. "Fuck, you're so hot."

"Kamryn," she warns.

"Are your boobs real?"

She lets out a laugh. "If I had a dollar for every time I was asked that... Yes, they're real. Stop looking at them. They're not on the menu for you."

I smile as I lay my head on the pillow and stare at her. "Do you think I'm being selfish by holding on to Cruz?"

She pinches her eyebrows together. "Why would you say that?"

"Because I don't want marriage and kids."

"Does he?"

"He says he doesn't care, but I think he does. It's in his genes. His family is single-handedly doubling the population of the state of Texas."

"He's a grown man. He can make his own decisions. He very obviously loves you. Do you love him?"

I nod.

"Then take him at his word. Or maybe you'll feel differently one day. Have you ever allowed for that possibility, or are you too stubborn about being stubborn?"

"What does that mean?"

"You have strong convictions, Kamryn. Like you're dead set on hating Tanner. So dead set that I can't get you to admit that you're starting to like him."

The corners of my mouth raise slightly. "All fungus grows."

"Not all fungus is bad. In fact, some of it's good."

I'm quiet before she continues. "She loves him, and he loves her. Whether you like it or not, and whether he can give her everything she thought she needed or not, they're going to end up together. He makes her happy. Maybe it won't be in the ways she had always imagined, and maybe it will, but she could do a lot worse than Tanner Montgomery."

"If you love him so much, why didn't you stay married to him?" I've asked her a million times about the end of her marriage, but she never gives me any answers.

She shakes her head. "I'm not *in* love with him, but I'll always love him and always want the best for him. He's the father of my child. *Nothing* will ever change that."

"Do you think he was the love of your life?"

She exhales a long breath. "Fuck. I hope not, Kamryn." She bites her lip. "If I tell you something, can you keep it between us?"

I nod.

"I've gone on a handful of dates with someone recently. The man I mentioned to you a while back. I said no to him at first, but he kept asking for months, and I finally decided why the fuck not. I have nothing to lose. Then Bailey's injury happened, and I moved in here. We finally went out recently and hit it off. Bailey will transition to outpatient soon. I'm going to tell Tanner that I'm moving out next week. Once I do, I want to see where things go with this guy."

"That's amazing, Fallon. Do you have any pictures of him?"

She scrunches her face. "I do, but—"

"But what?"

"You might recognize him. He's kind of famous."

I gasp. "Is it Vance? I can totally see you with him. He's hot."

She giggles. "In a million years, I wouldn't date a client of Tanner's. That's way too close to home. And I don't want to date someone younger than me who would want more kids. I'll be forty this year. I don't know if I can still have kids."

"Do you want more kids?"

She nods. "I do. Very much so, but each year that goes by I know what the odds are."

"I guess if I had a Harper, I'd want more too."

She lifts an eyebrow. "So if you were to have a Harper, you'd be interested in having kids?"

I twist my lips. "Hmm. There are no guarantees. And stop changing the topic. Let me see a picture of him."

She reaches for her phone and swipes away until she finally hands it to me. I look at the screen, immediately recognizing the photo. "You're dating *him*?"

She gives me a small smile and nods. "I suppose I am."

"How old is he?"

"Just a few years older than me. He has two adult kids, a daughter and a son."

I nod. "His daughter is a basketball player, right?"

"She is."

I've followed her career. She was a superstar college basketball player and played for the pro team out of New York for a few years before being traded to Philly this past season.

"Good for you, Fallon."

"It's new, but we clicked. We text several times a day and talk every night. We'll see what happens."

"I hope it works out."

"I didn't see it coming, but life takes unexpected turns. Sometimes you need to go with the flow."

I absorb her words. "Is that where you were tonight? With him?" She missed dinner tonight, which is unusual.

She shakes her head. "No. I had a board meeting. I sit on the board of a local battered women's shelter."

I give her an undoubtedly questioning look, and she shakes her head. "It wasn't me but someone close to me."

I want to ask more questions but decide it would be in bad taste. I simply say, "It's cool that you give back."

"You can't ever change the past, Kamryn, but you can always try to do your part in helping to pave a better road for the future."

CHAPTER THIRTY-FIVE

TWO WEEKS LATER

KAMRYN

L*ife takes unexpected turns.*

Fallon said that to me when we were in her bed that night, but little did I know how true it was about to become.

As it turns out, no one knew that Tanner had a vasectomy reversal before Bailey's accident. He never mentioned it because he was waiting on his test results to make sure it worked and that he could give her children. As luck would have it, Tanner didn't know that Bailey's IUD had been removed along with her ovary.

A full gas tank of sperm and no protection equaled a pregnant Bailey. I figured this out about a week ago. Yes, me. I realized she was pregnant before anyone else. In fact, Bailey was the last to know.

I laugh at the memory of how it went down. Fallon was the second one to figure it out, and we both ran into my room to freak out before cluing in anyone else.

I saw the moment it hit Fallon's face at the dinner table, so I grabbed her hand, and we ran into my bedroom at Tanner's house, shutting the door behind us. Tanner was clueless. Dumb shit. Bailey was in bed, feeling sick and not knowing why.

I nervously paced as reality set in, and I started to freak out. Running my hands through my hair, I muttered, "Holy shit, my sister is fucking pregnant. Oh my god. Can she even carry a baby with her injury? Will it cause issues for her back? Will she ever play ball again? Is he going to marry her? Will he be pissed? Will he break her heart? What if she's pregnant and he's not in the picture? I need to help her. And what if—"

Fallon's lips met mine at the same time she grabbed my face. Her tongue ran along my lower lip, and I moaned into her mouth. Fuck, she's a good kisser.

She momentarily deepened the kiss, moving her lips over mine and sliding her tongue through my mouth.

Still holding my face, she eventually pulled her mouth away, and her electric turquoise eyes stared into mine. "Relax. Everything will be okay. This is a good thing." She ran her tongue along her full lips. "Hmm, my friend Bianca was right. Women do taste different. And your lips and face are freakishly soft. I'm not used to that."

I smiled. "It's not all that's soft on me. Care to taste more?"

She giggled as she pulled away. "That will be my one and only sip of cooterade. Isn't that what you called it the other day?"

I let out a laugh. "Yep. Let me know if you change your mind." I grabbed my phone. "I need Arizona and Ripley to get their asses over here to help me deal with Bailey."

I texted them an update, and they both replied that they were on their way over. I then texted Cheetah, suddenly feeling a little guilty about kissing Fallon, though she kissed me.

> Me: Fallon just kissed me.

> Kitten: So fucking hot. Did you get a picture?

Because of course that would be his response.

Me: No, sorry.

Kitten: Can you get one? I'm hard as a rock right now.

Me: She did it to calm me down and said it was a one-time thing.

Kitten: Damn it. I miss all the good shit. Gotta go burp the worm.

Me: Come by later. Crazy shit going down at the Montgomery mansion.

Kitten: As long as you also go down.

Me: Deal.

After Arizona and Ripley arrived, we had to sit Tanner and Bailey down to explain that she was pregnant. They were both in shock but managed to cry tears of joy and get engaged all in the course of ten minutes. Later that night, Fallon, Bailey, and Tanner all sat Harper down to tell her about Tanner and Bailey getting married.

The next morning, Harper knocked on my door. Cheetah was already gone for a team workout, so I told her to come in.

"What's up, little prodigy?"

I could physically see the wheels in her mind in motion as she slowly entered my room. "My dad and Bails are getting married."

I nodded. "I know. How do you feel about it?"

She plopped down on my bed. "It's kind of weird, but my mom said that Bails is now my bonus mom, and I guess that's kind of cool. I spend half my time with my mom and half with my dad, but now I'll always have a mom wherever I go."

I couldn't help the tears that filled my eyes. "You're a lucky little girl. Some people don't have one good mom, but now you have two great ones."

She gave me a toothless smile. "You're right. I'm double as lucky as everyone else."

"Yep."

"Does it make you my aunt?"

Oh shit. I hadn't considered that. "I guess it does."

"What do I call you? Kam, Coach Kam, or Aunt Kam?"

"I would like you to call me Your Royal Highness, Queen Kam of Philly."

She giggled. "For real, what should I call you?"

"Call me whatever you want, Harper. Whatever makes you comfortable."

"Can I call you Aunt Kam?"

I nodded as I swallowed down the massive lump in my throat and somehow croaked out, "I'd like that."

Just before Bailey found out she was pregnant, she told me it was time for me to move home and that she was staying with Tanner. That she loved him and was willing to give up marriage and having biological kids of her own if it meant having Tanner and Harper in her life.

About two hours after that conversation, she had a positive pregnancy test in her hand and a diamond ring on her finger. I've never been more shocked in my life. Tanner loves her and decided that his love for her trumped anything else he thought he did and didn't want. The prince gave the princess what *she* wanted. He's giving her the happily ever after of her dreams.

The kicker? He's as happy as can be. Beaming. Radiating. I haven't seen a single moment of trepidation from him. He even let me plan the wedding, which is taking place at his house in a few days.

As for my sister, she's nearly back to herself. She has some residual hand issues. She can't grip things hard. For a regular person, it wouldn't be a big deal. For someone who needs to grip a bat for her career, it's everything. She spends hours in the batting cage every day but still can't get her grip strength back.

Her ability to play this summer wasn't looking good, but now that she's pregnant, it doesn't matter. She'll be heavily pregnant during the season and won't be able to play, regardless of her physical abilities.

Ironically, she now seems more determined than ever to get back up to snuff in time for the Olympics in a little over two years. She's never cared about making that team nearly as much as Ripley, Arizona, and me, but now that she's being told she can't, she doesn't like it.

There's not a doubt in my mind that she'll be standing with us on that podium when they put those gold medals around our necks.

As for her personal life, she's getting the full fairy tale. I have this lightness I've never felt before. Like the burdens I've carried for so long are finally being lifted.

I look at my computer screen and ask, "Dr. Pearl, do you think that maybe the Disney princesses' definitions of happily ever after changed?"

She stares back at me. "What do you mean?"

"I mean maybe Belle initially wanted her education but simply fell in love. Why can't she be educated *and* in love? Why are they mutually exclusive? Maybe Cinderella also fell in love. Maybe she wanted to get away from a shitty family situation *and* be with the man of her dreams. Aren't we supposed to be able to have it all?"

Her brow furrows. I feel like I've stumped her. She's rarely left without words. "It's certainly a thought-provoking question, Kamryn."

"I feel like that's a bullshit shrink response for the fact that you don't have an answer."

A small smile finds her lips. "Perhaps you're right."

"Maybe making the person you love happy can also make you happy. My sister's fiancé was dead set against marriage and having more children. He's about to have both, and I've never seen him look happier."

"What is it you're getting at, Kamryn?"

"I'm trying to decide whether or not to move in with Cruz. He asks every day."

Once Tanner and Bailey got engaged, Cheetah started talking to me again about moving in with him.

"I thought that he asked you to marry him every day."

I nod. "He does that too, but that's kind of become a joke. He's serious about us moving in."

"What's giving you pause?"

"The same thing that's given me pause since day one. I believe that, to his core, he wants marriage and children. I've always assumed I wanted neither."

"Interesting choice of words. You used to be more steadfast in that."

"I didn't do it on purpose."

"Your subconscious may have."

"Whatever. I don't want to waste his time. If I move in, he won't be searching for Mrs. Right."

"What if you're Mrs. Right?"

"What if I'm not?"

She sighs. "I feel like you're looking for guarantees. No such thing exists. Has he ever said to you that he needs marriage and children to be happy?"

She knows the answer. "He hasn't."

"I suppose at some point you'll have to decide whether or not to take him at his word."

I blow out a breath as I look at the time. "Fuck. Our session is over. Fastest hour of the week."

She places her notepad and pen on her desk and looks at me with more compassion than is normal for her. "Are you ready for today?"

I shake my head. "No, but I know this conversation needs to happen."

"Good luck, Kamryn. They'll believe you. I promise. For what it's worth, I'm proud of you."

I do my best to choke down my emotions. That means more to me than she realizes.

AN HOUR LATER, I'm at Kelly Drive, standing on the shoreline of the Schuylkill River. Kelly Drive is a nearly nine-mile loop around the river where people walk, run, bike, eat, and do all other kinds of recreational activities. In nicer weather, many people spend time here. It's a unique spot in the city, with the famous Philly Art Museum sitting at the very end, overlooking the water.

I see my father and Bailey approach. My father looks happier and healthier than he has in years. He's sporting a nice tan. For Christmas, I bought him and Ray a two-week Mediterranean cruise. I've never been prouder of a gift in my entire life.

They just returned a few weeks ago. My father said it was the best two weeks of his life. He's in town now for Bailey's wedding.

They both smile as they notice the pile of smooth stones I've assembled. Our father taught us how to skip stones on the water when we were little girls. It was often our quiet time away from the insanity of our mother, and we cherished it.

My father tentatively peeks over the edge into the water. "Is it safe?"

I let out a laugh. "No gators in Philly, Dad." Fresh water in Florida is full of them.

We spend a few minutes throwing the stones and letting them skip across the water. Bailey and I are much better at this now than he is. It was always the opposite when we were little girls.

Bailey eventually grabs my hand. "Why are we here, Kam?"

I point toward the bench. "I want to talk to you both. Let's sit."

We do, and I try to swallow down all the emotions that feel inevitable.

My eyes toggle between the two of them. "For the past year, I've been seeing a therapist to try to overcome some of my issues."

Tears immediately well in Bailey's eyes. "When? Where?"

"Electronically. My sessions are via video. She's always flexible around my schedule."

"Is that what you do all night?" she asks.

I shake my head. "No. We'll get to that. It's not that hard to find an hour each week to talk to Dr. Pearl. That's her name."

My father pinches his lips together. "I think it's great. I'm proud of you."

"Wait until you hear what I have to say before you declare that."

He gives me a small smile in acknowledgment, but says, "I'm proud no matter what."

"She said something in one of our sessions that resonated with me. She said depression is when you're worried about the past, anxiety is when you're worried about the future, and happiness is when you're living in the moment. I've spent most of my life toggling between the first two. Yes, I sometimes live in the moment, but I want to work toward letting go of the first two and focusing on happiness. It starts with me telling you two a few things I've kept hidden for a long time."

They both nod. I ask Bailey if she remembers that night when our mother told us we were about to be in a post-Super Bowl television show that never happened. She says she has a vague recollection but mostly remembers that as the time period when I completely soured on our mother. It's so interesting that a night impacted my entire life yet is barely a blip on her radar. I suppose that means I've done my job all these years of protecting her.

I tell them what I heard as they make no attempt to contain the look of shock on their faces. "I admit that I couldn't hear the whole conversation, but I know phrases like *Kamryn is too strong-willed,* and *Bailey will be more amenable* left Mom's mouth. I also know that the director responded with something along the lines of *Beverly, you'd sell your soul to the devil to get your girls to appear in my next project.* That's very real. And then Mom pulled only me away from the room, and the director was entering the room where Bails was alone."

My father openly sobs into his hands before apologizing over and over again that he never knew and never thought she'd take it that far. Bailey is shaking all over. I think she's in shock. I want to keep her calm. She's pregnant, after all.

I rub her back. "I know you've thought for all these years that I was selfish."

"I never—"

I hold up my hands. "Let me finish. I made you play softball. I made you come to college with me. I made you follow me into professional ball. I made you follow me to Philly. I need you to finally understand that it wasn't about me per se. It was about you. The anxiety I've felt since that night is very real. This all-encompassing need to keep you safe is real. I know you're an adult and can handle yourself, but you're also so pure-hearted. You only see the good in people. I couldn't live with myself if something bad happened to you. I'm so fucking sorry if you feel like I've held you back from anything in your life you've wanted to do. I promise that I won't do that anymore. It's your life to live as you please. The days of me manipulating things to keep you close are over. I swear to you."

She throws her arms around my neck as her voice cracks, "Kam, I can't believe all this. I can't believe you kept it bottled up inside. I'm so sorry if I've ever made you feel bad that I wasn't living the life I wanted to live. That's not true at all. I'm exceedingly happy with my life. I hope you know that. It's because of you. I see the good in people because you've always protected me from the bad. You didn't hold me back. You're my savior."

Tears spill from both our eyes. I wipe her tears from her face. "Fuck, I shouldn't make you cry right before your wedding. You'll have puffy eyes. At least you'll probably look closer to Daddy Tanner's age now."

She lets out a laugh as she sniffles and tries to wipe away more of her tears. "Bullshit. I'm gonna be a hot bride."

I nod. "That's for sure. Just wait until you see our entrances."

Her eyes widen. "What did you do?"

I wink. "Don't worry about it."

I turn to my father, who's still inconsolable. I knew this would be the hardest on him, but I needed to get it off my chest.

He shakes his head. "I...I didn't know. I hope you know that. It was *my* job to protect you. I've failed you as a father. It shouldn't have fallen on you, Kamryn. I robbed you of your childhood."

Fuck. This isn't what I wanted. His blaming himself isn't what's best, but some part of me feels validated that he's not suggesting I was wrong. He's not defending her. It would have hurt more if he did. I think part of me holding it in for all these years was thinking he wouldn't believe me.

I rub his back. "It doesn't matter anymore. It's all in the past." I think of Fallon's words to me. "You can't ever change the past, but you can always try to do your part in helping to pave a better road for the future. Daddy, thanks for believing me. It means everything to me."

He looks up at me with a bit of shock on his face. "Of course I believe you. You're a lot of things, Kamryn, but a liar isn't one of them. Your powers of perception have always far exceeded your age. I believe your version of the events, but this is just so hard to swallow as a father and as the man who married her and let her pull the strings for far too long."

"Unburdening myself of this will help me finally move past it. I hate that I'm burdening you with it, but I needed to do this."

He nods. "I'm glad you did. I'll need time to truly absorb the enormity of it."

Bailey and I do our best to make him feel better for a long while. We remind him that it may not have been the easiest road, but we're both in a good place right now, and that's all that matters.

I just dropped a major bomb. It's not like we'll have one conversation and it will be over. I know they'll both need time to process and react, especially him. As much as I want a quick fix, that's not how things work. Dr. Pearl taught me that.

I then let them know about the fact that I've been in law school for all these years. My father doesn't seem at all surprised. In fact, it gets him to perk up a bit. Bailey is in shock and doesn't understand why I never told her about it.

I suppose it's the only thing in my life that I've ever done purely for me. Right or wrong, I felt guilty about it.

AN HOUR LATER, I approach Cheetah's building and smile at my favorite doorman. "Hi, Evan."

He has an unusually enormous grin. "Good afternoon, Kamryn."

I narrow my eyes at him. "Why are you so happy?"

He pinches his lips together like he's trying to stifle his smile. "It's a beautiful day, and a beautiful woman is talking to me. Why would I be anything other than happy? Life is good."

I run my tongue over my top teeth. "Hmm. You and Sir Gonzales are up to no good. I can feel it."

He chuckles as he opens the door to the building. "He's awaiting your arrival, your majesty."

I walk inside and take the elevator to Cheetah's penthouse. As I exit, I see a bunch of packed bags in his foyer. He's leaving for Spring Training right after the wedding. It sucks. I prefer the off-season when we get to spend more time together. This off-season was rough but having him with me all the time helped me get through it.

He doesn't notice me at first while he exits his bedroom door and closes it behind him. I can't help but stare at him. Some people are human medicine. A little time with them cures everything. That's what he's been for me. Even if we part, I know that I'm better because of my time with him.

As soon as he sees me, he flashes me a huge smile. "Hey, Kam bam. How did it go?"

I nod. "It went well. They believed me."

He scoffs. "Of course they did. I told you they would."

I motion my head toward his bags. "All packed?"

He exhales a long breath. "Yep. I wish I didn't have to go."

"Me too. We need to talk."

He points toward the living room. I see a huge fort. "I thought you might say that."

We walk over, and he begins to undress but I stop him. "Can it not be a nudist fort today?"

He twists his lips. "How about we compromise? It can be a shark week fort." That means underwear.

I'm about to protest, but I'm learning to compromise. I simply remove my clothes until I'm in a bra and panties. Once he's in his boxer briefs and T-shirt, we crawl inside until we both lay our cheeks on the pillows facing each other. I find myself wondering if this will be the last time I'm in a Cheetah fort looking at his handsome face. My stomach twists at the notion.

I'm about to start my planned speech when he holds up his hand. "Don't. I know what you're going to say. You're always the one steering this ship. Today, it's my turn."

I nod. "Okay. Say what you need to say. I'm all ears."

"No less than a thousand times during the past year and a half, you've expressed that *I* want kids and marriage. That *I* need both to be happy. Have you ever heard me say that?"

I shake my head. "No, but you did ask me to marry you."

"I've asked you to marry me over two hundred times."

"The first time, Cruz. That proposal was real."

"Was it me being swept up in an emotional moment without an ounce of forethought, or was it as real as the night of the accident when you accepted my proposal thinking it was a marriage proposal?"

My eyes widen. "You knew?"

"You're not the only one with brains. I figured it out at some point that night while we were sitting in the hospital as I replayed it over and over in my delirious head."

"Okay, so maybe we were both swept up in moments, but haven't you always assumed you'd get married and have kids?"

He takes my hand and rubs his thumb over the back of my palm. "I think I assumed it because I hadn't considered differently. It's all I knew. But it wasn't my goal in life. I didn't run around looking for a child-bearing wife. I've never even been in a real relationship until you. I've never truly cared for a woman until you. Honestly, Kam, I was mostly worried that I'd never find someone who matches my crazy. Someone who loves to be silly and laugh like me. Someone who gets my euphemisms. Someone who loves me as I am. I know I'm not *normal* and never will be. There's only one thing in life I know for sure right now. I love you. I want to spend my life with you, whatever form that takes. There is not one ounce of doubt in my mind about that."

"What about kids? You'll push for that one day, and I don't know if I'll ever get there."

His blue eyes bore into mine. "Have I ever asked you to do something you didn't want to do?"

I shake my head. "Never."

"Other than giving our relationship a chance, have I ever once asked you to change anything about yourself?"

I shake my head again. "Never."

"Kam, I've never even asked you for monogamy. I made a personal decision not to be physical with other women because I don't want anyone else, not because we agreed to it. I'm not interested. It's not an effort. I've never asked you to give up women or men. You've done it because you want to. You don't want anyone else, just like I don't, but I never asked that of you."

What the fuck? I immediately replay all our relationship

conversations. It's true. He's never asked me for that. I did it because I only wanted him. Hell, before we even slept together, I couldn't look at other men because of him.

"W...what are you saying?"

"Do I make you happy?"

I nod as tears fill my eyes. "Exceedingly happy."

"I feel the same." He smirks. "I make me happy too. I'm a fucking riot."

I giggle as I playfully slap his arm.

His face turns serious again. "*You* make me happy. How about this? We spend time together as long as we both want that. No rules. I'm asking you to move in with me, not for any other reason than I want to live with you. I want to go to sleep with you. I want to wake up with you. I want to build forts with you. I want to make dinner for you. I want to pump you with dark chocolate when it's shark week. I want to pump you with my vanilla cream when it's not. If you don't want to—"

"I want the same. I want all of it. I just never want to hold you back from what you need, but I equally know that I'm not going to be forced into anything. But you're right, you've never once forced my hand...except down your pants at the dinner table a few weeks ago."

His dimples make an appearance. "Good, because I already made you a key, and that's three dollars I can never get back."

I smile. "What key? You don't have a front door, kitten. The elevator opens into your condo."

He feigns shock as he sucks in a breath. "Oh shit. You're right. The elevator keycard is like a hundred bucks. I'm not sure I'm ready for that level of commitment. Three dollars was my budget. Forget everything I said."

I let out a laugh.

He runs his fingers over my lips. "I love your smile, especially when I'm the cause of it." Exhaling a long breath, he says, "As for kids, I'm not sure I should be anything other than a fun uncle. A funcle, if you will. I don't have an overwhelming need to put more crazy into the world than I already do. Like you, I'm not closing the door, I'm simply saying it's not a deal-breaker for me. I've never once said to you that I need to have children to be happy."

I look into his eyes and whisper, "What did I do to deserve you? I didn't think men like you really existed."

He gives me an uncharacteristically intense look. "I exist to love you, Kamryn Hart. All you have to do is let me."

I have no words for that.

He stares at me as I let the enormity of what he just said sink in. "Did it ever occur to you that part of my attraction to you is that you make me a better man?"

"Me? I make *you* better? It's the other way around."

He shakes his head. "You're wrong. You're so much stronger than me. I see how you stand up for yourself and others. It's always been a weakness of mine, but now I'm aware of it and trying to stand up for myself and those I care about. For my whole life, I've let my post-baseball path be scripted into something that doesn't excite me. It's you who has pushed me to see that I have other options."

He rubs his thumb over my face. "If you don't want promises, we simply won't make any." He twists his lips. "Except one. I need you to make me one promise."

Fuck. Here we go. I blow out a breath. "What?"

He sits up. "I'll be right back."

What is he up to? This man is always full of surprises. Hell, it's one of the things I love most about him.

He disappears for about three minutes. I hear him approaching the fort, but when he bends down, I nearly melt into a puddle.

I honestly blink a few times to make sure I'm not hallucinating.

He's holding the cutest golden retriever puppy I've ever seen in my life. I gasp. "Oh my god."

He grins widely. "I need you to promise to take care of this guy while I'm gone. Also, I need you to name him because he doesn't like Little Dude at all. He thinks it's emasculating."

I breathe, "What? He's yours?"

"He's ours."

"What will happen when we're both in season? When we travel?"

The puppy adorably wiggles in his big arms. "Evan has two dogs. He said he'd take this cutie pie home with him when we're both on the road. I think Evan was more excited than anyone about this puppy."

That explains his cheery demeanor earlier.

I reach for the puppy. "Can I hold him?"

He happily and carefully hands the puppy to me. I take him into my arms and bury my face in his soft fur. The puppy smell invades my senses while he nibbles on my finger. "He's so fucking cute."

"Are you telling the puppy that I'm cute, or are you telling me that the puppy is cute?"

"Both."

"Fair enough. Any thoughts on names? Sixty-nine...since it's our two jersey numbers put together? Or something baseball and softballish like Dinger? Maybe Tater."

I scrunch my face. None of those feel right. I stare down at the sweetest little face I've ever seen in my life while I run through a few names in my head until the right one hits me. I look up at Cheetah. "I think I'd like to name him Chewbacca. We can call him Chewy."

Cheetah gasps before a huge grin forms on his handsome face. "For real?"

I rub my nose in the puppy's belly. "Do you like your name, Chewy?"

The puppy lets out a high-pitched bark, and I nod. "Yep. He loves it."

CHAPTER THIRTY-SIX

CHEETAH

Tanner narrows his eyes at Harper at the poker table. "Are you counting cards?"

Harper giggles. "What? Me?" She looks down at her full house and innocently shrugs. "It was a good time to go all in. I guess I got lucky."

Daylen blinks a few times as he stares at everyone's cards. "What the fu...dge? We were just hustled by a nine-year-old."

I'm realizing that she threw the first few hands until we upped the ante and assumed she didn't know what she was doing. She even folded a winning hand at some point and said she didn't realize it was a good hand.

There's only one person who could have taught her this.

Tanner's lip twitches as he grits out, "Kamryn *fucking* Hart."

Harper gasps. "That's ten dollars in the swear jar, Daddy."

She reaches her little hands out and collects all the chips

on the table, worth a few hundred bucks. "I think it's my bedtime."

Tanner accusatorily asks, "Since when are you excited about bedtime?"

"Since I have three hundred and forty-six dollars to put into my piggy bank. I see a trip to the candy store in my future."

It's the night before Tanner and Bailey's wedding. All he wanted was a poker night with his friends and Harper. They leave for their honeymoon right away, so including Harper was important to him because he won't see her for a while.

Harper walks around the table with a huge grin as she kisses everyone on the cheek. She whispers to me, "Text Kam and tell her that I hustled everyone."

I wink at her. "Will do."

When Harper leaves, Layton looks at me. "You were the last to arrive tonight. I didn't mention it in front of Harper because your fun facts are always dirty, but it's time to pay the piper."

I think for a few moments until something Kam mentioned a few weeks ago hits me. "Have you ever really considered the wording of Juicy Fruit commercials?"

I see them all deep in contemplation and notice the moment it hits each one.

I chuckle. "Yep. *Take a sniff, pull it up. The taste is gonna move you when you pop it in your mouth.* The Juicy Fruit marketing department are dirty fuckers."

Tanner rubs his beard. "That sounds like something Kamryn would know. Don't become as deranged as her."

That's now the third time tonight he's made a less-than-flattering comment about Kam. I'm a little fed up with it.

I fake a smile and say, "Wait until you see what she has in store for your wedding tomorrow."

Frankly, I can't believe he let Kam plan it.

I stick around after everyone has left. I'm helping Tanner clean up empty bottles when he turns his head to me. "Is something on your mind?"

I nod. "Yes. I get that you and Kam are a bit of a mismatch, and I'm cool when you two take playful jabs at each other when you're together, but I can't have you talking shit about my girl behind her back."

He jerks as if he's taken aback. "I didn't realize it bothered you."

"I know. That's my fault. I'm always one for keeping things light, but she's the woman I love, and she's about to become your sister-in-law. Find some common ground. I know she's going to bust your balls, and you have every right to give it back to her but keep the fighting clean."

One corner of his mouth turns up. "You're right. And I will." He rubs his beard. "I do have respect for her, Cruz. Did she tell you that I offered her a job?"

"What?" I couldn't possibly be more shocked right now.

"Yep. A few weeks ago, before we found out about the pregnancy. I did some digging and found out that she's been in law school. She told me that you were the only one who knew at the time."

"I was."

"She's the perfect person to represent female athletes, don't you think?"

I can't help the huge grin that finds my face. "I love this as her next act."

"I do too. So, yes, I bust her chops just as she busts mine, but at the end of the day, you should know I respect her. I wouldn't have offered her this huge job otherwise."

I nod. "I'm glad we cleared the air."

"Me too. I like this side of you. If Kamryn is to thank for it," he winks at me, "then perhaps she's not all bad. What are *you* thinking for your next act? You have time, you're still moving well, but it's never too early to plan for the future. Take it from Layton. Sometimes it sneaks up on you before you're ready for it."

I blow out a breath. "For the longest time, I thought I'd go home to Texas, start a family, and possibly do some coaching."

"Is that what you want?"

I shake my head. "I don't think it is. Not at all. It doesn't excite me in the least. Kam mentioned to me that she thought I'd be a natural in the broadcasting booth. What do you think of that?"

His face lights up. "I *love* that for you. You have both the personality and game knowledge."

"I think so too. I know I have time, but I was thinking I'd take a few broadcasting and communications classes in the off-season to get myself prepared. Kam emailed me local programs that offer it."

He pats my back. "She's good for you."

"She most definitely is."

THE WEDDING DAY HAS ARRIVED. Kam is with Bailey as they prepare for her big day. I'm in my elevator, about to walk Chewy before I head over to Tanner's house.

As I exit, I see Evan holding the front door open for me. He smiles down at my puppy, and Chewy jumps all over Evan's legs as he feeds him from his never-ending supply of doggie treats that now live in his pocket. "Is Sir Chewbacca Hart Gonzales, Prince of South Philly, excited about our evening walk?"

Evan is walking him while we're at the wedding.

Chewy lets out a high-pitched puppy bark and I nod. "He is. Thanks for helping us. We won't be back until late."

He rubs under Chewy's ear, much to Chewy's delight.

"My pleasure. Tell the lady of the house that anytime she needs help when you're gone, to please ask. I enjoy walking him." He pats his big belly. "I could use a little extra exercise."

"I will. Thanks, buddy." I wink at him. "You'll look after my family when I'm away, right? Keep the lady of the house out of trouble?"

He smiles. "I'll try. Trouble finds that one though."

I chuckle. "It sure does."

As I make my way onto the street, I pull out my phone and click on my mother's phone number. She answers right away. "Hola, mi hijo guapo."

"Hola, mi madre bonita."

"You must be excited for Tanner's wedding. Make sure you send pictures later today. I want to see Kamryn in her dress and you in your tuxedo."

Tanner has us dressing a bit more casually than that, but I won't burst her bubble.

"I will. I umm...need to talk to you, Mamá."

"Is everything okay?" she asks in a worried tone.

"Honestly? I've never been better. I have a few things to tell you, starting with the fact that Kamryn is moving in with me."

We moved a few of her bigger items while I'm still in town, but she'll gradually move in when I'm away. She had too much going on with the wedding this week, but her lease is up next month, and she told them she's not returning. I've never been more excited for Spring Training to be over so I can get back to her and *our* apartment. And of course, our baby boy.

Thankfully she agreed to find another home for that damn waterbed. Apparently, the girlfriend of the weird ginger neighbor was into it. She's moving in with him and loves the idea of them having a waterbed.

Mamá gasps. "That's wonderful. She'll accept your proposal any day now. I know it."

I sigh. "I know I'm going to spend my life with her, but —"

"But what?"

It's now or never. I'm laying all my cards on the table. "I don't know that we'll ever get married. I don't know that we'll ever have kids. But I do know that we probably won't be moving back to Galveston."

Three whammies all at once. I grab my balls as I wait for a response.

She starts yelling in Spanish, but I stop her in an unusually loud, harsh tone for me. "Mamá, let me finish!"

She's quiet, so I take a deep breath and calmly continue. "I know you've always had my future planned out for me, but I never saw it the same way as you. In fact, I never saw it at all until Kamryn came into my life. I never said anything to you because I didn't want to upset you, but it's my life, and I'll live it how I please. Kamryn and I have some post-ball career plans that won't work in Galveston. We've made our home here in Philly and don't plan on changing it anytime soon. As for marriage and children, I don't know exactly what the future holds for us, but I'm happy. She's the love of my life. That will *never* change. I can live without everything else, but I can't live without her."

"But you're sacrificing—"

"That's not how I see it at all. I'm only gaining." I exhale a deep breath. "I need you to be okay with this. I've spent the past ten years not wanting to come home because of the pressure you put on me. Pressure to do things I never really wanted to do but was always too afraid of hurting you to say. I want to visit with a clear mind. When Kamryn and I come to town, it should be fun and full of love, not expectations. I won't have you put pressure on me anymore, and I certainly won't allow you to ever put pressure on Kamryn. Whether you like my choices or not, they're mine. I don't ask that you agree with them. I ask that you respect them."

I hear her sniffle a few times. My stomach clenches at the thought of being the cause of it, but this conversation is overdue. *Long* overdue.

It's deafeningly silent for several long beats. She's a loving mother. She may have had a certain future in mind for me, but she ultimately loves me unconditionally. Maybe it will take her time to get there, but I know she will.

Chewy lets out a series of high-pitched barks at a few dogs that could swallow him whole. I love that he's unafraid to assert himself. He must get that from Kam.

My mother calmly asks, "Is that my handsome grandpup?"

I can't help but smile, knowing it's her way of letting me know we're going to be okay.

CHAPTER THIRTY-SEVEN

Ripley and Arizona are getting their hair and makeup done in another room, leaving me, Bailey, and Fallon alone in the master bathroom of Tanner's house. Bailey wanted Fallon as a bridesmaid. Gemma is off managing Fletcher somewhere. Harper is with Tanner and his crew downstairs. She's his "best woman."

Bailey is sitting on a vanity chair, reapplying her lipstick for the thousandth time. She looks a little off kilter. I'm surprised. I thought she'd be running down the aisle to get to Tanner.

She exhales a long breath, and our eyes meet in the mirror. "Are you nervous, Bails? You don't have to do this. People have kids out of wedlock all the time."

She shakes her head. "There's nothing in the world I want more than to marry Tanner. It's the stepmom thing that's got me on edge. Are we doing this too quickly? Harper just found out that we're together. What if she doesn't accept me as her stepmom?"

Fallon rubs her shoulders. "She loves you, Bailey. I think she was rightfully confused about you and Tanner at first. It had nothing to do with not wanting you as a stepmom. She's excited about that."

I nod in agreement. "She's super excited about that part of it. She worships you, Bails."

Bailey scrunches her face. "Maybe it's the word *stepmom*. The stepmom is always evil in books and movies. I feel like the word has this negative connotation when it should be the opposite."

I scoff. "Fucking Disney. It's all their fault. Growing up, they basically taught us to hate stepmoms." I wink at her. "It's a good thing that Pornhub has taken it in a completely different direction. They've redeemed the word stepmom for this next generation. They're true pioneers."

Bailey and Fallon both start laughing. Fallon shakes her head. "You're gifted, Kamryn. Your mind is a medical marvel. I've never seen another like it."

"I've been telling Bailey that since we were kids."

Fallon smirks as she turns to leave. "I'm going to check on Harper. I'll give you two a moment of privacy."

When I know she's gone, my eyes meet Bailey's in the mirror again. "Are you happy?"

She nods. "So darn happy. I feel like I'm getting everything I've ever wanted. I didn't expect it all to come in a rush, but I feel so fortunate. How about you? Are you happy?"

"Of course. You're getting everything you want and deserve."

"Not about my life, Kam. Yours."

I blow out a breath. "I can't believe I'm about to live with a boy and not you. It's weird."

She giggles. "I know. For me too."

"I'm happy, Bails. I'm a little scared about the future, but my anxiety is better than it used to be. I'll always be a work in progress, with good days and bad. It's just how I'm built. I'm learning to accept it and trying not to sweat the smaller things."

She nods. "I know. I'm proud of how far you've come." She swivels her head and looks up at me. "Tanner told me about the job offer."

I shake my head. "I don't know, Bails. He and I might kill each other. He's going to be your husband. What if we can't work together? I don't want issues with you."

She grabs my hands and looks me in the eyes. "Nothing and no one will ever come between us. You jump, I jump. I like this for your future. If you decide to retire after the Olympics, kicking ass on behalf of other female athletes is something I can see you doing. Think about how many women you can help."

"I know. I won't lie, it's appealing to me. I had never considered anything like it, but I've been thinking about it a lot since he mentioned the opportunity. He wants me to start right away, before I even graduate, to begin learning the business."

"You'll crush it. There's nothing you can't do."

I wink at her. "Including throwing a wedding. Are you ready?"

She lets out a laugh. "I can't believe Tanner let you plan it."

"I *loved* spending his money." And I think he didn't want to dump the responsibility of it all on Bailey with her still recovering and being pregnant. She's the one who wanted a quick wedding. Everything had to be planned in a mad rush. I was happy to bear that burden for her. Honestly, it was more of a privilege.

She rolls her eyes before taking my hand in hers. "Thank you for always protecting me. I know I've often made it seem like I was the one looking out for you, but I know we both look out for each other."

I squeeze her hand as I fight the tears. "That's why we're soulmates."

She nods. "The unbreakable Harts. I don't know if I'll ever fully recover from my accident, but for some reason, I'm more determined than ever to make it to the Olympics. It's like once the doctors told me they didn't think I could do it, it made me want it more than I ever have. After the baby comes, I'm going to need your help to get myself into game shape again. Push me, even when it looks like I don't want to be pushed. Even if I tell you I want to quit, don't let me."

"I'll be there every fucking day. I'm not playing in those Olympics without my sister."

I hear Arizona's voice, "None of us are. All four of us will wear those Team USA jerseys. All four of us will come home with gold medals around our necks. We told you once before, we don't play in the Olympics without Bailey Hart."

Bailey nods as she fights her emotions, which I know are bubbling at the surface. "You two look beautiful. Where's Kaya?"

Ripley answers, "She's with Quincy, my mom, and Dutton until showtime."

Dutton Steel, the sexy Cougars coach, is June's date. It turns out Mama June was secretly banging him for months and now lives with him. She's so iconic.

Bailey smiles. "Do you think she'll be able to handle her flower girl duties? She just started walking."

Ripley's lips curl up in amusement. "Kam has gotten her... assistance down the aisle."

Bailey narrows her eyes at me. "What did you do?"

"You'll see."

THE CEREMONY IS about to begin in Tanner's massive backyard. We're standing behind a curtain so no one sees my sister until it's time. Bailey peeks around the curtains and grits out, "Why are their four shirtless male strippers standing over there?"

I give her an incredulous look. "How else are Kaya and Harper supposed to get down the aisle? They have escorts. And they're not strippers. They're models...who probably also strip."

Our father rubs his temples. "God help me, Kamryn. I think I'm afraid of everything that's about to happen."

"Shh. It's about to start. We're hidden from view, but you can still see everything. You don't want to miss the show." I kiss Bailey's cheek. "You'll do great. I need to get into place. There's a...vehicle coming to help you down the aisle. Don't move until it arrives."

Bailey's face falls. "Dear god. What have you done?"

CHEETAH

I don't think I've ever been more excited about anything in my life. This is going to be epic.

Kam hurriedly makes her way over to me. She looks gorgeous in a short, tight, red dress. All the bridesmaids are in red, but they're all wearing different styles of their choosing, and none is as magnificent as Kam.

"You look sexy as fuck, Kam bam."

She flashes me her mischievous smile. "It's about to get even better, kitten." She reaches into her purse and pulls out two hair ties before fixing her hair into the Princess Leia buns she knows I love.

I adjust myself. "Fuck. I'm getting hard."

"You better tuck that shit in. It's game time."

Tanner stands at the top of the aisle just as the music begins. "Daddy's Home" by Usher starts playing on the speakers. Tanner snaps his head our way and scowls at Kam, but she simply waves and blows him a kiss.

He exhales a breath in defeat as he makes his way down the aisle. I'm not sure why he's shocked. He put Kam in charge. He had to know it would be a little... offbeat.

Four giant topless men then hold a cart in the air with poles as Harper makes her way down the aisle, Cleopatra-style. The small gathering of friends and family all laugh while Harper waves to them from six feet in the air like the princess she is.

Kam is beaming as she watches them go.

Next, it's Fallon and Tanner's father, Stan. They're both in kid cars as they race down the aisle, much to the enjoyment of the guests.

Due to numbers, Vance and Daylen have to walk down the aisle together with Ripley. "Lady in Red" by Chris de Burgh begins to play on the speakers. Daylen decided he'd also be the girl and is in a red dress being carried on Vance's back as the three of them dance their way down the aisle. I'm not sure how one finds a dress his size, but he did it, and the guys happily take their place beside Tanner while Ripley stands at the bride's side.

Trey and Gemma then ride a tandem bike with Fletcher strapped to the front as the ring bearer, followed shortly thereafter by Layton and Arizona, who ride down the aisle in ATVs.

Finally, it's our turn. I pull out our props and hand Kam hers. "Are you ready, Kam bam?"

She nods. "You bet, kitten."

Suddenly, strobe lights begin flashing in the backyard, and the Star Wars theme song starts playing. Kam and I hold up our lightsabers as we make our way down the aisle, doing the choreographed fight sequence we've been practicing all week. It might be the most fun I've ever had in my life.

I'm living the fantasy of every *Star Wars* fan. I know she did this for me, which makes it even more special.

Everyone is laughing hysterically. Tanner is simply shaking his head.

Kaya is then escorted down the aisle in the same fashion as Harper though, as the official flower girl, she drops rose petals along the way. I think she eats as many of them as she drops, but it's still adorable.

Now it's time for the bride. I knew about the rest, but

Kam kept this one a secret from me. She said it would be more fun if it was a surprise.

"My Heart Will Go On," the theme song from *Titanic* starts playing. That's not so unusual. I know it's Bailey and Kam's favorite movie, and it's certainly a popular love song.

I should have known there would be more.

Suddenly, our duck truck/boat comes into view, rolling down from the house with Bailey and her father standing on the bow of the boat, just like Jack and Rose in the movie.

I see the moment Bailey's eyes find Kam's as they share a look of mutual amusement. I think Bailey is fulfilling a lifelong fantasy too.

Harper starts giggling, and then everyone joins in on the laughter. Deep belly laughter from every single person in attendance, Tanner included.

Yep, this is Kamryn Hart's gift. Making everyone around her smile.

And she's all mine.

EPILOGUE

TWO AND A HALF YEARS LATER

CHEETAH

I'm awakened by three tongues licking my face. I blink my eyes open and see our three golden retrievers, Chewbacca, Princess Leia, and Luke Skywalker, all on top of me, begging for their morning walk.

I look over to the other side of the bed. Sadness blankets me at its emptiness. I miss her.

The dogs all sniff her pillow. "You guys miss her, don't you?"

Luke Skywalker barks and I nod. "Yep. Me too, buddy." I sit up. "Let's go for your morning walk. I've got a long day ahead of me."

I approach the front door of my building when Evan opens it. I pinch my eyebrows together. "You're working the early morning shift today?" He's been working the afternoon and evening shifts lately.

He nods. "I am. I've got a big game to watch later this afternoon. I switched shifts so I could watch it."

I mumble, "I wish I could do the same."

It's the gold medal softball game at the Olympics tonight. Per Major League Baseball's collective bargaining agreement with the Players' Association, only spouses are permitted to miss games for special circumstances like this. Kam and I are "only partners" as it was worded to us when my request for a leave of absence was denied. Quincy was granted a leave because he and Ripley are married. I wasn't because we're not. It's such bullshit.

I offered to pay any fine they could levy, but Kam was adamantly against it. She said it would tarnish my reputation, and she wouldn't allow it. I'm devastated to be missing the game.

What's worse? We play at the same time. Reagan Daulton promised to have the game playing on the big screen at our stadium. It's not enough.

As I'm walking the dogs, my cell phone rings, and I see that it's Kam. I accept the call. "Hey, Kam bam."

She smiles into the screen. "Hey, kitten. Are you walking the kids?"

I nod. "I am. I wish I was with you."

She gives me a sad smile. "I do too, but I'm in the Olympic village. It's not like we could spend time together. Bailey hasn't been allowed to spend time with Tanner and the kids, Arizona hasn't been allowed to see Layton and Ryan, and Ripley hasn't been allowed to see Quincy and Kaya."

"I know, but it still sucks. They get to watch the game in person."

She sighs. "Just another thing to fight for."

Kam ended up joining Tanner's company and built the women's division into the most successful one in the country. She's a full-fledged badass lawyer now, with every female athlete clamoring for her to represent them.

She and Tanner still go at it from time to time, but I know he appreciates what she's done for his company. She keeps threatening him that she'll go out on her own and take all her clients, but she won't. I think being around Tanner is her way of still keeping a protective eye on her sister.

Speaking of Bailey, it took a lot of time and effort, but she eventually got her game back just in time for the Olympics. Frankly, it wasn't quite back when the team was selected, but Kam, Arizona, and Ripley all told the committee that they wouldn't go without Bailey also on the roster. It was risky, but it paid off.

That was months ago. In the time since, Bailey has regained her form and has been playing extremely well. Kam is still the best player in the world and the reason they're in this game, but Bailey holds her own. Kam hit a grand slam in the semi-final to send them to the gold medal game. She's my hero.

We chat for a bit until it's time for us both to go. I make my way to the stadium and sit in the locker room with my head a million miles away.

I'm zoned out so I don't see Reagan Daulton walk in. She sits next to me. "I'm sorry about this, Cruz. It's shitty."

I nod. "I know your hands were tied."

"They were, but it doesn't make it okay. At the next owners' meeting, I'll be advocating for partners' rights. In the meantime, I have my jet waiting for you. As soon as this game is over, you can fly out to her. I know you'll miss the game, but at least you can be there for the celebration. I have no doubt there will be one."

I suppose I should better express my gratitude, but I only offer a solemn thank you before she leaves.

KAMRYN

We're in the dugout about to take the field for the gold medal game in the Olympics. All my friends have their husbands there as they warmly greet them in the stands for some pregame affection. I've never wished more that I had accepted one of the nearly thousand marriage proposals Cheetah has thrown my way over the past three years. Every single day, he finds some random way to propose. Every single day, I say no.

I make my way over to hug my father and my three nieces, Harper, Lorelei, and Rory. Bailey had twins, and she's freshly pregnant again. So is Fallon. I was with them when they took pregnancy tests together. I'm excited for them, but the moment confirmed for me that I'm still not ready to be a mother. I might have some marriage jealousy right now, but I don't have an ounce of pregnancy jealousy.

I told Cheetah how I was feeling about their pregnancies, and he was fine with it. We're sublimely happy with each other and our growing canine brood. Neither of us has any interest in changing things right now.

I haven't publicly admitted that I'll be retiring from softball after the Olympics like my three best friends have, but I'm going to. Why would I want to play without them? And my career is exploding at Montgomery Sports Management. I can hardly keep up with my current list of clients. Retiring would give me a little extra time in my life. It would also mean less time away from Cheetah. Conflicting schedules and weeks away from each other are wearing on me. I can't live for the off-season anymore. It's too hard.

After an emotional last-ever pregame huddle with my three besties, we take the field for what will be our final game. It's almost hard to believe that after all the years of dreaming of this moment, it's finally here. We're so close to our gold medal dream that I can taste it.

We almost didn't make it. We were down late in our semi-final game, but with the bases loaded, I did what I've done many times throughout my career. I played the part of the hero.

My sister has had a great Olympics. It took a lot of time, energy, and tears to get her here, but we did it. I initially feared she'd be relegated to the bench, but she's peaking at just the right time. Even better, her husband and three daughters are here to witness what hard work and perseverance look like. I'm proud of her. I'm in awe of her.

The game is underway, and it's a tight one. We're down one run as we enter the bottom of the sixth inning. Arizona uses her speed to get on base, as always. I watch the first pitch to enable her to steal second base, which she does.

I then look at the coach, waiting for a signal, even though I know what it will be. She's going to want me to swing away and bring Arizona home to tie the game. Or possibly hit a home run to give us the lead, once again making me the hero. I happen to have the best career batting average on my team against this particular pitcher. She's second only to Ripley in the world and shuts most batters down.

As expected, the coach gives me the signal to hit away. The batter after me will undoubtedly strike out. She's done that against this pitcher for her entire career. The coach should have moved her down in the batting order. Bailey bats after her, and she's a contact hitter, always putting the ball into play.

I decide to bunt Arizona over to third base and leave her there for Bailey to drive in. After laying down a perfect sacrifice bunt, I'm out at first base, but Arizona is now sixty feet away from tying the game. Both the coach and Arizona narrow their eyes at me in confusion. It's not often a power hitter like me bunts, but I had my reasons.

As expected, the next batter strikes out. Some pitchers just have the number of certain batters.

My sister has historically made decent contact against the pitcher. That's all we need right now. She needs to knock Arizona in. I have faith in my sister.

I stand at the edge of our dugout as I watch Bailey enter the batter's box for what will likely be the last time in her life. Everything we've been through in our thirty-two years flashes through my mind. We've had a lot of tough times, but we're finally at a point where the good severely outweighs the bad. She's so blissfully happy with Tanner and their girls. My heart bursts for her. I'd like to think I had some hand in helping her down this path.

She's told me many times throughout the past two years that she doesn't regret being pulled into softball. She doesn't regret anything in her life because it led her to where she is now. I want so badly for this to be her big moment. She's earned it.

She's got one ball and one strike in her count. She's laser-focused on the pitcher. Softball is a bit like poker. All pitchers have tells as to what pitch they're going to throw, you just need to learn how to read them. I think that's why I hit so well. I can usually figure out what pitch is coming. There's no bigger thinking person's sport than softball. It's what drew me to the sport in the first place.

I can tell the pitch is going to be inside and see the moment Bailey realizes it too. Come on, Bails, turn on it. Drive it down the left-field line.

The pitch is thrown, and Bailey begins her swing. The second the ball hits the bat, I know it's gone. It's like time momentarily stands still. We all watch as the ball sails *way* over the left-field wall for a two-run home run.

My sister undoubtedly just won the Olympics for us. Tears of joy immediately sting my eyes.

She hasn't moved. Her hands are on her helmet in shock. At some point, she realizes she has to trot around the bases and takes off in a sprint. She does some uncharacteristic twirly move. I can't help but laugh through my tears. It's so unlike her to showboat, but I'm happy she picked this moment to do it.

We all run out of the dugout to greet her at home plate, but I make sure I'm the first. I've never been so happy in my entire life.

She's got the biggest smile I've ever seen as she raises her fist in the air and stomps on home plate. I immediately wrap my arms around her and lift her in the air, shouting, "My sister, the hero. The unbreakable Bailey Hart Montgomery." I'm overwhelmed with emotion as I manage to croak out, "I'm so fucking proud of you."

We cry together as we make our way to the dugout. I can see Daddy, Tanner, Fallon, Harper, and the twins all jumping up and down in glee.

Our next batter grounds out, and then we take the field for the top of the seventh and final inning. If we hold them here, we win the gold medal. I glance at the stands, willing Cheetah to miraculously appear, but he doesn't. He can't. He was willing to be fined hundreds of thousands of dollars to skip their game, but I wouldn't let him. He's on the borderline of being a possible Hall of Fame player. Something like skipping out on a game without permission is one of those random things that would cause voters not to vote for him. I won't allow that to happen because of me. As much as I ache for him to be here right now, it's not best for him.

After Ripley strikes out the first two batters, our opponents are down to their last out. The batter steps in and Ripley winds up for the pitch. The batter swings and hits a missile toward the five-six hole. Fuck.

I tuck my glove, pivot, and take off as quickly as I can. Laying out until I'm completely parallel to the ground, I reach my glove all the way out and feel the ball hit it at the same time I come smacking down onto the unforgiving dirt.

Knowing I've got no time to spare, I pop up to my knees and throw the ball toward first base as hard as I can from this position.

The ball hits into the first baseman's glove a hair ahead of the runner.

Game over. We win.

We all run toward Ripley, as it's standard to pile on top of a pitcher after a huge victory. My sister runs toward me. Throwing her arms around my neck, she screams, "Best. Play. Ever."

The next thirty minutes are full of tears and celebration. My sister is being hailed as the hero. I couldn't possibly be any happier for her. I love seeing her get all the attention she deserves.

Harper is standing next to her, looking at Bailey like she hung all the stars in the sky. The twins don't totally know what's going on, but they know their mommy is a star. That's all that matters. When they're older, they'll be able to watch this moment over and over, knowing what it took for her to get here and how she rose to the occasion.

IT's late into the evening, and I'm sitting in a booth at a bar all alone. My friends are long gone, celebrating privately with their husbands. The younger players on the team are either already passed out or getting it on with some random person on the dance floor.

I stare at a few of them making out with strangers. That used to be me, but I've got no interest in that now. Not one ounce. A few people hit on me tonight, but there's only one person I want.

I try to focus on the ceremony earlier tonight when the four of us received our gold medals. We cried like babies at the moment our forever dreams became our reality.

The best part was right after the ceremony, when Bailey and I presented our father with our grandmother's gold medal, which our mother had sold. It took me a few years and a lot of money, but I was able to track it down and buy it back.

Even the memories don't fill the emptiness I'm feeling. I miss Cheetah terribly. The hole in my heart feels so real.

Suddenly, a familiar scent invades my nostrils and a voice whispers in my ear. "Want me to play a firefighter? You're hot, but when I'm done, I'll leave you dripping wet."

I can't help but smile as I respond, "Can I slide down your pole?"

My man chuckles as he slips into the booth next to me. I immediately wrap my arms around his neck and inhale him. I start sobbing as I mumble into his neck, "How are you here?"

"Reagan felt bad about everything. She sent the company jet for me. I left as soon as our game was over."

Tears freefall from my eyes. "I'm sorry you weren't here. It's my fault."

He squeezes me tightly. "Don't say that. I got to see most of the game on the screen in our stadium. That final play was sick. It substantiated all these years of me telling everyone how good you are on your knees."

I giggle. "How did it look?"

"Like my girl is the only person on the planet who could make that play."

I pull my head up and smile at him. "Did you see Bailey's big hit?"

"I did." He licks his lower lip. "Funny thing. I've watched every inning of you playing for this coach. I know the bunt signal. I didn't see her give it to you."

I pinch my lips together to hide my smile. "You must have missed it."

He lifts an eyebrow. He doesn't believe me.

I shrug. "I wanted Bailey to have this unforgettable moment in front of her three girls. She more than earned the right to be the hero this time around. It was her time to shine."

"That was a risky move. You're the best hitter in the world. She may not have come through."

"Twin intuition. I knew she would get it done."

He sighs as he cups my cheek. "I love you."

I bring my forehead to his. "I love you too."

His lips move over mine, and a sense of calmness and fulfillment runs through my body. It's like the moment you take a deep breath after you've been underwater for a little too long. Damn, I've missed him.

Before I know it, our tongues are in each other's mouths, teeth nipping at each other like we want to swallow the other whole.

Eventually, I break us apart. "Take me to your room. I don't want today's memories to be the only thing left inside me tomorrow morning."

He nods as he stands and pulls my hand to stand with him. As we walk back toward his hotel, arm in arm, I turn to him. "You didn't ask me to marry you today."

He smirks as he drops down to one knee, throws his arms in the air, and loudly shouts, "Kam bam, love of my life, want to do the divorce court foreplay and marry me?"

I laugh. "I haven't heard that one before." I run my lip through my teeth. "Hmm. Okay. Yes."

He shrugs, stands, and starts walking again. "Maybe tomorr—"

He stops dead in his tracks and turns to me. "Did you just say yes?"

I look down for a second before looking up at him. "I just…I wish you were there today. I truly wished you were my husband and not my boyfriend today."

He nods in realization. "It was a unique situation. I don't think we'll encounter anything like it again. You know I'm happy the way we are. I don't want you to do anything you're not comfortable doing."

I nod. "I know. I love you for that. You've never once pressured me."

"And I never will. I don't want this to be an emotional decision. Today was a big day. You've worked toward it your whole life. We'll see how you feel tomorrow. I promise to ask again."

I twist my lips. "I've got a legitimate reason though."

He smirks. "What is it?"

"Bailey is about to have her fourth kid. She'll never be available. I need a new *In Case of Emergency* contact in my phone."

He chuckles. "I can't argue with that logic."

I take a deep breath. "This isn't an emotional decision. I've been thinking about it for a long time. I've talked it through with Dr. Pearl a lot in the past few months as my feelings about marriage began to change. I'm ready, Cruz. I want forever with you." I grab his face. "I love every single thing about you. I no longer see marriage as a death sentence. I see it as a promise of great things. Thank you for waiting. Thank you for loving me exactly how I am. Crazy and all."

His dimples make an appearance as he wraps his arms around my waist. "I dig your brand of crazy."

I nod. "I know you do." Running my fingertips through the back of his hair, I say, "Our marriage will have to be a fifty-fifty partnership."

He rolls his eyes. "Obviously."

I smile. "You'll give me your last name, and I'll scream your first."

His smile widens. "Is this for real? You're not fucking with me?"

"I definitely want to fuck you, but I'm not fucking *with* you."

"We don't have to get married. It's not something you *have* to eventually get to. I know I'm going to spend my life loving you; I'm confident in that. I don't need a piece of paper. I just need you."

I love him so much for saying that. I kiss his lips. "Why don't we try being engaged for a while and see how that sits with me?"

He wiggles his eyebrows. "So you're moving from my live-in doggie mama bitch to my fiancée doggie mama bitch?"

I nod. "Exactly."

"Evan might cry tears of joy. He's going to be very excited."

I giggle. "I aim to please Evan in all my life decisions."

"Mamá probably won't let up."

I sigh. "I can handle her. She's all bark and no bite. She knows I love you and that I make you happy. That's all that really matters to her."

He nods as his face turns serious. "It's all that matters to me too."

Yep, because in my fairy tale, it's the prince who cares about making the princess happy.

He tugs on my red Team USA hooded sweatshirt. "You look like Little Red Riding Hood."

"I guess that makes you the Big Bad Wolf."

He roughly grabs me by the waist and brings his lips close to mine. "This Big Bad Wolf is going to kiss Little Red Riding Hood."

I shake my head. "No, kitten, in that story, he eats her. Get to work."

THE END

I hope you enjoyed Kam and Cheetah story. For a glimpse into their future, you can find their Extended Epilogue here:

ACKNOWLEDGMENTS

To Kam and Cheetah: I wasn't sure I was going to write your book, but I'm sure glad I did. You two are a riot.

To the Queen, TL Swan: This amazing journey would never have begun if not for you and your selfless decision to help hundreds of women. This crazy and unexpected new path in my life has brought me so much happiness. I owe it all to you. Please know that I try every single day to pay it forward. Getting to meet you in person was the icing on top. It's amazing when your mentor is even better in person.

To Lakshmi, Thorunn, Mindy, and Brittany: Thank you for being the best beta bitches in the world. You are available to me at all times of day and night. You truly lift me up when I'm suffering from imposter syndrome. I hope to one day repay your kindness. We added **Amanda Mijares** for this book. Thank you for making Cheetah's dirty talk so darn good.

To Jade Dollston: You are my Ambassador of Quan.

To Alyssa Boyle: Congrats on your new job as my CLO (Chief Lesbian Officer). I appreciate your openness and am forever grateful that you brought dildo stew into my universe.

To My OG Beta Readers Stacey and Fun Sherry: Thank you for being there for me since day one.

To The B!tch Squad Members: To both old and new friends, I appreciate you all so darn much. Katie G. brought a silly waterbed story to our group chat and look what happened!!!

To Chrisandra and K.B. Designs: **Chrisandra**: Thank you for making me feel illiterate. That's what makes you such a great editor. **Kristin**: Thank you for helping this artistically challenged woman. Thank you for your innate ability to read my mind.

To My Family: I truly feel bad for you. An immature mother and wife can't be easy. To my daughters, thank you for tolerating me (ish). Thank you for telling everyone you know that your mom writes sex books. I appreciate that by the time you were each six, you were more mature than me. To my handsome husband, thank you for your blind support. You never question my sanity, which can't be easy. But let's face it, you do reap the benefits of the fact that I write sex scenes all day long. Every single male main character has a little of you in him (only the good stuff - wink wink).

ABOUT THE AUTHOR

AK Landow lives in the USA with her husband, three daughters, one dog, and one cat (who was chosen because his name is Trevor). She enjoys reading, now writing, drinking copious amounts of vodka, and laughing. She's thrilled to have this new avenue to channel her perverted sense of humor. She is also of the belief that Beth Dutton is the greatest fictional character ever created.

As a former college softball player, she is forever grateful for this series. It will always hold a special place in her heart.

AKLandowAuthor.com

www.ingramcontent.com/pod-product-compliance
Lightning Source LLC
Chambersburg PA
CBHW031235310726
48971CB00004B/1024